How could she ever make it up to him?

"I'm sorry about your brother," Elise said.

"And now his daughter's missing. And you owe it to us to find her." Josh stormed toward the house. He turned back to say something when a car approached. As if in slow motion, the window lowered and an explosion of gunfire filled the air.

Josh threw her to the ground, shielding her with his body. The air around them was alight with gunfire, and there was the roar of a departing engine. Amid all that, Elise heard the rapid beat of Josh's heart, felt the warmth of his breath. In the middle of a firefight why was she aware of that?

The agent in her took over for the woman. "Did you see anything?"

"It's the same car that tried to run you down before," Josh replied.

She nodded. "Someone is trying to stop us from investigating your niece's disappearance. I think it's safe to say we're dealing with more than a runaway situation."

And safe to say they were in for the fight of their lives.

Margaret Daley, an award-winning author of ninety books (five million sold worldwide), has been married for over forty years and is a firm believer in romance and love. When she isn't traveling, she's writing love stories, often with a suspense thread, and corralling her three cats, who think they rule her household. To find out more about Margaret, visit her website at margaretdaley.com.

Debby Giusti is an award-winning Christian author who met and married her military husband at Fort Knox, Kentucky. Together they traveled the world, raised three wonderful children and have now settled in Atlanta, Georgia, where Debby spins tales of mystery and suspense that touch the heart and soul. Visit Debby online at debbygiusti.com, blog with her at seekerville.blogspot.com and craftieladiesofromance.blogspot.com, and email her at Debby@DebbyGiusti.com.

Virginia Vaughan is a born-and-raised Mississippi girl. She is blessed to come from a large Southern family, and her fondest memories include listening to stories recounted around the dinner table. She was a lover of books from a young age, devouring tales of romance, danger and love. She soon started writing them herself. You can connect with Virginia through her website, virginiavaughanonline.com.

Christmas Peril

USA TODAY Bestselling Authors

Margaret Daley

Debby Giusti

&

Yuletide Abduction

Virginia Vaughan

LOVE INSPIRED
INSPIRATIONAL ROMANCE

LOVE INSPIRED®

INSPIRATIONAL ROMANCE

ISBN-13: 978-1-335-42493-8

Christmas Peril and Yuletide Abduction

Copyright © 2021 by Harlequin Books S.A.

Merry Mayhem
First published in 2009. This edition published in 2021.
Copyright © 2009 by Margaret Daley

Yule Die
First published in 2009. This edition published in 2021.
Copyright © 2009 by Deborah W. Giusti

Yuletide Abduction
First published in 2015. This edition published in 2021.
Copyright © 2015 by Virginia Vaughan

This edition published by arrangement with Harlequin Books S.A.

For questions and comments about the quality of this book, please contact us
at CustomerService@Harlequin.com.

Love Inspired
22 Adelaide St. West, 40th Floor
Toronto, Ontario M5H 4E3, Canada
www.Harlequin.com

Printed in U.S.A.

CONTENTS

MERRY MAYHEM

Margaret Daley

To Aubrey with all my love

Trust in the Lord with all thine heart; and lean not unto thine own understanding. In all thy ways acknowledge him, and he shall direct thy paths.

—Proverbs 3:5–6

Chapter One

Annie Coleman almost dropped the phone at her ex-boyfriend's words, but she couldn't. She had to keep it together for her daughter. Jayden played nearby, oblivious to the sheer terror Annie was feeling at hearing Bryan's gasping warning. "Run. Disappear... Don't trust anyone, especially the police."

A scuffling noise on the other end of the phone sent her heartbeat slamming against her chest. What was going on? A swishing sound filled her ears, followed by something like a fist hitting flesh and a groan that iced her blood.

"Thought you could get away," a gruff voice said between punches. "You haven't finished telling me what I need to know."

Annie panicked. What was going on? What was happening to Bryan on the other end? Confusion gripped her in a choke hold, her chest tightening with each inhalation.

"I don't want—" Bryan's rattling gasp punctuated the brief silence "—any money. Just let me go. I'll—" a smack interrupted his words "—forget...everything."

"I'm not worried about you telling a soul." The menace in the assailant's tone underscored his deadly intent. "Now all I need is where you hid it exactly. If you tell me now, it will be a lot less painful."

"I can't—" Agony laced each word.

"What's that? A phone?"

The sounds of a struggle then a gunshot blasted her eardrum. Curses roared through the connection.

Fear paralyzed Annie in the middle of her kitchen. *Was Bryan shot? Dead?* she screamed silently, clutching the receiver until her fingers locked into place.

"Who's this? Annie? Who are you?"

The assailant's voice so clear on the phone panicked her. She slammed it down onto its cradle as though that action could sever the memories from her mind. But nothing would. Had she just heard her daughter's father being killed? What information did Bryan have? How did that man know her name? Question after question bombarded her from all sides, but inertia held her still.

The ringing of the phone jarred her out of a trance. She zoomed in on the lighted panel on the receiver and noted the call was from Bryan's cell. The assailant now had her home telephone number! He could discover where she lived. He knew what she'd heard.

The last time she'd talked with Bryan early this morning, he was finally paying his father a visit for the first time. What could have gone wrong with that? Why was he warning her? What was Bryan sorry about? What did he do? Why shouldn't she trust the police? The questions started all over again, slamming one after another into her thoughts.

"Mommy, what's wrong?"

Looking up at Jayden, Annie schooled her features into what she hoped was a calm expression while her stomach reeled. "You know I've been thinking, honey? We need to take a vacation. We've been working so hard this year. It's time for us to have…an adventure." Her daughter was all into having adventures, since her favorite book series was *The Brandon Twins' Escapades.*

"Where?" Jayden came to her and threw her arms around Annie.

She wished she could stay forever holding her child, pretending she hadn't heard what she had. But she couldn't.

Annie hugged her daughter to her, then leaned back. "That's a surprise—a Christmas surprise." Because she wasn't sure herself, but she couldn't get Jayden's father's words out of her mind. *Run. Disappear. Don't trust any-one, especially the police.* Nor would she forget the gunfire that followed.

Grief and fear swamped her. Although she and Bryan had never married and were only friends for Jayden's sake, he'd tried to do right by his daughter in his own way. Had that led to him doing something foolish? Deadly?

"When are we going?" Jayden stepped back from Annie.

"Right now is as good a time as any. It's Saturday. I'll get some money and then we'll hit the road."

Jayden whirled from her and started across the kitchen. "Wait till Mandy hears I'm going on an adventure."

"We don't have time for you to call Mandy." They might not have much time for anything. She didn't even know where Bryan had been calling her from. "I'll get our suitcases. Let's see how fast we can pack. Take only your favorite things." Although she tried to make it sound like a game, her voice quavered, and Annie curled her trembling hands until her fingernails dug into her palms.

At the door her daughter paused, cocking her head. "When will we be coming back?"

Not until I figure out what's going on. I can't take the risk that Bryan has gotten caught up in some scheme and somehow involved us. He'd done some foolish, impulsive things in the past. "I'm not sure. But we'll probably be gone for a few weeks." She hoped only that long.

Jayden whirled around. "Then I'll need my new doll and my treasure chest."

The memory of when Bryan had given his daughter an antique porcelain doll for her birthday last month jolted Annie as though she'd stuck her finger into a socket. He'd even given them his mother's family's Bible, a surprise, since he wasn't a Christian, but he'd wanted his daughter to have it when she got older. Would Jayden ever see her father again?

Annie passed the sign for Christmas, Oklahoma. After two days on the road, driving long hours and crashing at night, she needed a place to stay for a while to figure out what was going on. She didn't even know if Bryan was dead or alive or where he'd been when he'd called her.

"I'm tired, Mommy."

"We're almost there."

She prayed that her mother's cousin, one she hadn't

seen in fifteen years, still lived in Christmas. After
racking her brain, she'd finally come up with Sara
McLain's place as a possible refuge until she did some
investigating and came up with a plan. Fond memories
of a holiday season spent in a town called Christmas
kept creeping into her thoughts as she drove toward
Oklahoma.

In the motel rooms along the way, she'd spent each
night after Jayden had gone to sleep reading Bryan's
mother's family Bible, looking for guidance on what to
do. But the Lord hadn't answered her prayers in years.
So why had she thought He would now?

On the outskirts of Christmas, Annie stopped at
Speedy Mart to get some gas and directions to her
cousin's house. As she filled her tank, Jayden danced
around, happy to be out of the car.

"Honey, stay right next to me." Annie envisioned
the unknown assailant on the other end of the phone
call suddenly appearing and grabbing her and her
daughter. Would she ever feel safe again?

She searched her surroundings, looking for anyone
who appeared suspicious. A car pulled in behind her,
and a man got out to get gas. Didn't she see that Chevy
behind her on Interstate 40 back a hundred miles? Not
sure, she massaged her temples, trying to rid herself
of the constant fear that had engrained itself in her.

When she was through filling her tank, she took
Jayden's hand and hurried toward the building to pay.
A bell rang as she opened the door. She glanced back
at the man finishing up putting gas into his car. He
caught her gaze, grinned and got back into his Chevy,
then pulled out of Speedy Mart. Relief slumped her
shoulders. False alarm—she hoped.

At the counter she started to pull out her credit card out of habit, but she stopped herself and instead withdrew some cash from her quickly dwindling savings. She smiled at the older woman who took her money and gave her change.

"You just passing through?"

"No," Annie said, stuffing the dollars into her purse, her gaze slanting toward her daughter, who was holding her porcelain doll and exploring the candy rack next to the counter. When she fingered one, Annie said, "Jayden, no candy right now."

"But I'm hungry."

"We'll get something in a little bit."

"Here visiting?" the attendant asked and slid her cash drawer closed.

"Yes." Behind Annie the bell over the door jingled, and she automatically turned to see who was entering. For the past two days she'd been constantly looking over her shoulder and checking out all the cars behind her on the highway. She'd never been paranoid before, but fear was taking over her life.

A tall man in a navy-blue police uniform came into the store and grinned at the woman behind the counter. Annie breathed a sigh. Then she remembered Bryan's warning, and tension whipped through her.

The police officer's gaze swept the store as though checking to make sure everything was all right before settling first on Jayden then Annie. The sharp, assessing look moved down her length before coming back to her face. A smile crinkled the corners of his cobalt-blue eyes and lit their depths with a glitter. He nodded a greeting toward her.

Uncomfortable with his scrutiny, Annie turned her

attention back to the cashier. "I need directions to Sara McLain's house on Bethlehem Street. Do you know her?" She was over a thousand miles from Crystal Creek. This man had nothing to do with what had happened in Florida.

The older woman glanced behind Annie.

"Maybe I can help you." The police officer stepped up to the counter a few feet from Annie. "Sara's a neighbor of mine."

"Oh, good, you know where she lives. My name is Annie Madison." Which was true but Madison was her middle name. She'd decided the first night on the road that was the name she would go by as a precaution in case anyone was looking for Annie Coleman.

"I'm Caleb Jackson, the police chief of Christmas." He offered his hand.

She fit hers in his and shook it. "Nice to meet you. Can you give me directions to Sara's?" Annie snagged her daughter before she wandered toward another rack with chips. "I'm her cousin."

"Cousin?" Skepticism sounded in his voice. "She's always talking about her family. I don't remember her mentioning you."

"It's been a while since I've seen her." She hated explaining herself to a stranger, but she didn't need the police chief becoming suspicious.

A grin eased the wariness from his expression. "Sara will be thrilled. She was just talking about how none of her nieces or nephews could come for Christmas. Have you ever been here?"

"Yes, the last time was when I was ten during the holidays, but I don't remember much about the town, except all the lights downtown and the huge Christmas tree in the park." She glanced out the large picture window, a blanket of clouds darkening the late afternoon. "I need to talk with Sara this evening and then find a place to stay. My daughter is tired and hungry." She hoped Sara would let her stay with her, but she hadn't seen her in years and she might not open her home to her. If that were the case, she didn't know what she would do. Her money was limited. Fear, always present since she'd last heard from Bryan, wormed its way deeper into her mind.

"Sara fell a few weeks ago. She could use some help around the house, but she hates asking anyone to. Maybe you are an answer to a prayer. I'll show you where she lives. You can follow me." He turned to the lady behind the counter. "I just need a cup of your coffee, Marge."

"Already have it for you." The woman took the dollar the police chief set on the counter.

"Ready, Mrs. Madison?" He snatched up the cup.

"It's Ms. Madison. I'm not married."

She'd never been married. Although Bryan and she had discussed marriage when she discovered she was pregnant in college, she'd decided against it when he was arrested for driving under the influence. Too many red flags kept popping up in their relationship. When she'd met him as a freshman, he was an upperclassman with arresting blue eyes and an easy smile. He'd whisked her off her feet, and she'd given herself to him. She deeply regretted her choice back then, but one good thing had come from it: Jayden.

Taking her daughter's hand, she started for the door. "I appreciate you showing me where Sara lives. I probably could have wandered around until I stumbled onto

Bethlehem. I remember what a big deal the holidays are here in Christmas."

"Yeah, the town grows at this time of year. We get people from all over Oklahoma and the surrounding states visiting during the season. We go all out."

"The thing I mainly recall is the festival of lights," Annie said as she helped Jayden into the back and slipped behind the steering wheel of her ten-year-old Ford Mustang.

"We added fireworks about twelve years ago." He shut her door and strode toward his police cruiser.

As she followed Caleb Jackson through the town, holiday spirit was evident everywhere she looked. Every street's name had a Christmas theme: Noel Avenue, Candy Cane Lane, Mistletoe Street, Nativity Road. Usually Christmas had little meaning for her. She only celebrated it for Jayden's sake.

Although Bryan tried to help as much as he could, it had been a struggle supporting her daughter on an office manager's salary. She was thankful when she called her employer, Ron Adams, that he'd been understanding about her suddenly taking some time off. She'd been with him for five years, and this was a slow time of the year for his roofing business. She hoped by the first of the year that she could go back to Crystal Creek and her old life. She wanted to believe that Bryan was all right and there had been no reason for her to flee.

Six blocks off the main street through downtown where one store after another dealing with Christmas edged the thoroughfare on both sides, the police chief turned onto Bethlehem. Large houses—some Victorian, all decorated for Christmas—lined the street.

He stopped in front of one of the Victorian homes, painted a powder-blue, with a black wrought-iron fence along the sidewalk. The lot Sara McLain's place sat on was at least half an acre. In fact, all the houses on the street had sizeable yards. Memories of running and playing on the lawn flashed into her thoughts. She remembered feeling safe here.

Annie stared at the three-story structure with a Christmas tree positioned in the center of a floor-to-ceiling window facing the street. White lights draped the pine with gold bows and white ornaments. "We're here. Remember, your last name is Madison, honey. It's important you don't forget."

"Why, Mommy?"

She didn't want to tell her daughter the reason, but she had to say something or she would continue to ask. "That's our new last name now. We're on an adventure and in disguise."

"Oh, great!" Jayden unsnapped her seat belt and hopped from the car, hugging her doll.

As Annie climbed out, she heard Caleb Jackson introduce himself and ask her daughter, "What's your name?"

Annie stiffened, gripping the door handle.

"Jayden Madison."

Annie expelled a deep breath and rounded the front of her Mustang. She knew he was a police chief, but the words *don't trust anyone, especially the police* had kept her up most of the past two nights, listening to every sound passing her motel room door.

His gaze captured hers. "This is Sara's."

"Yeah, I remember playing here, making—" Annie

pointed toward a spot in the front yard "—a snowman right there."

"A snowman. I wanna make one." Jayden looked up at the sky. "When's it gonna snow?"

Caleb chuckled. "In Oklahoma, if you don't like the weather, just stick around a day. It most likely will change. But right now, there isn't any snow forecasted."

Jayden's mouth turned down in a pout. "I was hoping for snow. I've never seen any."

He winked at her little girl. "Maybe while you're visiting, there will be some." When he shifted toward Annie, Caleb gestured down the street. "I don't live far from here. The last house at the end of the block."

"Thanks for showing us where Sara lived."

Taking her daughter's hand, she started to open the gate that led into the front yard, when the police chief reached around her and swung it toward him. His arm brushed up against hers. Jolted by the contact, she stepped back, aware of the man only inches from her. His smile encompassed his whole face and made his eyes gleam.

But she'd learned the hard way to be wary of strangers. Look what happened when she'd given into Bryan and his smooth-talking ways. She would love to trust the police chief with what was going on in her life, but at the moment she didn't even know what that was. In a tight crunch she would appreciate someone like Caleb Jackson watching out for her. She hoped she never had to find out just how good he would be defending someone. The very thought sent a shiver down her.

"Cold?"

She nodded, although her chill had nothing to do with the weather.

"It's getting nippy. So, Jayden, you might get that snow after all. I've learned not to take the forecasters too seriously." He mounted the stairs to the porch that wrapped around one side of the house and pressed the bell. "It'll take Sara a bit to get to the door." He leaned back against the wall, crossing his arms. "What do you think of our little town?"

"I've never seen so many Christmas decorations in one place."

He quirked a grin. "Yeah, it does take some getting used to for newcomers. We go all out for a good three months a year. Personally, I like what Christmas stands for. We could use it year round."

"What? Rampant commercialism?"

He laughed, a warm sound that Annie responded to. "A cynic. Before you pass judgment on the town, you need to experience the holidays here." He straightened as the door opened. "And I wasn't talking about the commercialism of Christmas but the celebration of Christ's birth. It all started something awesome."

All words fled Annie's mind at his answer. She hadn't expected it. But the appearance of her cousin in the entrance gave her a reprieve from making any comment.

A small woman, about five feet, her totally white hair pulled back in a bun, pushed open the screen and smiled at the police chief. "Goodness, I didn't expect you for another hour, Caleb."

"I'm not here to fix the leak in the sink, but I'll be back later to take care of it. Right now I brought you Annie and Jayden Madison." He gestured to each of them when he said their names.

Sara's gaze took both she and her child in, a puzzled expression on her face.

"I'm your cousin. Alice's daughter." Annie held her breath, hoping Sara remembered.

"Ah, it's been years since I've seen you or your mother. How is Alice?"

"She died seven years ago."

"Oh, I'm sorry to hear that. We lost touch when y'all moved to Miami." Her forehead wrinkled in thought, Sara studied Annie with a sharp alertness in her brown eyes. Then she swept her attention to Annie's daughter. "What an adorable little girl. You and your mother look a lot alike. I think I've got photos from her visit when she was a little girl. If I can find them, I'll show you." She grinned at Jayden and stepped to the side. "Come in. It's getting cold." After Annie and Jayden entered, Sara asked Caleb, "Coming in?"

"No, I have to get back to the station." The police chief peered at Annie, who stood next to Sara in the entrance. "Nice meeting y'all."

When her cousin closed the door, she faced Annie. "Hon, what brought you to Christmas, Oklahoma?"

Annie's stomach constricted, her grip on her daughter's hand tightening. She didn't know how to answer Sara. The woman's kind eyes made her long to share what happened, but words refused to take hold in Annie's mind. How could she explain anything to Sara when she herself didn't understand? This was her problem, not Sara's. She'd always managed on her own in the past. This would be no different.

Sara waved her hand. "When you're ready, you'll tell me." Then using her cane, she headed toward the room off to the right of the foyer. "Come in, and make yourself at home."

Annie remained rooted to the floor.

Finally Jayden tugged on her hand. "Mommy, okay?"

Annie blinked and glanced down at her daughter—her whole life. Everything she did she did for Jayden. If they were in danger, she had to protect her daughter at all costs. "Yes, I'm fine. Let's go see what Miss Sara has to say."

"We could tell her we're on an adventure."

"Let's keep that a secret between us." Annie placed her forefinger over her lips.

Jayden pulled her down so she could whisper, "This house is *big*."

"Yeah, it is. I bet there are great hiding places in here." She just hoped she never had to use them.

Chapter Two

As Annie checked the meat loaf and placed the vegetable casserole in the oven, the doorbell rang. Jayden was so absorbed in her new coloring book she didn't even notice when Annie hurried from the kitchen.

Earlier she and Sara had talked and the older woman had shown Jayden the photos of Annie as a little girl and then given her one to put in her treasure chest. Annie had volunteered to cook dinner. Although Sara was a relative and had opened her home to her gladly, she wouldn't freeload off her. She was determined to help her cousin as much as possible in exchange for giving her a place where she could decide about her future.

A few seconds later, she swung the door open to the police chief standing on the porch with a puzzled expression creasing his forehead. His gaze locked on hers.

"Did something happen?" she asked, trying not to react to the man. But for some reason her heartbeat accelerated, and it really had nothing to do with the assessing look he sent her. Although no longer in his uniform, the man commanded a person's attention even wearing jeans and an Oklahoma University sweatshirt.

His features smoothed into a grin. "No, just surprised to find you here."

"You are? You brought me here."

"Yeah, I did," he said in a thoughtful tone. "Your car isn't out front."

"I parked it around back by the detached garage." No sense leaving it on the street for anyone looking for her to find. Little by little she was trying to learn caution, but she'd never even watched a crime show on TV or read a suspense book.

"When I didn't see it, I thought maybe you'd left."

"Nope. Sara insisted Jayden and I stay with her through the holidays. Come in." Annie opened the door wider and stepped to the side. "Sara's in the living room resting her eyes, she says, but I think she's really taking a nap."

Caleb entered with his toolbox. "Ah, in her lounge chair, which she calls her command post." He sniffed the air. "You're cooking dinner?"

"Yes, meat loaf."

"It smells great." He followed Annie to the kitchen. "What are you coloring, Jayden?" Stopping next to the table, he peered over her daughter's shoulder. "You like animals?"

"Yes. We were gonna get a puppy for Christmas. I guess we won't since we're on an adven—" Jayden's gaze flew to Annie, and her daughter snapped her mouth closed.

Caleb glanced from her daughter to Annie. For a few seconds his forehead crinkled as though trying to come up with the right question to ask. Then a smile leaked back into his expression as he turned his attention to Jayden. "I have a dog. Ralph is a mutt and loves children. You'll have to come visit him. He's deaf, which doesn't make him a good watchdog, so I'm glad not much happens around here."

Jayden twisted around in her chair and looked at Annie. "Can I see Ralph? I can finish coloring later."

Annie laughed. "Honey, I think Mr. Jackson means some other day. He's here to fix a leak."

Her daughter's pout descended. "We aren't home now for me to get my puppy."

"We'll get a puppy later." When she knew what was going on and she had a game plan. Tomorrow she needed to go somewhere and use a computer. Maybe if she surfed around, she could discover what had happened to Bryan.

"I'll bring Ralph down tomorrow for you to meet him." Caleb put his toolbox on the floor in front of the sink. "Will I interfere with you cooking dinner?"

"No, I just finished preparing the meal right before you came. Great timing."

"I aim to please. Don't let me stop you from doing whatever you need to do." He knelt on the floor and opened the cabinet door, then reached in.

Annie sat next to Jayden, trying her best to ignore the police chief's presence. Taking up the crayon nearest her, she started to color until her daughter said, "A cat isn't blue."

Annie glanced down at the paper and noticed what she'd done. "Oh, you're right. Sorry, honey."

A commotion behind her drew her attention to Caleb. He took a wrench to the faucet, his movements a study in economical action. Transfixed for a moment, she watched until he peered back at her. One corner of his mouth tilted up, a gleam in his startlingly dark blue eyes. She'd always had a thing for blue eyes. Bryan's had been—were—blue.

Over the years her ex-boyfriend had schemed to get rich, tired of being poor, not supporting his daughter as he wanted. Going to meet his wealthy father had been his latest ploy to get rich quick. His mother's death six weeks ago had affected Bryan. Before she'd passed away from a heart attack, he'd thought his father was dead. Not long afterward, he'd discovered he was very much alive and had lots of money. He'd intended to reintroduce himself and benefit from his father's wealth. He'd never gotten the chance to tell her what had come of that meeting.

"I'm partial to blue," Caleb said with a wink, drawing Annie back to the present.

Heat scored her cheeks, and she quickly returned to the paper between her and Jayden. This time she noticed the crayon she selected, making sure it was an appropriate color.

It was only because she was in unfamiliar surroundings with an unknown future stretching before her and Jayden that her nerves were frazzled. Caleb had nothing to do with the fact that her hand quivered as she grasped the crayon and tried to color within the lines and was not succeeding very well.

"I think that should take care of the leak," Caleb said as he closed the cabinet door under the sink.

Annie knew the exact second he stood behind her and looked over her shoulder. His spicy scent vied with the aromas of the cooking meat loaf and vegetable casserole.

He pointed to the blue kitten left abandoned on the page. "There are some cats with a bluish tint to their fur."

"There are?" Jayden's green eyes widened.

"Yeah, Harriet, the receptionist at the station, owns one."

"Can I see it?"

"I'll say something to Harriet and see what I can come up with—that is, if it's okay with your mother." Caleb moved to sit in the chair next to Annie at the oak table.

"That's fine." Annie slid her gaze away from Caleb's. "So should we finish coloring the kitten blue?"

Her daughter giggled. "I will, Mommy." After she grabbed the crayon, she bent over the paper and concentrated on finishing the animal, the tip of her tongue peeping out of the corner of her mouth.

The sound of Sara's cane hitting the hardwood floor in the hallway preceded her entrance into the kitchen. "I heard laughter and wanted to see what was going on." Slowly she lowered herself in the last chair at the table.

"I took care of the leak. Is there anything else you need fixed?" Caleb leaned toward his toolbox to shut the lid.

"This place is old. There's always something."

"Sara, all you have to do is call." Caleb inhaled a deep breath. "That meat loaf just gets better smelling by the minute."

"You know you can always stay for dinner. We don't stand on ceremony around here." Sara hooked her cane on the back of her chair. "And I agree it smells wonderful."

"I checked it a while ago. It should be ready shortly." Annie turned to her daughter. "Which means you need to put your coloring book and crayons in our room, then wash your hands."

"Do I hafta? I haven't gotten them dirty."

Annie took her hand and showed her the black smudges from the pencil she'd used earlier. "Go, young lady."

Jayden leaped up from the chair and raced from the room.

"Walk. Don't run." Annie waited to hear that her daughter had slowed down and then said, "Running is her favorite mode of traveling."

"Don't worry about Jayden. It's nice to have a child in the house again. I used to have nieces and nephews who visited all the time before they moved away and got so busy. I enjoyed watching them grow up. To this old lady—" Sara patted her chest "—seeing the world through a child's eyes is like being young again."

"You aren't old."

"Goodness me, Caleb. Have you gone blind? I'm feeling every one of my years right now."

"Age is all up here." Caleb tapped his temple. "By the way, how many years are we talking about?"

"That said, Annie, by one of the young," Sara said, then shifted her sharp gaze to Caleb. "And, young man, it's none of your business. I'm not telling, and you know that." The stern tone belied the gleam dancing in Sara's eyes.

"Ah, but age has nothing to do with how you look at life. And yes, ma'am, I know, but I was trying to help the townspeople." He angled toward Annie. "Her age is a town secret many in Christmas have been trying to figure out."

Sara's laughter filled the kitchen. "It will go with me to my grave."

The humor in Caleb and Sara's exchange touched a much-neglected part of Annie. Working hard as a single mom, trying to make ends meet, had left her without much hope. And now with the threat looming over her and her daughter, she felt weighted down. If she had to disappear as Bryan had insisted, what did she know about doing that? There had been a time in her life when she would have turned to the Lord for help, but maybe the Lord had really forsaken her when she'd lost her direction as a teen.

A few hours later, after a delicious home-cooked meal, Caleb dried the last dish and put it in Sara's cabinet. "I keep forgetting Sara doesn't have the conveniences like a dishwasher for just such an occasion."

"Now she does. At least for the time being." Annie wiped her hands on the tea towel hanging on a hook near the sink. "Me."

"The prettiest dishwasher I've seen." The second he said it he wanted to snatch the words back. His comment produced a pink flush on Annie's cheeks that highlighted her beauty. Caleb tried not to notice. Annie probably wouldn't stick around Christmas long, so why become interested in her? He didn't want his heart broken a second time. Once was enough.

"Thanks." She ran the wet dishcloth around the sink.

Busywork, as though she were nervous. "I just ap-

preciate a home-cooked dinner I don't have to make."
Caleb folded the towel and placed it on the counter.
"I've got a question for you."

She stopped in mid-rotation, her body tensing. Then
as if shaking it off, she completed her turn, throwing
a glance over her shoulder.

"Jayden has red hair, but yours is light brown. Was
Jayden's father redheaded?" *Great going, Jackson.
Why don't you just ask what happened to her mar-
riage? Is the guy still in the picture?*

"Yes." Lowering her eyelashes, she veiled her expression. "I'd better get Jayden to bed. Can I see you
out?"

He deserved that. The subject wasn't one she wanted
to discuss. Which only piqued his interest. "I can find
my way to the front door." He tried to inject humor
into his voice, hoping to see Annie's smile.

Instead, she said in a serious tone, "I know Sara's
been recovering from a fall. Did she break anything?
Was she in the hospital?"

"She fell but didn't break any bones. Her hip is
bruised, and she pulled a muscle in her leg. Her doctor forbade her getting up on a ladder anymore. It happened two weeks ago." Caleb passed the front room
and gestured toward the eight-foot tree that could be
viewed from the street. "Decorating that." At the door
he faced Annie, rubbing his hand along the stubble of
a day's growth of beard. "Sara tends to want to do everything herself."

"I can understand that."

Caleb stepped closer, taking a whiff of her flowery
scent. "The dinner tonight was great."

"Thanks." A dimple appeared in her cheek, enticing him to touch it.

Caleb curled his hands and kept them at his sides. "Good night, Annie. I'll bring Ralph down tomorrow for Jayden to see."

The crisp night air surrounded him as he left Sara's house and strolled toward his smaller home at the end of the block. He'd enjoyed himself a lot tonight, but something wasn't right. He felt it in his gut. During the conversation at dinner Annie had revealed little about herself and her life in Florida, as though she wanted to avoid anything having to do with her past. And really, telling them she was from the Sunshine State wasn't a big secret since her Mustang sported Florida tags.

He would keep an eye on Annie Madison. Even though she was Sara's cousin and his longtime friend hadn't had a problem with an unexpected guest appearing right before Christmas, that didn't mean something wasn't going on. Sara hadn't been expecting her to show up today. This evening Annie had been nervous whenever anything remotely personal came up. Sara hadn't seen Annie in fifteen years. A lot could have changed in that time.

Inserting the key into the lock, he wished he could turn off the cop in him, but it had been drilled into him from his years on the force in Tulsa and now here in Christmas. He would never forgive himself if something happened to Sara.

He was protecting Sara by being vigilant. Or was he really protecting himself? He'd been in a serious relationship in Tulsa, but when he'd asked the woman to marry him and move to Christmas, she'd decided there was no way she could live in a small town, especially one so kitschy. And he'd known better than to date a woman who wasn't a Christian, but he'd thought it might work out. Wrong! And he'd paid for that assumption.

Caleb had been the police chief for two years, ever since he came back to Christmas to take care of his ailing father, who died last year. His death left a hole in Caleb's life. His dad had been his best friend, and he was glad he could help ease the last few years of his life.

He tossed his keys on the table in the foyer and set his toolbox down, then made his way to the den. Ralph lay in front of the fireplace and stood when he saw Caleb. His pet wagged his tail so much that his whole back wiggled in his excitement. Greeting his dog was a great way to end his day.

Tonight while Annie had gone to get Jayden for dinner, Sara had told him she had a gut feeling Annie was in need of a good friend. That the Lord had sent Annie to Sara so she could help the young woman with the adorable child. Caleb wasn't so sure about that. Since her grandniece had moved away last January, Sara had been lonely, even depressed, which definitely could be coloring Sara's perception of Annie.

It was up to him to make sure she wasn't taken advantage of.

Annie rolled over and pounded her fist into the pillow. She should have fallen asleep hours ago, but instead she couldn't shut down her thoughts long enough for sleep to overtake her.

She kept replaying the evening with Caleb. A look he sent her. The touch of his hand. A wink, as though they shared some secret. And then there was his smile. She must have contemplated that for a good thirty minutes. Remembering it bathed her in warmth. She had no business being interested in a man right now. She didn't even know if she would stay in town long after Christmas. After all the commotion of the holidays passed, she needed to decide what she should do next. She had a life back in Crystal Creek she wanted to return to and didn't know if she could.

Frustrated, Annie flipped back the covers and slowly stood, making sure she didn't disturb Jayden sleeping on the other side of the queen-size bed. She paced to the window and pushed the curtain back to peer outside. The blackness of night only reinforced her fear of the dark. She shivered and turned away from the window, letting the drapes fall back into place.

She needed to do something now. Was Bryan alive somehow? How could she find out? Call all the hospitals in that part of Florida? She didn't know their names, but maybe information could help her.

Her gaze fell on her cell, which she'd finally started charging when she'd unpacked earlier. The green light indicated she could use it. She turned it on for the first time since before she'd fled Crystal Creek. When she'd gotten up Saturday, it had been dead, but she hadn't gotten around to charging it before everything changed after Bryan's phone call to her apartment. She'd been too tired to charge it on the road. Annie stiffened. Two messages were on her cell. Afraid of what she might find because few knew her new cell number—one being Bryan—she couldn't keep her hand from trembling.

"Annie, my meeting with my father went badly. He won't acknowledge me. I'm coming to see—" A pause of several seconds then, "I'll call you back. I guess I was going too fast. A cop is behind me and wants me to pull over."

She punched the next message, hoping it was Bryan to explain further, to help her to make some kind of sense of all that was happening. "Annie, you can't run forever. I'll find you, just as I found Bryan."

Listening to the second message from a gruff-voiced man, the same one she'd heard as Bryan was being beaten, only strengthened the terror that was a constant companion. There was no going back to Crystal Creek.

Chapter Three

The next day at the library computer, Annie stared at the screen, rereading the words of the small article from the Daytona paper: "The body of 28-year-old Bryan Daniels of Daytona was found in a Dumpster behind the McKinney Apartment Complex. The victim was badly beaten and died from a gunshot wound to the stomach. His apartment was later discovered to be ransacked."

He's dead. His place robbed. Tears blurred the words on the screen. Her relationship with Bryan had ended six years ago, but he'd tried to do the right thing concerning Jayden, even if he'd totally messed up his life. How was she going to tell Jayden about Bryan? She had to find a way but make sure her daughter didn't say anything about Bryan to anyone. Maybe when she moved on after the holidays.

Beaten and shot. The facts in the article taunted her. *Oh, Bryan, what have you done? What have you gotten Jayden and me into?*

A noise behind her prompted her to click off the computer before Sara or Jayden found her looking at it. She watched a lady at the counter cross to a cart and place a stack of books on it. Annie scanned the library's large room with rows and rows of shelves and found Jayden sitting cross-legged on the carpet flipping through a book with Sara behind her in a chair peering over her daughter's shoulder.

Shifting back around, she stared at the blank screen. She'd figured after the message last night that Bryan was dead. Reading the news in black and white hammered home that she couldn't go back to Crystal Creek, only fifty miles from Daytona, until she knew what was going on. Had Bryan's visit with his father had anything to do with him being killed? She couldn't go to the cops with what little she knew—not yet, not until she knew whom she could trust. Her life and Jayden's might depend on her silence. She couldn't risk it, especially after Bryan's last message about being pulled over by a cop. That had only been an hour before he called her at her apartment. What had happened in that hour?

What was her next step? Find out more about Bryan's father, Nick Salvador. It had all started with Bryan's visit with him. Who was he? What kind of power did he wield? Where did his money come from? How wealthy was he? Was he capable of killing his own son?

Her head pounded with all the unanswered questions that seemed to demand responses immediately. She rubbed her temples, unable to alleviate the tension.

First, she needed to know if whoever had picked up Bryan's cell and talked to her had found where she lived in Crystal Creek. She dug into her purse and pulled out her cell to call her apartment manager, Trey Johnson.

When he came on the phone, she said, "Trey, this is Annie. I—"

"Where have you been? I've been trying to find you. I don't have your new cell number."

"What?" Annie gripped the cell tighter, again peering around her to make sure no one was nearby. "Why are you looking for me?"

"Your apartment was broken into a few days ago. It was destroyed."

The man found our place in Crystal Creek not long after we'd left!

Her nerveless fingers released her cell, and it dropped to the tile floor making a loud sound in the quiet of the library. Several patrons, including Sara and Jayden, looked at Annie. A flush heated her cheeks as she retrieved her cell and said, "Sorry, I dropped my phone." The rapid thumping of her heartbeat made her voice sound breathless.

"Where are you?"

Light-headed, Annie tried to drag enough air into her lungs, but the room swirled before her. She closed her eyes for a few seconds.

"Annie, are you there?"

"Yes. Do you think anything was taken?" As a friend and manager of the apartment complex, Trey had been in her place several times.

"That's hard to tell, since it was trashed so badly. Even the stuffing in the couch was torn out. Most of what is left isn't salvageable. The police have been here. They aren't saying much, but I haven't heard of any other robberies like yours in town lately."

And Trey would have known. Little crime happened in Crystal Creek—until now.

"When are you coming home? Where are you? I thought you might be dead or something when no one could find you, but your boss told the police you left town for a while. They've been looking for you."

The police, looking for her? The thought escalated her fear and panic even more. "Jayden and I," she began in a voice that quavered, "are okay." *If you don't count having someone hunting us.* "I can't tell you anything else. I'll get back to you later. Thanks, Trey." She clicked off the cell before she told him something that could give her location away. What if the person who had killed Bryan had gotten to Trey?

Don't trust anyone. That included her friends and the police in Crystal Creek.

She turned off the cell, realizing if she was on it long enough they could trace her through the GPS in it. Half the time she didn't have it on because she left it off at work and often forgot to switch it back on. Now all she wanted to do was throw it away, as though the assailant had come through the connection to touch her with evil. She shuddered.

"Mommy, I've got my books. I'm ready to go. Sara wants to take us by the police station to meet Harriet and her blue cat."

"Her cat is at the station?" Annie stuffed the cell into her purse and rose, smiling as Sara made her way to her at a slower gait than Jayden.

"Yeah, isn't that cool? Sara said she's the station mouser."

Fifteen minutes later they entered the police station. The instant Annie saw Caleb, her heartbeat increased as though she'd been given a shot of adrenaline. His gaze latched on to hers and didn't release it.

He disengaged himself from a conversation with an older woman at the back of the station and sauntered toward them, coming around the counter, his eyes sparkling with pleasure. "What brings y'all by here?"

"Jayden said something about wanting to see Harriet's cat, and I told her Samson stays at the station when she's here." Using her cane, Sara moved toward her friend. "Jayden, Samson's usually in his basket near Harriet's desk."

Her daughter trailed behind Sara. The second Jayden saw the cat she stooped next to the large wicker basket and touched the blue-gray animal. Its loud purrs resonated through the room. Jayden grinned and stroked her hand along his back over and over.

"I hope you don't mind us visiting like this. Are you busy?" Annie swiveled toward Caleb.

"I was just taking a break for lunch."

"It's almost two."

"I was busy this morning. We had some vandalism last night." He leaned against the counter, placing his elbow on its top.

"Have you found out who did it?"

"I've narrowed it down to a specific group of teenage boys. Their antics won't last much longer."

"What did they do?"

"Took the ornaments off the town Christmas tree." One corner of his mouth lifted.

"And broke them?"

"Thankfully not. They left them carefully on the ground all around the tree."

Annie chuckled. "Where do kids come up with things like that?"

"The mayor wasn't too happy." Caleb shoved away from the counter. "C'mon and meet Harriet and Samson."

"I was thinking I needed to rescue her from my daughter's endless questions."

"You kidding? Harriet is loving this." He gestured toward the woman with short brown hair and a huge smile on her face.

"Yep, every ornament was on the ground. It took me and some others most of the morning to redecorate the tree. I think Caleb should post guards around it." Harriet peered at Annie as she stopped at the side of the desk near her daughter. "You must be Sara's cousin, Annie." The woman took Annie's hand and pumped her arm.

"I'll see you tonight," Caleb whispered close to Annie's ear. "I have to pay a visit to one of the boys I think is responsible for the mess in the town square. But first I'll have to deal with the mayor again. He just came in."

Caleb strode toward the middle-aged, stocky man whose dark gaze lit upon Caleb. The town leader's beet-red face attested that his anger was still present. But Caleb's calm demeanor slowly eroded the man's wrath until he let out a deep breath and followed Caleb into his office.

Maybe she could tell Caleb what happened in Florida. Maybe he could help her figure out what was going on and what to do about it.

But as she, Sara and Jayden left to finish their errands, another police officer entered the station. Annie almost ran into him when she opened the door. She quickly sidled away. Although dressed in the same blue uniform as Caleb, this man brought to mind Bryan's warning not to trust the police. As much as she wanted to trust Caleb, she couldn't.

While Sara was reading to Jayden in the living room and the stew was in the Crock-Pot, Annie stepped outside onto the back stoop. Although the temperature was a little above freezing, she relished the crisp air, the perfectly still wind. The sun sank below the tree line, a rosy hue tinting the few clouds in the sky.

The line of fir trees along the back of Sara's property caught her attention. She strode across the yard to get away from the house. She didn't want anyone to overhear her as she made a call. She withdrew her cell from her pocket and called information to find out the police department number in Crystal Creek.

When someone answered, she said to the woman on the other end, "I'm calling about a break-in at my apartment a few days ago."

"Just a moment please."

"Can I help you?" a deep, baritone voice asked a minute later.

"This is Annie Coleman."

Before she could continue, the man said, "We've been looking for you. Where are you?"

"I'm on vacation. Have you found out who broke in?"

"No. Do you have anyone angry at you? Your valuables seemed to still be there, but they were destroyed. Television smashed to pieces, pearl necklace broken

and scattered all over the floor. It was more vandalism than a robbery."

Because Bryan's killer was looking for something.
"When I return I'll come see you. Thanks." She clicked
off quickly, praying she hadn't made a mistake by calling them. She'd kept hoping they might have a clue to
who had trashed her apartment. Now she realized that
that was wishful thinking.

She turned at the sound of the back door slamming
closed and a yelping dog. A big, black mutt bounded
toward her with Jayden not far behind. Annie braced
herself, but a few feet from her, the dog skidded to a
stop.

Her daughter halted next to the animal and threw
her arms around him. "Isn't Ralph great? He can even
do tricks. Caleb showed me."

At a much more leisurely gait, the police chief approached, again dressed in casual jeans, a blue T-shirt
and an open sheepskin coat. "Your daughter wanted
to show you Ralph."

"Will you show Mommy how he can roll over?"

"You can get him to by pointing your finger and
making a circle in the air," he said with a grin.

Jayden squared her shoulders and inhaled a deep
breath, then drew a circle. Ralph performed the trick
while Jayden clapped.

Caleb retrieved a rubber ball from his coat pocket.
"He loves to fetch. Do you want to throw the ball for
him?"

"Yes!"

As Caleb gave the toy to Jayden, Annie's throat
closed at the excitement that brightened her child's
face. She ran a few yards, winding up her arm, then

lobbed the ball as far as she could. Ralph shot after it. It bounced several times and landed by the back door. Her daughter ran after the dog.

"I'm gonna have to get her a dog. This will cinch it."

"Kids should have a pet. It teaches them responsibility and how to care for something other than themselves."

"Thanks for bringing Ralph over." While Jayden continued to throw the ball for Ralph, Annie started across the yard. "I'd forgotten how quiet this town is. A good quiet. Sara says this is a great place to raise children, that it's so peaceful a lot of people don't lock their doors."

"Yeah, I'm trying to convince them to lock them at least at night, but most of the older folks never have." Caleb paused, his intense gaze skimming her face. "That includes Sara."

"I know. That's when we had the discussion last night about not locking the doors. I did. I told her I couldn't sleep with one eye open." When she did sleep, which had been little lately. "Are you staying for dinner?"

"Of course. I could smell that stew the second your daughter opened the front door. I didn't even have to beg Sara. She asked when I set foot in the living room."

"How did you know it was stew?"

A gleam twinkled in his eyes. "I looked."

Annie stopped at the bottom of the back steps and swung around to watch her daughter. "Jayden, it's time to go in."

Her daughter trudged toward the stoop with the dog bouncing across the yard much like the rubber ball he held in his mouth had.

Five minutes later, Annie entered the living room after checking on the stew in the Crock-Pot and setting the table. Sara sat in her favorite lounge chair while Jayden sprawled on the area rug, busily drawing a picture of Ralph stretched out before the fireplace.

"Caleb, would you be a dear and build a fire?" Sara pulled the edges of her shawl together.

"Sure. I'll need to move some of the items away from the fireplace."

Jayden leaped to her feet. "I'll help." She headed straight for the figure of the baby Jesus, gently lifting it from the manger and cradling it against her as if she were playing with one of her dolls that she'd had to leave in Crystal Creek. "Miss Sara says I can hold him. But I hafta to be *real* careful."

"Are you sure, Sara?" Annie held her breath watching her child handling the eighteen-inch-long figurine, beautifully painted.

"She's fine."

"Here, hon, I'll move the manger for you." Annie tried not to think about the things they'd left behind in the rented apartment. And according to Trey, all destroyed because someone had searched and trashed her place. Looking for what?

A thoughtful expression slashed her daughter's face. "What's a manger?"

"Child, it's a place where animals eat." Sara rubbed her hands together.

"Why was baby Jesus put in one?"

"Because there was nowhere else for Mary to give birth to Him. The inn—motels were full, so they stayed in a stable." Caleb stacked the logs on the grate then turned the gas on and put a match to it. Flames burst about the wood.

Jayden tilted her head to the side, her eyebrows crunched together. "But isn't Jesus special? He should have a big bed."

"Yeah, Jesus is special, but He didn't mind the manger." Caleb rose and caught Annie's look.

In that moment she knew she had let her daughter down. She might be upset with the Lord because He wasn't answering her prayers, but she should have at least given her child a chance to learn about Him so she would be able to make up her own mind when she was older. At breakfast this morning Sara had talked about going to church on Sunday and had asked them to go.

At one time she had believed that all things were possible through God. She'd been active in her youth group at church, had gone on mission trips. Then she'd made wrong choices when her father had walked out on the family. She'd thrust herself into a murky pattern of self-destruction. She was thankful Jayden's birth stopped that slippery slope downward. But was the Lord mad at her because of her actions?

"Give me about five minutes to get the dinner on the table." Annie averted her gaze and hurried from the room. She wouldn't be using that excuse on Sunday; she needed to take her daughter to church.

In the kitchen she had begun spooning the stew into a serving bowl when Caleb came in.

"Here, let me help." He held the Crock-Pot over the bowl so she could slide the stew into it. "Are you okay?"

"No. I just realized what an injustice I have done to my daughter. I should have taken her to church, but I was angry with God. I still am."

"Why?"

"My life wasn't going the way I thought it should.

I prayed and prayed for help, but He didn't answer me. I was basically alone, struggling to pay my bills, raising my daughter with little support…" When she realized what she was telling him, she peered at him to read his expression. Compassion greeted her look.

"What happened to Jayden's dad?"

"He's dead."

"I'm sorry. That makes it tough."

If you only knew.

Caleb set the Crock-Pot on the counter and took her hands. "Look at coming to Christmas as a fresh start. The Lord hasn't forgotten you. He doesn't. He answers in His time, not ours. I'd love for you and Jayden to come to church with me on Sunday."

For a few seconds Annie couldn't concentrate enough to form a coherent reply to his invitation. All her senses were centered on the feel of his hands around hers, the rough texture of his thumb rubbing her skin, his spicy scent wafting to her, putting to shame the aromas of the stew and rolls baking.

"Will you come, Annie?"

She stepped back, grabbing for the pot holders to take the bread out of the oven. "Sara said something about it." She didn't want to care for Caleb. She would be moving on when she could come up with a plan. She needed to return to the library and begin researching how to get lost and stay hidden.

"That's okay. We go to the same one. I'll come by and pick everyone up."

The next afternoon, late, Caleb rang the bell at Sara's. He really didn't have an excuse for visiting, but he was here because he found himself drawn to

Annie and Jayden. Since his father's death last year, he'd been going through the motions of living, but something was missing. He wanted a marriage like his parents had.

Whoa. He'd gone from thinking about Annie to thinking about marriage. He still couldn't shake the feeling something was wrong with Annie. Had someone hurt her? Her deceased husband?

Annie swung the door open. "Hi." Her smile encompassed her whole face, pushing away the vulnerability he'd glimpsed for a few seconds. Now he realized why he was here. He wanted to pump Sara about information concerning Annie. The investigator in him couldn't let go of the fact Annie was harboring pain. He wanted to know what caused it and help.

"What brings you by?"

He pulled his thoughts back to the task at hand. "I came to see Sara."

"Oh, that sounds serious. Is there a problem?"

He schooled his expression into a neutral one, hoping he hadn't given anything away. "No." He should elaborate, but what could he say to Annie? *I've come to find out all I can about you and what made you visit a relative suddenly right before Christmas. One you haven't seen in fifteen years.*

"Were there any more teenage pranks pulled last night?"

"All's calm right now. I issued my warning to the one I think is behind it. Hopefully he heeds it. If not, I may sic the mayor on him," Caleb said with a laugh as he crossed the threshold.

"Is that your secret weapon?"

"No, my art of persuasion is."

Annie closed the door. "Sara is in the living room in her usual place."

"Are you going out?" He noticed she had her coat on, her purse sitting on the table in the foyer.

"Yeah, as soon as Jayden washes up. She had some chocolate and managed to get it all over her face and hands."

Carrying her doll, Jayden bounded down the stairs in her jacket, her hair pulled back in a ponytail that bounced with her lively movement. "Is Ralph here?"

Caleb responded to the little girl's smile with one of his own. "Sorry. I left him at home. I can bring him by later if you want."

"Yes!" Jayden pumped her arm. "We're goin' to the liberrie."

"We've already read the books we got yesterday. We're getting some more. And Sara wanted me to pick up one for her." Annie grabbed her purse. "Ready?"

Jayden hurried across the foyer, snatched up her pile of books and rushed out the door.

Annie shook her head. "I guess she's ready. See you later."

"Bye." He waited until she was gone before proceeding into the living room and taking a seat.

Sara closed the magazine she was reading and placed it in her lap. "I heard you at the door. Did you know Jayden is already reading? She loves books 'bout as much as I do."

"You really have enjoyed having them here, haven't you?"

"I didn't realize how until today. When they first came, I sensed they were lost and looking for something. Well, at least Annie. But so was I. These past few days have brought me back to life. So yes, I've enjoyed them being here. I'm so glad she decided to visit me."

"Did she ever tell you why she suddenly decided to come see you?"

"No, other than she'd always had fond memories of the couple of times she had when she was a child. Especially that last visit, when she and her family came at Christmastime."

"She told me her husband was dead."

"Husband? She said that?" Sara's wrinkles deepened on her forehead.

"Well, not in those words. I asked about Jayden's father."

"Annie has never been married." Sara leaned forward in her chair. "I've been meaning to talk to you about that. I'm concerned about Annie. I think she's in trouble. Earlier today when I asked why she didn't wear a wedding ring, she told me she'd never married the man who fathered Jayden. I'd thought that first day she'd come the name you used to introduce her was her married name, so I didn't say anything. But her real last name is Coleman, at least that was it when she was ten."

Caleb inhaled a deep breath and held it. This was what he'd come for, to find out what was going on with Annie, but he didn't want to hear that she was in trouble. He wanted to be wrong about his gut feeling that something was wrong with her. "Did you say anything about it to her?"

"No. Every time I start asking about what she's been doing she manages to change the subject as quickly as possible. I think my question about the wedding ring threw her, or I'm not sure I would have gotten that much information. Something's not right."

"Are you worried about yourself?" He hated asking that question because his gut told him Annie wasn't someone who would hurt Sara, but he was a cop and Sara was a friend. He *had* to ask.

Sara chuckled. "Absolutely not. I'm a good judge of people, and I see a woman who is hiding something because she's afraid. I catch glimpses of fear in her eyes every once and a while. For instance, yesterday in town a car backfired. She went deathly pale, grabbed Jayden and shielded her. It took her several minutes to calm down, although she tried to hide her fright at the sudden sound. And right after that, Annie was talking on her cell in the library. Her face went pale, and she dropped the phone." Sighing as though relieved she finally shared her concerns, she sat back.

"What do you want me to do?"

"Do some investigating like they do on TV? See if you can find out anything? Most people don't leave home, drive halfway across the country and show up on someone's doorstep they're not even sure is still alive or living where they used to. What made her leave Florida?"

"I'll see what I can find." After hearing what Sara had discovered, his concerns spiraled upward and alarm bells pealed loudly in his mind.

"You said something about bringing Ralph down this evening. Come for dinner, too. Annie is planning spaghetti. We're eating at six."

"Sold." He came to his feet. "I best be going. See you later."

Outside he paused and drew in a deep breath. What

kind of trouble could Annie be in? First thing he would do was drive by the library and get her license plate number and find out where she lived in Florida.

He drove to the library, jotted down her number and then left, not wanting to hang around and have her find him there. He went to his office and ran her tag number. After discovering she lived in Crystal Creek, Florida, he placed a call to the police there.

"This is Caleb Jackson, of the police department in Christmas, Oklahoma. Can I speak to your police chief?"

When the man came on the line, Caleb explained who he was and asked, "Are there any outstanding warrants for a Annie Coleman. She lives in Crystal—"

"I'm familiar with who Annie Coleman is."

Caleb straightened in his chair. "You are? How?"

"Someone broke into her place a few days ago and I'd been trying to locate her ever since. She finally called me yesterday afternoon and told me she would handle it when she got back to town."

"Do you know who did it?"

"No, but they destroyed just about everything in her apartment. It appears to have happened late Saturday night or the early hours of Sunday morning. Is she in any kind of trouble there in Oklahoma?"

"No, not with the police." When Caleb hung up, he couldn't shake the warning bell going off in his mind. What was Annie into?

He decided to make a call to a friend on the police force in Orlando. Maybe he could dig around and find out what kind of trouble Annie was in? Because everything pointed to a woman on the run. Why?

When Don answered, Caleb took a few minutes to

catch up with what was going on with him, then Caleb said, "I have a favor. I need you to find out what you can on Annie Coleman. She lives in Crystal Creek. There was a break-in at her apartment, but from what the police say it sounds like someone that is angry with her or looking for something. They tore her place apart."

"Will do. It may take a few days because I've got a tough case I'm working on, but on my first day off, I'll go to Crystal Creek and do some poking around. Talk with her neighbors. Where she works. I'll even check in with the local police and see if there are any new developments on the break-in."

"Thanks. I owe you." Caleb's hand lingered on the phone after he returned it to its cradle. *Lord, whatever problem Annie is having, let it be one I can help her with.*

Chapter Four

On the computer at the library after searching on the Internet for twenty minutes for information on Nick Salvador, she found an article in a Florida newspaper about him being indicted for murder several years ago. She went through the archives of later issues until she discovered what the verdict in the Salvador trial had been.

She stared at the screen. Terror seized her. He had been acquitted of the murder charge, but the reporter noted that a key witness had never showed up to testify. He'd disappeared. She ran a name search on the witness but didn't find anything pertaining to him. Was he dead? Or living somewhere else?

She pictured something like that happening to her. For a second, panic gripped her. She quickly looked around the library, her heartbeat rapping a mad staccato against her ribs.

"I've got my books," Jayden said, cradling her doll against her chest.

Annie cleared the screen and turned toward her daughter, forcing a smile to her mouth while inside terror still ruled. All she wanted to do was grab her child, hug her tightly and find a way to vanish. Next time she came she would have to research ways to disappear without a trace. There was no way she would risk going back to Crystal Creek now.

"Ready?" Clutching her five books to her chest, Jayden rocked back on her heels.

"Yep, let's go check these out. I need to get back to Miss Sara's and cook dinner." She'd come back tomorrow and do some more searching. She still didn't have any idea what was going on. Maybe the thugs who had trashed her apartment had found whatever they were looking for. What if they weren't looking for an object but for her, because Bryan had called her and she'd overheard some of what happened to him?

On Monday afternoon, Annie grabbed her jacket and hurried into the hall upstairs. She'd promised her daughter she would go for a walk with her today and explore the area. Jayden was taking the idea of being on an adventure seriously, whereas Annie wanted her life back. She'd finished her research today on how to disappear and knew it wouldn't be easy, especially since she had little money. She didn't even have a cell phone anymore. She'd thrown it away after receiving another message from Bryan's killer two days ago. He used Bryan's cell phone again to call her.

His message, "I'm coming to get you," echoed through her thoughts, producing beads of sweat on her forehead and upper lip. She swiped her hand across her face. She couldn't let her daughter see how upset she was. Acting as though nothing was wrong wearied her to the point where she was getting no more than a few hours sleep at night.

Annie descended the staircase, composing her features into a calm countenance for her daughter. Jayden was probably already on the porch waiting, since she wasn't the most patient child. As Annie emerged from the house, she paused. A sudden sense of being watched crawled up her spine, an unpleasant tingling following in its wake.

The last message left on her cell popped into her mind again. She went weak-kneed and clutched the post to steady herself.

Jayden hopped up from the porch swing and skipped to her. "Ready, Mommy? Let's go."

"Sure," she whispered, her throat tight, her mouth dry.

But Annie held her ground for a moment while she scanned up and down the street. There wasn't one car out of place or anyone hanging around. She had been letting her imagination run rampant ever since she listened to her cell phone messages and discovered the type of father Bryan had—one who would go to any lengths to get what he wanted. One who could afford to hire thugs to take care of the messy stuff.

Bryan's killer's messages unnerved her. His taunts indicated he was getting closer. She knew he was doing that to throw her off balance so she would make a mistake. There was no reason to think anyone had found her here in Christmas. She shook off the sensation that someone was out there keeping track of her movements, waiting for the perfect moment to pounce on her.

"C'mon. You promised." Jayden tugged on Annie's hand.

"Fine, but we can't be gone long." When her daughter started to pout, Annie added, "Caleb could still bring Ralph over today. I'm sure you'll want to be here when he does."

Annie followed behind Jayden, who skipped ahead. The feeling she was being watched stuck with Annie all the way around the corner and never ceased, even when she and Jayden started down the road behind Sara's property. What had happened at her apartment had happened in Florida. Not here.

As she strolled near the curb because there was no sidewalk, Annie glanced around at the houses, smaller than those on the street where Sara lived. Fifty feet ahead of Annie, Jayden paused for a second in front of a place and then darted forward. The border of bushes and trees obstructed her view of her daughter.

"Jayden, wait for me." Her shout reverberated down the street.

She hurried her pace, rounding the overgrown hedge in time to see Jayden disappear behind a run-down house that appeared vacant. Her pulse rate increased as her steps did toward the place.

"Jayden, come here."

"Mom*eeee*," her daughter yelled, the sound sending a streak of panic down Annie and propelling her into a flat-out run.

Annie came around the side of the house and heard her daughter whimpering. Fear draped her in an icy sweat, and she rushed toward the sound, her heartbeat roaring in her ears. Blocked by a large holly bush up against the wooden structure, Annie didn't see where Jayden was until she skirted the shrub and found her daughter down on the ground, one leg stuck in a hole that had been boarded over.

Tears in her eyes, Jayden looked up. "I can't get up. It hurts."

Part of her wanted to wail at her daughter for running ahead of her, but she kept her words inside for later, when she was calmer. "Don't move. Let me see what I can do."

Annie approached Jayden as a large black dog bounded around the corner of the house, barking. Caleb appeared right on his pet's heels. Surprised to see him but relieved to have help, she knelt next to her daughter and began checking out the situation.

"What happened?" Concern on his face, he stooped beside Annie.

"I thought I saw something inside. I was looking in when I fell." Tears rolled down Jayden's cheeks.

"Honey, we'll get you out," Annie said, while she couldn't shake the words her child had uttered. *Something inside? What?* Again the threat in the message played across her mind. No, she couldn't show her panic. She wouldn't give in to what the killer was trying to do. Her call to the police couldn't have been traced to Christmas. And she hadn't left a trail to the town.

"This looks like a hole that the previous owner covered up with some boards. It's been here a while, and most of the wood is rotten. I'll pull Jayden straight up while you try to keep her leg from being scraped any more with the jagged pieces." Standing and leaning over, Caleb put his arms around her child. "Are you ready?"

Jayden nodded.

Annie wedged one hand down between her daughter's leg and the worst broken piece of wood. With the other, she clasped Jayden to help guide the leg straight up. "Ready."

"On the count of three. One. Two. Three." Caleb slowly lifted Annie from the hole.

The action pressed Annie's palm into a sharp, jagged point. Pain flashed up her arm. She bit down and pulled her hand free as soon as her daughter was out. Blood trickled from a cut on her skin.

Ignoring the wound, she angled toward her daughter on the ground, where Caleb examined the gash visible beneath the torn, ruined cotton pants. She moved to Jayden.

Caleb ripped off a part of her daughter's slacks and tied the strip around her calf to stop the bleeding. "We should have Doc look at this. It might need stitches."

"Stitches!" Jayden's eyes grew round as a full moon.

Ralph licked her child's face, producing a giggle. Jayden threw her arms around the dog's neck and plastered her cheek against his fur.

"Let's get her back to my house. I'll call Doc and let him know you're coming in. Are you ready? I'm gonna carry you, Jayden." Caleb slipped his arms under Jayden and lifted her in one fluid motion.

Balling her throbbing hand, Annie rose. "We need to let Sara know we'll be late. She'll worry."

"Get my cell from my left jacket pocket. Call Sara, then I'll give you Doc's number to dial for me."

She stepped nearer to reach for the phone. When she pulled it out, he started for the front of the house while Annie called Sara and told her what happened and where they were going.

When she hung up, Caleb stopped and spun toward

her. "Doc's number is—" His gaze latched on to something over her shoulder. A frown descended.

Annie pivoted and saw the front door of the abandoned house open slightly. "Jayden thought she saw something inside." Annie again felt as though eyes were on her.

His jaw set in a grim line, he handed Jayden to Annie, took his cell, then headed toward the porch. "Wait by the street." He signaled to Ralph to go with Annie, then he cautiously entered the house.

"Mommy, what if the ghost gets him?"

With Ralph next to her, Annie followed his directions and stood at the edge of the property along the road, comforted by the fact a big dog was with her. "Honey, there's no such thing as ghosts. If there was someone in the house, he was very much alive. And while we're on this subject, don't ever run off from me again. Understood?"

"I'm sorry. The house looked haunted."

"It isn't." Annie inched closer to Ralph.

Caleb emerged from the house and crossed the yard to them. The scowl on his face didn't bode well. He'd found something he didn't like.

"Did you see anything?" Jayden asked.

"Nothing to concern you. Let's go get you patched up. That's my priority now."

What did you find? Annie wanted to demand details but clenched her jaw and kept quiet. She would revisit the subject when Jayden wasn't listening.

Caleb started to take her daughter from her when his gaze caught sight of her injury. "You're hurt, too." He paused and took hold of her hand. "You should have said something."

"It's nothing." The feel of his fingers touching her momentarily wiped the dull ache emanating from her wound.

"Doc's gonna have two patients." Caleb took Jayden. "I've already called him, and he'll be at his office."

Two hours later Annie sat in Caleb's car heading back to Sara's with a bandaged hand, a sleepy daughter and a sack of food from the café for dinner. Darkness had fallen over the town, but the Christmas lights lit the night.

Annie peered into the back of the vehicle and saw her daughter nodding off until she slumped over onto the seat. "We didn't get a chance to talk about what was inside the house."

"Someone was using the house to stay in. I suspect some teens are using it to party. I'll have a word with them tomorrow and put the fear of the law into them."

"Do you think they ran out the front while we were in the backyard?"

"Maybe. I didn't notice if the door was open when I arrived. I was focused on you disappearing around the corner. More likely they forgot to shut it all the way, and the wind blew it open." Caleb pulled up to Sara's and opened his door. "Grab the food, and I'll get Jayden."

Caleb carried her daughter toward Sara's, Jayden slowly waking up and rubbing her eyes. Her wrapped leg testified to her "adventure," one Annie hoped she didn't repeat. The tears in the doctor's office as well as the stitches her daughter had were bad enough, but she didn't know how she was going to pay the bill. Although Doc didn't seem too concerned, she knew the state of her finances wouldn't take many more of these little mishaps, especially if she had to start over somewhere new.

"Sara's probably starved by now. She's used to eating early." Annie took out her key and unlocked the front door then entered.

"I imagine she's more concerned about Jayden than anything."

Before Annie closed the door, Sara stood in the entrance into the living room. "How's Jayden?" Worry lined her wrinkled face as she moved toward them.

"Miss Sara, I'm okay." Jayden yawned, then stuck her leg out. "See. I got four stitches."

Sara made a production out of examining the bandage. "Doc did a great job fixing you as good as new."

Annie headed for the kitchen. "I'll have dinner on the table in a few minutes. Jayden, go wash up."

Caleb gently set her daughter down, and she limped toward the small bathroom under the staircase.

"Annie, let's have a picnic in the living room." Sara moved toward the room. "I already have a blanket spread on the floor in front of the fireplace. Caleb can fix a fire."

Ten minutes later Annie sat on a large red-and-green plaid blanket eating fried chicken and all the fixings, from biscuits to coleslaw to green beans. With a huge grin, Jayden put her drumstick down on her paper plate, grease smeared around her mouth. Annie handed her a napkin, which her daughter swiped across her face.

As Annie settled next to Caleb, the fire warming her back, he captured her gaze and held it. Her stomach tightened at the gleam that glinted in his eyes. She searched for a safe topic of conversation—one that didn't make her regret her decision to leave after the New Year, all brought on by her fearful feelings and the messages she'd received. She couldn't stay long in any one place. That would give the man time to find her. How she was going to be able to disappear with her daughter was still a question she couldn't really answer.

This town had taught her one thing. If she had to disappear, she needed a place where she could keep to herself. It was much easier that way. There were too many times she wanted to confide in Sara and Caleb. The burden of an unknown enemy out there was taking its toll on her. Especially when she had to seem perfectly fine so as not to arouse any suspicion.

If Nick Salvador or one of his goons were after her, she never wanted to subject the townspeople, especially Caleb and Sara, to someone like him with unsavory connections and accusations of murder in his past. They had all been so kind, accepting her and her daughter.

"How did you know we were on the other block earlier today?" Annie finally asked, although her words held a whispery quality at the intensity flowing from him, all directed at her.

"Sara told me. I just missed you."

"I'm glad you came," Jayden said before Annie could open her mouth. "You saved me."

The admiration in her daughter's eyes probably mirrored her expression, Annie thought. She wasn't good at relationships. The one person she'd really fallen for in the end hadn't been who he'd first appeared to be. She'd thought Bryan was kind, honest and caring, but the only person he'd really cared about was himself. He'd been in Jayden's life when it suited him. And she'd caught him in enough lies while they had dated that when she'd discovered she was pregnant she knew she couldn't marry him. So why was she responding to Caleb? She'd learned her lesson, hadn't she?

"I hope you know now not to go off exploring on your own, especially vacant buildings. They can be dangerous," Caleb said in his police officer voice.

Jayden hung her head. "I won't." She lifted her chin and looked right at Caleb. "I wasn't gonna go in. Promise."

Sara leaned forward and gave Annie her plate. "Remember those marshmallows I got at the store the other day? Let's roast them over the fire. I used to do that as a kid."

Caleb rose then tugged Annie to her feet. "Do you have some metal coat hangers?"

"In the hall closet." Sara waved her hand toward the foyer.

"I'll get them while you get the bag of marshmallows." Caleb picked up the trash Annie couldn't, snagged a mint from a jar on Sara's end table and headed toward the foyer.

After rummaging through the cabinet in the kitchen, Annie found the chewy treat and pulled the bag out. She turned to go back in the living room and nearly collided with Caleb standing behind her.

He hadn't needed to steady her, but his hands clasped her upper arms anyway. The smile deep in his eyes warmed her more than the fire had earlier. Tired of being alone and doing everything herself, she wanted to snuggle into his embrace and feel its protective touch about her.

"How's your hand?" He slid his down her arm to clasp her injured one. Turning it palm up, he peered at it.

"It's quit throbbing," she managed to whisper, although her words came out breathless.

"Good." His gaze stole the rest of her breath. "I worry about you."

The huskiness in his voice constricted her throat, and the intensity in his expression seized her and held her motionless. Worry about her? Bryan certainly hadn't. Somehow he'd dragged her into a mess that might cost her life. "You don't need to. I'm fine." She tried to interject conviction behind that declaration, but Caleb gave her a slow appraising glance.

He combed his fingers through her hair. "If you're in trouble, I can help you."

"In trouble?" Her mind could hardly wrap itself around his words. All she wanted to do was block the world out and just enjoy this man's attention for just a moment in the middle of the nightmare her life had become.

He leaned in, his mouth inches from hers. The scent of peppermint teased her senses. "I take my job seriously."

The whispered words tickled her lips. She closed her eyes, the anticipation of his kiss tapping a fast tempo against her rib cage. When his mouth finally settled over hers, she melted against him, her legs going weak. He wound his arms about her and held her upright while deepening the touch of their lips.

When they parted, he rested his forehead against

hers, and she tried to bring some kind of order to her thoughts. But all she could think about was the dynamite kiss that had been gentle but demanding at the same time. She was in such trouble, and it had nothing to do with Nick Salvador and Bryan's killer. Caleb had the ability to steal her heart. She'd had it crushed once before and because of Bryan might never be able to go home again. That scared her.

The reminder forced her from Caleb's arms. She stepped back against the counter and gripped the edge. "I'll be moving along after the holidays. I'm thinking of heading out west." As far away from Florida as possible.

"Why? If you're looking for a new place to live, what's wrong with settling down in this town?"

Nothing. "Too small." Hard to get lost in. According to what she'd read on the Internet, a big city might be easier to disappear in.

"Oh, I see." Caleb took the marshmallows from her and pivoted toward the hallway. "We better get into the living room before Sara sends out a search party."

Annie stayed for a moment, her grasp on the counter the only thing holding her up. That kiss and her response changed everything, but she couldn't allow it to. She'd fought her battles alone. Nick Salvador could destroy people's lives with his questionable connections, money and hired thugs. She wouldn't do that to Caleb.

By herself, she would keep Jayden and her safe.

By herself, she would find a way to disappear and a place to live.

But as she contemplated the loneliness stretching before her, her thoughts strayed to the kiss that had taken a piece of her heart. She doubted she would get it back. Caleb was the marrying kind of man, one who would protect the people he loved to the end.

Tell him what's going on. Get his help.

She didn't know what was going on. How could she explain it to another?

By herself, she firmed the resolution in her mind and pushed off the counter.

As she entered the living room, she came to a stop just inside and took in that man helping her daughter roast marshmallows over a blazing fire. Jayden's giggles filled the air. Her megawatt grin brightened the room more than the lights. Caleb glanced back at her. His veiled expression didn't reveal anything that had happened in the kitchen, but when she had said Christmas was too small for her, she'd seen the quickly masked hurt in his eyes.

As Jayden and Caleb prepared the treats for everyone, Sara pushed herself out of the lounge chair and shuffled toward the long table behind the couch. She plucked the ceramic Christmas tree from it and carried it back with her.

"Jayden, I usually decorate every room in the house, but I didn't this year because of my fall." Sara set the tree with colorful painted ornaments down beside Jayden. "Put this in your bedroom. In fact, tomorrow we can drag out the boxes I put away and see what else I have that will add a touch of Christmas to your room."

"Do you have a manger with baby Jesus, Mary and Joseph? I learned about them yesterday in Sunday school class."

"I think I have several in those boxes somewhere."

Jayden clapped. "Yippee. This will be fun."

Sara chuckled. "Christmas is so much better with children around. Too bad you have to work, Caleb, or you could come over and help."

He gave Sara her plate with a roasted marshmallow on it. "I'll stop by at the end of the day, and if there's anything I can hang and put up for you, I will."

A warm, cozy living room with a large Christmas tree in front of the floor-to-ceiling window, garland draped along the fireplace, a blaze in the hearth with the scent of wood permeating the air, snowman figurines everywhere, bright twinkling lights on the tree and intertwined in the wreath hanging over the mantel. She wanted to savor the evening for as long as she could.

"I'm glad you came over tonight." Annie slipped out the front door later and stood with Caleb on the porch. "It'll be fun decorating tomorrow. We didn't get to do much this year at home."

"You didn't want to because you were going to be gone?" He took her hands in his, the touch warm.

Now she realized her mistake. She shouldn't have walked him to the door or come out onto the porch to say good-night. Without Sara or Jayden around, she was afraid Caleb, a police officer who was probably a master at interrogation, would grill her. The whole evening he had asked questions about her life. She'd given him a few tidbits, but not much.

She shrugged. "Why decorate when you aren't going to be around? We didn't have much anyway."

He pulled her toward the porch swing and sat, tugging her down next to him. "I feel like tonight all I did was talk about myself. You know about my father's death last year. About the reason I left Tulsa. But I didn't tell you the whole story. I was dating a woman seriously in Tulsa and when my father became ill and I knew I needed to return home to help him, I asked her to marry me."

What would it be like married to someone like Caleb who cared about others, was honest and decent? If she had to live her life on the run, she'd never find out. "It's obvious she didn't. What happened?"

"She told me no, said she couldn't live in a place like Christmas. She hated small towns. I was floored. I thought I knew her, and I didn't. It made me question my judgment."

Ah, so when she'd said that this evening, it had brought back memories of the woman in Tulsa. "How do you feel now?" She knew exactly what he had gone through, because she had with Bryan.

"I finally decided the Lord had a hand in it. He had something else in mind for me."

"I wish I had your faith. I did at one time." In more ways than one. He believed good would triumph over evil in the end. She wasn't so sure, especially with evil lurking out there ready to pounce on her.

With his finger under her chin, he drew her face around so she had to look him straight in the eye. "What happened?"

This she could tell him, and he still wouldn't know what was really going on. Maybe then the questions would stop. "I've made some bad choices, ending with getting involved with Bryan, Jayden's dad. My father leaving sent my mother into a severe depression. She never recovered. Nothing I could do made a difference. She died brokenhearted."

"I'm so sorry, Annie."

Tears crowded her eyes, her throat aching. "I know tragedy happens, but why does it have to?"

"Because we aren't meant to spend eternity here. This is the place where we grow and learn. Sadly that doesn't always happen, when everything goes along merrily with no obstacles to surmount."

"What doesn't break you makes you stronger?"

"Something like that." He used his thumbs to brush away the rivulets of tears flowing from her eyes, then he cupped her face. "Thank you for trusting me with that. You don't know how much it means to me." He bent toward her and kissed her.

In that one gentle kiss he branded her his. From the very beginning he had accepted her, no questions asked. That fact awed her. He hadn't gone behind her back but had waited for her to tell him her story— even if he didn't realize it wasn't the whole story. For the first time in a while she felt hope for the future. Maybe she should say something to him about Bryan's murder and father.

Pulling away, Caleb looked long and hard at her. "I'd better call it a night. See you tomorrow."

As he strolled away, he felt her gaze on him as though she had brushed her hand down his spine. She had trusted him only partially. But she hadn't said a word about the break-in at her apartment in Crystal Creek or the fact all her possessions had been trashed. Why not? Why would that make her flee her home and travel across the country right before Christmas? What else was she keeping from him? He was developing deep feelings for her, and he couldn't allow them to go any further. She wasn't staying in town after the New Year. But mostly even if she was, he had to have total trust.

Chapter Five

Wednesday afternoon, Annie rocked back and forth in the porch swing while Sara took an afternoon nap and Jayden sat on the steps and drew pictures. Bright sunshine and warm temperatures made the day beautiful, promising. But inside Annie couldn't unwind. Her stomach remained in a tight knot, as though a nest of vipers lay curled in a lump, waiting to strike and inject her with their poison.

With a glance at her watch, she rose. "Honey, I have to put the clothes into the dryer. I'll be right back."

She hurried into the laundry room and transferred the wash to the dryer. What little clothes they'd brought with them she'd cleaned several times since they'd arrived last week. She'd never had a lot of clothing, but she'd had to leave at least half behind in Crystal Creek. In that moment, the thought of having to start over in a new place—get a job somehow, find a cheap place to live—overwhelmed her. She slammed the dryer door closed and leaned into the appliance to steady herself.

Why, Lord? Why me?

No answer came to mind. She couldn't give in to

self-pity. It wouldn't change her situation or produce a solution. She would survive and protect Jayden. She had no other choice.

She pushed off the dryer and scrubbed her hands down her face as though that could miraculously wipe any fear from her expression. She made her way to the foyer, stopping halfway across it when Jayden came into the house, carrying a wrapped present.

"Where did you get that?" Annie covered the few feet to her daughter.

Jayden held it up to her. "He gave it to me and told me to tell you it was from a secret Santa."

"Caleb?" Annie took the gift from her.

"No." Jayden shook her head several times to emphasize the point. "A stranger. I promise I didn't say anything to him. You told me never to talk to a stranger."

Chills encased Annie. "What did he look like?"

"Big."

"Anything else?"

"He wasn't Santa. He had dark hair. He came in a car, not a sled."

"What color was the car?"

"Black and big."

He could have taken Jayden. The rapid beating of her heart thundered in her ears. "Thanks, honey. Let's get your stuff and come inside." Somehow she'd managed to keep her voice level, the panic from sounding in it. But inside it raged, squeezing around her chest until she could hardly breathe.

When she stepped onto the porch again, Annie surveyed the street. As it was two days before, nothing was out of place—no strangers, no cars that shouldn't be. She'd only been gone five minutes.

After Jayden collected her pad, Annie hurried her inside and locked the door. "Why don't you go draw in our room? I'll be up there in a few minutes."

As her daughter bounded up the stairs, Annie peered out the small window in the foyer. Still nothing. She strode to the kitchen, made sure the back door was locked, then looked outside the window there. No sinister man lurking around the yard.

She sat at the table and slowly opened the package. Her hands quaked so badly she fumbled, taking twice as long as she should have. Inside the box lay a 5x7 photo of Bryan, Jayden and her he'd taken last summer. Jayden had a smaller version in her treasure chest she'd brought with her, while Bryan had framed a 5x7 picture and put it by his bedside. At least that was what he'd told her.

On the glossy page a big X was marked through Bryan. The words, You're next, were written across her image. She dropped the photo, so cold she couldn't contain her trembling. Rubbing her hands up and down her arms, she tried to erase the goose bumps from them, to warm herself. She couldn't.

Bryan's killer is here.

Caleb pushed to his feet and scooted his desk chair back. When he exited his office, he peered at the wall clock and noted the time. 2:00 p.m. He needed to grab something to eat and try to straighten out what was going on in his town. Heading toward the door to the station, he went over his earlier interview with several of the teens he'd thought had used the vacant house behind Sara to party in. None of them had, according to their protests. The three boys had seemed genuinely surprised when he had questioned them. If they were telling the truth, then who had used the house? He'd sent Jeremy, one of his police officers, over to see if he could get any fingerprints. He hadn't bothered yesterday, but now he'd give it a try, although the chances of finding the culprit's prints were slim.

Looking up and down North Pole Boulevard, Caleb started across the street for the café. Suddenly he heard the shriek of tires and peered to his left. A black SUV with dark tinted windows came barreling around the corner and headed right toward him. He dove between two parked vehicles on the other side of the street as the car whizzed by him. Scrambling to his feet, he tried to make out the tag number. Mud covered the license plate.

His palms stinging, he flipped open his cell and made a call to Tyler, another officer on patrol. He gave him what information he could on the vehicle and had him keep an eye out for it. If he hadn't reacted quickly, he could have really been hurt. Lunch forgotten, Caleb limped back across the street to the station to get his keys, which he'd overlooked on his desk. He would do his own patrolling, too.

Annie rushed into the bedroom she shared with Jayden and went to the closet, pulling out their suitcases then stuffing the still wet clothes from the dryer into one of them.

Jayden looked up from drawing at the small round table. "Are we going someplace?"

"Yes, a new adventure. C'mon. Start packing your stuff."

"I don't wanna leave." Jayden threw down her crayon.

"We're playing a game to see how fast we can get everything in the car. I think we can in ten minutes. What do you think?"

Jayden's eyes brightened. "Maybe. What do we get if we win?" She leaped up from the chair and raced toward the dresser to get her clothes.

To stay alive. "It's a surprise," Annie said, frantically trying to think of anything to say to get her daughter to cooperate. She wanted to be gone before Sara woke up from her nap. She didn't want to answer any questions.

All she knew was she needed to leave Christmas. She couldn't stay. He was here! Her heart hammered so quickly the room spun. She paused and inhaled a fortifying breath. *I can't fall apart. I can't fall apart.*

I can do all things through Christ, who strengthens me. The verse infused itself into her mind, and a calmness descended.

Ten minutes later, Annie stopped at the back door and searched the yard and driveway. Empty. She released a breath through pursed lips. She and Jayden left the house and covered the distance to her car parked in front of the detached garage. After stuffing their suitcases into the trunk, she got into the front and inserted her key into the ignition. When she turned it, nothing happened. She tried again.

Dead. As dead as she was going to be if she stayed.

Desperation drove her to try yet a third time. Nothing. She pounded her fist on the dashboard. That was when she saw the piece of paper that had slipped down near the windshield.

She read it. *You can't hide. You're mine anytime I want.*

"Mommy, what's wrong?

What should I do?

Tell Caleb. Get help.

That calmness still clung to her. She turned to Jayden and smiled, although the effort to maintain it made her lips quiver. "Let's see, how long did it take?" She checked her watch. "We did it in eleven minutes."

"We lost?"

"No, we didn't. And I think there's some ice cream in the freezer that has your name on it."

"Chocolate."

"Yep."

Jayden leaped from the car and raced for the back door. Annie exited and popped the trunk, taking their suitcases and following her daughter inside. Trying desperately to remain calm for Jayden, she fixed her daughter a large bowl of ice cream and then went to the hall phone and dialed Caleb at the police station.

"Annie, it's nice to hear from you after the bad day I've had."

"What happened?" She fought to keep her voice from wavering but her hands shook.

"A few minutes ago I almost got run over right outside the police station."

Annie straightened. On purpose? "Did you catch the person?"

"No, but I'm leaving and going out to look. What do you need?"

She couldn't tell him over the phone. "I hope you'll stop by later. Let me know what happens."

"I'll see you this evening and we'll talk."

She started to go back into the kitchen when the phone rang. She snatched it up, not wanting to disturb Sara. "Hello."

"Hi, Annie. Did you get my little present? I know it's a little early for Christmas, but I didn't want you to think I'd forgotten you," the deep, gruff voice of her tormentor said.

She shuddered at the implication of his words. "What do you want?"

"You know. And just so you don't get any ideas about telling your boyfriend about what's going on, I wanted you to know I'll actually kill him the next time. Today was your one warning."

"You tried to run him down."

"It was so much fun. Or maybe he's not enough of an incentive to keep quiet. Maybe instead, I'll take Jayden. She's a pretty little girl. Not very talkative, though."

"You wouldn't."

His cackle right before he hung up was her answer. With the receiver in hand, Annie sank to the floor and leaned her head back against the wall. She couldn't leave. And she couldn't tell Caleb.

Thursday night, Caleb turned off the ignition to his police cruiser in the church parking lot and laid his head against the steering wheel. The last few days had been hectic, especially after nearly being run over yesterday. His body still protested his contact with the asphalt surface of the street.

This morning the black SUV had been found outside of town, ditched in a field. It had been stolen the day before and all prints had been wiped clean. On the other case, Jeremy had found some usable fingerprints in the vacant house and was running them for a match. But that could take time.

He didn't like everything that was happening in Christmas lately. He had someone he was falling for obviously in trouble and not saying anything to him. Last night he'd tried again to get her to talk, but she hadn't. He had someone who had deliberately headed right toward him on the street. And he had someone, maybe more than one, using the vacant house without the knowledge of the owners, who he'd contacted yesterday.

The ringing of his cell cut into his thoughts. "Jackson here."

"I've got something else for you, which may or may not be connected to your Annie Coleman," his friend Don from the Orlando Police said.

Caleb sat up straight, peering toward the doors to the church. "What?"

"Her landlord is in the hospital in a coma. Someone beat him up bad. Nearly killed him."

"When?"

"Middle of last week."

"Any suspects?"

"No. I also discovered her daughter's father was found dead—beaten up and shot in the stomach."

Caleb's gut constricted into a hard ball. "No suspects?"

"You got it. This doesn't bode well for your Annie."

My Annie. The woman who wouldn't say a word

to him about what was going on. One way or another he would get to the bottom of this tonight. He was through waiting for her to tell him. "If you hear anything else, call."

He slipped from the front seat and crossed the parking lot to find his Annie.

"I was gonna borrow Harriet's car to go get the box of garland. I'm glad you showed up," Annie said as she walked toward Caleb's vehicle parked in the church lot, not five minutes after he arrived. "You look tired."

"Just working hard." He took her hand, a frown creasing his forehead. "You are shaking. Are you okay?"

No, my life is in shambles. I don't know what to do about the man who murdered Bryan. He could be anywhere. Watching. Waiting. But if I say anything, he'll hurt someone I care about. "Too much caffeine."

"You look like you're not getting much sleep."

"I never sleep well in a new place." She slipped into the front passenger seat. When Caleb had come into the rec hall, the grim look on his face concerned her. Had the killer tried something else with him? "Did you find out anything about who tried to run you over?"

"No," he clipped out and started the engine, then backed out of the parking space. "What happened to your car? Why did you come with Harriet this evening?"

Ah, the questions again. She delayed answering as long as she could. "I went to try it and it was dead. I had it towed this morning to the garage. They haven't told me what's wrong yet. It's ten years old."

He turned down Bethlehem. "We need to talk."

"We can after the greening of the church. I don't want to leave Jayden too long with Harriet. She'll talk the woman's ear off about her cat. Besides, with all those kids running around, they need all the adults they have to get the job done before the party Saturday night."

"Fine. I'll bring you and Jayden home this evening instead of Harriet. You get the box of garland Sara called about and I'll get the stepladder they need."

She opened the door. If she kept busy, maybe she could get through this evening at church and not fall apart in front of everyone. "It shouldn't take long, but I want to check on Sara. I think she overdid it yesterday and her hip is giving her trouble."

"I'll grab my ladder and be back here."

Annie jogged to the porch and dug into her jeans pocket for the house key. When she entered, the glow from the Christmas lights Sara liked to leave on would give her enough illumination to see her way toward the small storage room off the kitchen. Sara must have gone to bed right after she called her at the church.

As Annie passed the living room, she froze. Inside it, Sara was tied up in her chair with a gag over her mouth, her eyes wide with fright.

Chapter Six

Annie whirled toward the front door and took a couple of steps when someone slammed into her. His beefy arms snaked around her, trapping her against his large body.

"Well, well, you came quick, Annie."

The sound of the intruder's voice generated a rush of memories. Of holding the phone listening to Bryan being beaten up. The noise when the gun went off. The same deep, gruff voice taunting Bryan, demanding answers. His threat to find her. To kill Caleb or take her daughter.

Panic seized her in a stranglehold, her body washing in hot and cold flashes almost simultaneously.

He killed Bryan. And he was here for her.

The assailant held her up off the floor, the upper part of her stuck to him like glue. But her legs were free. She swung one back and whacked him in the shin. He groaned. She struck him again, one of her shoes flying off. That didn't stop her. She kept hammering at him.

He groaned and muttered a few words that fired

her determination to get away. "What did Bryan give you? Where is it?"

"I don't know what you're talking about," she screamed as she swung back her foot with her slip-on shoe to hit him again. Not expecting the sudden release when he dropped her, she crumpled to the floor.

"I'll get it from you one way or another. We've looked everywhere else. We know you have it." He blasted her with his fury, towering over her. "Remember what happened to Bryan. I can do the same to her and you," he said, indicating Sara in the chair.

"I don't know what you're talking about." She poured all her confusion into her voice and expression. She couldn't give the man something she didn't have. *Lord, help.*

Hauling her to her feet, he pushed his face into hers, the scent of garlic and onions assaulting her. "Bryan gave you something to keep for him. Where is it?"

She screamed again.

He slapped her, sending her head reeling to the side. Her ears rang with the sound of his hand striking her cheek, reminding her of what he'd done to Bryan. Cold fury and fear tangled together, vying for dominance.

"If you scream again, you'll regret it." He pulled a knife out of his pocket then put it back. "Where are your things?"

"Upstairs." She balled her hands in preparation to punch him in his belly and then run.

But before she could, he hefted her over his shoulder and started for the stairs. "Show me."

The air swooshed from her lungs as her stomach connected with his shoulder. The blood rushed to her brain. She managed to kick off her other shoe while trying to hit him.

Where's Caleb?

As the intruder climbed the steps, her cheek impacted with his back with each jostling move. The farther away she was to the shoe at the bottom the more her fear grew that Caleb wouldn't reach her in time. She had to do something. She fisted her hands and pummeled his back.

On the second level he unceremoniously set her down, and she grabbed for the banister to steady herself.

"Which room?"

"That one." With a shaky hand, she pointed to her bedroom where she and Jayden were staying.

He gripped her arm and yanked her down the hall. She tugged in the opposite direction, dragging her feet. The assailant had killed once before, and she wasn't a fool who thought she would make it out of this alive if she gave him what he wanted.

Caleb sat in his car out in front of Sara's listening to the radio with the stepladder lying across the backseat. For the fifth time he checked the clock on the dashboard.

Where's Annie? She should be out here by now.

He shoved out of his vehicle and headed for the house. On the porch he found the front door ajar and pushed it open. He scanned the foyer. His gaze riveted to one of Annie's shoes lying on its side near the stairs. Then he caught sight of the other one in the entrance into the dining room. Alarm bolted through him. Still dressed in his uniform, he drew his gun.

As he eased toward the living room, warning bells clanged full force in his mind. When he peeked inside, he spied Sara tied up. He rushed to her, removing the gag.

"Where's Annie?" Caleb started untying her.

"A man took her upstairs. He's looking for something. Go. I'm okay."

He quickly undid the last knot, saying. "Call the station," then moved out into the foyer. He quickened his pace and climbed the stairs two at a time.

The assailant tossed Annie on the bed. He withdrew the switchblade from his pocket again, the movement exposing the gun strapped to his belt under his jacket. Her panic surged to a level that threatened to incapacitate her.

"I don't have time for games. Where is it?"

While his gaze swept the room, she inched toward the side away from Bryan's killer.

His steely look fell on her, his forehead puckered. "I'd hate to cut that pretty little face. Move again and I will. Where is it?" He shouted the last sentence.

"I've been trying to tell you I don't know what you're talking about. Bryan hasn't given me anything to keep for him. What is it you're looking for?"

"You know. I have a way of loosening the tongue." He caressed the length of his knife as though he were stroking a woman he loved.

Every muscle locked in place. *Where's Caleb?*

Bryan's killer knelt on one knee on the bed, his dark eyes pinning her down.

Terror crammed her throat. She crawled to the side and back, trying to get away from him.

* * *

Plastered against the wall outside the bedroom, through the crack in the open door Caleb saw the man kneel on the bed near Annie, her eyes wide, her face as white as the coverlet she was on. He shifted to pivot into the entrance and aim his gun.

Protect Annie, Lord.

With a calming breath, Caleb swung into the entrance and pointed his weapon at the man's chest. "Police. Drop the knife, now!"

The intruder hesitated, his gaze flying toward the door.

"Don't make me use this," Caleb said as Annie scrambled from the bed, out of reach of the man.

The clunk of the knife as it hit the hardwood floor echoed through the room.

"You're okay?" Caleb asked Annie without taking his eyes off the intruder.

"Yes." She hurried toward him. "He has a gun in a holster on his belt."

Her brave front that vied with her quavering voice made him want to hold her and reassure her he wouldn't let anything happen to her. But he couldn't until he took care of the man. "I untied Sara. Make sure she's okay."

"Will you be okay alone?" Annie skirted around Caleb.

His chuckle eased some of his tension. "I think I can manage."

As soon as Annie made her way down the stairs, Caleb said to the intruder, "Kick the knife under the bed, then lie facedown on the floor in the middle of the room, arms outstretched."

The second the assailant complied, Caleb approached him, his gun at all times pointed at the man's back. After patting him down and removing his Glock, Caleb withdrew his cuffs and snapped them on the suspect and then jerked him upright. It took all his willpower to keep from slamming the man a few times up against the wall.

As he descended to the first floor with his suspect, Caleb heard Annie in the living room talking with Sara. Her voice still shook, but with each word it grew stronger. The thought of what this man in front of him could have done to Annie twisted his gut in a hard knot.

Later that night, when everyone had left and Jayden and Sara went to bed, Annie came down the stairs, the soft glow from the fireplace and the lights on the Christmas tree in the front window drawing her toward the living room and Caleb, who was waiting for her. When she entered, she found him poking the blaze, sparks flying up the chimney.

Putting the poker up, Caleb rotated toward her. For a long moment, he didn't say a word, but his visual tether roped her to him. Words fled her mind.

Slowly the corners of his mouth inched up. "Is Jayden tucked in?"

"When her head hit the pillow, she was almost instantly asleep. I wish I could go to sleep that fast." Exhaustion cleaved to her. The past few hours had been hectic, but she was happy to be alive. She could have ended up dead, like Bryan.

"Sara?"

"She's fine. Told me she was made from sturdy

stock." She wished she could say the same about herself. She clasped her hands together to still their quivering.

"That man acted like he knew you. What was he after? He isn't saying anything except he wants a lawyer." His perceptive gaze held her again.

Tell him everything, not just part of it. You can't do this alone anymore, and it's not over. What if the assailant's acting on Nick Salvador's orders?

Caleb's forefinger whispered a path across her face, along her cheekbone. "I can see your worries in your gaze. He can't hurt you anymore."

She closed her eyes. "I know I'm an open book. I wish I wasn't."

"I like you the way you are."

His words weaved their way through her mind, tantalizing her with the idea she could put down roots in Christmas, be a part of the town, be a part of Caleb's life. She lifted her eyelids and looked at him. The warm expression, as if she were special to him, only added fuel to that fantasy.

"Annie, you can trust me. I care for you and Jayden. You can't do everything alone. We all need others." He took her hand and led her toward the couch. "What's going on? I can help you."

She couldn't resist his enticement. He was offering her something she hadn't had in a long time: someone to confide in. *Did You lead me to Christmas for this, Lord? Is Caleb Your answer to my prayers for help, for a solution to my problem?*

He sat so close his leg pressed against hers. He slipped his arm along the back of the couch, cocooning her in the shelter of his embrace, loose but protective. "I see a look in your eye that tells me you've been hurt. You're still hurting and it goes beyond what you told me a few days ago. It has something to do with the man I have in my jail."

Dropping her gaze to her lap, her hands twisting together, she nodded, the pain of the past swelling in her chest. "And with Jayden's father."

"Tell me about him. You said he was dead. When?"

She sucked in a fortifying breath. "He died twelve days ago."

"I'm sorry, Annie."

The words she needed to say lodged in her throat. She was so tired of holding everything inside. "I wasn't ever married to him. In fact, he didn't live in the town I lived in but Daytona. I saw him occasionally because of Jayden." Trying to prepare herself for a disappointed look in Caleb's eyes, she glanced toward him. What she saw stunned her. There was no condemnation, only sympathy. "We met in college. I fell head over heels in love. Until I got to know the real Bryan. He was exciting, charming and in the end totally focused on himself. He partied too much. He drank too much. He even went to jail for a DUI. He asked me to marry him, but I couldn't, not even when I found out that I was pregnant. It would have been a marriage doomed from the beginning. He didn't have much money, so he didn't help much with raising Jayden except to sweep into her life every once in a while, give her presents, then sweep back out."

"I'm sorry you had to go through that alone. I don't understand a man chucking his responsibilities, especially to his own daughter."

"I learned to take care of things myself."

"But you don't have to. I'd like to help. Sara cares about you, too."

She wouldn't think of what his words implied—that he cared about her possibly more than a friend. "You don't really know me."

"I know a woman who loves her daughter and has done a great job raising her. I know a woman who's been wonderful with Sara, giving her a reason to look forward again to Christmas. You don't have to worry about going it alone anymore. You don't have to leave town when your car is fixed."

"I'm used to going it alone. That's not what I'm worried about." She collapsed back against the cushion, tired of holding herself so tense that her muscles ached. "Bryan got into something bad and somehow pulled me into it. I got a call from him the day he was killed—murdered."

"Murdered?" Caleb pulled her into the crook of his arm as though to prove to her she wasn't alone, that he was right there with her.

"I wasn't sure exactly—I'm still not—what was happening when he called. But I read later he was found beaten and shot. I heard it happen, and the man you have in jail is the one who killed Bryan, although I didn't see him do it."

Caleb tensed. "What happened?"

"The killer interrupted the call to finish the deed. Bryan called me to warn me not to trust anyone and to run and hide." She turned toward Caleb. "And before you ask me why, I have to tell you I don't know the reason. All I know is that he was going to finally pay his father a visit. The father he didn't know he had until after his mother died last month."

"So that man is Bryan's father?"

"No, but I think his father sent that man after Bryan. After what I learned about who his father is, it's definitely a possibility. But then again, why would the man do that to his own son, even if he didn't know about him? I know that Bryan thought this was the answer to all his financial woes, but still..." She let her voice fade into silence, still perplexed by the whole situation.

"Who's his father?"

"Nick Salvador, a man who lives in Tampa and is basically a wealthy criminal from all I can learn. The last thing I knew, Bryan was in Tampa to meet him."

"So he got mixed up with the wrong guy? I've seen that before, and I've even seen a father kill his son, but you're right that there are definitely questions that need answers."

"From what I could tell, the person with Bryan in the end wasn't his father. The little I heard didn't indicate that at all. The reason I didn't go to the police is that Bryan warned me not to even trust them. And the last message he left me on my cell phone was he'd left his father's disappointed. The meeting went badly with Nick Salvador. Bryan started to tell me something else when he was pulled over by a cop. Then not an hour later Bryan called me at home. He was running for his life. That's when I heard him being killed."

Caleb sucked in a deep breath, his face paling. "So somehow Bryan thought the police might be involved?"

"That's why I didn't know where to turn. When the man called me, I panicked and fled Crystal Creek. After about a day on the road, I decided to come here and hide. Sara was my mother's second cousin. When we came to Christmas all those years ago, it was really to see Sara's mother. My mother and hers were close at one time. I just ended up over here a lot because I loved Sara's house. Great places to hide. That's what made me think of Sara and Christmas." Palms sweaty, she rubbed them on her jeans. "I know I can't stay long. I don't want to in any place until I figure out what's going on."

"Why didn't you tell me?"

"Because the man you caught tonight threatened to kill you. He's the one who tried to run you down. He was making a point to me that anyone I cared about could be hurt if I said anything to you."

"No more running, Annie. It ends here. I'll protect you." Anger laced his voice, the muscles in his arms still bunched. "If Nick Salvador is behind this, we'll deal with it on *my* turf."

She inhaled a soothing breath, and yet it did nothing to calm her.

"And until we get to the bottom of this whole situation, I'll be with you, or one of my men will." He patted the couch cushion next to him. "I'm a light sleeper. This will serve nicely as a bed. I'm staying here at night. Sara would be the first one to agree to that."

"I can't ask you to do that."

"You aren't. I'm insisting, as the police chief of Christmas. There won't be a repeat of this evening." Caleb brushed his hand through her hair, then leaned down and kissed the tip of her nose, saying, "You're safe in my town." Then he proceeded to graze his lips over each corner of her mouth.

The sensations bombarding her from all sides made

it difficult to think straight. All she managed was to nod her head. Everything else took too much thought.

After sampling her lips in a deep kiss, he framed her face. "Let's go out together tomorrow night to take your mind off all that's happened."

"A date?" She hadn't been on one since Bryan, and look what happened there. Wariness inched into her thoughts.

He chuckled. "Yes, a date. How about it?"

"Yes," she whispered, right before he kissed her again.

Chapter Seven

Sitting at his desk on Friday, Caleb scrubbed his hands down his face. He hadn't slept at all the night before. Sara's couch had been comfortable enough, but his mind kept going over and over all the facts and questions concerning Annie and what had happened the evening before. Bruce Downey, the suspect, still hadn't said a word, and from what Caleb understood, a lawyer was arriving later today. An expensive, high-powered one from Oklahoma City.

What bothered him the most was that Downey was an ex-policeman for the Tampa Police Department. That ate at his sense of fair play. Had he stopped Bryan and pretended to still be a cop? It appeared Bryan knew his attacker had a connection to the police.

A match for a fingerprint found at the vacant house came back a little while ago. It was Downey's. How long had he been in town watching Annie? Waiting for his chance to get her alone.

He flinched at the sudden ringing of the phone cutting into the silence. Snatching it up, he said, "Jackson here."

"I got some more information for you," Don said.

Caleb had called his friend in Florida first thing when he'd arrived at the station this morning. "Shoot."

"Nick Salvador has disappeared. No one has seen him for the past day. Someone thought he might be on vacation in Mexico."

"You think he's fled the country?"

"No, I don't think anyone knows where he is. He's bad news. I'm warning you to keep your guard up. Someone I know on the Tampa police force said it's been rumored that Downey went to work for Salvador. Downey was basically kicked off the force three years ago."

"Thanks. If you hear anything else, I'd appreciate a call. I feel like I'm flying in the dark."

"I'd hate to see you crash. I'll call if I hear anything."

After Caleb hung up, he stared at his phone and decided to call Tyler, the police officer watching Annie. "Everything okay?"

"Quiet. Well, not exactly quiet. Jayden is dancing to some Christmas music in the living room and Sara is keeping time to the song."

"Where's Annie?"

"Fixing us lunch. She's serving us leftover homemade chicken pot pie."

Remembering when she served it the first time, Caleb licked his lips, his stomach churning his hunger. "I'll be there in a few hours. The man who might be behind what happened last night has disappeared in Florida. Don't let down your guard."

As soon as Caleb finished with Tyler, the questions returned to plague him. What had Downey been looking for? The only thing that Bryan had given Annie lately was the family Bible and he'd checked that out. Nothing.

Christmas lights strung everywhere illuminated the downtown area in a glittering fairy-tale setting. The last burst of fireworks Friday night sprayed across the dark sky, a multicolored display that stole Annie's breath.

"You guys go all out here in Christmas." Annie made another visual sweep of the square at the south end of the main thoroughfare. All it needed was a blanket of snow to complete the effect of a twinkling winter wonderland. "First a great meal, and now this light celebration."

"Kinda goes with what we're doing this evening, celebrating." Caleb clasped her hand and began walking toward his car. "Tomorrow is our last fireworks display. Let's bring Sara and Jayden down here after the Christmas party at church. I'm sure they're watching from the house, but it's better from the town square."

"Sounds nice." *Making plans for the future.* She wanted to be able to do that, but after all that had happened in the past few weeks, she realized how quickly her life could change.

At his vehicle he opened the door for her. "I'm hoping Downey decides to talk, but even if he doesn't, he'll be going away for a long time with what we have here. And I talked to the FBI late this afternoon about Nick Salvador. They'll be sending someone down from Oklahoma City tomorrow to talk to you and Downey. They are interested in what happened. Nick Salvador has been on their radar for years." He stepped closer, cupping one cheek. "Put your worries in the hands of the Lord. Between Him and me, you'll be all right."

"I'm trying. It isn't always easy. I want to control every aspect of my life so I don't have any more surprises like what happened with Bryan."

"But we aren't really in control. God is and He's perfect for the job. He knows the future. We don't."

She gave him a smile. "Thursday night I asked for help, and He sent me you."

He roped her against him. "I'm glad I could help. I want to be there for you."

A parishioner Annie met at church passed by on the sidewalk and greeted them. Caleb backed away from Annie. A red tinge, highlighted by the streetlamp a few yards away, colored Caleb's cheeks.

"I guess we'd better go to Sara's." Caleb gripped the doorframe.

"We can finish our…talk there."

Annie slipped into the passenger seat, the heat from her own blush warming her face. She hadn't flirted in years, and yet that was what she'd been doing. As she watched him round the front of the car, she realized she was falling in love with him. She didn't know if their relationship was possible, because if she had to leave Christmas to protect Jayden she would. After Christmas she needed to reassess her situation concerning Nick Salvador.

Behind the steering wheel, Caleb started the car and pulled out of the parking space along the main street. He scanned the area as he drove by.

"You won't be able to keep protecting us indefinitely," Annie finally said, disturbing the comfortable silence between them.

"We'll deal with that when we have to. Let's see what the FBI have to say about the situation. They may be able to locate Salvador and keep an eye on him."

"If you say so."

"I'm not gonna let Salvador win." He pulled into Sara's driveway.

When Caleb climbed from his vehicle, Annie started to open her door but stopped. He liked to do that, and she was learning to let him. She was so used to opening her own door that she had to work to curb the impulse.

On the walk to the porch she relished the crispness in the night with the scent of burning wood from the neighbor's fireplace lacing the air. With Caleb's arm around her, she mounted the steps. Sara had left the outside light off, but the Christmas ones all around them lit the dark shadows.

At the top of the stairs she turned toward him, not wanting the evening to come to an end yet. "I can fix some hot chocolate, if you want."

He framed her face, his amiable gaze fixed on her. "I'd better try to get some sleep tonight. Tomorrow will be another full day, especially with the FBI here." He moved closer, his arms winding about her. "Are you and Jayden gonna stay after Christmas?"

"It's a possibility." One she wanted to make happen with all her heart. Caleb made her feel cherished. No one had made her feel that way, not even Bryan when they had been dating. She didn't want to give that up, but so much depended on what Nick Salvador did. Even if she was falling in love with Caleb, her daughter had to come first, and she couldn't live her life with him always having to protect her. She would have to have another solution—even if that meant somehow disappearing somewhere else.

"I'll just have to keep working on you. I can be very determined when I need to be."

"If I stay, I'll have to find a job soon. I can't continue to live at Sara's. I don't want to outstay my welcome."

"In the few weeks you and your daughter have been in Christmas, Sara has become her old self again. She'd probably have something to say about that."

"Maybe I could find a job and rent a room from her. Still be here and even help her."

He nestled her against him. "I like how you think. What kind of work have you done?"

"I went to college for a year but had to leave when Jayden was born. I've recently been an office manager of a roofing company in Crystal Creek."

"I'll see what I hear through the grapevine." He bent closer. "But you've given me inspiration to see what I can find."

His last words whispered across her lips, tickling them, right before he touched his mouth to hers, quickly lengthening the kiss. In that moment Annie knew she wasn't just falling in love with Caleb but that she was in love with him. Her heart soared with the thought, only to plummet a few seconds later when she realized the implication. She might have to walk away from the best thing that had happened to her besides the birth of her daughter.

When they parted, he took her hand and they walked the couple of paces to the door. She scrambled to mold her features into an expression that didn't reveal her fear of the unknown future.

Put your trust in the Lord. Those words slipped into her mind. She was trying, but for so long she'd only relied on herself.

"Good night," she murmured after entering the house and crossing to the staircase. "Tell Tyler thanks for watching Jayden and Sara tonight. It was nice getting out by ourselves."

Caleb gave her a quick kiss then stepped back. "He owes me."

On her trek up the stairs she hugged her arms to her, savoring the memory of being in his embrace, experiencing again the feel of his lips on hers.

"I can't believe I got talked into playing Santa Claus. I think the mayor got sick on purpose just so I had to do this." In the church classroom, Caleb turned from the mirror after examining the white beard Annie had glued on his face. "How do I look? Do you think anyone will know it's me?"

Taking in his youthful appearance that the beard couldn't disguise and his dark hair still not completely hidden by the wig, Annie pressed her lips together, trying to contain her laughter. "Yes, but the kids won't. All they'll see is the bundle of presents you're carrying and your jolly belly." Patting his padded stomach in the red suit, she finally released the chuckles she'd held inside since he'd asked her to help him with his beard.

"I'm consoling myself with the fact that this is for a good cause. This party is for the disadvantaged children in the area. The presents I'm delivering will often be all they'll get. This is what makes Christmas so special, giving to others, especially those who don't have anything."

Annie stepped close and adjusted his wig to cover his hair. "Yes, you keep telling yourself that and everything will be fine. You know, I think I have just the right touch to make you look official."

His white eyebrows slashed down. "I don't think I like your tone. What?"

"You're way too suspicious." She rummaged in her purse.

"That's a good thing for a police chief."

She retrieved what she'd been looking for and turned back to him. "And I'm glad. I appreciate all you've done for me, especially bringing the FBI in on what's been going on. With them looking for Salvador for questioning, I feel better."

"Their resources extend further than mine."

"And maybe they'll be able to crack Downey."

"I'm not too sure about that. The man is scared. He's trying not to act that way, but I see it in his expression. According to the FBI, people who cross Salvador die."

"And Bryan somehow had. If Downey worked for Salvador, I can't see Downey killing Salvador's son without him telling him to. Maybe the FBI will find what someone was searching for in my apartment. Bryan could have hidden something there that I'm not aware of."

Caleb gestured toward her balled hand. "What are you hiding there?"

She produced a tube of red lipstick. "This."

His eyes widened. "You want me to wear lipstick?"

She laughed. "Just on the cheeks."

He swiped his hand across his brow. "For a minute I thought you'd gone loco." He fastened on her a pinpoint gaze. "Are you crazy? I'm not wearing lipstick anywhere."

"It might make you look older, disguise you some."

"Well, guess what? Santa has just gotten younger and looks remarkably like Christmas's police chief." With a final glance at the mirror in the church classroom, he headed for the door, grabbing his big, black bag full of presents for the underprivileged. "Let's get this over with, then on to the fireworks celebration. Remember, stay near me."

"Aye, aye, captain." She saluted him.

When Caleb entered the rec room, saying, "Ho ho ho," the kids' eyes brightened, and they rushed toward him, an onslaught of twenty-five children ranging in age from three to ten.

Annie crossed to the kitchen entrance and stood with Sara, watching the joy on the little girls' and boys' faces. Annie spied Jayden with some of the kids from the church standing behind the refreshment tables waiting to serve the food after the gifts were given out. "This is all Jayden talked about today. The party. The presents. She helped make cards to go with the gifts."

"I loved helping y'all bake the sugar cookies today then decorate them. I hadn't done that in years." Sara flashed her a smile. "Look at the turnout. The town does love a good party. I hope we have enough food for everyone."

Annie scanned the large room, full to capacity. Quite a few people she recognized. She wanted to stay in Christmas after the holidays and had prayed about it last night after saying good-night to Caleb.

In the short time here, Jayden had blossomed. She trusted Caleb. He believed in her and she'd never really had that.

"Is all the food out?" Annie asked over the claps and giggles coming from the children as Caleb handed out the presents.

"I think so…" Sara snapped her fingers. "Except the dip I stuck in the refrigerator in back. No room in the front one. I forgot about it."

"I'll get it." Annie turned into the entrance.

The large kitchen was now empty, but twenty minutes before she'd had a hard time moving around as different church workers took out all the food and made the punch for the party. Making her way around the corner and toward the backup refrigerator and freezer, she listened to the noise coming from the rec hall. Joy. Laughter. The sounds gave her a peace about her decision to stay if the FBI could find Salvador. If not…

She wouldn't think about that right now. Opening the refrigerator door, she saw the large bowl of dip that Sara had prepared for the feast. As she reached for it, a hand snaked around her mouth while an arm slammed her back against a hard body.

"Don't make a sound. I don't have a beef with anybody else, but if I have to, I'll use my gun. Understand?"

She nodded.

His tanned hand eased from her mouth, but he kept his arm locked about her. Something poked her in the temple, cold and metallic. She slanted her look and nearly collapsed at the sight of the gun to her head.

"We're going for a ride, so we can have a chat undisturbed."

His gravelly voice chilled her to the marrow of her bones.

"If you try anything, I'll shoot you and anyone who tries to interfere. I have nothing to lose."

He dragged her toward the back door at the end of the short hall. That door had been locked earlier but now it stood open. She shouldn't be surprised a criminal knew how to get into a locked building, but surrounded by lots of people she knew and Caleb a room away, she'd felt safe. All an illusion.

At the end of the deserted alley behind the church, a car sat parked. If she got into the vehicle, she would be found dead. She couldn't let that happen.

Chapter Eight

Mobbed by children, Caleb looked toward where Sara and Annie had been talking. Sara stood alone. His gut tightened. Where was Annie? She wasn't supposed to leave his sight. He'd made that clear, and she'd been good about it all day. Either him or a police officer at all times.

"This is my last one." Caleb dug into the bag, grabbing the lone present and pulling it out. "This one is for Danny."

The five-year-old jumped up, waving his arms, with the biggest grin on his face. "I'm Danny."

Caleb waded through the crowd of kids and handed the child his gift, then said, "You can open your presents now."

While they tore into the wrapping, bits of paper flying everywhere, Caleb covered the distance to Sara. "Where's Annie?"

"She just went into the kitchen to get the dip from the back refrigerator." Sara's forehead scrunched. "She's only been gone a minute or two."

Too long. His gut knotted.

He pivoted into the kitchen and scanned the area. No Annie. He headed toward the back refrigerator. He hurried down the short hallway and checked the refrigerator. The bowl of dip was inside. Slamming the door closed, he went to the exit nearby and tested the handle. Locked.

Caleb swung around, surveying the corridor, and spied the storage room off it. He strode toward the slightly open door.

"What do you want?" Annie asked as Nick Salvador dragged her toward the car. She'd recognized him from a photo in the newspaper.

"I want the information Bryan Daniels had."

"What information?"

The large man stopped a few feet from the vehicle and jerked Annie around to face him. "Don't play dumb with me. He said it was in safekeeping, that if something happened to him it would go to the police. It was photos, a tape and a gun." The laugh that erupted from Salvador's mouth scared her worse than the gun he held in his hand. "Just like in the movies. Fool. He thought I would cower at his threat. I've killed men for less than that."

"I can't give you something I don't have. Your man searched my apartment and didn't find anything."

"It was too important to leave behind. You two probably thought that I would bow down to the blackmail and give him everything he wanted when I didn't accept him as my son."

"But he was your son. How could you send someone after him?"

His laugh froze her. "I can't have children. Never

have been able to. He isn't my son. His mother just tried to claim he was."

Bryan, what in the world did you do? Frantic to find a way to convince the man she was telling the truth, she lifted her chin a notch and met his gaze. "Bryan didn't give me anything."

"I know all about your relationship with him. He had no friends. He called you when he knew he would die to tell you to send the information to the police. Downey managed to stop him before he could. I want the information."

What gun, photos and tape? Again she searched her mind trying to think where or when Bryan would have done that. But all her thoughts centered on the gun Salvador pointed at her.

"Get in." He waved the weapon at the back of the car, then took his key out and popped the trunk.

"In there?" Her squeaky words reverberated through the silence.

"Now." He pushed the lid up and gestured with the gun where he wanted her.

Annie stared at the dark hole he wanted her to crawl into, and fear mushroomed. A band stretched around her chest and contracted. He moved toward her. She scrambled into the trunk before he could lay a hand on her.

The last thing she saw before he slammed the lid was the light at the end of the alley by the closed kitchen door of the church. Then nothing but darkness. Her black surroundings hammered terror into the fiber of her being. Her quaking started in her hands and spread so quickly it consumed her in a matter of seconds.

Sucking in deep breaths that never filled her lungs, she closed her eyes, hoping to trick her mind into thinking she was just resting. But the tight confines pressed in on all sides. Like being in a coffin.

Lord, help. What do I do?

Part of the twenty-third Psalm came to her, weaving its way through her thoughts. *Yea, though I walk through the valley of the shadow of death, I will fear no evil; For You are with me; Your rod and Your staff, they comfort me.* In the wake of those words, calmness cocooned her in a sense of peace. Her rapid breathing slowed.

The motion of the car stopped. Hearing the door shut, Annie braced herself. The trunk popped open and the lid flew up.

"Get out." Salvador stood like an avenger, bent on having his way no matter what it took.

When Annie climbed from the black hole, she hadn't fallen apart as she would have in the past when greeted with darkness like that. Because God was with her. She wasn't alone. Even at the moment when she faced Sara's house, the sense of the Lord's arm about her shoulders cloaked her in a composure she would need if she were going to make it out alive.

"What are we doing here?"

"Your stuff is here. Downey didn't get a chance to go through it. We are now. Either you will give me what I want or I'll kill you. It's that simple."

Caleb, where are you? By now you have to know I'm gone.

"And your cop won't be able to save you. I've got a surprise for him."

The storage area off the kitchen was empty, other than two cigarette butts on the floor by the door. Caleb closed the door and turned into the kitchen. Since he was protecting Annie, he had his service weapon on him. He pulled it out of his holster under his red coat then his cell from his pocket. Had someone been waiting in there? Salvador or someone else he sent?

He called the station. "Tyler, I need you here at the church to watch Jayden and Sara. Annie's gone. I'm going to check the rest of this place. Have Jeremy swing by Sara's house and make sure everything's okay there."

The sound of an explosion roared through his connection. Caleb jerked his cell from his ear for a few seconds before shouting into it, "Tyler, what happened?" Nothing. "Tyler?"

Salvador shoved Annie through the entrance into Sara's house. Suddenly a blast rolled through the air like thunder. She peered behind her and saw a flash light the night toward downtown.

She stopped and pivoted. "What have you done?"

"Got rid of a liability before he decided to talk."

"You blew up the jail?"

He chuckled. "A most effective way to cause a diversion and take out Downey. He had his chance to fix his mistake. He wasn't supposed to kill Bryan until after he got all the information I needed."

I'm a liability, too. Even if I could find the information and give it to him, he'll kill me.

She had to stall as long as she could until someone finally came or she could think of a way out of this situation.

"How did Downey find me?"

Salvador stepped through the entrance and kicked the door closed. "That was easy. Your cop friend led him to you."

Caleb betrayed her? No, he's lying. "You're lying."

The man's laughter erupted. "For once I'm not. He called the Crystal Creek police and introduced himself and then asked about you. If that wasn't enough, he sent someone to check up on you. That someone talked to the police in Crystal Creek about you. It was only a matter of putting a few things together to find where you went. At least Downey was good for something. His police connections helped. Now enough of this, where's your things?"

Again Annie found herself trudging up the stairs to her bedroom with a madman behind her, wanting something she couldn't give him. She and Caleb had discussed what she'd brought and couldn't come up with anything.

At the top of the steps she swung around, and the action was so sudden, it took the man by surprise. His hand shot out and grasped the banister. "Back off." He lifted the gun and pointed it right at her face.

"I don't have what you want. At least tell me why you want them." If she were going to die, she wanted to know why.

He scowled, his eyes narrow. "Bryan's mother, years ago gathered a tape, a gun and photos that tied me to a murder. When she ran away from me, she used it as her insurance to keep me in line. Believe me, I still looked for her, but it's much easier to track a person today than it was twenty-eight years ago."

"Maybe she was lying and there wasn't anything." Bryan certainly had lied to her enough.

"It's possible, but I don't think so. In the note she left me it was clear she knew too much. I don't let people live who know too much about my...affairs." A smile pulled the corners of his mouth in an evil line.

"You don't think I know what you're doing. You're stalling. No one's gonna come. Show me your room."

In his vehicle, Caleb called Jeremy. "I need you at the station. The back of the jail was blown up and the fire department is there."

"How's Tyler? He was there."

"Okay. A few cuts and bruises, but he says he can handle the situation. I want you to help him. Downey is dead. Thankfully we didn't have anyone else in jail. Two FBI agents were on the way out of town. They're coming back. They'll help you. I'll take care of Annie."

"Sure, Chief."

Caleb turned down Bethlehem Street and saw Sara's house at the end of the long block. And he also glimpsed an unknown car in front. He gunned his and came to a stop a few seconds later. After confirming Annie wasn't in the church, he knew where Salvador would take her. Annie wouldn't leave the party without letting him know unless the man had taken her.

Thrusting open his door, he hit the ground in a run and headed toward the porch. With his weapon in hand, he snuck into the house. Pausing in the foyer, he listened, trying to get a feel for where Annie and Salvador were. A floorboard squeaked above the dining room. Annie's bedroom.

He took the stairs two at a time, making sure he avoided a creaky step.

Pages of Bryan's mother's Bible lay scattered all over the bed. Annie's heart pounded in a mad tempo at the sight before her. Every item, even clothing and the suitcases, that she and Jayden had brought from

Florida was being torn apart before her eyes. Salvador took hold of the antique porcelain doll Bryan had given her daughter for her birthday last month.

"Please, not Jayden's favorite doll." The words tumbled from her mouth before she could stop them. She knew the man wouldn't listen to her pleas. He hadn't when he'd ripped through the Bible.

He glared at her and proceeded to tear it apart—first the head then the limbs and finally the body. Nothing. He tossed it down at his feet. "That's it. Everything." He scanned the room. "How about that?" He pointed at the ceramic Christmas tree nearby.

"Not mine."

He picked it up and smashed it against the floor then toed the pieces to see if there was anything hidden among them. His scowl deepened into an almost desperate look when he peered toward her. "It's got to be here. I've looked everywhere I could—Bryan's apartment and car, anything I could tie to him. You're my last link." He covered the few feet between them and slammed her up against the wall by the bed. "Where is it? You've hidden it in this house. If I have to and can't find it, I'll burn this place down rather than let anyone find the evidence. I don't leave evidence around to be used against me." His hand gripped her neck as he held her pinned with his body.

Nor witnesses, from all she'd read about him. "Bryan never gave me anything that would hold photos, a tape and a gun. Believe me, I would know that."

"Maybe it's something smaller—a note about the location of where the items are." Frustration toughened his voice to a growl.

Frantic, she searched the chaotic mess strewn about

the room and zeroed in on Jayden's treasure chest sitting undisturbed on the dresser, as though part of Sara's belongings. Salvador squeezed her neck, the glint in his eyes feral. Slowly he cut the flow of air to her lungs. Her mind swirled from the lack of oxygen.

"Box," she choked out, shifting her gaze to the item on the dresser, peeking out from some clothing pitched onto its top.

He eased the pressure about her burning throat. "Where?"

"Dresser." She dragged air into her oxygen-starved lungs as his hand fell away and he turned toward the piece of furniture a few feet away.

Quickly crossing to it, he snatched it up and lifted the lid, throwing Jayden's treasures—a polished rock, a picture of her, Bryan and Jayden, a necklace, her favorite hair ribbons—onto the floor. He checked the box's bottom, but it was solid wood, then his gaze latched on to the satin lining of the lid. He ripped it off and a key and a piece of paper fell out.

As he picked them up, flinging the box to the side, Annie saw her chance while his attention was riveted on the small paper. She grabbed the alarm clock on the nightstand next to her and swung toward Salvador. He started to turn toward her when she smashed the metal-and-plastic object into his head as hard as she could. He swayed.

Then she ran as quickly as she could for the door. His curses propelled her faster and faster as she hit the hallway and saw the staircase only ten feet away.

Caleb heard the sound of pounding footsteps coming toward him as he climbed the stairs. He swung toward the noise, and through the slats in the banister he saw Annie. He increased his speed. She rushed toward him, her eyes wide, her face pale. Then she spied him and lengthened her strides even more.

He looked behind her. Salvador emerged from her bedroom, his expression contorted with rage. The man planted his feet and lifted his Glock, aiming for Annie. Caleb stopped and sighted Salvador through the railing.

Caleb squeezed off his shot a split second before Salvador could. Annie dove the last few feet toward the staircase. Salvador's bullet whizzed by her and hit the wall. Caleb's struck the man in the chest. Salvador staggered back, tried to lift his arm to shoot again, but Caleb fired again and Salvador crumbled to the floor.

Caleb scrambled up the two remaining steps and gathered Annie into his arms. "Are you okay?"

Tears streaked down her face. She threw her arms around his neck and sobbed.

"May I have a word with you, Annie?" Caleb's voice held no emotion in it.

She paused and turned from the front door as Sara and Jayden were finally allowed into the house after the scene upstairs had been processed and Salvador's body carted off. "Sure. Jayden, can you go with Miss Sara for a few minutes? I won't be long."

"I've got some cookies left over from church tonight and some milk. Wanna share some with me?" Sara offered her hand to Jayden. "Then I imagine you'll want to take a hot bath. You and your mom are gonna camp out downstairs in the living room. Won't that be fun!"

Jayden hesitated, clinging to Annie.

"I won't keep her but a few minutes. I just need to check out some things." Although Caleb grinned at Jayden, a tic twitched right above his jaw line.

"Mommy, I'll save a coupla cookies for you."

"And some milk." Jayden didn't know what had happened that evening upstairs. Sara had kept her at the church helping to clean up. Annie would have to explain part of it to her daughter. The past hours had been filled with people in and out, and all she wanted to do was collapse on the portable mattress Caleb had set up for her and Jayden and sleep for the next twenty-four hours.

Jayden leaned back and looked up at Annie. "Okay?"

"I am, honey. I just had some things I had to take care of here at the house, but everything's okay now. Enjoy the snack."

Jayden fit her hand in Sara's while the older lady kept a running commentary going about how successful the Christmas party at the church was and what a big help Jayden had been.

"Let's go into the living room," Caleb said in that matter-of-fact voice he'd been using since that brief time he'd held her at the top of the stairs and let her cry.

When she settled on the couch, he remained standing, facing her. "Why did you leave the rec hall this evening? What part of 'you need to stay with me at all times' did you not understand? He had you in his sights tonight. You could be dead right now instead of Salvador. You could—" Frustration and anger poured off Caleb, his hands curling into fists and uncurling at his sides.

He was angry with her for going into the kitchen

when he was the reason it all happened. She drew herself up tall, lifting her chin a notch. "I know exactly how Downey found me. Salvador told me you sent someone to Crystal Creek to check up on me. What did you think? I was a criminal running from the law?" When guilt flickered across his face, his gaze sliding away for a few seconds, her own fury surfaced. "You did think that."

"No, not really, but I could tell you were in trouble, and you weren't talking."

"It wasn't any of your business."

"Ah, the 'I can do everything by myself' attitude. How far did it get you today?"

His question wounded her more than she ever wanted him to know. She narrowed her eyes and pinned him with her look. "I've learned the hard way not to depend on others."

"And yet today, you had to."

She fisted her hands. "Yes, today I did. But that's not the issue here. You didn't trust me, or you wouldn't have gone digging into my life." Annie surged to her feet, needing to get away from the anger she saw in his eyes. "I have a daughter who needs me. Good night." She strode toward the foyer and opened the front door for him.

He walked passed her without looking at her. He stopped, started to turn back. Quickly she shut the door, too tired to go into her feelings concerning Caleb. She half expected him to pound on the wood and demand she let him in. But he didn't, which spoke volumes to her.

How did she expect him to be any different from

Bryan? He had her investigated, so when she was spilling her guts to him, he'd known all about her past.

"Is Jayden finally asleep?" Sara asked in the kitchen, where she was cleaning up after their snack.

"Yes, I laid down with her and held her until she drifted off." Annie collapsed into a chair at the table, too weary even to sleep with her daughter in the living room on the air mattress. When she'd tried to close her eyes, all she saw was Caleb's furious face.

"Did you tell her anything about what happened tonight?"

"Not yet, but I'll have to tomorrow when she sees all her things were destroyed. I just couldn't deal with it after…" After the scene with Caleb.

"How about you?" Sara sat across from Annie.

"I've made a mess of everything. Caleb is mad at me for leaving the rec hall." Tears blurred her vision.

"That's his frustration lashing out. He was frantic when he couldn't find you this evening. He kept saying he shouldn't have been Santa. I think he blames himself for everything that happened."

"It wasn't his fault. It wasn't mine, either. Salvador would have come after me one way or another. He was crazed. I'm glad the FBI took the safety deposit key and the box's location. Let them deal with what's in it. Not that it makes much difference, since Salvador is dead. So much death." She shuddered, several tears rolling down her cheeks. She didn't even try to stop them. "I can't believe Bryan hid something so potentially dangerous in one of Jayden's possessions."

"What are you gonna do now? You have a home here for as long as you want."

"I don't know. I guess I could go back to Crystal Creek, but that never really felt like my home. What do I do about Caleb? I care for him so much."

"It's sounding like much more than that. Are you falling in love with him?"

"I—yes."

"You won't find a better man."

"I know, but we can't have a relationship without total trust. And I don't think he really trusts me. He had me investigated like a criminal."

Sara peered down at the table then up into Annie's eyes. "I think I had a part in that happening. I told him I thought you were in trouble. He said he would do some poking around and see what he could find out. I'm so sorry. It wasn't that I didn't trust you. I was worried about you. You weren't sleeping. I could tell something was really troubling you. Please forgive me."

"Always. You have been so kind to me and Jayden." Annie reached across the table and covered Sara's hand. "I'm still not sure how much Caleb really can put his trust in someone. For that matter me. I've been so scared to do that, especially after Bryan. After years of not trusting others, I finally trusted Bryan and let him get close. Look what happened because of that. He put me in danger as well as his daughter." She averted her gaze, the scene with Salvador replaying in her mind.

"Do you trust the Lord?"

Do I? The whole time she'd been with Salvador she'd prayed to God to protect her. And He had. He'd answered her prayers and had even given her a sense of peace in the midst of her panic in the trunk. She used to think He'd forsaken her because of her past, but He hadn't. He'd been with her the whole time, even at the end, when she'd dove toward the staircase. Something instinctively had compelled her to drop suddenly. "Yes, I do. I couldn't have said that a few weeks ago."

"Then trust He's there for you always. Turn your dilemma over to Him concerning Caleb. Ask Him for His advice on what to do."

Annie pushed to her feet and came to Sara, giving the older woman a hug. "I will. Thanks for listening. Thanks for opening your home to Jayden and me."

"You've helped this old lady feel young again. I should be thanking you."

Annie trudged into the living room, wishing she could collapse onto the makeshift bed but knowing from past experience she wouldn't. One light still on, she found Sara's Bible on the end table by Sara's lounge chair and let it fall open. Annie began reading the first chapter of Nahum.

The Lord is good, a strong hold in the day of trouble; and He knoweth them that trust in Him.

As in the trunk, a peace descended as she continued to read the Lord's words. Had He led her to Christmas? To Sara and Caleb? She'd come to care for the people in this town in a short amount of time.

The next evening when Annie saw Caleb come home from work, she hurried down to his house and rang his bell. When he opened his door, she drank in the sight of the man she loved and was determined to fight for. Shadows under his eyes declared the toll the past few weeks had taken on Caleb. The urge to throw her arms around him inundated her, but the closed expression on his face stopped her.

"May I come in?"

He stepped to the side. "Have you come to tell me you're going back to Crystal Creek now that you're free of Salvador?"

"What if I told you I wanted to stay in Christmas?" Her heartbeat accelerated as she tried to read his emotions behind his neutral countenance. "Would you mind?"

"You don't need my permission." Wariness still touched his voice, but there was a warmth inching into it.

"I know, but I felt like we should talk about it."

"For how long?"

"Talking or staying?"

"Staying."

Hearing the note of hurt in his words and remembering about his past relationship with the woman in Tulsa, she advanced toward him. "I'm staying for good. I don't want to move on or go back to Crystal Creek. I want to call Christmas my home. But I don't want to stay if it'll make you uncomfortable or—"

He reached and dragged her the remaining few feet to him. "You mean that? You want to live in Christmas?"

"Yes. I love the town, the people—but especially you." She peered up into his endearing face, seeing his neutral expression melt into a look of joy.

"Say that again."

"I love you, Caleb. I know last night we were both exhausted, upset at how close we came to the outcome being different. I want us to trust totally in each other. That takes time. I want to stay and fight for your love."

He framed her face, burying his fingers in her hair. "You don't have to fight for my love. You have it already." He brushed his lips across hers. "You really didn't do anything wrong last night at church. I think toward the end when everyone was leaving the crime scene I began to figure you had nothing to hold you in Christmas, that you'd want to go back to Florida and pick up your old life. I began to distance myself from you because I didn't want to be hurt again. I started to come by several times today, but I just couldn't bring myself to find you packing or for you to tell me you were leaving, so I stayed away."

"I trust you with my heart. I'm not going anywhere." She pulled his mouth down onto hers and kissed him.

Epilogue

Jayden rushed into Annie and Caleb's bedroom. "C'mon, Mom. It's almost time for the celebration to start. We can't be late. You're supposed to turn the lights on the Christmas tree tonight."

When the town council had given her the honor of being the Mistress of the Festival of Lights, she'd been surprised and speechless. Her husband of ten months had accepted before she could get the words out of her mouth. "I'm coming. Where's Caleb?"

"He went ahead and picked up Miss Sara since you were taking forever."

Her daughter disappeared, but her pounding footsteps could be heard throughout the house as she went down the stairs. She had grown up so much in the year they had lived in Christmas. Annie pushed herself to her feet, her back hurting. She placed her hand on her rounded stomach and felt the baby kick beneath it. He was going to play soccer or maybe football. Caleb would like that. He'd already bought some sports equipment, but it would be years until their son would be big enough to use any of it.

"It won't be too much longer. Maybe you'll be a New Year's baby. I know your daddy can't wait."

As fast as she could she made her way to the front door, grabbed her overcoat and shrugged into it. A minute later she sat in the passenger seat of an SUV that Caleb had recently purchased for his expanding family.

Annie peered in the back and gave Sara a smile. "It's gonna snow tonight. I feel it in the air."

"Perfect. A little snow during our opening celebration would add just the right touch." Sara patted Jayden's hand on the seat between them. "Don't you think?"

"Yeah. I love making snowmen."

"If so, I'll probably have to work later helping people." Caleb threw Annie a warm look.

Sara chuckled. "The townspeople aren't too great driving on snow. Maybe it'll hold off until everyone's home for the night."

When Caleb parked near the town square, where the huge Christmas tree was erected, Jayden thrust open the door, saying, "I see Lisa. Be back in a minute."

"I don't think I'll see her for the rest of the evening," Annie muttered, watching her child disappearing into the middle of a group of children.

Sara pushed open her door and slowly stood, reaching in for her plate of goodies. "I'll be at the refreshment table if y'all need me."

"Mrs. Jackson, we're finally alone." Caleb took her hand and lifted it to his lips to kiss her knuckles.

"But not for long. Isn't that the mayor heading for us?"

Caleb scanned the crowd amassing around the

square. "I do believe it is." He tugged Annie toward him. "Let's give him something to talk about."

Her husband settled his mouth over hers and kissed her long and hard while the revelry took place around them. When he leaned back slightly, a smile encompassed his whole face.

He smoothed her hair back behind her ears. "I'm thinking the Mistress of the Festival of Lights is now properly charged and ready to do her duty."

* * * * *

YULE DIE

Debby Giusti

To my mother

Betty Willoughby

With love and gratitude

"Behold, the virgin shall be with child and bear a son,
and they shall name him Emmanuel,"
which means "God is with us."

—*Matthew* 1:23

Chapter One

"Christmas should be a time of joy, not sorrow," Callie Evans whispered as she pulled into the parking spot directly behind Lazarus House. The news she'd just heard over the radio made her heart heavy. Reaching for the control knob, she paused to listen to the rest of the report.

"Two of the three gunmen wounded in yesterday's east Atlanta shootout died during the night," the announcer said. "Hospital personnel decline to comment on the lone survivor."

Callie sighed with regret. Turning off the radio, she climbed from the Magnolia Medical van, dropped the keys into the pocket of her lab coat and hustled up the rear steps of the nursing home. Without warning, her mind flashed back fifteen years to another Christmas—the unlatched gate, the swollen pond, her sister's tiny body.

Stamping her feet to ward off the bitter cold and the memory, Callie opened the back door, stepped inside and hurried toward the narrow front lobby.

Nurse Tamika Bryant's broad face cracked into a

welcoming grin and her eyes twinkled like the lights on the small tree in the corner. "You're amazing to help us out on Christmas Eve."

Callie smiled back at the day-shift supervisor. Tamika had a heart big enough to embrace the fifteen men who, without family to love them, found comfort and care under her watchful eye.

"Mr. Petrecelli needs a digoxin level drawn, and we've got a new guy in room seven." Tamika handed her the lab request forms.

Opening the storage cabinet, Callie grabbed the bulky phlebotomy tray and glanced at the slips. "Harry Potter? It's a joke, right?"

Tamika's smile faded. "Atlanta Police Department's idea of humor. They're trying to keep the guy's identity under wraps. He was involved in that shootout on Foster Street yesterday."

Callie had heard the initial report on the television last night. "The news mentioned a lone survivor."

The nurse nodded. "That's our guy. He had surgery at Grady Hospital. According to the night-shift supervisor, they transported him here at two this morning when the cops got word his pals wanted to spring him. Rumor has it the Exterminators were involved."

"But why would the police bring him here?"

"To hide him from his Exterminator buddies." Tamika pursed her lips. "Look, if you don't feel comfortable, I can draw his blood."

Callie shook her head. "No. It's okay."

"Offer up one of those prayers you're famous for. Maybe you can change his heart."

Callie smiled then glanced around, seeing none

of the aides who usually worked the weekend shift. "Where is everyone?"

"Sam called in sick, and Barb got tied up in that holiday parade snaking though the city."

"Santa and his elves. A little ho-ho-ho on Christmas Eve."

Tamika lifted her brow. "That invitation still holds. You know we'd love to have you spend Christmas with us."

"Thanks, but my brother called a few days ago and asked if he could come over."

The nurse's eyes widened. "You haven't seen Robbie in years."

"Three to be exact. I'm not sure what he wants. He didn't have time to chat."

Tamika smiled. "Maybe his sister's good influence finally rubbed off on him."

"Either that or he needs money and thinks he can rip me off again."

"I hear you. Someone who took my credit card and treated himself to a weekend fling wouldn't find me welcoming him back with open arms."

But Callie's arms weren't open. They were crossed over her chest and her foot was tapping with a "let's see if you've changed" attitude.

Truth was, despite what he'd done, Callie loved her younger brother. Separated as kids when their parents divorced, Callie had drawn the short end of the straw. Not that her mother had been a bad woman, just unforgiving.

Her mother had cut all ties with the male side of the family, changing her last name and Callie's to spite the husband who'd wronged her. Then, true to her narcissistic nature, she'd heaped the underlying blame on her daughter's shoulders. Callie accepted the guilt for her sister's death but not for her parents' failed marriage.

"I told Robbie to come back when he straightened out his life." Callie arranged the Vacutainer tubes on her tray. "Maybe he has."

The head nurse shrugged. "Things don't work out tomorrow, you come over to my house. You know James and the girls consider you family."

"I've got presents for the kids. I'll drop them off after church in the morning."

"You're spoiling them for sure." The phone rang and Tamika reached for the receiver as Callie placed the lab slips on her tray and headed down the side corridor.

She'd draw the new guy's blood first then spend time with Mr. Petrecelli, a cancer patient who could use a visitor, especially on Christmas Eve. Tamika had mentioned an anonymous donor who, unbeknownst to Theo, took care of his medical expenses. The only other person in his life was an estranged brother. She and Theo would pray for his younger sibling as they always did. *Please, Lord, bring him back into Theo's life.*

Glancing out the window, Callie noted the string of older homes lining the neighboring residential streets. Someone in the Atlanta PD must have realized the out-of-the-way care facility would be the last place the gang would look for their buddy.

Rounding the corner, Callie saw the officer sitting on a folding chair at the end of the hallway. Face flushed, the guy packed at least twenty pounds of extra weight along with his weapon. Hopefully, he had Christmas off to spend with his family.

The cop stood as she neared. "I've gotta check your tray, ma'am."

"Don't bother." Callie pointed to a bookcase in the nearby alcove. "I'll grab what I need and leave everything else out here." She shoved a needle and three Vacutainer collection tubes into the pocket of her lab coat along with a tourniquet, alcohol swab and a bandage. After placing the metal tray on the bookshelf, she stepped through the door the cop held open for her.

Closed venetian blinds covered the window, throwing the room into shadow. The patient lay under a pile of blankets, face to the wall, his chest rising and falling in sync with the labored pull of air through his lungs.

"Sir?" Nearing the bed, she touched his arm. "I need to draw your blood."

The patient groaned then shifted and turned toward her.

Callie's heart hydroplaned against her chest.

"Robbie?"

Chapter Two

Joe Petrecelli drew in a lungful of cold December air and checked his watch. He'd run the two miles from his condo in fourteen minutes. Not his personal best, but decent and a strong indication he'd max the annual PT test again this year. Unless some dirtbag perpetrator decided to do a little target practice with Joe in his sights.

Seven years on the force, and he'd been lucky. A flesh wound to the shoulder and a broken collarbone. Not bad, when he considered the odds.

Joe had the holiday weekend off, but he'd be back at his desk by 9:00 a.m. after he jogged home to shower and change out of his sweats. Not that anyone expected him at work.

He glanced up and down the street. Quiet. No traffic. He'd been right. Lazarus House was a safe hideaway. God willing, the Exterminators wouldn't find their man here. Not that the Lord had much control over the gang of extortionists ravaging Joe's part of the metro area. Still, he wouldn't turn down help no matter where it originated, even from a God he'd shoved aside years ago.

Pulling open the front door and stepping into the warm interior, Joe made a mental note to call headquarters for more security. The nursing home was out of the way, but he wouldn't underestimate the Exterminators.

One nurse on duty. Joe flashed his badge, and the woman pointed him toward the side corridor, not realizing he'd been there in the middle of the night when the patient transported over from Grady.

Joe's footsteps sounded on the polished hardwood. He spied Phil Rogers, pulling duty at the end of the hallway. Glancing beyond the cop to room 10, Joe's gut tightened. Theo's room.

He still couldn't forgive his older brother. Joe had been thirteen when their parents died. He'd expected Theo—twenty-one and living on his own—to be his guardian. Instead, Theo had moved on with his life of carousing and drunkenness and abandoned Joe when he'd needed his brother the most. Forced into foster care, Joe had vowed to cut all ties with his self-centered sibling, and to this day, the two brothers had never met face-to-face again.

Acknowledging the officer on duty, Joe stepped into the patient's room and closed the door behind him. Movement caught his eye. He turned.

A woman stood in the shadows. White lab coat, swarm of black curls, alabaster skin. Troubled blue eyes captured his gaze.

Joe's gut tightened and warmth flooded over him. He spied the tourniquet in her clenched fist and tried to override the conflicting signals pinging against his heart.

Glancing at the patient, he asked, "Is the kid okay?"

"He...he appears stable." She stepped into the light.

Pretty, in a fresh, wholesome way, the woman stared back at him with an intensity that made his world shift.

Instantly aware of his own less-than-stellar appearance, he glanced down at his sweats, wishing he'd already showered and shaved. Needing to introduce himself, Joe pulled out the leather case he carried on his waistband in lieu of a wallet and held out his badge and police identification.

"Atlanta PD," he said, as if that would explain the reason he'd ventured into the patient's room.

She took the case.

A name tag hung from her lab coat. Callie Evans, MT(ASCP). Magnolia Medical.

Atlanta's state-of-the-art laboratory complex. Joe hadn't expected their techs to work at the home.

"Joseph X. Petrecelli." She read his name off the ID then glanced up as if seeing him clearly for the first time. Her eyes appeared almost turquoise.

"Joseph *Xavier* Petrecelli?" Her forehead wrinkled. "You're Theo's baby brother?"

Now Joe was the one to furrow his brow.

"Room ten," she continued. "Three doors down on the left."

Before Joe could respond, a scuffle sounded in the hallway. Joe hesitated for a second too long. The door crashed open.

Callie's eyes widened and the badge fell from her fingers and slipped under the bed.

Joe stepped in front of her. His hand searched for the service revolver he'd left back at his condo. Stupid mistake. Dropping to the floor, he pulled Callie down with him and reached for the .38 strapped to his calf.

Not fast enough.

Three men stormed into the room armed with automatics. Black ski masks covered their faces. Latex gloves encased their hands.

The tallest of the three kicked Joe beneath the eye.

"Augh!" Thrown off balance, the gun flew from his grasp. Joe grabbed the bedrail, pulled himself upright and lunged, crashing into the torso of the lanky guy who belonged to the boot. He followed with a fist to the guy's gut.

Callie screamed. The shortest of the three men wrapped his arm across her chest and jammed an automatic to her head.

"Let her go." Joe went for the gun.

A stocky guy slammed the butt of his pistol into Joe's neck.

Callie's mouth opened, but the ringing in his ears muffled her screams. Joe gasped for air.

The tall guy twisted Joe's arms behind his back, forcing him upright and opening his airway.

The patient's eyes blinked open. He struggled to rise off the bed.

"No," Joe warned, earning a knee to the small of his back. He doubled over, his face close to the kid's ear. "Don't move!"

Hands jerked Joe away.

The stocky perpetrator appeared in charge. He pointed his gun at Callie. "Rocky needs medical care. You come with us."

"What about the jock?" the short gunman asked. Deep voice, Latino accent.

The leader turned his eyes—piercing slits in the otherwise faceless mask—on Joe.

"Kill him."

Chapter Three

"You'll need help moving the patient." Joe grasped for anything that could slow down the action. "Leave the woman. Take me instead."

"He smells like a cop, Arnie," the Latino snarled. "He was packing a snub nose in his ankle holster."

Arnie? Arnie Frazier? One of the Exterminators' chief musclemen. *Keep talking,* Joe thought. *Draw attention off the woman.*

"Must be the sweat you're smelling." Joe's lips twisted into a grin. "The gun's for protection. Did you get a look at the neighborhood around here?"

Callie's face blanched. Her eyes glazed with fear. His first priority was to get her out of the mix.

"The woman's bound to slow you down," Joe continued. "Lock her in the latrine."

"Sanchez, I told you to kill him," Arnie spat back at the Latino.

"But he's a…?" Callie glanced at Joe for help. "A doctor."

Doctor was good. At least she hadn't mentioned he was a cop.

"You need both of us to keep Robbie alive." She struggled to free herself from Sanchez's hold.

"His name's Rocky," the Latino sneered, jerking her back against his chest.

Arnie turned to the tall dude. "Frisk him, Malachi." Joe clenched his jaw while the guy patted him down.

"He's clean."

Where was Rogers, the guard? Bound and gagged? Or dead?

Malachi shoved Joe toward the bed. "You carry Rocky."

"He...he's just had surgery," Callie pleaded. "There's a transport gurney in the alcove."

"She's right," Joe seconded, not that they appeared interested in anything he had to say.

"Please," she begged.

Arnie aimed the gun at Joe. He got the message. Wrapping one arm under the patient's shoulders and the other beneath his knees, Joe raised the kid off the mattress, making the shift as smooth as possible.

Malachi stepped into the hallway. The Latino followed, shoving Callie ahead of him.

Arnie eyed Joe. "You're next."

Holding the wounded patient, Joe moved forward. The guard lay in the alcove. His chest moved but only slightly. He needed medical care stat.

Arnie jammed the gun into Joe's back. "Keep walking."

The entourage snaked along the hallway toward the lobby, where the nurse sat slumped over her desk. Blood stained her scrubs, verifying her need for immediate medical care, as well. She moaned.

Ten steps to the back door. Joe ran through their options.

Get outside where someone would see them. A passing motorist. A next-door neighbor.

Take it slow and easy. Buy time.

Any distraction could be the opportunity they'd need to escape.

"You got a car big enough for all of us?" Joe asked, doubtful the thugs drove a minivan. He hoped his question would throw them off track.

The Latino looked back over his shoulder.

Joe shrugged, a smirk on his lips. "Sorry, guys, but I left my wheels at home."

Malachi inched open the back door. A white utility van with the words *Magnolia Medical* painted on the side panel sat at the base of the steps. The tall gunman glanced at Callie's name tag, making the connection.

"Looks like the woman can help us out," Malachi said.

Joe's optimism deflated. He caught Callie's gaze. *Do what they say, honey,* he tried to warn her. The terror he saw in her eyes made him realize she was scared to death.

The patient struggled in Joe's arms, his breathing labored. Death hovered close to him. Close to all of them.

If Joe didn't do something and do it fast, three of the six people walking out of Lazarus House wouldn't live to see Christmas day.

The cold air whipped around Callie as she stumbled down the back steps, urged on by the gunman's hand around her upper arm. She jerked away from his touch.

"Watch it, lady," he growled.

Squaring her shoulders, she shoved out her jaw with

determination. No matter how much she was trembling inside, she wouldn't let them see her fear.

Once again, she glanced over her shoulder at the cop, a man she'd prayed for countless times with Theo. Cancer had wasted the older brother's body into soft flesh that hung on a bony frame. In contrast, Joe was bulk and brawn and raw emotion that made her heart quicken and her pulse race. Dark eyes matched his hair and the shadow of beard that outlined his angled jaw.

Theo sought forgiveness and a chance to reconnect with the brother who couldn't forgive the sins of his past. Something Callie and Joe shared in common. They'd both shut out their siblings and closed the doors to their hearts. Although every time she caught Joe's gaze, her door creaked open.

When Callie had approached her brother's bed earlier to draw his blood, Robbie had shown no sign of recognizing her. Probably the post-surgery medication coupled with the seriousness of his injury.

Now his body hung limp in Joe's arms. Robbie's prognosis couldn't be good. Concern for her brother enveloped her like a winter fog. How had he gotten involved with these despicable men?

And Tamika? Would she survive her injuries?

The guard? *Oh, Lord, help all of them.*

Callie had left her purse and her cell phone in the van. Maybe she could call 9-1-1.

But how? *Think. Think.*

"Keys?" The guy at her side held out his right hand. His left tightened on her arm.

"In my pocket." She slipped her hand into her lab coat, pulled out the bundle of keys and dropped it into his outstretched palm. He unlocked the rear door. Plastic containers filled with supplies cluttered the transport area in the rear of the van.

"Clean out the back so we can lie Rocky down." Sanchez nudged her forward.

Hands trembling, she stacked the plastic interlocking containers and shoved them aside. A thin pad of industrial carpet covered the floor.

"I've got a coat in the front passenger seat," she said. "Toss it back here."

The tall guy did as she asked. Callie arranged her wrap and helped the cop place Robbie on the makeshift pallet. Her shoulder rubbed against Joe's, sending a jolt of awareness through her body. Dwarfed by his size, she was surprised by his control in the midst of chaos. His fingers touched hers and a surge of hope coursed through her veins. At least they were in this together.

"Don't do anything foolish," he whispered, his voice low, determined. "I'll take care of everything."

Callie nodded ever so slightly, noting the flecks of gold that rimmed his eyes. His left cheek looked bruised and swollen. A gash marked his neck, but his smile of encouragement warmed her in spite of the frigid wind that swirled around them.

She pulled a blanket from one of the crates that contained supplies for blood draws and covered her brother. Joe started to climb into the rear to adjust the fabric.

Arnie grabbed his shoulder. "No way, buddy. You drive."

Joe stepped back and supported Callie's elbow as she crawled in next to Robbie. Releasing her arm, his fingers swept against the small of her back before he stepped to the front of the van.

The assurance in his touch strengthened Callie's resolve. If they worked together, they'd get out of this alive. Refocusing her attention on the problem at hand, she tucked the blanket around her brother, keeping her gaze on anything except the handbag wedged in the corner.

Sanchez hoisted himself onto the bench seat. Malachi slipped in beside him. The cop and the other man claimed the captain's chairs up front, the bulky guy riding shotgun. He tugged his ski mask off his face and discarded the latex gloves. He was white, middle-aged, his faced pocked with scars. Probably acne as a kid.

"Pull onto the street, turn left and take it nice and slow," he said to Joe.

The engine turned over and hummed to life. The two men directly ahead of her ripped off their masks and gloves. The tall guy, Malachi, had mahogany skin, short hair and a slender face that fit his lanky body. He glanced back, his black eyes flicking from her to Robbie. He was close to her brother's age. Twenty-three, twenty-four.

Probably ten years older, Sanchez had a round face, square jaw and black hair. His skin appeared a few shades lighter than Malachi's but still dark.

Sanchez turned to check on her, his eyes scanning the rear of the van. "Whatcha doing, lady?"

"Taking care of my—" no reason to let them know Robbie was her brother "—my patient."

"You treat him real good, make sure he stays alive. Okay, doll?"

"I'm not your doll."

He glanced at her name tag. "Easy, Callie. You cool down. Don't give me no trouble. You understand?"

Joe's gaze caught hers in the rearview mirror. At

this distance, she couldn't read him. Maybe he was telling her to keep quiet.

Callie wiped her hand over Robbie's cheek. His skin felt warm. Infections often followed surgery. No telling what had entered his body along with the bullet.

Sanchez shifted and glanced nervously out the front window, giving her time to dig into her handbag. Her fingers touched the cool metal of her cell. Hopefully, the gunman wouldn't hear the call go through.

The van bounced along the road. Callie could feel the ruts in the pavement. The jarring motion wouldn't help her brother.

Malachi said something to the Latino.

Now or never.

She tapped in 9-1-1 and pushed Send.

"Emergency Operations Center. Please state your problem." The operator's voice sounded from the phone.

Callie glanced at the men up front. Had they heard anything?

Sanchez turned, perhaps sensing her gaze. "You say something, doll?"

He spied the phone. Spanish expletives flew from his mouth, and he yanked the cell from her hand.

Arnie looked back. "What's goin' on?"

The Latino held up the phone.

"Toss it," the leader ordered.

Sanchez rolled down the window and threw the phone into a wooded area. Swiveling to face her, he raised his hand and struck Callie across the jaw.

She reeled back, and her head slammed against the wall of the van.

"Next time you do something loco," Sanchez sneered, "you'll die."

Chapter Four

Adrenaline shot through Joe. He swerved to the side of the road, stomped on the brake and turned ready to pound some sense into Sanchez. "Don't touch her."

Arnie jammed the muzzle of his gun into Joe's side.

"So, Doc, you wanna be a martyr?"

Joe wanted to shove his fist down Sanchez's throat, but that wouldn't help the situation. Callie needed protection, not a hotheaded madman who would make matters worse.

Clamping down on his jaw, Joe pivoted forward, grabbed the wheel and ground his foot onto the accelerator. Gas surged through the engine. The tires screamed in protest.

Sanchez cursed from the backseat. The fingers of Arnie's left hand snaked around Joe's neck. His right hand forced the gun deeper into Joe's side.

"Blow off steam again—" the warning shot from Arnie's mouth "—and the girl dies."

Joe flicked his gaze to the side mirror. "An SUV's passing on the left. My advice is, you take your hands off my neck."

"He's right," Sanchez said. "A guy and his two kids. Christmas tree strapped to the roof."

Arnie's fingers released their hold. He adjusted himself in the passenger seat, keeping his gun low.

Joe eased up on the accelerator so the SUV could pass. No reason for the man and his kids to suspect anything amiss. They didn't need to get involved. Let them have their merry Christmas. Too many people had already been hurt by the Exterminators.

Once again, Joe looked in the rearview mirror. Callie stared back at him. The mark of Sanchez's hand was on her jaw. Tears glistened in her eyes, but she blinked to keep them in check.

A sense of helplessness swept over Joe. He had to bide his time. Outnumbered, without a weapon, he couldn't let his emotions get the best of him. He had to use every bit of training and experience to outsmart the three gunmen and gain control of the situation. The wounded patient was important, but Joe's number-one priority was to get Callie Evans out of the situation alive.

Callie's jaw burned where Sanchez had slapped her, but what hurt worse was seeing her brother's declining condition and the worry that they might kill Joe. Surely a cop would know to play along with the bad guys until an opportunity arose to escape. She didn't have a degree in criminal justice, but she'd watched enough cop shows on TV. Keep the bad guys thinking they were in control. Try to establish a relationship with them so they'd let their guard down. With a gun aimed at his heart, this wasn't the time to be Mr. Macho Cool.

Of course, Callie hadn't followed her own advice. Making a 9-1-1 cell call had been a risk, and she'd been caught. That was her mistake—at least the be-ing-caught part. She'd seen a story on a television re-enactment about a carjacked woman who'd done the same thing. Only that gunman had been oblivious to the call and the woman had been saved.

To save Robbie, she needed Joe's help. Callie looked down at her brother. For all the trouble he was in, Rob-bie might not want help. He seemed to be in league with these gang members. If they got out of this situ-ation alive, he'd have to face the consequences of his crimes.

He'd been a kid when their parents separated. It was doubtful their dad had been the best of role mod-els. A bitter man, he'd been verbally abusive, often scoffed at the concept of a loving God and died with-out a change of heart.

No wonder Robbie had made bad choices. Callie hadn't helped. For all her talk about God's love, she'd turned her back on her brother three years ago when their mother had died. Callie should have surrounded him with love. Maybe then, he would have been able to turn his life around.

Callie looked forward, once again catching Joe's gaze in the rearview mirror. The cop seemed to glance back more than he focused on the road. His dark eyes burned into hers. Heat warmed her cheeks, and the soft flesh at the base of her neck tingled.

"Rocky feels hot," she said, raising her voice to be heard over the sound of the motor. "He can't travel far."

Sanchez turned and glanced down at Robbie. "We'll stop soon."

Maybe he had an ounce of decency hidden under all that anger after all. She grasped her brother's hand and squeezed, hoping he could feel the encouragement and support in her touch.

Through the window, she saw the Atlanta skyline to her left. The golden dome of the State Capitol was visible in the distance. The turnoff for the Interstate 75-85 connector lay ahead.

Chilled from the cold, she wrapped her arms around her chest. As if sensing her discomfort, Joe reached for the heater. A blast of warm air blew from the overhead duct.

Arnie mumbled something from the front seat, and Joe switched lanes. If they exited downtown, they'd be caught in the holiday parade. Crowds of people lined Peachtree Street and International Boulevard.

Gridlock might provide the opportunity to escape. Once the van stopped, she could throw the door open and scream for help.

A surge of hope filled her. She inched toward the door. Joe turned onto the connector, heading north. Three exits until International Boulevard and the throng of holiday merrymakers. Not that she wanted anyone else to be hurt.

A cell chirped from the front of the van. Arnie fumbled for the phone and pulled it to his ear. "Yeah?"

He grumbled. "Right." Flipping his cell closed, he glanced back at Sanchez and Malachi. "Streets downtown are closed." He reached for the radio knob.

Christmas music piped through the speakers: "Peace on earth, goodwill to men..."

Peace? Goodwill? The three gunmen, holding them hostage, had an opposing point of view.

Once again, her gaze settled on Joe. Did he believe in peace on earth, or had he been warped by the crime and depravity with which he came into contact in his line of work? Hard to be optimistic about man's nature when all he saw was the underbelly of society.

What had happened to the world? Callie sighed, their situation heavy on her heart. Joe looked at her in the mirror as if he understood her frustration and upset. Despite the odds, she felt a wave of confidence sweep over her.

The Christmas song ended.

"This just in." The radio announcer's voice cut over the hum of the motor and the sound of the wheels spinning along the asphalt. "A shoot-out at a local nursing home has left an officer and the facility's head nurse severely injured. Police were unable to question the wounded, but the gunman involved with the local gang, the Exterminators, has been kidnapped. Police have set up roadblocks to all routes leaving the city. The group is armed and dangerous, and citizens are asked to notify police if they see anything suspicious."

Arnie clicked the radio off. "Leave the connector at the next exit."

Joe steered the van into the right lane and decelerated onto the ramp. Callie's heart plummeted. They were heading east, away from the parade route.

Arnie turned to catch her eye. "You live close by?"

"Not far," she said, wondering if he planned to hole up at her apartment. She thought of the elderly gentleman who sat by his window and watched everyone's comings and goings. If anything seemed amiss, he'd knock on her door to check on her. Another neighbor, a sweet widow, had promised to bring over a plate of holiday cookies this afternoon.

Callie couldn't let them be brought into this situation, yet riding in the back of the utility van wasn't good for Robbie. He needed bed rest and time to heal. For her own peace of mind, she wanted to run the lab tests that would tell how his condition was progressing.

She adjusted the blanket around Robbie and pulled her hand back, noticing blood on her fingers. Tugging the blanket and hospital gown aside, she saw the bright red stain on the gauze dressing, covering his incision. Robbie needed to be stabilized to stop the bleeding. A complete blood count, or CBC, would determine the amount of blood he had already lost.

"Magnolia Medical isn't far from here," she blurted out before she could weigh her words.

The three gunmen turned and stared at her.

Joe shot her a cold glance from the mirror.

"The main lab's closed over the holiday weekend," she explained. "No one will think to look for us there. We can park the van behind the building and out of sight. I'll be able to run Rocky's lab tests. There are medical supplies, blood for transfusion."

Arnie snorted. "I don't like labs."

"Rocky's bleeding bad," Sanchez confirmed, gazing at the stained bandage.

"All right, all right." The ringleader nodded. "We'll hole up at Magnolia Medical."

Joe turned left at the next intersection and headed for the large medical complex situated on the edge of town. The cop looked back, his eyes hooded.

Callie's heart quickened, realizing too late she had

provided the gunmen exactly what they needed—a safe place to hide out.

Her stomach dropped. What had she done? Reacting too quickly, she'd provided the gunmen with the perfect solution to their problem—a problem that had just grown worse for Callie, her brother and the driver, whose neck muscles were already tensed with frustration.

She touched Robbie's side as fresh blood stained the gauze. If only she'd learned when to keep her mouth shut.

Long ago, she'd suggested her sister play outside. Callie had made a mistake then that had led to her sister's death. Hopefully, she hadn't made a second mistake that would cost her brother's life, as well.

Chapter Five

Joe gripped the steering wheel, trying to override the frustration that was bubbling up within him. Cute as she was, Callie had a stubborn determination that might get them all killed. Most folks would be cowering back in silence, afraid to mumble a word. Not this gal. She was becoming more vocal by the minute.

"Turn left at the next intersection," Arnie directed. Driving away from the busy downtown, Joe steered the van through an industrial area. Empty parking lots signaled plant employees had the Christmas weekend off. No one would notice the van snaking along this deserted back road toward the laboratory.

In the distance, Joe saw the top of the Magnolia Medical complex above the barren treetops. A few doctor's offices and small medical clinics bordered the side roads. A drugstore appeared to be the only place open for business. A couple of cars were parked out front.

Arnie grunted for Joe to turn into the laboratory lot and steer toward the rear of the main building, where the parked van would appear to be waiting for employees, returning to work on Monday morning. If this situation wasn't resolved by then, the medical personnel going into the lab would be put in danger, as well.

Following Arnie's direction, Joe parked near a side entrance. Sanchez climbed out and opened the driver's door, his gun trained on Joe as he stepped to the pavement.

"Get the kid," Arnie ordered.

Rounding the van, Malachi opened the rear door. Joe held out his hands and helped Callie climb out. A scent as fresh as sunshine swirled around her, so different from the smell of death that clung to the gunmen.

He squeezed her fingers. "Are you okay?" Standing close, he could see her long lashes, which fluttered over her cheeks, the curve of her lips, the arch of her brow. His breath caught, and for an instant he thought only of how smooth Callie's skin felt to his touch.

"Move it," Arnie barked.

As she stepped aside, Joe glanced into the van, seeing the kid's pain-stretched face wedged between the plastic containers. A small, clear area had provided Callie room to kneel at his side, which must have been uncomfortable for her as well, yet she hadn't complained.

Sensing her gaze, Joe turned. She stood next to Malachi, arms wrapped around her chest for warmth or to ward off the dread that lined her pretty face. Joe raised his chin, hoping she'd see the gesture as acknowledgment of her courage.

Wind swirled through the parking lot, scattering the last of the autumn leaves like lost souls looking for a place to rest. Joe quickly studied the surrounding area. Nothing indicated a source of help. Callie's words echoed in his mind: "No one will find us here."

Arnie dropped the bundle of keys he'd pulled from the ignition into Callie's hand and pushed her toward the side entrance. "Open the door," he ordered.

Joe lifted Rocky into his arms, and the kid's head rolled back. His eyelids fluttered but failed to open. Trying to keep him steady, Joe followed Arnie and Callie into the first floor of the laboratory's main building.

The ringleader shoved Callie along the corridor. She stumbled forward then caught herself and straightened. He grabbed her arm, but she jerked free.

Glancing right, then left, Joe familiarized himself with the building. Biohazard signs hung on various doors that undoubtedly led to labs off a central main corridor. He noticed a stairway at each end of the hallway. Water fountain. Public restrooms.

"The therapeutic donor room is on the third floor." Callie glanced back at the patient. "He'll be comfortable there."

She stopped at a bank of elevators and pushed the up button. The door whooshed open. They filed in, wearing strained expressions on their faces, and rode in silence to the third floor. The only sound was the kid's heavy breathing.

"This way." Callie took the lead when the elevator stopped. The lab was her home turf, and she walked with determined steps as if taking charge of the situation.

All that assertiveness could get her into trouble. Arnie Frazier wasn't known as a nice guy. He'd hurt anyone, including a woman, who didn't follow his directions.

Callie opened a steel door, which bore an Authorized Personnel Only sign and a biohazard logo. The smell of chemicals wafted past Joe, sharp, acidic, not totally unpleasant but distinctive in an antiseptic way. He followed Arnie across the threshold and into an expansive clinical lab. Rows of slate countertops and overhanging cabinets filled with laboratory supplies occupied the greater portion of the room.

The ringleader hesitated. "This place filled with germs?"

"Depends. Watch where you put your hands." Callie kept moving past a number of freestanding automated analyzers and a row of refrigerators.

Arnie caught Sanchez's eye and motioned him forward. "Check it out. Make sure no one's around to disrupt our privacy. Cut the phone lines while you're at it."

Sanchez grunted and headed off on his own.

Joe spied a smaller room to the right. The sign above the door read Micro Lab.

"In here." Callie pointed them forward. A fire extinguisher hung on the wall behind her.

Still carrying the kid, Joe stepped into the windowless room about the size of a two-car garage. Four padded contoured donor chairs sat two-by-two in the center. The walls were edged with the same slate counters and overhanging cabinets as in the main lab area.

A small Christmas tree stood dark in the corner. On the nearby countertop, ceramic figures of Joseph and Mary huddled around a tiny infant in what appeared to be a handmade stable.

"You draw units of blood in here?" Arnie asked as he looked around.

"Not the blood used for transfusions," Callie explained. "This room is for patients who have hemochromatosis—too much iron in their blood. Every so often they need a unit drawn off to drop their levels into normal range."

Arnie nodded as if he understood about iron levels and therapeutic blood draws. Opening a door on the far side of the room, he peered into the corridor at the stairwell directly opposite. Evidently satisfied, he closed the door.

Callie pulled a bedsheet from the wall cabinet and slipped it over the leather recliner then helped Joe lower Robbie onto the chair, his hips angled into the contour. Pushing aside the hospital gown, she checked the blood-tinged gauze that covered the incision on his side before she drew a blanket from another cabinet, covered him and tucked the fabric under his legs.

Joe walked to the sink, searching for something—anything—that could serve as a weapon.

Malachi raised his gun. "Whatta think you're doing?"

"Washing my hands." Joe turned on the water and lathered his hands with soap. "I need to examine your buddy."

Lowering his weapon, the mocha-skinned gunman leaned against the counter and shrugged. "Watch your step."

Once Joe dried his hands, he reached for the latex gloves on the counter and held the box out to Arnie, who stood with his back against the wall.

The gunman hesitated for a moment then pulled out

two gloves and slipped them over his hands. Evidently he didn't like germs.

Callie handed Joe a disposable lab coat and held another one out for Arnie. He shrugged off the offer.

"Doing okay?" Joe whispered, his voice muffled by the running water as she washed her hands.

"Scared."

The tremble of fear he heard in her voice cut into his heart.

"Anyone expecting you home today?"

She shook her head.

"What about at Lazarus House? Won't someone realize you were working today?"

"I got a call about an hour ago. I visit the patients most weekends. I was asked if I could fill in by drawing some of the lab work."

"So no one would suspect you've been taken hostage?"

Once again she shook her head. Joe didn't want to sound an alarm, but it seemed neither he nor Callie would be missed by anyone today. From the news report, he knew the cops hadn't been able to question the guard or head nurse, so the responsibility of escaping rested solely on Joe's shoulders.

"Stay out of their way and keep quiet," he told her. "Let me handle the gunmen."

Their gazes locked. Her eyes were clear as a mountain stream.

Wanting to focus on something other than Callie Evans, he glanced at the supply cabinet in the corner. "I need a weapon. A scalpel, scissors. Anything sharp that can inflict a wound."

Sanchez returned to the donor room. "The lab

checks out, Arnie." He caught sight of the wall phone hanging in the corner. "You want me to cut that phone line, too?"

The ringleader shook his head. "Leave it. We might need it later."

Spying the reclining chairs, Sanchez smiled. "I'm gonna stretch out and relax for a while." He holstered his weapon and pointed to a wall-mounted television. "How 'bout turning on the tube?"

Malachi raised his hand and flipped the power switch. A Spanish variety show came on. The sounds of Christmas carols—some sung in English, some in Spanish—filled the room.

"Help me out when I examine the patient," Joe whispered as he slipped into the lab coat and gloves then stepped to the donor chair where Robbie lay.

Noticing how Arnie was staring at them, Callie raised her voice for his benefit as she pulled on gloves. "I'll draw the CBC you ordered and the chemistry panel."

"Perfect." Joe took the kid's pulse then checked the whites of his eyes, felt the lymph glands on his neck and palpitated his lower abdomen. At least he knew the basics. Hopefully his act would convince the gunmen he was a qualified physician.

Callie pulled a stethoscope from the cabinet drawer. Wrapping the cuff around the kid's upper arm, she pumped up the pressure and watched the indicator slowly drop. "One hundred over seventy-five."

"We need to keep him stable so his blood pressure doesn't drop," Joe said.

Callie pulled the blood-drawing supplies she'd grabbed at Lazarus House from her pocket. Tying a tourniquet around the patient's arm, she swabbed his vein and inserted the needle. Joe glanced over his shoulder at Arnie. The gunman's face blanched, and he averted his gaze as the color-coded tubes filled with blood.

Working swiftly, Callie unsnapped the tourniquet and jabbed a gauze square against the point of entry before discarding the needle into the special receptacle for sharp objects hanging on the wall.

The kid's eyes fluttered open. "Cal...?"

Sanchez stared at the television. Malachi asked a question that deflected the ringleader's attention. Turning back to the patient, Joe leaned down. "What is it, kid?"

Still dehydrated from surgery, he tried to swallow. "Cal...?"

Callie grabbed his hand. "I'm here, Robbie."

His lips broke into a strained smile. "Callie," he whispered, and then his eyes closed, and he slipped back to sleep.

A sinking feeling settled in the pit of Joe's stomach. "You know the kid?"

Face drawn, she pulled back ever so slightly. "He... he's my brother."

The air knocked out of Joe's lungs. Callie and the kid were related? Now *that* was a complication he hadn't expected.

Up to this point, Callie had trusted him, but that might change if she found out the truth. Joe had ordered the middle-of-the-night transfer to Lazarus House to keep Robbie out of the hands of the Exterminators. Unfortunately, his strategy had backfired.

As much as he wanted to explain everything to Callie, he couldn't. The stakes were too high, and emotions were stretched too thin. It was easy to see how much she loved her brother. If anything happened to him, she would never forgive Joe. Even though they'd been together only a short time, he wanted to ensure their fragile relationship stayed intact.

His job was to get her out alive.

Maybe then he would be able to share the secret Robbie's sister needed to know.

Chapter Six

Working as efficiently as possible under the trying conditions, Callie smoothed the blanket over Robbie and tucked the edges under his legs. When her hand brushed his calf, he jerked and groaned with pain.

Alarmed, she pulled back the blanket. The side of his leg was scraped. Normally, she wouldn't be concerned, but a small open sore, no larger than a dime, had erupted in the center of the irritated skin. A circle of angry, red tissue surrounded the opening, indicating infection. Something Robbie didn't need.

Callie grabbed a transfer tube and culture swabs from a nearby cabinet and rubbed them against the wound while Joe held Robbie's leg in place.

Arnie stepped out of the room. Despite his tough-guy facade, he apparently had a problem with body fluids and open sores.

"How long will it take to know what's causing the infection?" Joe whispered. At least he understood the seriousness of this new complication.

"Depends how fast the organism grows. I'll make a smear and look at it under the microscope. If we're

lucky, it may give me a clue about what bug we're dealing with. A more definite identification comes once
the culture grows out, which could take twenty-four
to forty-eight hours." Time they didn't have.

Lowering her voice, she added, "I've got scissors in
the micro lab. I'll get them when I set up the culture."

Once she covered the sore with a gauze square, Joe
helped her smooth the blanket back into place.

His fingers touched hers. "Be careful, Callie."

Warmth spread through her and a sense of gratitude
for the concern she saw in Joe's dark eyes. His calm
in the face of crisis reassured her. Somehow he'd get
them out of here.

She thought back to all the times she and Theo had
prayed for his cop brother. God must have a sense of
humor to allow Callie and Joe to meet under such trying circumstances.

Her daily prayer for so long had been for the Lord to
bring Joe back into Theo's life. Either Joe or God had
missed the mark at the nursing home by three rooms.
She almost smiled, knowing the cop had been the one
with the bad aim.

If the hostage situation ended on a positive note, she
would do everything in her power to ensure the two
brothers reconnected. Reconciliation might be asking too much, but God worked in mysterious ways,
and His timing was perfect. Maybe He would even
use their present predicament to bring about change
for the better.

"Theo was right," she said, seeing confusion wrap
around Joe's handsome face. "Your brother said you
were a good man."

An edge of vulnerability flashed in Joe's eyes.

There was a lot of hurt in his past, Callie knew. Every family had problems. Some more than most. Her own proved the point.

She'd made a mistake the last time she and Robbie had been together. This time she'd ensure her brother knew she loved him. She'd let him know the Lord loved him as well. From what Theo had said, Joe might need that same message.

Malachi peered down at the patient. "How's he doing?"

"Rocky needs to be in a hospital," Joe insisted.

"Forget it." Arnie stepped back into the donor room, appearing somewhat composed now that the wound was covered.

Callie gathered the tubes of blood and culture swabs. "I need to run these lab tests."

"Malachi, go with her." Arnie pointed Joe to the corner. "Sit on the floor, Doc."

"If I help her, we'll have the results faster," Joe said.

"Malachi, aim your gun at her head. One wrong move and she dies." Arnie glared at Joe. "Got it?"

He fisted his hands. "Yeah, I've got it."

Callie sent him a reassuring glance, hoping he got the message. She'd be okay as long as he didn't do anything rash.

Malachi followed her into the small microbiology lab and plopped down on one of the tall swivel chairs.

Callie pulled in a calming breath, hoping to ease some of the tension that tightened the muscles in her neck. She labeled three petri dishes then touched the end of the cotton swab, containing the discharge from the sore on Robbie's leg, to the gel culture media. Lighting a Bunsen burner, she sterilized a tiny steel loop in the flame and streaked the discharge across each plate.

When Callie opened a drawer under the work area, she spied the scissors Joe needed. Turning ever so slightly, she found Malachi staring at her.

"Something wrong?" he asked.

"No, of course not." She pulled a microscope slide from the drawer. Callie rubbed the swab over the glass and allowed it to air-dry before she placed it onto the automatic staining machine.

As the slide dropped into position and was covered with the first of a series of dyes, Callie returned the plates to the incubators. As attentive as Malachi was, she'd have to come back later for the scissors.

Motioning for him to follow her into the main laboratory area, she headed for the chemistry analyzers. As she prepared her brother's blood specimen for testing, Malachi leaned back against the slate countertop. The tension in his face eased. Away from Arnie, he seemed to let down his guard.

"You from around here?" she asked, hoping to develop a rapport with the youngest gunman.

He nodded. "Decatur's home. My mama and grandma live there."

"Bet they'd like to see you on Christmas."

"Yeah. There's a big family get-together. My mama's been cooking all week."

"Turkey and dressing?"

He nodded and smiled. "Corn-bread stuffing, collard greens, sweet-potato-and-pecan pie." Malachi swallowed as if tasting the holiday treats, his eyes wistful. "My mama's gonna be disappointed if I'm not there for supper."

"Ask Arnie. Maybe he'll let you leave."

The gunman straightened. Perhaps she'd said too much.

Callie programmed the tests into the analyzer before she spoke again. "Smart guy like you could make a difference in the world. Ever think of going straight?"

He shrugged. "My mama said I should be a preacher."

Callie almost dropped the tube of blood she held. Either Malachi's mother didn't know the depth of his gang involvement or she had extraordinary confidence in God's redeeming love to change her son's heart.

"Sounds like your mama wants you to be right with the Lord."

"I believed when I was a kid. Don't have time for God no more. Gotta job to do. Gotta stay strong, you know what I mean?"

Evidently Malachi had a flawed view of what it meant to be a Christian. "So you think believing in God would make you less of a man?"

"I'm just sayin' I've got other things to do."

"Like holding people hostage?" she asked.

He stiffened. "We didn't start out to do anybody no harm. Just needed to get Rocky. Make sure he was safe."

Robbie would have been safer remaining at Lazarus House, but Callie doubted the gunman would agree. "He needs medical care."

Malachi waved his arms in the air. "But you've got all these medical machines to make him better right here." He pointed a finger at her chest. "You're a nurse. The doc's with him now."

"I'm a medical technologist," she corrected. And

the doc's a cop. A fact she wouldn't mention. "The tests will determine the seriousness of Rocky's condition, but he needs intensive care that he can only get at a hospital."

"He wasn't in a hospital when we grabbed him. He was in an old folks' home."

"Lazarus House is a long-term nursing facility where he had full-time care," Callie explained.

"But they moved him there from Grady, the biggest hospital in the city."

Malachi was right. Under the cops' insistence, no doubt. Tamika had said the transfer was in response to information law enforcement had received about the Exterminators.

Callie would like to meet the wise guy who suggested her brother would be safe at the residential care facility. She'd give him a piece of her mind. He'd made a mistake—a big mistake that could cost three people their lives.

Once the chemistry analyzer was running, Callie focused on the CBC. The results confirmed that Robbie's red blood count was low. Any additional loss of blood would be life threatening.

Conversely, his white blood count was elevated, indicating a possible infection. Callie turned back to the chemistry analyzer as the results flashed across the monitor. She printed off a hard copy of all the tests and shoved them into Malachi's hand.

"Take these to the doc while I see if the slide's finished staining." She motioned him into the donor room, relieved when Malachi complied with her request.

Slipping into the small side lab, Callie grabbed the

scissors and shoved them into the pocket of her lab coat just as the young gunman stepped back into the room.

"Arnie wondered what's keeping you," he said.

"I'll be there in a minute." She extracted the now-stained slide from the drying rack, added a drop of immersion oil and placed it on the microscope. Cells swarmed into focus. She pulled her eyes away and invited Malachi over.

"Take a look," she said.

He leaned down to peer through the ocular, his gun close to her hand. Callie edged closer. Her fingers touched the cold metal.

Malachi jerked his head up, and his right hand went for the gun.

She pulled back just in time, keeping her gaze neutral. Inside she was shaking. "Did you see bacteria?"

Malachi stared at her for a long moment then nodded.

Callie kept talking, hoping to distract Malachi. "Bacteria with a circular shape are called cocci. It they appear in a chain, they're called streptococci."

Footsteps sounded at the doorway, and Sanchez stuck his head into the room. "Arnie wants to know if there's a problem."

"She's almost finished," Malachi said.

The Latino narrowed his eyes at Callie. "The doc's explaining the test results to Arnie. He wants to hear what you have to say."

Butterflies fluttered through Callie's stomach. If she contradicted Joe's assessment, the gunmen would realize one of them was a fraud.

Malachi grabbed her arm and shoved her toward the door, suddenly needing to assert his authority. Callie

would let him save face in front of Sanchez. For all
Malachi's attempt to be tough, he had been raised by
a God-fearing woman. Surely some of her prayers had
rubbed off on her son.

The Christmas message could move the hardest
heart. Maybe it could allow the youngest gunman to
realize the error of his ways. Callie stepped back into
the lab and glanced at her brother. If only his heart
could change, as well.

She turned to Joe, their eyes locking. Once again,
a sense of hope flowed over her, along with the confidence that God had brought them together for a purpose.

Arnie shoved the lab sheets into her face. "Tell me
what these numbers mean."

Keep it simple, an inner voice cautioned. Callie
knew that even if she provided a very basic overview
of her brother's condition, without medical training,
Joe would be hard-pressed to do the same. Providing
contradictory information could prove fatal.

She took the papers and swallowed the fear that
struggled to overpower her. Arnie aimed his gun at
Joe's temple. The cop never blinked but continued to
stare at her. His lips curved into a confident grin that
made her pulse race and her frustration bubble anew.
Why'd he always have to be so sure of himself?

"Come on, Callie," Arnie sneered. "Tell us what
we need to know."

Chapter Seven

Joe wished he could reassure Callie. Trust your instincts, he'd tell her if he could. Arnie questioned Joe's medical expertise. Hopefully, the information Callie provided would wipe out any doubts the gunmen still harbored.

"Go on," Arnie insisted.

Callie swallowed. "Rocky's dehydrated, and he's lost blood. He has a scrape on his leg, which is infected. I saw a number of organisms present under the microscope that could produce a serious complication."

"As I told you, Arnie, your man needs IV antibiotic therapy as well as hydration," Joe said, confirming Callie's findings. "We're watching the wound on his chest. If he loses much more blood, he'll need a transfusion, as well."

Arnie grunted. "Rocky stays here. There are two of you and one of him. Keep him alive." He waved the gun between them. "If he dies, you will, too."

A smirk crossed his face as he glared at Joe. "I'm a gentleman, Doc. Ladies first."

Joe wanted to grab Arnie and squash him like a bug, but he needed to do things by the book. Let the rule of law deal with him. Fact was, Arnie Frazier deserved solitary confinement for the rest of his life. Forget parole.

Unfortunately, with a .45 waving in the air, Joe had to ignore Arnie's cocky rhetoric and try to be a voice of reason in the midst of chaos.

Stepping around the gunman, Joe moved back to the patient's side. "Callie, if you'll help me, we'll check his leg again."

Worry pulled at her pretty face, but she appeared to muster an inner strength as she followed Joe's lead.

Malachi approached Arnie. "Hey, man, it's Christmas Eve. Maybe we should split up tomorrow."

Sanchez moved closer. "I told my wife and kids I'd be in Juarez late Christmas night."

"I'm in charge," Arnie scoffed. "We stay here until I say otherwise."

"Ah, man," Malachi groused.

Sanchez muttered something in Spanish.

While the gunmen bickered, Callie whispered to Joe. "What did you tell Arnie about the lab test results?"

"The same thing you said."

She looked up. "But how did you know what the test results meant?"

"EMT training while I was in the military. Basic medical triage. Nothing sophisticated or high tech. Evidently, it was enough to satisfy Arnie."

"Thank you, God," Callie whispered.

"While you're sending up that thank-you, better ask Him how we can get antibiotics for your brother."

"There's a drugstore not far from here. Arnie might let me get a prescription filled."

Joe remembered seeing the pharmacy earlier.

"Our lab pathologist keeps a prescription pad in his office," Callie continued. "I'll write the order for an antibiotic and pain medicine. You'll need to sign his name."

"Arnie won't let you out of here alone."

"I'll see if Malachi can go with me. He's not as hard-hearted as he likes to pretend."

"If you can get away from him, call the cops. Tell them where we are. They'll send in a SWAT team."

She slipped her hand into her lab coat pocket. "I got the scissors."

"You're amazing." He smiled. Callie *was* amazing. She was strong and determined and resourceful. Hopefully, she'd find a way to get away from Malachi.

Joe shoved the scissors into the pocket of his sweatpants, comforted to know he had a weapon. He'd wait until she left the lab before he executed his next move. Hopefully one that would end the hostage situation once and for all.

Together, he and Callie checked the kid's blood pressure. Still low.

"How bad is it?" Arnie asked from across the room.

"He needs an antibiotic and pain medicine," Joe insisted. "If I write a prescription, you can send one of your goons with Callie to get it filled at the nearby pharmacy."

"The prescription pad is in the lab office. I'll get it." She started for the main lab.

Arnie glared at Malachi. "Go with her. Don't let her out of your sight."

As the two left the room, Sanchez adjusted the volume on the television and lowered himself onto the donor chair.

Joe checked Robbie's side. The bleeding had eased. He pulled back the sheet that covered his leg. The skin around the scrape appeared swollen and hot, worse than when Joe had first seen the gash just a short while ago.

Callie returned with the pad and ballpoint pen. "I wrote the prescriptions as you told me to do," she said for the gunmen's benefit. "A broad-spectrum antibiotic and high-dose painkiller." She had also traced the pathologist's signature lightly in pencil to guide Joe's hand.

Arnie and Malachi continued to argue about when to leave Magnolia Medical. Malachi was determined to have Christmas dinner with his mother and family. Arnie seemed increasingly aggravated with the tall, lanky gunman's plans for Christmas Day.

"Remember, Callie, get away from Malachi as soon as you can," Joe whispered. "Call the police. Tell them about the stairway that leads to the back hallway. The phone's still connected in this room. Tell them to call and let the phone ring twice to warn me they're ready to charge the lab. I'll distract the gunmen until they arrive."

She nodded, her eyes wide, but she showed no sign of fear. He admired her courage and hated putting her in danger.

Once he signed the prescriptions, she turned to Malachi. "Are you ready?"

Arnie held up his hand. "Not so fast." The ringleader nudged Sanchez. "You go with her. Take the van. If she tries anything, shoot first, ask questions later."

Joe's gut tightened. Callie had developed a rapport with Malachi and had a better chance of getting away from him. Sanchez wouldn't let down his guard even for a second.

Sanchez grabbed Callie's upper arm and shoved her toward the door. "Let's go, doll."

She glanced over her shoulder at her brother then raised her eyes to Joe. He nodded with encouragement, feeling the weight of the scissors in his pocket.

"Get her out alive," Joe mumbled, wondering to whom he was addressing the request. Certainly not God. With his track record, the Almighty would never answer Joe's prayer for help.

Sanchez's fingers were tight on Callie's arm. As hard as she tried, she couldn't jerk free from his grasp. Joe was counting on her, but she wasn't sure she could do anything heroic. Hopefully, the pharmacist—a man she knew—would recognize the forged signature and come to her aid.

Callie remained optimistic until she and Sanchez walked into the drugstore. Within a few seconds, she realized the pharmacist was preoccupied with a cute blonde who seemed to strike his fancy as she waited for her prescription. With his focus on the woman instead of his work, the pharmacist overlooked the incorrect answers Callie gave to some of his questions as well as the *Call Police* message she wrote instead of her signature at the bottom of the credit card sales receipt. He shoved the slip of paper into the bottom drawer of his cash register without noticing her cryptic plea for help.

Sanchez hovered close by, his weapon aimed at her from the pocket of his jacket. Children scurried through the store dangerously close to the Latino gunman and his weapon. As much as Callie needed to get help, she couldn't do anything that would endanger the little ones.

Her heart plummeted as they left the store and climbed into the Magnolia Medical van. She had the medication Robbie needed, but she hadn't been able to warn anyone about what was happening at Magnolia Medical, nor had she been able to get free from Sanchez.

"Grab the drugs," he ordered when they parked in the rear of the laboratory. He yanked the keys from the ignition and held the gun on her as they both dropped to the pavement.

When he rounded the front of the van, she took off running, her eyes focused on the wooded area at the far end of the parking lot.

Sanchez cursed and raced after her, his footfalls slamming against the concrete. "Stop or I'll shoot," he shouted.

He could kill her as easily inside the lab as out here. Callie had to get away. The muscles in her legs burned, and she gasped for air, feeling tightness in her chest.

Sanchez's labored breathing sounded in her ear. He was gaining. Calling on an inner strength, she increased her pace. Twenty feet more and she'd enter the wooded area surrounding the lab complex. A small gate would take her out of the fenced compound. Fifty yards beyond that she could see a gas station, where help hopefully waited.

His hand grabbed her shoulder. She screamed and stumbled to the pavement. Her knees scraped against the cement, ripping her skin open. Gravel cut the palms of her hands when she tried to break her fall.

Sanchez wove his fingers through her hair and pulled her to her feet. Callie cried out in pain. Hot tears stung her eyes. She'd failed. Joe was counting on her. Robbie wouldn't last much longer. Their survival depended on Callie, and she'd let them down.

Oh, God, I'm so sorry, she moaned. Sanchez shoved her toward the lab. If the gunmen killed Joe or Robbie, their deaths would rest on her shoulders. Right now, the thought of losing them and the guilt she would carry was too much for her to bear.

Joe knew everything would happen fast once Callie contacted the police. The two-ring hang-up phone call would signal that the SWAT team was in place and ready to storm the lab.

His plan was straightforward. He'd attack Arnie with the scissors before Malachi went for his gun. Caught off guard, the gunmen would be overpowered once the SWAT team stepped through the door.

Relieved that Callie wouldn't be in the middle of the milieu, Joe's heart warmed thinking of her courage. Hopefully she'd gotten free from Sanchez.

Malachi lounged on the chair Sanchez had vacated and watched an old rerun of a classic Christmas movie. Arnie's eyes were heavy as he glanced between the overhead screen and the floor where Joe sat. Robbie moaned occasionally and called out twice in pain.

The phone rang sooner than Joe had expected, and before he could dig the scissors from his pocket. Callie must have gotten away from Sanchez immediately after leaving the lab. Both gunmen looked up, but neither made an attempt to answer the phone.

"Want me to get that?" Joe stood and stretched.

"Sit down," Arnie demanded.

"I need to use the restroom."

The ringleader nodded to Malachi. "Take him to the men's room. Watch him."

Malachi's eyes were fixed on the TV. He laughed at something one of the characters said as he slid off the chair.

Arnie glanced at the screen, giving Joe the chance he needed.

He lunged for the weapon jammed in Malachi's waistband. Taken off guard, the lanky Exterminator fell back against the donor chair. His gun clattered to the floor.

Joe slammed his fist into Malachi's jaw. Stunned, he tried to stand as Joe bent to retrieve the handgun.

"Back off," Arnie yelled.

Ignoring the warning and unable to grab the dropped weapon, Joe jabbed his shoulder into Malachi's gut. The gunman's fingers circled Joe's neck, constricting his airway.

He gasped and pulled the scissors from his pocket.

Arnie raised his weapon. Instinctively, Joe shifted, pulling Malachi off balance.

In that split second the gun went off, the sound deafening.

Joe sucked in a lungful of air, expecting pain. Instead, Malachi slumped to the floor, a gaping wound to his side. His face twisted. He stretched a hand out to Arnie. "Why...why'd you shoot me, man?"

Arnie stared at him as if dazed, his mouth open, eyes wide.

Spying Malachi's gun under the donor chair, Joe dropped to his knees and reached for the weapon.

"No," Arnie screamed. He fired again.

Pain sliced though Joe's shoulder. The scissors dropped from his hand.

Arnie slammed the barrel of his gun into the base of Joe's neck.

He gasped and fell to the floor.

Where was the SWAT team?

The door to the lab opened. Relief spread over Joe.

He looked up, but instead of the well-trained team of law enforcement professionals, he saw Sanchez with his hand around Callie's neck.

Chapter Eight

"Oh, dear Lord, help us all," Callie cried, taking everything in as she entered the donor room. Her gaze flicked from her brother to Malachi to Joe, who struggled to rise off the floor.

The phone rang, the shrill sound echoing through the lab.

Sanchez released his hold on her, reached for the receiver and brought it to his ear.

"Yeah?" He shook his head. "You've got the wrong number, dude."

Callie raced to Joe's side.

"I'm okay," he whispered, his voice raspy.

"What happened?"

"Guess I was in the line of fire." His crooked smile pulled at her heart.

"Looks like you had a little problem," Sanchez said to Arnie.

"The doc got carried away."

"What about Malachi?"

"Lift him onto that reclining chair."

Sanchez's eyes were wide. "He's bleeding real bad, Arnie."

The older guy shrugged. "Shove a towel against his wound."

"There's one in the bottom drawer." Callie pointed to the metal cabinet.

Sanchez lifted the moaning gunman onto the chair. Opening the drawer, he grabbed a white terry-cloth towel and held it against the wound.

Callie pulled two plastic pill bottles from the shopping bag. Arnie grabbed them out of her hand. "Give me those. I say who gets the drugs and when."

"Rocky needs the antibiotic."

"He's asleep. Tend to Malachi first."

She wasn't a doctor, but she knew the wounded gunman's condition was critical. The bullet had entered his back and exited through his chest. Using the basic supplies on hand, she bandaged the wound. Robbie was sleeping, so she quickly moved back to help Joe.

"It's only a flesh wound," he said, trying to make light of something that had to be painful. "I'll be okay, Callie."

"Would you stop with the macho male routine," she said under her breath. "Your wound needs to be cleaned."

Daring Arnie to stop her, she reached for the scissors where they lay on the floor. The way she felt, if he objected, he'd get a piece of her mind. She cut through the sleeve of Joe's shirt then placed the shears on the counter.

Arnie grunted as he shoved them into his back pocket and focused on the television. Sanchez stood against the wall, equally distracted.

Callie examined Joe's torn flesh. "Trying to take two men with a pair of scissors wasn't smart. Anyone ever tell you to think before you act?"

"You sound like you're angry."

"Peeved, not angry."

"Because I tried to get the upper hand?"

"The odds were against you, Joe."

"I had to do something."

She raised her gaze and realized too late that their lips were only inches apart. As much as she tried to focus on what he was saying, her mind kept thinking about the way his mouth twitched when he tried to smile and the hint of limey aftershave mixed with the smell of hardworking male that drew her like a moth to flame.

"Don't talk to me," she finally insisted.

"What?"

"You're distracting me."

Once again, his mouth curved into a cocky grin that sent her heart into arrhythmia. Wounded, outnumbered and still he had a magnetism that made her internal compass spin out of control.

"Close your eyes," she whispered.

"You gonna kiss me?" His voice was low and husky and stretched with tension that caused her inner thermostat to rise.

She opened a small first-aid kit. "I'm going to clean out your wound. It'll be easier for me if you don't watch."

"Yes, ma'am. But I'll be thinking of you."

His thick lashes dropped over his eyes, giving her time to examine his angular face. His cheek was swollen and a growth of beard darkened his jaw, which for some reason she suddenly wanted to touch. Instead, she turned back to his wound and cleaned the injured shoulder.

"Tell me when you're finished," he said.

"Almost done."

His eyes blinked open. "Thanks," he whispered, flashing a megawatt smile that sent a surge of static electricity dancing along her spine.

"I tried to get away," Callie said, needing to turn her mind to something other than the way he looked and smelled and how much she wanted to rub her hands over his injured shoulder.

"The pharmacist should have realized something was wrong," she said. "But he was looking at a pretty face and ignored my efforts to get his attention."

"A pretty face like yours?"

She touched the back of her hand to his forehead. "No fever yet, but you sound delusional."

"You are beautiful, Callie." He stole a glance at the two gunmen who seemed mesmerized by the television program before he turned his gaze back to her.

Raising his right hand, Joe touched her cheek. "Very, very beautiful."

For a second, the donor room, the gunmen, her injured brother—everything faded into darkness until she and Joe were the only people in the light.

Neither of them spoke. They didn't need to. For this split second in time, they were joined together. Their future, their destinies intertwined. Life or death? Everything depended on what happened next.

"We need a plan," Callie whispered when her heart had stilled enough for her to form a thought and express it in words.

Joe wrapped his fingers through hers. "Keep a low profile. I'll take care of everything."

"Which you keep saying, but from the looks of your shoulder, you're not my vote for most likely to succeed."

He smiled. "Straightforward, aren't you?"

"Determined to find a way out of this hostage situation. It's not how I want to spend Christmas."

"Why, that hurts my feelings." Playing along, he feigned a pout.

The guy was crazy. Crazy cute with an attitude that made her want to hug him, injured shoulder or not. "I can take care of myself, you know, Joe."

He rolled his eyes. "Yeah? What's that on your knee? Looks like you and Sanchez didn't see things eye to eye."

"I told you I tried to get away."

Suddenly, he became serious again. "Let me handle the bad guys. Okay, Callie? I'm trained at this."

A commercial came on the television. Arnie motioned to her. "See what you can do for Malachi before he bleeds to death."

When Joe started to stand, the ringleader shook his head. "Stay where you are, Doc."

The towel shoved against Malachi's wound was soaked with blood. Callie changed the dressing then drew a few tubes of blood from Malachi's arm. The lab tests confirmed his red blood count was dangerously low.

"He needs a transfusion," she told Arnie.

Relieved when the ringleader allowed her to move unaccompanied into the blood bank without Sanchez, Callie quickly set up the crossmatch. Once completed, she hurried back to Malachi, a unit of blood in hand. Joe was sitting near the wounded gunman taking his pulse and blood pressure. Even with the bandaged shoulder and swollen eye, he looked professional in the lab coat and latex gloves. Her heart fluttered with the memory of their moment together.

Starting an IV wasn't in her job description, but she'd drawn enough blood to be able to hit the vein. Joe had EMT training, and between the two of them, they managed to get the job done. Luckily, the gunmen kept their eyes on the television instead of Joe and Callie's fumbling attempts to hang the unit of blood.

Once the life-giving blood was dripping into the gunman's arm, Arnie stepped closer.

"He needs a couple of those painkillers," Joe said. Arnie shook two caplets into Joe's hand.

"Sanchez." Arnie glared at the Latino. "Get a glass of water for Malachi."

"Get it yourself," Sanchez groused.

Arnie rested his hand on the gun jammed in his waistband.

Sanchez threw his hands in the air. "Okay, man. I'll get water. Next time, just ask pretty."

"You'll find bottled water in the employee break room." Callie pointed him in the right direction as she headed into the micro lab to check Robbie's culture.

She pulled the petri dishes from the incubator and removed the lids. The muscles in her back tightened. A faint clear halo surrounded the tiny clusters of bacteria overgrowing the plate.

Working quickly, she ran a few more tests.

"No," she moaned, when the results confirmed her suspicion.

Rushing back to the donor room, Callie jerked the blanket off her brother's leg. The scrape that had appeared red and swollen just a few hours earlier had tripled in size to a black hole of raw flesh. The surrounding skin had darkened and dried like seaweed on the outside of a sushi roll.

Joe stared at the blackened flesh.

Arnie spied the wound and backed toward the door.

"Callie?" Joe reached for her hand. "What is it?"

"A fast-acting bacteria. Necrotizing fasciitis is the medical term. You may have heard it called by another name."

Tears swelled in her eyes. She blinked to keep them in check but was unsuccessful. As they streamed down her cheeks, she shook her head.

"Robbie's infected with flesh-eating strep."

Even without medical training, Joe knew Robbie's condition had taken a drastic turn for the worse. "At least he's on an antibiotic."

"Oral antimicrobials won't work." Callie wiped her hand across her cheeks, drying the tears. "He needs IVs pumping through his body. Even the strongest antibiotics might not make a difference."

Sanchez moved closer. "How come you don't know that, Doc?" He glanced back at Arnie. "We got a problem with the medical guy. He's not up on his treatments."

Callie put her hands on her hips and glared at the Latino. "For your information, *Señor* Sanchez, physicians rely on medical technologists' expertise to help with diagnoses based on laboratory testing."

"Yeah? Whatever." He shrugged and returned to the donor chair.

Ignoring Sanchez, Joe moved to Robbie's side. "Callie, you'll have to assist me in caring for this wound."

She found a sterile debriding kit in the main lab and opened it for Joe.

"Guide me," he whispered, keeping his back to Arnie.

"I'm winging it, too." She handed him the round-tipped scissors. Using the tweezers, she lifted up an edge of the skin. "The dead flesh needs to be removed."

Joe rolled his eyes. "If you've got an in with someone upstairs, this might be the time to let Him know we could use help."

"I'll pray while you work." She paused then said, *"Dear Lord, help us. Help Robbie."*

Joe worked around the wound, relieved that Robbie seemed oblivious to what they were doing. Arnie stood in the doorway, arms crossed over his chest. A biohazard trash receptacle sat near his feet.

Once the necrotic skin had been removed, Callie dressed the wound with sterile gauze. Joe slipped the round-tipped scissors into his pocket and bundled the refuse into the towel and stepped toward the biohazard receptacle.

Arnie backed away. "What are you doing?"

Joe tossed the refuse in the special container. Unable to resist, he smirked at the gunman. "Just protecting you from germs."

The ringleader's face reddened. "I've had it with you, Doc." Arnie turned to Sanchez. "Tie him up."

"But—" Callie objected.

"Tie her up, too."

"I need my hands free to help Rocky and Malachi," Callie insisted.

Ignoring her request, Sanchez drew cable ties from his pocket. "I'll tie your hands in front so you can tend to the wounded. Okay, doll?"

Using a second tie, Sanchez bound Joe's wrists, taking pleasure in slapping his wounded shoulder when he was done.

Their chances of getting free had gone from bad to worse. Joe's shoulder ached, but his heart hurt more. He hadn't been able to protect Callie. Sanchez said they planned to kill the hostages before they left the lab, and the only weapon Joe had was a pair of debriding scissors he'd managed to slip into his pocket.

Chapter Nine

Joe sat next to Callie on the floor, their hands bound, their moods sober. She laid her head against his good shoulder and closed her eyes. More than anything, he wanted to wrap her in his arms and hold her tight. She had to be exhausted after working so hard to help her brother and care for Joe and Malachi. Before long, her breathing slipped into the gentle rhythm of sleep.

Sanchez lay on the donor chair, snoring. He, too, had succumbed to the long afternoon that had moved into an even longer night. The two other gunmen had done nothing except watch television and argue. Arnie had tuned to a variety show and seemed to enjoy the colorful costumes and larger-than-life theatrics. At some point in the afternoon, he'd grabbed a folding aluminum chair from the break room and now sat with his feet crossed at the ankles and his back against the wall.

With Callie sleeping next to him, Joe treasured the few minutes of quiet time he had with her. Eventually she sighed, and her eyes fluttered open. He shifted and tilted his head so his cheek touched her hair. The scent of her shampoo refreshed him like a spring rain.

"I'm sorry you had to be involved in this," he said.

"It's okay, Joe. Robbie is the one we need to worry about. His cheeks are flushed, and he has to be in a lot of pain. If only I could help him."

She shook her head. "Growing up, Robbie was a good kid. But now—?"

"Maybe you're jumping to the wrong conclusion."

"Oh, Joe, as much as the truth hurts, we're in this situation because of my brother. If he hadn't been working with the Exterminators, we wouldn't be held hostage."

Joe wished he could tell Callie the truth, but her brother's life and probably her own safety depended on the gunmen's need to get Robbie out of the city. If only Joe could find out who was running the operation. Once the head man was captured, law enforcement would be able to end the gang's corrupt hold on Atlanta.

"When was the last time you saw your brother?" Joe asked, hoping to learn a little more about their sibling relationship.

"He showed up at my door three years ago." She swallowed hard, as if the memory was painful. "We hadn't seen each other since our parents had divorced a number of years earlier. Our mother had died, and Robbie was grieving, which I didn't realize at the time. All I noticed was a twenty-one-year-old who had his hand out for money. When I said no, he paid me back by running up debt on my credit card."

"But you didn't press charges?"

She shook her head. "I couldn't. Jail wouldn't have

been the answer. I told him I didn't want to see him again until he straightened out his life."

"Sounds like you were using tough love to help him," Joe volunteered.

"I wish my motive had been that honorable. When families break apart, there's a lot of pain. Kids feel responsible or caught in the middle. I hadn't gotten over my parents' divorce. For so long, I'd cried myself to sleep at night missing my dad, missing Robbie. I thought my mother was to blame for their breakup and was convinced Dad and Robbie felt the same."

She bit her lip. "According to my brother, I had it wrong. My dad hadn't missed me at all."

Tears sprang to her eyes, but she blinked them back, once again showing the strength Joe had seen throughout this hostage situation.

"Robbie's lucky to have you for a sister," he whispered. His lips brushed her hair.

Joe had longed for a strong relationship with his own brother. Unfortunately, all that had ended when his parents died.

Callie shook her head. "If Robbie had a caring sister, a sister who truly considered what the Lord wanted, my door would have stayed open for him. Instead I slammed it shut and warned him that unless he worked to improve his life, I wanted nothing to do with him."

"You were reacting to the pain you carried and to the way he'd tricked you. He expected you to save him when he really needed to save himself." Joe stared at the kid. "Something tells me he's learned his lesson."

Callie bit down on her upper lip. Her fingers caressed Joe's arm. His shoulder ached, but he didn't want to move for fear she'd pull away. Having Callie next to him made his world seem complete.

"What about Theo?" she finally asked. "He said you never forgave him."

Joe tensed. "My relationship with my brother is different."

"Is it?" She stared at him with a level gaze. The door to his past that had remained closed for so long opened ever so slightly.

Staring deep into her eyes, Joe knew Callie only saw the good in his brother. She didn't know about the other side of Theo.

"You expected Theo to take you in after your parents died," she said.

"Is that what he told you?"

"He told me he was twenty-one and living on his own. You thought he'd step into your dad's shoes, but Theo wasn't ready for that type of responsibility."

"You believed him, didn't you, Callie?"

"What I think isn't important. The real issue is what you think, Joe. Theo needs you."

He shook his head. "He didn't want me when I was a kid. Why would he want me in his life now?"

"He's all the family you have left, except for your foster parents. Theo said they're good people."

"Then that's one thing my brother and I agree on."

"He had his reasons for sending you to foster care, Joe."

"Did he tell you he was putting my needs first?" He bristled, angry that Theo convinced Callie he had done the right thing. There was nothing right about breaking a thirteen-year-old's heart.

Callie had bought into Theo's lies just as she'd

bought into the lies about her own brother. Not that Joe had set her straight about Robbie. Did that make Joe the same as his brother?

The Petrecelli boys weren't known for the goodness in their hearts. They were known for making tough decisions. Sometimes they got it right. Sometimes they didn't.

He shifted his weight, trying to ease the pain that throbbed along his arm.

Sensing his discomfort, Callie called out to Arnie. "The doc needs a couple pain pills."

Joe started to shake his head no, but she nudged him. "Hush," she warned out of the corner of her mouth. "Let me handle this."

"I don't want medication."

"Got it. But I've got a plan."

Arnie pulled his focus from the television and stretched. "What do you want?"

"The doc's in a lot of pain. The pills might help him sleep."

Arnie snorted. "As much trouble as he's caused, might be good if he did sleep. One pill. He doesn't deserve to feel too good." He shook a caplet into Callie's outstretched hand.

"Would you mind handing me a bottle of water?" she asked.

Why'd she have to be so polite to the gunmen?

Arnie grabbed a bottle from the counter, and when he handed it to Callie, she looked imploringly up at him. "Arnie, would you mind cutting this tie so I can check on Rocky?"

Arnie grunted but cut the plastic that had bound her hands, freeing Callie to open the water bottle. Climbing to her knees, she held it up to Joe's lips. He drank deeply as Arnie returned to his chair.

"Now pretend you're taking the pill," she instructed, her voice a whisper.

Playing along, he took another large gulp of water.

"I gave Malachi one pill earlier and pocketed the other one. It could be useful to us later." Joe pulled a caplet from his pocket and dropped it into Callie's hand.

Arnie glanced back at the twosome, but she had already slipped both pills into her lab coat.

Leaving Joe and moving to her brother's side, Callie touched Robbie's forehead then eased the sheet aside.

Joe could see the wound had grown larger, killing more tissue as it ate through Robbie's flesh.

Her face whitened. Joe wanted to comfort her.

She turned to catch his eye and shook her head ever so slightly. He knew from the sorrow he saw in her expression and the sense of discouragement he read from her stance that the kid's condition had grown increasingly worse.

Joe needed to do something, but tied up, he didn't have many options. "Look, Arnie, I'll make a deal with you. Let Callie drive Rocky to the nearest hospital, and I'll stay with you as a hostage and do everything I can to get you out of the city. Without intensive IV antibiotic therapy, he won't survive."

"Yeah? Tell me how you can help."

"I'll drive the van. You and Sanchez hide in the back. The cops won't expect you to move on Christmas. They'll be understaffed with most of the guys at home, spending the holiday with their families."

Arnie rubbed his hand over his chin. "You've got a point."

Hopefully, the ringleader would buy into the hype. Truth was, many of the guys would have the day off, but departments throughout the greater metropolitan Atlanta area would still have adequate coverage to handle any emergency.

Once behind the wheel and with Callie and Robbie on their way to the hospital, Joe would do whatever was necessary to stop the two thugs. He wouldn't let Arnie and Sanchez get away.

Having overheard the conversation, Callie started toward the main laboratory. "There's a transport gurney in the histology department. I'll use it to take Rocky to my car. You take the lab van. If we all leave together, you'll be out of the city before I get to the hospital."

Sanchez's eyes blinked open. "What? We're leaving?" He raked his hand through his short hair.

Arnie grabbed Callie's arm, and she stopped and stared at him. "Is there a problem?" she asked.

Joe clenched his fist. The problem was Arnie. If only Joe could get the upper hand on that guy. Shoulder injury or not, he'd teach him a lesson about not touching Callie.

Arnie loosened his hold on her arm. "Get back to the corner."

"Rocky will die if he doesn't get to the hospital," she said.

"Let me worry about Rocky, okay?" Arnie said.

"What about Malachi?" Joe pushed. "He needs medical care as well."

"Shut up." Arnie wiped his hand over his jaw. "I need to think about what we're going to do."

If only he'd accept Joe's suggestion. Callie sighed as she dropped to the floor next to him. Her brother came first, and Joe knew she'd do whatever it took to get the medical care Robbie needed.

Arnie looked anything but concerned about either of the injured men and quickly turned his attention back to the television show. Despite his aversion to germs, he seemed to enjoy the entertainment and even laughed out loud a few times, a sound so opposite the feelings Joe harbored.

The night ahead would be difficult for everyone involved. Callie's discouragement, Robbie's wound that was eating at his flesh, Malachi's breathing, which had grown more labored—there would be nothing merry about this Christmas Eve.

Callie wouldn't give up. She couldn't. Her whole life, she'd believed good triumphed over evil, even when her sister had died. As much as she hadn't understood what had happened or why, she knew God was a loving Father and didn't want suffering and despair for His children.

Resting her head on Joe's shoulder, she thought back to that other Christmas Day. Her mother had been getting the turkey out of the oven and would soon make the thick gravy that they'd spoon over the creamy mashed potatoes.

Her sister had been four, almost five. Rains had been heavy that December, and a morning shower had kept the children in the house. When the sun came out,

Callie had asked if Becky could play in the fenced backyard.

"Make sure the gate is locked," had been her mother's only request.

From the back porch, Callie could see the gate was latched and too high for Becky's fingers to reach. Yet, fifteen minutes later, when her mother called the little girl for dinner, the backyard had been empty.

Callie closed her eyes, trying to block out the memory of her mother's screams and their frantic search. The police, the flashing lights, her sister's tiny body floating, facedown, in the nearby pond seemed too real even after all these years.

An accident, a gut-wrenching tragedy, cut their family in two. Callie never understood how her mother could turn on her father so mercilessly. He was grieving as much as any of them. Besides, her mother made it perfectly clear who was to blame.

"Forgive me, Lord," Callie whispered as she'd done a million times before. But nothing, not even the Lord's forgiveness, could absolve her of the guilt she carried.

Callie raised her eyes to her brother's feverish face. She'd been the reason one sibling had died. She couldn't let Robbie die on her watch, as well.

As if sensing her struggle, Joe nuzzled her with his cheek. "You okay, honey?"

She nodded. Having Joe's support made the pain of the past more bearable.

The closing credits for the show flashed on the television screen. Arnie stood and stretched. Sanchez rubbed his hand over his face. "Anything to eat around here?"

"There's some leftover food from the holiday potluck we had yesterday," she said. "I can fix a plate for everyone."

"Oh, Callie," Joe groaned. "I wish you'd stop trying to be so helpful."

She patted his arm. "Don't worry. I'll be okay."

As she stood, Arnie nodded to Sanchez. "Help her out. And like I said before, if she does anything strange, shoot first and ask questions later."

Stepping into the main lab, Callie looked back, catching Joe's eye from where he sat on the floor. With the wound to his shoulder and the infection in Robbie's leg getting worse, Callie had to act.

She just hoped Sanchez wouldn't get in the way. *Shoot first and ask questions later.* Arnie's words rumbled through her mind.

Oh, Lord, help me do the right thing.

Chapter Ten

Joe stood as Callie and Sanchez left the donor room. "Malachi needs another unit of blood."

"We'll wait for Callie." Arnie glared at him. "Sit."

Joe crumbled back to the floor. If he couldn't do anything else, he'd pump the ringleader for information that could be used later, once the hostage situation was over.

Joe had a sickening thought. Suppose the resolution didn't go the way he planned?

For an instant, he saw Callie's body lying on the floor. His stomach roiled from the mental picture that he forced from his mind. Attitude was half the battle. He had to stay focused on success.

"I heard someplace that the brains behind the Exterminators is a big money tycoon from Atlanta."

Arnie sniffed. "You always so nosy?"

Ignoring the comment, Joe continued. "Some speculate the guy calling the shots is Martin Osborne." Osborne was only a middleman, but Joe wanted to hear what Arnie would say.

Joe hadn't expected him to laugh.

"Osborne's a lazy fool who thinks he's more important than he really is."

"What about Jiles Forest?"

"What about him?" Arnie stiffened.

"Some say he's in charge."

The gunman pursed his lips. "Jiles would like to think he's important."

"So someone else is in control?"

Flipping the channels on the television, Arnie stopped at the local news, sending a sickening feeling through Joe's gut. One mention of Officer Joe Petrecelli having been taken hostage and any hope Joe had of saving Callie and her brother would end.

He had to do something to force Arnie to turn the channel. Looking down at his bound hands, he realized embracing Callie's technique of peaceful harmony to affect change might be the best tactic.

"There's a Christmas special on Channel 12 based on the Nativity story," he suggested.

Arnie groaned. "I don't buy into religion."

"Neither do I, but Callie might be interested." Evidently she had some influence on Arnie, because he changed the channel to the children's story.

Callie returned, with Sanchez in tow, pushing a cart laden with serving dishes. The smell of baked turkey and all the trimmings filled the donor room. She glanced at the television and then turned a questioning gaze at Joe.

He raised his brows and shrugged.

"I heated the food in the microwave," she said, filling a plate, which she handed to Arnie.

He hesitated.

"Everything has been in the refrigerator. Away from the germs," she assured him.

He took the plate and began to eat.

Callie prepared a second serving and glanced at Joe. He shook his head. "I'm not hungry."

"You have to eat."

"Yes, ma'am." Joe was beginning to realize that when Callie made up her mind, there was no changing course. He accepted the plate she offered and, in spite of his bound hands, managed to get the food in his mouth. The meal nourished his body and brought a renewed sense of hope to his faltering spirit.

She offered food to Malachi. He didn't eat more than a couple bites but seemed to appreciate her care and concern.

Callie was the most selfless woman Joe had ever known. Her entire focus was on others. She was even trying to change the gunmen's hearts through kindness. What was it about Callie that allowed her to be so hopeful and optimistic? Could it be her faith in God?

Joe's foster parents were believers. His foster mom told him she prayed daily for his safety. If something happened to him, he hated to think how it would affect her. His foster dad was a quiet, reserved type, but they had a good relationship. Joe wouldn't want either of them to be hurt, especially after everything they had done for him.

Callie wet one of the towels, wrung it dry and then wiped it over Malachi's forehead. He took her hand and smiled. She leaned down and whispered something in his ear. He nodded as she continued to talk to him.

Once Malachi's eyes closed, she pulled on a pair of gloves, checked her brother's leg and then walked into the other lab. Arnie was focused on the television and didn't object to her leaving. She returned with a light, which she set up to shine on Robbie's wounded calf.

"What's that for?" Sanchez asked as he piled a second helping of sweet potatoes onto his plate.

"It's a UV lamp. One of the researchers is experimenting to see how UV rays retard the growth of bacteria. If it works in the petri dish, it may work on Rocky's leg. At least that's my hope."

Once she made Robbie comfortable, Callie pulled off her gloves and washed her hands. As she returned to the corner, Joe looked up. "Fix a plate for yourself."

"I'm not hungry."

"You need to keep up your strength." He flicked his gaze to Arnie and Sanchez, both glued to the television, hoping Callie understood what he meant. The night ahead would be long. Food would sustain them both no matter what happened.

She nodded, a look of understanding on her face. She placed a few items on her plate and came back to sit next to him again.

"Were you successful?" he asked.

Her lips quirked into a hesitant grin. "Meaning?"

"Meaning the pain pills. You pocketed two of them. I noticed you didn't put any sweet potatoes on my plate, but you gave Arnie and Sanchez double helpings. Hopefully you mixed the pain pills into their food."

Callie's face broke into a smile. "The two oxycodone would probably do the trick, but I added a couple of muscle relaxers to the potatoes, as well. One of the techs has a back problem and leaves some pills in the break room. I gave Sanchez a piece of pie to keep him occupied while I grabbed them."

She snuggled closer.

"Way to go, Callie. Now we have to wait until they fall asleep."

But Arnie and Sanchez's eyes were wide open.

Arnie's phone rang. Flipping off the television, he pushed the cell to his ear.

"Yeah?" He nodded a few times as the person on the other end spoke.

"Okay. We'll leave before dawn. Malachi's in bad shape. He might not make it through the night. Sanchez wants to head south to see if he can meet up with his family."

Arnie nodded again. "Yeah. I'll bring Rocky with me. What about the woman and the doc?"

He stared at them. "Kill both of them? Yeah. When we leave the lab."

Callie swallowed hard and laid her plate on the floor.

Joe fisted his hands. What could he do? He'd always been able to handle any bad situation and turn it to his advantage. After Theo had abandoned him as a child, Joe had vowed to always come out on top. But now, with Callie at his side and their fate in the hands of two gunmen, Joe knew this was one time he couldn't change what would happen.

With no place else to turn, he hung his head. *Lord, if you can hear me, I'm asking for Your help. Save Callie. She doesn't deserve to die. Neither does Robbie. If possible, give me an opportunity to overpower the gunmen before it's too late.*

Callie continued to check on her two patients into the night. The growth of the wound on Robbie's leg seemed to slow a bit, although she couldn't be sure. Perhaps she was imagining the slight improvement.

Malachi wasn't faring well. Blood oozed from the wound whenever he moved. Callie started another unit of blood, but his red blood count remained low when she ran a second CBC.

"Malachi, you need to keep fighting. Don't give up." She bent close to his ear. "You want to see your mama."

He moaned and grabbed her hand. "Don't…don't tell her…what… I done. I… I didn't mean to hurt no one."

"Ask God to forgive you, Malachi. He loves you."

"I wanna get right with the Lord. Cross my heart. Say a prayer for me."

"We'll pray together." Callie held his hand, and began to pray.

"There's something I need to tell you," he said when the prayer ended. Callie leaned down once again and listened as the youngest gunman bared his soul. When he finished, she drew the blanket over his chest. He smiled feebly and mouthed "thank you."

Wetting a second towel, Callie sponged Robbie's hot forehead. She took his temperature. The thermometer registered 104 degrees. Sadness wrapped around her.

The overhead fluorescent lights glared in her eyes. Needing to focus on life rather than death, Callie lowered the switch, leaving only a small light on near the doorway.

She plugged in the lights to the Christmas tree. The tiny colorful bulbs flickered on and off, catching Robbie's eyes. His lips twitched ever so slightly, as if he enjoyed seeing the tree aglow.

Callie glanced at the wall clock. Almost midnight. Just a few more minutes and it would be Christmas. No matter what happened, they needed to celebrate the birth of the Christ Child.

Feeling someone's gaze, she turned. Joe stared at her from across the room. Callie's cheeks warmed. Even his spirits seemed buoyed by the Christmas lights. She clicked on a small CD player that sat on the shelf against the wall, and the soothing sounds of Christmas music played.

Arnie turned off the television and watched as she pulled a Bible from one of the drawers and padded across the lab back to where Joe sat. Lowering herself to the floor, she stared at the clock until the two hands pointed to twelve.

Opening the Bible, she began to read with a strong, clear voice from the beginning of Luke's gospel. "In those days, Caesar Augustus published a decree ordering a census of the whole world…"

Joe tipped his head back and closed his eyes.

Arnie and Sanchez listened as she read. Even Malachi seemed to understand the significance of the story.

Robbie calmed, and his face filled with peace. The UV light streamed down on his leg, like the star that had hovered over the tiny stable.

"While they were there the days of her confinement were completed. She gave birth to her first-born son and wrapped him in swaddling clothes and laid him in a manger…"

More than two thousand years ago, Joseph had tried to find shelter for his pregnant wife soon to give birth, but there had been no room in the inn. Did Callie have room in her heart for the Lord? Or did she have a

Do Not Enter sign nailed across the entryway? She'd closed her door to Robbie, and he'd ended up with the Exterminators.

As she read, she glanced from one gunman to the next. Had doors closed on them long ago? Is that why they had chosen the darkness of a life of crime instead of the light of Christ? When she finished the narrative, she shut the Bible and listened to the soft strains of the Christmas music.

Digging a cell phone from his pocket, Sanchez slid from the chair. "I'm gonna call my wife." He stepped into the larger laboratory. "*Hola*, Maria? *Feliz Navidad*."

Hopefully the message had gotten through to him. What about Arnie? Would the Christmas story affect him in a positive way? Or was he the same man who had shoved Callie along the laboratory corridor earlier today? *Lord, change his heart, and help us stay alive.*

Chapter Eleven

Callie watched Arnie wrap his arms across his chest and stare at the ceiling. No telling what he was thinking.

Joe's fingers touched her arm. "The Scripture made me remember the real meaning of Christmas."

She smiled at him, seeing the warmth in his gaze. "Amazing, isn't it? Christ came as a child born so long ago, yet the Christmas message holds the power to heal troubled hearts even today. All of us need to hear that message and allow it to transform our lives."

He scooted closer to her. "There's something I need to tell you, Callie. It's about your brother."

She shook her head. "I don't want to hear about jail time or years in prison today, Joe. It's hard enough knowing I'm the reason he strayed."

"You?" He looked surprised. "But you told him to make something of himself."

"A lot of good that did."

"You're wrong, Callie. What you said to Robbie caused him to change. That's what I needed to tell you. Robbie's not part of the gang. He infiltrated the Exterminators as an undercover cop."

She shook her head, confused by what Joe had just said. "He's a cop? Why didn't you tell me, Joe?"

"Because one slip and—"

"One slip? You didn't trust me?"

"Of course I trusted you, but I was responsible for your brother's safety. I'm the one who insisted he be moved to Lazarus House. I got him and both of us into this mess."

All this time, Callie had felt responsible for her brother's actions.

"You gave your brother a mandate to change," Joe continued. "Your tough love opened his eyes. He told me he cleaned up his life because of what Callie had told him. I didn't realize the Callie he was talking about was his sister."

"Rob… Robbie said my words made a difference?"

Joe nodded. "The problem isn't with Robbie, is it? The problem is with you. You still can't forgive yourself."

Joe was right. She'd carried the guilt for her sister's death and Robbie's failures for too long.

"You believe in the Lord," Joe said. "Don't you believe He forgives?"

"Of course I do."

"But you can't accept that forgiveness in your own life."

"You should talk."

Callie had prayed with Theo, asking the Lord to change Joe's heart. The man who now questioned her ability to forgive should look more closely at himself. Scripture said it was easier to see a splinter in another's eye rather than the plank in one's own eye. That Biblical message certainly applied to Joe.

"I need to check on my brother." Callie couldn't think, sitting so close to Joe. She needed space and time alone. Robbie was a cop? The words she'd said to him three years ago had made a difference in his life? Was Joe telling her the truth?

She took the damp cloth and wiped her brother's brow. His forehead felt even hotter than before. Surely, he couldn't survive much longer with the aggressive infection eating away his flesh. *Please, Lord, let him live.*

She moved to Malachi's side. He needed to be sponged off, as well and his dressing changed, but that might not be enough. Just like for her brother, this Christmas could be Malachi's last.

Sanchez ended his conversation with his wife and came back into the donor room, his bravado somewhat mellowed. "I talked to Maria."

Arnie looked in his direction. "So?"

"So the kids want to know when their dad's coming home. I'm leaving soon."

"I don't like it."

"It's Christmas, man. Don't you have family?"

Arnie rubbed his jaw. "Not anymore."

"Parents?"

"I left home a long time ago and never looked back." He shook his head. "We were dirt-poor. No money. Not enough food. The only thing different about Christmas was a little candy on our dinner plates."

"What about church?"

The ringleader laughed. "Church? The only time

I went was on my wedding day." He shrugged. "My wife said old habits die hard. When she left, she took the baby. Now I've got money but no one to spend it on." He chortled. "Maybe I'll buy gifts for your kids, Sanchez. How many you got?"

"Five. One on the way."

Joe listened as the gunmen talked. Sad to think of the bad choices they had each made. What about his own choices? As a thirteen-year-old, he'd reacted the only way he knew how. If something hurt, cut it out of your life. Theo hadn't wanted him. Stood to reason that Joe wouldn't want Theo, either.

But years had passed, and the fast living that had been Theo's reason for closing his door to Joe had done damage. Because of the cancer, his brother's medical condition was fragile at best. Yet the two of them had never reconnected.

Forgiveness? The word flickered through Joe's mind. He'd told Callie to forgive herself. Truth was, Joe needed to forgive Theo.

Something he couldn't do.

Callie wiped a cloth over Malachi's forehead and lowered her ear as he whispered something to her. Adjusting the blanket around his shoulders, she patted his hand and then went back to her brother and once again examined his leg. The wound had grown.

Callie's face was drawn as she returned to the corner and sat a few feet away.

Joe was filled with regret. "I didn't tell you about your brother, Callie, because I wanted to keep you safe," he whispered as Arnie and Sanchez talked.

"You didn't trust me."

"I didn't know you, Callie. We only met a few hours

ago." He looked into the depth of her soul and saw the purity and beauty of this woman he'd been waiting his whole lifetime to find. "Now it seems like I've known you forever."

"Did you give Robbie the undercover assignment?"

Joe nodded, knowing he had to tell her everything, even if it would turn her against him for good.

"Your brother asked to infiltrate the Exterminators, but the decision to use him was mine. He's made a difference, Callie. His actions have been courageous and self-sacrificing. That's who he became after you challenged him to grow into a man."

"I told him I'd pray for him to be the man God had created him to be."

"Your prayers paid off. Robbie's a fine and noble person. A person I'm proud to know."

Tears swelled in her eyes, and she scooted closer. Placing her hand in his, the two of them sat for a long moment. "You know Theo loves you," Callie finally said.

Joe's throat thickened.

"Theo said his life was mixed up when your parents died. He was into things he didn't want you to know about. That's why he didn't take you in. He wanted something better for you."

"Better?" Joe thought of his foster parents and the brick two-story house where they lived—a place he now called home. Good people, they had given him love and acceptance, guidance and respect. Under their care, he had moved from a troubled adolescence into a stable adulthood.

Joe tipped his head back. His eyes rested on the hand-hewn stable where the ceramic figures of Joseph and Mary gathered around the manger. *Peace on earth, goodwill toward men.* The words played through his mind. Maybe he could at least have goodwill toward his brother. It would be a start.

Callie squeezed his hand. "You've been doing a very good thing, and it's probably worth more because of the way you feel about Theo."

"Worth more? What do you mean?"

"You're his anonymous donor, aren't you? Tamika mentioned that someone paid Theo's bills, but she never told me it was his estranged brother. Theo doesn't even know."

"It needs to stay that way. It wouldn't do any good for him to know his younger brother is supporting him."

"Probably not. But you're a good man, Joe. Theo's lucky to have you in his life."

Joe looked into her eyes as their fingers entwined. "If I've learned anything during this hostage situation, Callie, it's that life can't be taken for granted. Certain things are important, like relationships and family and someone to love."

Chapter Twelve

Joe watched the two gunmen for some sign of fatigue. Callie had mixed the pain medication in with the sweet potato casserole, which the men had eaten, yet neither appeared tired.

"We need to leave," Sanchez said. "The middle of the night is our best chance to get out of the city."

Arnie nodded. "But I say when."

Grumbling, Sanchez retreated back to the donor chair. Settling into the contour, he closed his eyes and soon fell asleep. At least the medication had worked on one of the gunmen.

Callie padded quietly to Malachi's side. Once again, she wiped his hands and brow then bent down to whisper in his ear. One lone tear fell from his eye and rolled down the side of his face.

Before long, the Exterminators would claim another fatality. Heaviness settled over Joe. *Lord, no more deaths. Protect us from harm.*

Callie checked her brother's leg and wiped his forehead. Robbie's eyes blinked open. He raised his hand off the bed and pointed to the crèche. She smiled and nodded.

The action between brother and sister signaled reconciliation and forgiveness. Callie's face reflected love and acceptance. Robbie, even through his fever and pain, seemed renewed, as if the action brought healing.

Joe's eyes fell on the tiny manger and the babe who came so that all might have eternal life.

Malachi? Would he see the face of God?

Robbie? *Oh, Lord, he needs medical care. Keep him alive.*

And Callie? *Keep her safe.*

Take me instead, Lord.

Callie came back to the corner and sat next to Joe. Without having to ask, she whispered, "Robbie and I used to act out the Nativity when we were young. He liked to pretend he was the lamb following the shepherd to the stable."

"The shepherd—the Good Shepherd—protected him from harm," Joe said aloud.

Surprise registered on her face. "That's right. He always asked God to protect both of us when our parents argued."

"Protected by a God who loved you," Joe added. Hearing his own voice made the words real to him.

Had it only been hours since he and Callie had met? He loved her courage, her determination, her optimism. Fact was, he was starting to love Callie.

She wouldn't let anyone control her life nor would she back down about her relationship with the Lord. Joe wanted that confidence in a loving God as well.

"Pray with me," he whispered. "I want the fullness of God's love."

Tears filled her eyes. "He already lives within you, Joe. You just didn't recognize Him."

Callie placed her hand in his and prayed with him. Love filled his heart like he'd never known before. Love for Callie. Love for the Lord.

He finally saw clearly. Theo hadn't abandoned him all those years ago. He'd made a decision about what would be best for Joe. Tough love.

As a young teen, Joe had only thought about his immediate pain. He hadn't thought about needing a good home life and stability, which is what his foster parents had provided. If Joe hadn't shut Theo out of his life, perhaps the loving family that had raised Joe and provided for his every need could have influenced his brother. Instead, Joe had excluded Theo.

If only he had a chance to ask his brother's forgiveness. From the depths of his heart, Joe knew the Lord forgave him. Now if only he'd have the opportunity to ask Theo's forgiveness.

Arnie stood and turned on the overhead television. He flipped the channels to the all-night news. The order of stories appeared in a sidebar on the screen. The Atlanta hostage segment was next in the lineup.

Malachi moaned.

"You think he caught Rocky's infection?" Arnie asked Sanchez, but he was still asleep.

Squeezing Joe's hand, Callie whispered, "This might be what we've been waiting for. I'll try to get into the micro lab and come up with some type of disruption. I grabbed vinegar and baking soda from the break room. It'll sound worse than it really is."

Arnie motioned Callie toward him. "My throat hurts," he said as she neared. "You think I could have that flesh-eating bug?"

Callie hesitated, throwing a quick glance back at Joe.

"I'm not sure. Let me do a throat culture." She pulled a sterile swab from a drawer. "Open your mouth."

Arnie complied. While she swabbed his throat, Joe pulled the debriding scissors from his pocket and snipped through the tie that bound his hands.

"I'll test this right away." Callie headed for the micro lab.

Holding his hands together as if they were still bound, Joe stood up.

Arnie glared at him. "What are you doing?"

"I need to stretch my legs."

"Forget it."

"Really, Arnie. My legs are stiff. I just need to stand."

"I said no."

Robbie jerked, knocking the UV light to the floor. Joe leaned down to pick up the lamp and unplugged the cord at the same time.

Callie stepped back into the donor room. "I've got bad news, Arnie. You've got the same infection as Rocky."

The ringleader raised his hands and clutched his neck. His eyes widened.

Knowing she was setting Arnie up, Joe prepared to act.

Sanchez blinked his eyes open and stared at the television screen as the news report continued.

"Law enforcement provided a photo of the Atlanta police officer thought to have been taken hostage," the newscaster said. "His name is Joe Petrecelli."

Joe's picture flashed on the screen.

"Yikes, Arnie." Sanchez slid out of his chair and pointed to Joe. "He's a cop."

Behind them, an explosion tore through the micro lab.

Arnie and Sanchez turned toward the doorway.

"Fire," Callie screamed, grabbing the extinguisher from the wall.

In one swift motion, she pulled the pin and aimed the flow of retardant at Sanchez. The spray hit him in the face, knocking him back against the counter. His head hit the overhead cabinet.

She slammed the canister against his chest. With a loud moan, Sanchez doubled over and slid to the floor.

Joe struck Arnie with the metal base of the UV lamp as he fumbled for his gun. The rapid motion tore at Joe's wound, and pain, hot as lightning, ricocheted down his arm.

Arnie pulled his weapon free. Turning, he aimed at Callie. She readjusted the canister in her hands, oblivious to the immediate danger.

Joe had to save her. Gathering strength from deep within him, he lurched forward, slamming his good shoulder into Arnie's side. Air wheezed from the gunman's lungs. Joe grabbed his wrist, and the two men fought for control of the automatic.

"No," Callie screamed. She raised the extinguisher and slammed it against Arnie's head.

Staggering backward, he crashed into the biohazard trash container, knocking it over as he fell to the floor. The gun dropped, and the contents of the receptacle spilled onto Arnie's lap.

He covered his face with his hands and screamed.

Joe grabbed the gun and aimed it at Arnie. "Call the police, Callie. Tell them we've got the Exterminators under control."

Chapter Thirteen

Callie stood at Robbie's bedside, praying that the massive doses of antibiotics threading through his veins would combat the flesh-eating strep. When they'd arrived at the hospital in the middle of the night, the doctors hadn't been optimistic. Now as the sun began to set on Christmas Day, Callie felt especially discouraged and alone.

A knock at the door caused her to raise her eyes. "Come in."

Her heart fluttered as Joe stepped into the room. His arm was in a sling, his eye had swollen shut and a large bandage covered his neck, but he looked more handsome than ever.

In his good arm, he carried a small artificial Christmas tree decorated with tiny lights and shiny ornaments.

"I thought you could use a little cheering up." He placed the tree on a table in the corner and pushed a switch.

"Battery operated and hospital friendly." The lights flickered, sending colorful spots dancing along the walls.

"It's beautiful, Joe."

Stepping to Callie's side, he rubbed his hand over her shoulder and stared down at her brother. "Any change?"

"Not that I can tell. They drew another CBC a short while ago. The nurse said she'd let me know his white blood count once she hears from the lab."

"Why don't you take a break, Callie? I'll stay with Robbie."

She shook her head. "No, I need to be here."

"You've got to be exhausted."

"I'm okay, Joe."

"Which is what you always say. I do have some good news. Tamika and the police guard are stable and should make full recoveries."

"Oh, that's wonderful."

"I met Tamika's husband and girls in the hallway outside her room. They said they're praying for Robbie."

"That's what he needs right now. Did you find out about Malachi?"

"He made it through surgery, and the doctors expect him to pull through. His mother and grandmother were relieved."

"Did you tell them he'd have to stand trial?"

"No, not yet. That discussion can wait until after Christmas. Sanchez and Arnie are being questioned, although it's doubtful either of them will divulge the name of the man at the top." Callie heard discouragement in Joe's voice. "The Exterminators won't be stopped until their leader is apprehended."

"His name's Sanders Brown."

"What?"

"Malachi thought he was going to die and wanted to come clean. He told me Brown was in charge of the Exterminators. I should have mentioned it sooner, but after everything that happened, it slipped my mind."

"Oh, Callie, you are amazing."

Another knock sounded and the door opened. A nurse peered into the room. "The lab called. Robbie's white blood count has dropped a bit."

Relief swept over Callie.

"What's that mean?" Joe asked.

"It means the antibiotics are working," she explained.

"He's not out of the woods yet," the nurse added. "But there's improvement."

"Which is what I've been praying for." Callie waved her thanks as the nurse left the room.

Joe wrapped his arm around Callie. She felt Joe's strength once again and was uplifted by his presence. They'd been through so much in the last thirty-six hours. It seemed they'd been together for a lifetime, which is what she hoped might unfold for their future. Of course, she didn't know how Joe felt. Things would be different once they both went back to their normal workday routines. Not knowing what tomorrow would bring, she closed her eyes, wanting to hold on to this moment forever.

"Callie?"

She looked down. Her brother's eyes were opened.

"I… I'm sorry," he whispered.

"Don't worry about anything right now, Robbie. The antibiotics are working, and you're going to get better." Callie was sure the Lord had heard and was answering her prayer.

"I… I was wrong, Callie. Mixed-up. Dad had died. And Mom."

"Shhh," she soothed. "We all make mistakes. I shouldn't have closed my door to you three years ago,

Robbie. Then I thought you had joined the Exterminators. Joe told me your were working undercover."

Her brother tried to smile as he looked at Joe. "How are you, sir?"

"Better now that you're getting the medical care you need. Oh, and by the way, I think your sister's the greatest."

Callie's heart went into overdrive, but she knew the offhanded remark was only a figure of speech.

"So do I," Robbie said.

Tears burned her eyes. She'd wanted to hear something positive from her brother for so long.

"There's something I need to tell you," Robbie said, his voice growing stronger. "I was cleaning out some old letters and things of Dad's after he died. One letter was addressed to Mom."

"Written after they divorced?"

Robbie nodded. "But he never mailed it. Dad wrote that he had been working on the gate the morning Becky died. He'd taken out a bolt on the latch and should have replaced it, but he'd gotten distracted since it was Christmas. The latch looked like it would work but sprung open when any weight pushed against it. He said he was to blame for Becky wandering off."

All these years, Callie had carried the guilt for her sister's death. "Why didn't he mail the letter to Mom?"

"Maybe he thought she wouldn't forgive him."

Forgiveness. Callie hadn't been able to forgive herself. She'd missed so much in life because of the guilt that had eaten into her like the flesh-eating strep had eaten into Robbie's leg.

This Christmas was the time for new beginnings. She wanted to put all the pain and guilt behind her and start fresh. Joe's hand was on her shoulder. She reached out and entwined her fingers with his.

Once again the door opened and a young woman stepped inside. She was pretty with long blond hair and big blue eyes. "Robbie?"

Haltingly, she stepped toward the bed. "I just found out what happened." Tears spilled down her cheeks.

He took her outstretched hand. "Everything's going to be okay, Missy."

She kissed his forehead then wiped her hand over her face and smiled at Callie. "You must be Robbie's sister. He's talked so much about you. I'm Missy Adams. Robbie and I are—"

She smiled down at him.

"Planning to get married," Robbie completed her sentence. "That's why I wanted to see you, Callie. So you and Missy could meet."

Seeing the love so evident in her brother's eyes when he looked at Missy, Callie knew he would have a complete recovery. She and Missy would get to know each other in the days ahead, but right now, the young couple needed a bit of privacy.

Joe took Callie's hand as they moved to the corner. "In spite of everything that happened, this is the best Christmas of my life," he said.

She turned to face him.

A warm glow tingled her neck.

"I don't want this to end, Callie." He rubbed his fingers over hers. "I want every day to be Christmas. Not the hostage part, of course, but being together. I want to see you tomorrow and the next day and the next. I want to call you from work and tell you how my day went when my shift's over. I want to share birthdays and holidays and go to church with you every Sunday."

Her head swirled and she wanted to laugh with joy. "Aren't you moving a little fast, Officer Petrecelli?"

"Hmmm? Maybe. But who knows what the future holds?"

A life together was her dream, and she was beginning to think it was Joe's, as well.

He hesitated for a moment then glanced at Robbie and his girlfriend. Callie followed his gaze. The young couple was totally occupied.

"I stopped by Lazarus House this afternoon," Joe finally said.

"Room ten?"

He nodded. "I told Theo I'd met a very special woman. I said I didn't deserve you, and that we must have met because of his prayers. Then I asked his forgiveness for closing him out of my life. Only he said he was the one who'd been wrong."

Callie sighed with contentment as Joe wrapped his arm around her and drew her close. Being careful of his wounded shoulder, she snuggled into his embrace and, without hesitation, raised her lips to meet his. Their kiss was long and lingering and filled with the promise of a lifetime of Christmases to come.

The tree twinkled, bathing them in light, but it was the light of Christ, the light of a child born so long ago, that reflected in their hearts.

Forgiveness and reconciliation, healing and wholeness were all wrapped up in the Christmas message. Callie's heart sang with joy, and in the distance she heard a joyous chorus as if the angels were singing on high: "Peace on earth. Goodwill toward men."

* * * * *

YULETIDE ABDUCTION

Virginia Vaughan

This book is dedicated to my boys, Josh and Chris,
for all the years you put up with me
while I tried my hand at this writing thing.

Your word is a lamp for my feet, a light on my path.
—*Psalms* 119:105

Chapter One

She should have brought her gun.

FBI agent Elise Richardson slowed her jogging pace then stopped and knelt down, pretending to tie her shoelace. She glanced over her shoulder at the car that had been following her for three blocks. An older-model gray sedan with one occupant. She stood and stretched her arms and legs, casually scanning the early-morning downtown area. The buildings had been decorated for Christmas, but the streets were uninhabited at this time of day. Stores were locked up and secured. Only the street lamps lit the sidewalk as her feet pumped against the pavement once again. And she was exposed without her gun and without her cell phone.

Who knew an early-morning jog would necessitate weaponry?

She rounded a corner and found more of the same. Christmas adornment. Empty streets. Locked shops. No one in this sleepy town of Westhaven, Mississippi, was at work yet.

Except the guy in the car following her.

She kept her speed consistent, but her legs and her

lungs were already burning from the run. If she could circle the block perhaps she could make it to her hotel. She pushed through the pain and quickened her pace. The car matched her speed. She rounded another corner. The slow-moving car did the same.

She had no idea who was following her or what they wanted. Who even knew she was in town? She hadn't checked in with the local police department yet since she'd arrived last night. She turned her head and glanced at the car again. Sunglasses and a hat hid his face, but he flinched as if realizing he'd been spotted. He gunned the engine. Elise took off running and this time the driver made no pretense. He swerved onto the sidewalk, barely missing her before she jumped over a concrete barrier and across a grass partition. The car rammed the barrier then backed up and sped toward her, its wheels squealing against the asphalt and metal screeching as it swiped the pavement.

She ran past an outdoor café, taking a moment to fling the metal chairs into the path of the oncoming vehicle that swerved to miss them but didn't stop pursuing.

She heard a horn blare and tires squeal from a different direction. She turned to look and saw a black truck swerve into the path of the car then slam into it. Elise dived into the alcove of an office building to escape the debris. Her head hit the hard glass doors and the mounted Christmas wreaths fell on her. Blinding pain exploded in her head and the world spun. The howl of metal on metal roared in her ears. She tucked her head into her knees and used her arms to shield her, but shards of glass and metal bit into them. Another blinding pain ripped through the back of her leg. She cried out, realizing a fragment had lodged in her upper thigh.

Tires screeched again, and she peered out to see the sole figure in the gray sedan shake his head and regain his composure before ramming the car into gear and speeding away as fast as possible with the damage done to the driver's side of the car.

The truck's driver stumbled out, obviously shaken by the crash but heading unsteadily toward her. Elise braced herself for a confrontation and rummaged beneath fallen lights and garland for a piece of metal matching the one in her leg. Could this man be trusted? He had just saved her life, hadn't he? Had he not rammed his truck into the sedan, she would be roadkill. Still, she hesitated, her instinct melting into her fear. She felt naked without her gun, and the blinding pain in both her leg and her head could be hampering her judgment.

Before she could decide if he were friend or foe, he was beside her. "Are you injured?" He glanced at the weapon in her hand then where her other hand cradled the piece in her leg. "You are hurt." He knelt and examined her wound. "Can you speak?"

She had to be delirious. Perhaps she was already unconscious because the man before her was someone who couldn't possibly be there. She recognized the strong, triangular jaw from the image on her faded newspaper cutout and even more vividly from the night that had changed her life ten years earlier. She remembered those intense blue eyes gazing at her from beneath dark, brooding eyebrows that matched his black hair, sideburns and the hint of a stubbled beard—the face of her own personal hero.

But it couldn't be.

Max Adams had died ten years earlier...the night he'd saved her life.

The piece of metal slipped through her fingers as her mind swirled. "Max?"

His head jerked as she said the name, and his eyes grew dark and inquisitive. "Max was my brother. My name is Josh Adams."

She cried out as a sharp pain pulsed through her, and Max... Josh...grabbed her hand.

"Hang on. Help is coming."

She chuckled at the idea. What were the chances of being rescued by another of the Adams brothers?

"Stay with me," he commanded, doing his best to keep her conscious. "Talk to me. Tell me how you knew my brother."

She struggled with the memory of another man stepping between her and an armed assailant. "He saved me." *And died doing it.* She didn't need to verbalize that part. He knew his brother had died.

His eyes widened in surprise. "What's your name?"

She struggled to fight off the darkness but finally gave in to it. "Elise Richardson," she managed to mumble before the shadows overtook her.

Sitting in the ER waiting room, Josh gingerly touched the goose egg on his forehead from where the air bag had deployed. He'd rammed his truck quite hard into the car gunning for Elise, but he was no worse for the wear.

Elise Richardson?

It wasn't possible, was it, that this woman was the same girl whom his brother had rescued from an attacker ten years ago? The woman he'd died protecting? He'd imagined her many times—the woman who'd caused his brother to step to his death—but he'd never imagined the thin, toned body, the dark hair and olive complexion or the beautiful hazel-green eyes with specks of golden brown glancing up at him. In his mind, she'd always been a caricature of a coed who'd selfishly placed herself in danger. But he'd remembered her name. He'd held on to it as a target for his anger through three tours of Afghanistan.

And now she was in danger again.

He folded his arms as he stared through the windows into the ER room where she lay unconscious on the bed. Why had someone been chasing her? He thought he knew most folks in Westhaven even if just in passing, but he didn't recognize the dark-haired beauty who'd passed out in his arms, or the driver of the car that had tried to run her down, as locals.

Daniel Mills, the current police chief and his brother's childhood friend, approached him and glanced into the room. "She had no ID on her and no cell phone."

"She said her name was Elise Richardson, but I don't think she's local. She could be visiting someone in town for the holidays." He hesitated, wondering if he should mention her connection to Max. His brother had worked on this police force and was well known and liked by guys still on the job. There might still be some hard feelings from them about this woman who'd cost him his life… At least for his part there was.

Daniel's eyes widened. "Seems like you two had a nice conversation before she passed out. Did she happen to say who ran her down or why?"

"No. I didn't recognize the car. It was a gray sedan with darkened windows. Mississippi plates but I couldn't see the county or catch the tag number. But the car was like a hot rod, probably custom-rebuilt."

"Did you get a look at the driver?"

"He was male but I mostly just saw his outline."

The chief nodded. "Why don't you come by the office later and give a full statement. I'm going back to the scene and see what's left of your truck. I'll have it towed to Carr's Body Shop." He pressed a set of keys into Josh's hand. "Use my Jeep until you get your truck back. I'll drive the squad car."

"Thanks, Daniel."

"You probably saved that woman's life today."

At least he could save someone.

Josh bit back that negative thought and nodded at Daniel as he walked off, but frustration tinged him. His niece, Candace, had been missing for nearly two weeks and he was at a loss to find her. It seemed she'd vanished from the face of the earth while walking home from school. The police, including Daniel, believed she'd run away, but Josh knew better. Something had happened to Candace and, despite his best efforts, he was frustrated he hadn't yet brought her home.

He would never be the hero his brother had been.

Elise moved in the bed and her eyes fluttered. Josh stepped into the room as she opened them and examined her surroundings.

She glanced his way. "Max? No… Josh, right?"

"Right. And your name is Elise." She struggled to sit up and he saw pain flit across her face as she moved her bandaged leg. "Maybe you should take it easy. You've been through a lot. I'll get the doctor to come in and speak to you, and I know Chief Mills will want to take your statement, too. Do you remember what happened?"

Her full lips pressed into a line. "Absolutely. Some maniac tried to run me down with his car."

"Did you know him?"

She thought for a moment as if trying to recapture the incident. "No. I have no idea who it was."

"Well, I'm glad I was in the area."

She turned her inquisitive eyes upon him and suspicion filled them. "What were you doing in the area? I know I'm an early bird, but why were you out so early?"

"I was on my way to the Randolph Hotel. I heard an FBI agent was in town and I wanted to speak with him. My niece is missing and I was hoping the FBI was here to investigate her disappearance. But then I saw the car chasing after you. I didn't even have time to dial the police. I knew I had to do something or you would be killed." He glanced down at the bloody shirt he was still wearing and knew he'd made the right call. Someone had tried to kill her. "Why would someone want to hurt you, Elise?"

She gave a haggard sigh. "I suspect it's because I'm the FBI agent you were going to speak to."

"You're FBI?"

Elise didn't care for the incredulous tone of his voice, but she was in no mood to chastise him. Her brain hurt—actually hurt—and she was having enough trouble putting words together for a rational conversation. The doctor who looked to be thirty years past retirement age had told her she'd suffered a concussion, but he might as well have said she'd scrambled her brains. It felt the same.

"I've been with the Bureau for six years. In fact, I owe my career to your brother in a way. I changed my major to criminal justice after my attack."

"Are you here because of Candace's disappearance? I know she didn't run away. She wouldn't do that, especially not right before Christmas."

Elise visualized a photograph of a young, redheaded girl the police had classified as a runaway. How had she not realized it before? "Max's daughter is the girl that vanished?"

"That's right."

Determination settled inside her. She pushed back the blanket and pulled her injured leg over the edge of the bed, struggling to balance as she stood.

Josh rushed to her side, steadying her with his arm. "What are you doing?"

"Getting out of here. I have work to do."

She owed it to Max to find his daughter.

The doctor and a nurse rushed into the room. "Agent Richardson, we need to keep you for observation," the doctor insisted.

"I'm fine," she said, wishing her legs were just a bit more steady. But Josh slipped his hand under her elbow and acted as her support. Beneath his gentle touch, she sensed strength and power and was confident he wouldn't let her fall.

The doctor sighed. "Well, I can't keep you, but you'll have to sign something saying you're leaving against medical advice. And I insist on having one of my nurses phone you every few hours just to check on you. Leave your number with Nurse Stringer here," he stated before walking out.

Elise wrote down her cell phone number then changed into a pair of borrowed hospital scrubs with the nurse's help.

"Are you sure you're up for this?" Josh asked her as they exited the hospital. "You did sustain head trauma."

She grunted, already tired of hearing that question. "I'm fine. Candace may not be. Now, please take me to my hotel. I'd like to change my clothes." She glanced at the shirt he was still wearing, stained red with her blood. "I'm sure you'd like to go home and change, too."

He opened the door to a black, four-door Jeep and helped her into the passenger's seat. "Daniel—Chief Mills—loaned me his Jeep while my truck is in the shop."

He walked around and slid behind the wheel then donned aviator sunglasses similar to ones Elise had seen military men wear. He didn't have the clean-cut look of most of the former military types she knew, but there was something about his manner that was orderly and neat and made her wonder about him.

"Since I guess I owe you my life, tell me about yourself. What do you do for a living?" She felt silly asking, like a schoolgirl digging for information about the boy she liked, but she tried to keep her tone matter-of-fact because she wasn't a schoolgirl and Josh wasn't the object of a girlish crush. She was an FBI agent and he was the brother of the man she'd got killed.

"I'm a security consultant for an oil company. I arrange and oversee security for the executives when they have to travel overseas."

That only confirmed what Elise suspected. "Isn't that the kind of job former military usually take?" She'd been around enough former military men to recognize the signs.

He nodded. "I served fourteen years in the army. Discharged last year."

"Why did you leave? You could have stayed and retired in only a few more years."

He shrugged. "Things change. People change."

His guarded expression and suddenly rigid body language told her there was more to that story but he wasn't going to share it. That piqued her curiosity. Vague people generally had something to hide.

But she hadn't come to town to learn about Josh. "Tell me about your niece. When did she go missing?"

His entire demeanor changed in an instant. His eyes perked up as he spoke about his niece. "Candace is smart and funny and so kindhearted. She often tutored other students." His smile faltered. "That's what she was doing the day she vanished. It was a Thursday afternoon and she'd stayed after school. I spoke to her before she left, but she never made it home."

"And why do the police think she ran away?"

"Her best friend, Brooke Martin, told the police Candace was planning to leave home, but Candace never said anything to me to make me believe that."

"Fifteen-year-olds don't always share everything with their uncles."

"She did. She talked to me about a lot of things. I would know if she was planning to run away."

Elise suspected that might not be the case, but she

didn't bother arguing the point. Her work had taught her that teenage girls were notoriously secretive with adults. What made Josh's relationship with his niece so different? More important, what made Josh believe their relationship was different?

He turned into the hotel and parked beside Elise's blue SUV.

She got out, careful not to place undue weight on her injured leg. "I'll have to go to the office and get the spare key."

"That won't be necessary." Josh's gaze stopped her. She followed it and saw her hotel room door standing open, the lock busted and the wood splintered.

Movement caused them both to jump. Whoever had broken into her hotel room was still inside. Elise stumbled to her SUV and keyed in her security code. The lock released and she opened the door, grabbing her gun from beneath the seat. She ignored the pain in her leg and the dizziness raking over her and headed for the hotel room, ready to pounce on whoever was inside.

Gun raised, she rushed into the room. "Don't move!" she shouted, causing the short, sandy-haired man inside to jump and raise his hands quickly.

"Don't shoot, Agent. It's only me, Bobby Danbar, the hotel manager."

Josh pushed past her. "Bobby, what are you doing in here?"

"I saw the door was busted and I was worried about Agent Richardson, especially since I hadn't seen her since she checked in."

Elise lowered her gun as the vague memory of this man filtered through her scrambled brain. She'd met him yesterday in the office. "You found my room this way?"

"Yes. Someone must have kicked in the door. Whoever did this was gone before I came along."

Elise surveyed the room. Her clothes were scattered as if thrown from where she'd neatly folded and placed them into the dresser drawers. Her makeup bag was overturned on the bed and her briefcase had been cracked open.

Josh motioned to the dresser where her badge and ID still sat. "Why didn't they break into your car? Steal your gun or your FBI credentials?"

"Who knows? Maybe they couldn't break the lock on my car. Or maybe they got interrupted before they could finish ransacking the room and ran. Regardless, they got what they came for."

"How do you know?"

She picked up her briefcase and held it open for Josh to see.

"It's empty."

"Exactly. My laptop is gone, and so are my case files. They're the only things missing, as far as I can tell." All her files on missing girls in three states. All the evidence that pointed toward a human trafficking ring operating in this area. Gone. "These intruders knew what they were looking for."

"Seems like you brought some trouble to town with you, Agent," Daniel commented.

Elise was still dressed in the scrubs the hospital had furnished her with since she'd been careful not to move anything in her hotel room before the police arrived to work the scene for prints and trace evidence.

Josh hoped she felt more confident than she looked. In truth, she looked young and vulnerable, her dark hair curling around her cheeks, her face devoid of makeup, revealing a faint but cute line of freckles on her cheeks and nose, and her hazel-colored eyes wide with surprise at the comment.

"I'm sorry to have been such a burden to you, Chief Mills." The bite of sarcasm in her tone belied her sincerity. "Tell me, do you treat all victims of crime in your town with this regard?"

"I meant no harm, ma'am. It's just that first my officers spent all morning cleaning up that mangled mess downtown and now this. It's taking a lot of man-hours we aren't accustomed to in our sleepy little town. Besides, now we know you're not any ordinary crime victim, are you? When were you planning to inform the police that the FBI was conducting an investigation in our jurisdiction?"

Elise pushed a runaway curl behind her ear, folded her arms and stared coldly at Daniel, and Josh got his answer. Even bandaged, bruised and dressed in hospital scrubs, she demanded the full respect due an FBI agent. "I am not required to inform you of anything, Chief Mills. The FBI has the jurisdiction to investigate any crimes that intersect your city line. Your duty right now is to gather and collect the evidence of two crimes that have occurred within your city limits. And I will expect and demand a full accounting of said evidence. And let me make myself clear. If I find any stone left unturned, you will wish you had never laid eyes on this FBI agent." Her expression was firm and fierce, and Josh noticed Daniel stiffen at her threat.

He replaced the hat on his head and nodded to her.

"I already regret that, Agent Richardson." He walked out, leaving his crew inside dusting for prints.

Josh suddenly felt the need to apologize on behalf of his hometown and his friend. "He shouldn't have said that."

She turned those green eyes on him, but they seemed to soften a bit, the golden-rimmed fire going out. She gave him a wiry smile. "He's not wrong. I am certainly not your normal crime victim."

He saw no anger or bitterness in her eyes. She had compassion and he liked that. But that didn't excuse Daniel's behavior. "Elise, someone tried to run you over and now they've broken into your hotel and stolen files. FBI or not, that has to affect you."

She stepped out into the breezeway and gripped the guardrail as if determination alone could keep her going, but he noticed the slight tremble of her hands and the cringes of pain she tried so hard to cover. "I don't have the luxury of letting it affect me."

He stared at her a long moment, impressed by her tenacity. Another time or place and his opinion of her might have grown into more than attraction, but he wasn't interested in a relationship. And besides, this was the woman who'd taken his brother from him. No amount of tenacity and determination could ever overcome that.

He heard her name and saw Bobby rushing toward them, waving a card in his hand.

"Your new room is ready, Agent Richardson. It's on the second level whenever you want to move your belongings. I just spoke to Daniel and he said we could clean this room in another hour or so. Of course, it's no rush because I have to have the door replaced before I can rent it again."

Elise took the card, thanking him with a nod of her head. "I'm sorry for all this, Mr. Danbar."

"I'm only glad you're okay," he said before walking off.

The officer dusting for prints appeared at the doorway. "We're finished here. We found several good prints, so maybe we'll get a hit."

Elise didn't look enthralled as he walked off.

She walked back inside and began gathering her belongings, her full lips pressed together grimly. Josh followed to help. "That's good news that they found prints. Maybe they can figure out who did this."

"Assuming the person is in the system, it will probably only be someone who stayed in this room before me, or one of the cleaning crew."

"Is Daniel right about someone following you to town? Is this fallout from another case you've investigated?"

"I'll know more when I get the preliminary reports, but I don't believe it is. I think whoever was driving that car was keeping an eye on me while his partners broke in here and stole my files."

"But who knew you were in town?"

She stopped sorting clothes and turned to him, realization dawning in her eyes. "You did. How did you know?"

"I overheard Bobby telling someone last night that an FBI agent had checked into his hotel. I figured you had to be here about Candace."

The fire in her eyes reignited. "Where were you when you overheard this?"

"At the steak house. I was picking up supper for my sister-in-law. She's been a mess ever since Candace vanished."

"So if you overheard it and put two and two together, there's no telling who else overheard and did the same."

"You think whoever did this could be responsible for Candace's disappearance?"

"I think it's one possible scenario until I can rule it out."

His mind whirled at the idea of all those he'd seen at the restaurant last night. "The restaurant was crowded. Half the town was there. And Bobby was drinking and talking loud."

She settled her hands on her hips in a way that made Josh feel sorry for his friend when she got ahold of him. "Then half this town just became suspects."

Elise rechecked the door locks to ensure they were secure. Despite what she'd told Josh, her nerves were on edge and the pain in her head pounded like a jackhammer. Per doctor's instructions, she wasn't supposed to sleep for more than a few hours at a time. Josh had offered to stay up with her, but she'd politely declined his offer. She didn't know him well enough to impose that way, and it wasn't appropriate for her to have a man stay in her hotel room. Besides, the hospital staff would be calling her cell phone every few hours to check on her. Nurse Stringer had informed her that if she didn't respond, they were sending the paramedics over to break down the door.

She smiled now, realizing she couldn't let that happen. Two broken doors in one day? She couldn't do that to Mr. Danbar.

Then again—her sympathetic feelings for him faded as she remembered he was the one telling folks she was in town in the first place—it would serve him right to have another room damaged because of his big mouth. She would have to remember to write a letter to whatever board governed hotel operations. Certainly it went against some code to announce who was staying in his hotel? What had ever happened to privacy rights?

She'd hoped to have at least one night of peace then show up bright and early at the police station to gather information about the missing girl. So much for her surprise. And so much for her quiet investigation into Candace Adams's disappearance.

Was the attack on her this morning the result of the trafficking ring trying to get her to back off the investigation? Or simply someone who'd got wind that the FBI was in town and wanted to find out why?

Either way, she needed to replace her missing files.

She reached for her phone and called Lin Wildwood, her partner in the FBI for the past three years. "Elise, where are you?" His voice was full of concern. "I haven't heard from you in a while."

"I'm in Westhaven, Mississippi, looking into the disappearance of a teenage girl."

He sighed wearily. "When are you going to give up on this futile quest and come back to work?"

Elise had been expecting this reaction. Three months ago, she'd taken a leave of absence from the Bureau to pursue evidence of a possible human trafficking ring operating in the Southeast. She didn't yet have enough proof to support an official FBI investigation, and many of her colleagues believed she was chasing at shadows, but Elise was certain something was going on. She just had to gather enough facts to support it.

"I can't, Lin. I'm close to uncovering this ring. This missing girl might be the key." But she wouldn't know if she didn't have her files. "I need a favor." She filled him in about the break-in, being careful to downplay the seriousness of this morning's events. "I have backup copies of all my most recent files on a flash drive in my apartment. Can you send it to me?"

"Fine, but only on the condition that you'll come back to work if this investigation doesn't turn up anything. I have a stack of cases—actual reported missing persons cases—that need to be investigated."

She was hesitant to make such an agreement, but if it would get her the files… "I'll consider it," she told him. "If I don't turn up anything here."

He seemed to take what he could get. "I'll swing by your apartment on my way to work."

She gave him instructions for where she'd hidden both the spare key to her apartment and the flash drive, and he promised to have it sent first thing in the morning.

She hung up then lowered herself into a chair by the window. She had a long night ahead of her before she was supposed to meet Josh and get started with the probe into his missing niece.

How weird was it that the girl she'd come to town to investigate was Max's daughter? But then, the University of Southern Mississippi, where she'd gone to college, was less than an hour's drive from Westhaven. Elise knew many people from these small Mississippi towns lining the highway made that drive to attend classes. She thought back to that terrible night ten years earlier when she'd been walking to her dorm room and had been greeted by a man with a gun. Max Adams, a complete stranger, had stepped between her and the assailant, taking the fatal blow. As the attacker had run off, she'd held the dying man in her arms, thanking him and assuring him that everything would be fine. She would never forget his face or his bright blue eyes.

She got goose bumps remembering seeing those same blue eyes staring at her this morning on the street. But it hadn't been Max. It had been Josh Adams.

If she believed in God, she might believe in some sort of spiritual connection and feel as if God had allowed her to live so she could someday help Max's daughter. But how could she believe in a God that allowed such terrible things like Max's death and the abduction and trafficking of young girls to happen?

Her mother had been a believer and had taken Elise to church regularly, but a car accident when Elise was fourteen had taken her mother from her. She had been sent to live with her father and the new family he'd started after her parents' divorce. She'd been an outsider there throughout her teenage years, offered food and shelter but never love. In fact, Elise's stepmother had made a point of reminding her daily that she didn't truly belong. Elise had worked hard to make the good grades required to earn a scholarship to college and had fled that house, never once looking back. In fact, the only contact she had with them now was the yearly Christmas card she received complete with holiday family photos proving how happy they were without her.

She had never been able to mesh her mother's idea of a loving God with her own experiences. Where had God been during her teen years? And why had He allowed a lonely girl to suffer alone? The painful truth was that because of her, Max's daughter had grown up without a father and his wife had gone ten years without a husband, and Josh had lost a brother.

If there was a God, He obviously didn't care enough to intervene.

But Elise cared.

She turned her focus back to the investigation and dug through her purse for a pen and paper. She needed to get the names of everyone in the restaurant that night Bobby had spilled the secret of her arrival. Someone had known she was here, and she was determined to discover who had tried to run her down and had stolen her files.

Her cell phone rang, startling her. She didn't recognize the number but saw it was local, so she answered it.

"Agent Richardson, this is Nurse Stringer from the Westhaven Hospital. Just calling to check on you."

"I'm fine, Nurse Stringer."

"Any dizziness or blurred vision?"

"I said I'm fine." Her tone was a bit harsher than she'd intended, but Nurse Stringer either didn't notice or didn't let it bother her.

"Very good, then. I'll give you a call again in another few hours. Have a blessed night."

Elise hit the off button and threw down her phone. That woman sounded way too chipper for it to be so late. She knew she'd been abrupt with her, but the truth was she was feeling dizzy and her eyes were blurring. But she wasn't about to admit it and be hauled back into the hospital. She had a job to do, and she wasn't going to allow a little thing like a mild concussion slow her down.

Chapter Two

Josh stopped by the bakery and purchased coffee and breakfast sandwiches before heading to the hotel. He still couldn't believe he was turning to Elise for help. He'd wrestled with the decision all night and was still having trouble reconciling the image he'd carried in his mind all these years of the girl responsible for his brother's death with the flesh-and-blood woman who'd appeared out of nowhere yesterday.

It had been a difficult enough decision to seek out the FBI for help in finding Candace given his distrust for any of the three-letter government agencies after his army-ranger squad was betrayed by a CIA-vetted translator, but he'd had to concede that finding his niece outweighed his dislike for the agency. He needed FBI resources.

He needed Elise.

She was up and dressed when she answered his knock, having traded the secondhand scrubs for slacks and a white blouse. He was stunned at first glance. He'd seen her yesterday probably at her worst and she'd been beautiful, but now… His heart kicked an extra beat as he stepped in and closed the door.

He held up the paper bag in his hand, glad to have something to distract him from his own racing heartbeat. "I brought breakfast."

Her face paled at the sight of the sandwiches, and only then did he notice the draw of weariness beneath her flawless hair and makeup. Yesterday's ordeals had indeed taken their toll on her. "Thank you, but I don't think I could eat anything."

He placed the bags on a round table by the window, pulled out a cup of coffee and gave it to her. She cupped it in her hand, took a whiff and smiled a big wide smile that caused his heart to hitch again.

"Thank you. This is just what I need this morning."

"Rough night?"

"You could say that."

"Maybe you shouldn't have left the hospital."

She glanced up at him, her eyes full of determination and persistence. "I'm fine. Besides, your niece might not have time for me to lie in a hospital bed."

He could see she needed a day or two to recover from her injuries, but it was obvious she wasn't going to take it, and he couldn't deny he was glad. At least someone was taking Candace's disappearance seriously.

"I need to go to the police station and get a copy of their missing persons file then find somewhere to purchase a new laptop. My partner is overnighting me a copy of the files that were stolen." She pulled on her suit coat, stumbling backward as she did. She glanced up at him, her reassuring smile as shaky as her balance. "I'm okay."

It was obvious to him she wasn't, but he needed her

to be and he was prepared to do whatever it took to keep her going. "There's an office-supply store on the highway where you can buy a laptop. I'll drive you."

"That's not necessary," she said, but after fumbling a few moments with the buttons on her jacket, she gave a weary sigh and resignation colored her tone. "On second thought, maybe that's not such a bad idea."

He was pleased she'd accepted his offer. She had determination, and he admired that, but he was also glad to know that she wouldn't try to push him out of the investigation. As long as she needed him to drive her, he was assured of being kept in the loop. He slipped his arm around her waist as he helped her outside. Had he missed yesterday how easily she fit into his arms? The top of her head met his chin and he caught the scent of her shampoo, sending his senses swirling. He couldn't help noticing how slim and trim she was as he helped her to the Jeep. He was putting all his hope in this petite powerhouse, and that should worry him, but he'd already seen how she'd commanded respect from Daniel when she needed to. If he had to work with the FBI, maybe Elise wasn't a bad choice.

They drove to the police station first and Daniel wasn't pleased to see them. He ushered them through to his office, but his tone was almost adversarial as he turned his gaze on Josh. "Is this your doing? Did you call in the FBI?"

"No, but I'm thankful she's here and willing to look into Candace's case."

"Why are you so convinced she didn't run away, Josh?"

Josh had always known him to be a good cop, but

he'd dug in his heels with this case, determined he was right. "Why are you so convinced she did?"

Daniel looked exasperated. "You know why."

"The letter? Daniel, you've known Candace her whole life. Did that letter really seem like something she would write? She and Patti have a great relationship, but that letter made it sound like Patti didn't have time for her." His sister-in-law was a good mom and Josh knew Candace adored her. That was why the tone of that letter baffled him so.

But Daniel pressed on. "It was her handwriting. Her mother confirmed it. She wrote that letter. I know you don't want to accept that, but it's the truth."

"Something isn't right, Daniel. You have to see that."

"I am doing everything I can to find her, Josh. I've sent her picture out on the wire to police agencies all across the state. I entered her name into the missing persons database. I've even driven to New Orleans to hang flyers and search the shelters for her. But I haven't found one clue to indicate she didn't leave on her own."

Elise stepped forward and interrupted their heated discussion, probably sensing the futility of it. Josh wasn't going to change his mind, and without more proof, neither was Daniel.

"I'm going to need to see that letter, Chief."

That note had convinced Daniel that Candace had left home on her own, and Josh had to admit it was hard to dispute. He hoped Elise wouldn't write off this case because of it, too.

"What's the FBI's interest in a runaway case?"

Josh hadn't told Daniel her connection with Max and hoped she wouldn't let it slip. He still worried about the reaction this police force—this community—might have if they knew the truth about who she was.

He needn't have worried. She was all FBI business. "Actually, I'm here as part of a larger ongoing investigation into missing teens in this part of the Southeast. I'm trying to establish a pattern that may indicate a human trafficking ring operating in this area."

Josh's gut twisted at her revelation. "You think Candace was abducted by a trafficking ring?"

Sympathy shone in her eyes and she quickly responded to the terror she must have seen on his face. "This is only a preliminary investigation. I've identified some characteristics that may suggest a pattern. I obtained Candace's information through the National Center for Missing and Exploited Children database when it was entered, but I still need to see if her disappearance matches any of the criteria I've uncovered in other cases."

Daniel shook his head. "You're barking up the wrong tree in this case, Agent. Candace ran away. I know Josh doesn't want to believe that, but all the evidence supports that."

Nothing about her demeanor as she handled Daniel suggested that she had been barely able to stand on her own a half hour ago. He was impressed with the strength she'd garnered from somewhere in order to maintain her composure in front of others. No one in this office would see how the events of yesterday had affected her.

"Regardless, I still need to see that file, including the letter."

Daniel sighed wearily, but conceded. "I'll have someone make you a copy of the file. I'm sure once you examine it, you'll concur with our findings." He picked up the file folder and walked out.

Josh sank into a chair as the enormity of the situation hit him. Elise wasn't here by accident. Something about Candace's disappearance had caught her attention during her investigation into human trafficking.

She touched his arm and he glanced up at her. Her lips curved into a gentle smile that said she understood better than anyone what he was feeling. Her hand on his arm was small but reassuring. "I know it looks bleak, but I promise you if something did happen to Candace, we will find out."

He was thankful for her words and for her presence here in town. He hadn't even considered that something sinister must have brought her here because Daniel was right—the FBI did not normally investigate runaways.

Her cell phone rang and she glanced at the screen then stood. "I have to take this."

He watched her slip from the room and realized she'd become his lifeline. He was depending on her. He'd known fear during his time with the Rangers, but nothing like the fear that gripped him now. He'd seen parts of the world no one in this town would ever see. He'd seen the incredible beauty of God's handiwork across the world, as well as the unbelievable corruption of man. And his time with the Rangers had assured him of one ultimate truth—good and evil existed.

They had to find Candace, and he was relying on Elise and her FBI resources to make that happen.

It was the hospital number calling…again. Three hours on the dot, just as Nurse Stringer had promised…all night long and into the morning. She considered letting it go to voice mail but then remembered Nurse Stringer's warning about sending the paramedics. Maybe Bobby Danbar deserved it, but she didn't feel like changing rooms again.

"We're just checking on you, Agent Richardson," the nurse who sounded much younger than Nurse Stringer had said. "How are you feeling this morning?"

Honestly, the blurred vision and ever-persistent headache were more of an obstacle than the pain ripping through her leg with every step. She didn't know how she would function without Josh's help and was glad he'd insisted on driving her. But she couldn't tell this to the nurse, not if she hoped to remain able to investigate Candace's disappearance…and she couldn't stop, not until she brought Candace home.

"I'm fine," she said, hoping she wouldn't probe more.

Fortunately, this nurse took her at her word. "Okey-dokey. Talk to you in a few hours, then."

She breathed a sigh of relief as she put away her phone. But it was short-lived. On the wall, she spotted a memorial to fallen officers, including a photograph she recognized from her newspaper clipping. She stared at the memorial to Max Adams, his bright blue eyes clearly noticeable in the photograph. She shuddered, flashing back to that night ten years ago when she'd held him in her arms as he gasped for his last breath.

A tear slipped from Elise's eye and emotion threatened to overwhelm her. She glanced around at the bull pen visible from where she stood and was struck by the realization that this was where Max had spent his days. All these men and women had probably known him and had loved him…and she had killed him.

"That's Josh's brother and Candace's father," Chief Mills said, coming up behind her. "This office lost a good man. He was one of our own, and we all consider his daughter's disappearance a loss."

Elise shuddered, suddenly feeling anxious. What would these people do if they knew who she was—who she really was? Had Josh told him she was the person who'd taken their fallen brother away from them? Was that why Chief Mills was so cold toward her? She was used to seeing the local police posturing whenever the FBI arrived in town. She hoped that was all this was. She couldn't worry about pacifying Chief Mills. Too much was at stake.

She took a deep breath and pushed her focus away from Max and from the pounding in her head as she followed Chief Mills back into his office, where Josh was waiting for them both.

"Here are those copies you wanted."

She took the folder he offered. "Have you gotten the fingerprint results back from my hotel room?"

"We have." He pulled up a file on his computer and Elise moved around his desk to read over his shoulder. That was a quick turnaround, which meant his department was efficient. Good.

"Only one print raised any flags. It was pulled off the door. We matched it to a local thug named Taylor Johnson. He's been on our radar since he was a teen, in and out of trouble. He just returned to town after serving three years in the state correctional facility for breaking and entering."

"I want to question him."

"I sent an officer to his house to bring him in, but no one was home. I'll let you know when we pick him up."

"What about the car that tried to run her down?" Josh asked.

He pulled up a grainy image on the computer. "A bank security camera caught an image of the car, but the driver's face is obscured and the plates are unreadable. I've issued a Be On the Lookout for cars matching this description, and I'll have someone run a check of stolen vehicles. I've also alerted the body shops in the area to watch for anyone coming in with vehicle damage matching what we know your truck did to it."

Elise nodded, certain they had covered all avenues available to them. "Keep me informed, Chief."

She really wanted to speak with Taylor Johnson to find out exactly what he'd been doing in her hotel room. Why would a B and E criminal target the FBI? Was he involved in something bigger that might get the FBI's attention? Or was he simply curious to know what the FBI was doing in town? She might have chalked it up to a simple burglary if her case files hadn't been taken. Taylor would have done himself a favor if he'd helped himself to other valuables in addition to the files and her laptop.

"Where to now?" Josh asked as they walked toward the Jeep. "To the electronics store?"

She was about to agree when her strength gave out, her knees buckled and she stumbled. Josh's arms went protectively around her, steadying her. Elise stared up into his blue eyes and saw concern and compassion in them, causing her heart to skip a beat as they locked gazes. She'd already been in this man's arms more often than she had in any other man's in a long time.

"Maybe I should take you back to the hotel so you can rest."

She shook her head and started to protest. "I'm—"

"Don't tell me you're fine again, Elise. I can see that you're not." His tone was firm but caring. "You're pushing yourself too hard."

She hated that he could see through her so easily. She thought she'd held up quite well in the chief's office. But she wasn't going back to the hotel. "Fine, but let's go to the café instead. I think I'll be okay if I just sit down for a few minutes."

Josh helped her into the Jeep then drove them to a café and walked around to open her door. Elise grabbed the file Chief Mills had given her.

He didn't mask his surprise. "Really? I thought you were resting, not working."

"No reason I can't do both."

He kept his hand on her back as they walked inside, and Elise was grateful. She did feel better knowing he was there to keep her from stumbling and was strong enough to catch her if she fell. It was comforting to have someone looking out for her…even if it was only so that she could investigate his niece's disappearance.

He led her toward a booth in the back and Elise slid into one side.

"Do you feel like something to eat now?" Josh asked.

She still blanched at the idea of food. She probably needed something, but she wasn't sure her stomach would agree. "Just coffee, please."

While Josh walked to the counter to place their orders, Elise pulled out the runaway note and examined it.

Dear Mom,
By the time you receive this, I will be gone. I
can't take it at home anymore. There is no room
in your life for me. The tension is unbearable
and I just want out. I need some time away to
clear my head and you need to be able to move
on with your life without me. Please don't try to
find me. You won't. And don't involve the police.
That will only make things worse for both of us.
Please know that I still love you. I just think this
is the best option for me right now.
Love,
Candace

She noticed patterns of words and phrases similar
to the ones she'd seen in the other letters written by
girls believed to be runaways. It was almost as though
someone was dictating the letter for each girl. She'd
suspected as much before. A letter written by the missing girl in her own hand stating that she was running
away from home was often the key detail that ruled out
abduction in these cases, but this letter seemed proof
enough to Elise that Candace Adams was caught up
in a net that stretched through several states.

Even though her mother had stated it looked like her
writing, Elise still wanted to get a handwriting sample of Candace's for confirmation. She suspected that
like the others, the sample would confirm Candace's
penmanship wasn't as sloppy and haphazard as the
writing on this note. Other officials had chalked the
scratchy scribble up to haste or the girls being upset,
but Elise suspected it was more than simple discomfort. She suspected something far worse—someone

was standing over these girls dictating to them what to write. They'd all been written under duress and it showed in their penmanship.

She couldn't wait to get her files and compare this letter to the others. She was certain she would find similarities. The part about involving the police was suspiciously similar as was the focus of the letter, which was primarily to blame the parent. Elise had found that parental guilt was a wonderful way to paralyze otherwise caring, grieving parents.

"Does seeing that letter make you change your mind about Candace?" Josh asked as he returned to their table with two cups of coffee. He handed one over to Elise and she took it.

"Not at all. In fact, it makes me believe more than ever that Candace might be in trouble." She saw relief in his face. Josh was the only one who seemed adamant that Candace hadn't run away, despite this letter. "It didn't convince you either, did it? Why?"

"It just didn't seem like something Candace would write. That part about Patti not having room in her life for her? That's crazy. Patti is a terrific mom."

"Surely that's not the only reason."

"I've shared this with the police and the school board, but none of them seemed too interested in my concerns. There's a man, a teacher at Candace's school, whose behavior worries me. I don't like the way he looks at the female students, and he seems to give too much attention to them. I think he might have had something to do with Candace's disappearance."

So he'd already suspected something sinister had happened to his niece before he even saw this letter.

"I thought you said you worked security. How do you know what goes on at the school?"

"My sister-in-law, Candace's mother, is the principal. I volunteer with after-school programs when I can."

"Did Candace have any regular contact with this man you suspect?"

"He's her biology teacher. And I know he's kept her after school on several occasions. She said it was for tutoring."

"Did the police question him?"

"Of course. I shared my suspicions with them." He raked a hand over his face, obviously weary of the lack of attention his niece's case had received. "I know what Daniel thinks. And I know what this note suggests. But I also know my niece. She wouldn't have been gone this long without a word. She's in trouble."

Elise already suspected she was a victim of the trafficking ring, but she couldn't rule out other possibilities, like this teacher Josh mentioned. Was it possible he was part of the ring she was investigating? She had to consider all avenues if she hoped to find Candace. "I would like to interview this teacher, as well as some of Candace's friends from school."

"She didn't have many. Brooke Martin was her closest friend, and she's only been at the school a few months."

Elise recognized the girl's name from her conversation with Josh yesterday. "That's the girl who said she was planning to run away? I'd still like to speak to her and any other students who had contact with Candace during the school day."

"That shouldn't be a problem. The whole town is upset over the disappearance of Candace."

Elise wasn't so sure she believed that. Most towns where girls had been abducted would be on full alert, organizing searches, and the newspaper headlines would announce updates of the search. From what she'd seen of this town, the townspeople had continued on with very little concern for Candace. It broke Elise's heart to see that a girl could go missing with so little fanfare.

Except for Josh. He was concerned enough to be seeking her out, to be excited to have the FBI join the search. She hated to disappoint him with the news that no one else was coming. She was the lone agent looking into this case, and if she didn't find any evidence of an abduction quickly, she would have to move on.

"I'll mention the interviews to Candace's mother when I speak to her."

"Interview Patti?" He seemed surprised by her suggestion.

"Of course. I'd like to go right over there after the electronics store."

Josh's expression fixed firmly. "No."

"No?" What did he mean no? Speaking with the parents was always the starting point.

"I need to speak with Patti before you interview her. Can it wait until later this afternoon?"

Elise frowned. Why would Josh want to speak with the girl's mother before she spoke to Elise? "Is there some reason your sister-in-law doesn't want to speak to the FBI?"

"It isn't about being FBI, Elise."

She realized where he was heading…her connection

with Max. She felt herself flush, suddenly realizing what an awkward interview that would be. Still, she was a professional and she would conduct herself as one despite what had happened between her and Max. "It's not necessary that she knows. I can be discreet."

"I'm sure you can, but she deserves the truth and she's at school until this afternoon. I'm asking you to please wait."

She nodded her agreement, understanding his reservation and suddenly fearful of facing this woman. After all, her husband might still be alive if it wasn't for Elise.

Suddenly a wave of dizziness rushed through her and Elise gripped the table as the seat beneath her seemed to fade in and out.

Josh saw and stood up, holding out his hand. "That's it. I'm taking you back to the hotel."

"No."

"No arguments, Elise. You need to rest for a couple of hours. I'll talk to Patti then come by later and take you to get the laptop. We'll swing by her house and you can ask your questions."

She finally conceded and took his hand, thankful again for the strength he displayed as he helped her to her feet then drove her back to her hotel.

Elise tried to manage the hotel steps alone, declining his offer to help. He stayed beside her just in case and was glad he did. Her injured leg buckled three steps from the top and she slipped and fell right into his arms.

Josh took the remaining steps easily and set her down, careful of her injured leg, but didn't immediately release her. She glanced up at him, her green eyes ablaze with speckles of brown darkening them. He pulled his eyes away from her gaze only to find them focused instead on the fullness of her lips and wondering what it would feel like to kiss her.

He took a deep breath and let it out, making himself remember who she was. Besides being the woman Max had died for, she was also someone who placed her life in danger every day. Working for the FBI meant you were always aware of the danger you placed on yourself—you could never promise to come home to your family each night. He'd left the army because of that very reason. He certainly wouldn't now place himself in a situation of getting involved with someone in the same predicament.

When he released her, she pulled out her hotel card key, opened the door then turned to thank him.

"I'll come back in a few hours and we'll go see Patti together," he said and she nodded. "Try to get some rest."

"Thanks for your help today, Josh."

"Thank you for being here, Elise."

He turned and jogged back down the stairs, grateful to be free of the pull she seemed to have on him. He had to remind himself that Elise Richardson was everything he'd determined he didn't want. She was the "jump first then look to see if it was safe" type of person. He knew those people. He used to be one of them. He'd lost army brothers, good men who'd left their wives widowed and their children without a father all for the sake of the job. He'd lost Max, who'd placed himself in danger to protect someone he didn't know.

Elise was the type of woman he would spend his

life worrying about because of the danger of her job and the risks she took. Even if he was looking for a relationship, it would not be with someone like her.

Josh heard his name and saw Bobby heading his way. "How is Agent Richardson?"

"I just dropped her off to rest. She's one tough lady." He smiled, realizing that pretty much summed her up.

"Is she really here because of Candace? I didn't realize the FBI was interested in cases of runaways."

"Candace did not run away from home." He gritted his teeth, tired of people so easily jumping to that conclusion.

"But I heard she wrote a letter to her mom. Has Agent Richardson seen that?"

"She saw it. I've been saying all along there is something fishy about that letter and Elise agrees with me. She thinks Candace might be a victim of human trafficking."

Bobby's eyes widened. "Human trafficking? Here in Westhaven? That's hard to believe. This is such a small town. I thought things like that only happened in big cities."

"Me too, but I'm still suspicious of Candace's teacher Mr. Larkin. I know he had a hand in Candace's disappearance. Whoever took her is going to pay. I'll make sure of it."

"I hope you find her safe," Bobby said.

"Thank you."

Bobby headed back toward the hotel office and Josh slipped behind the wheel of the Jeep and headed home.

He spent the next few hours following up on a background check of a staff member at the hotel housing one of his security clients on an upcoming trip. It was probably nothing, but he liked to be thorough. No one understood better than he the importance of fully vetting those surrounding his clients. Perhaps if the CIA liaison to his ranger unit had done a more thorough job of checking the credentials of his translator, Josh's squad wouldn't have suffered such calamity.

He pushed that thought from his mind. He couldn't focus on the past. That part of his life was over now and he was trying to work through his bitterness at the CIA and the other three-lettered agencies that had let them down. An image of Elise this morning when she'd opened her door popped into his brain and he smiled. Perhaps working with Elise would help restore his faith in the government agencies.

Trusting her seemed to come easily to him. She'd impressed him and he couldn't deny it. She sent his senses rumbling, reminding him that he was hungry for life and ready to step back into a world where it was okay to laugh and love and live again.

That realization terrified him as much as it excited him.

Lord, please don't allow her to build up our hopes only to let us down.

He was used to the disappointments, but he didn't think Patti would be able to take it.

He glanced at the clock and realized he couldn't wait until later to talk to Patti. He needed to see her now, to warn her about Elise and her connection to Max. But could he make her understand how much they needed Elise to do her job? Would it even be a concern for Patti? She didn't seem to harbor the same anger over Max's death that Josh did. She'd told him several times that she'd let go of that pain a long time ago.

But Josh hadn't been able to let go. He'd carried it with him through years of dangerous missions with the Rangers, through years of top-secret raids and rescues that shouldn't have succeeded. But Max's death had always been there in the back of his heart, the mission shielding him from the pain of it. Until the last mission, when his pain had finally encompassed him.

He picked up the phone and dialed the school, hoping she could find a few minutes to speak with him. She always turned off her cell phone when she was at work, so he knew the main line at the school was the best way to reach her. When the school's secretary answered, he asked to speak to Patti.

"I'm sorry, Josh," she said. "Patti wasn't feeling well, so she went home early."

Now he was worried. Patti never left work early. Ever since Candace's disappearance, she'd been a trouper, insisting that work kept her mind off the situation. Was it possible her facade of strength was finally crumbling?

"I'll swing by her house." He thought about calling Elise and putting off the interview until Patti was feeling better, but he hated to postpone it any longer than he already had. Finding Candace had to be priority one, and Patti was a tough lady. But maybe it wasn't the right time to break the news to her about Elise's connection with Max. Maybe that information was too much for her to handle right now.

Elise hated being so weak. Why was this affecting her so? She should be able to push past the pain and dizziness. Too much was at stake. Lives hung in the balance, and she had to return to her hotel to rest? It didn't make sense to her why she couldn't muster the strength she needed to push through this.

After all, Josh had rammed his truck into another car and he seemed fine. He amazed her with his determination to find his niece. It so reminded her of Max stepping between her and that gunman. Was strength and character a family trait? Or was it something he'd picked up in the army? Either way, it was good to have someone on her side. Since taking on this project, she'd lost her backup at the Bureau. Everyone thought she was searching for patterns that weren't there. Even Lin believed she was stretching, an adverse reaction to a difficult situation.

Allie Peterson.

Elise had ignored her gut on that case and Allie had been found dead. Why had she allowed the opinion of others to sway her from doing what she knew needed to be done? Finding Allie's body had been the breaking point. She'd taken this job with the FBI to help locate these girls, not bring them home in body bags. She'd delved into cases that matched Allie's, searching for patterns, and when her supervisors had insisted she move on to other cases, Elise had taken a leave of absence to follow her gut. Maybe she was committing professional suicide. And maybe, as Lin believed, she would turn up nothing, but she had to try. She owed it to the Allie Petersons of the world.

But this case was different. Now she owed more than a missing girl. She owed Max's family.

Josh's belief in her meant the world, but she couldn't deny his determination was likely misplaced. In all probability, they wouldn't find Candace in time and Elise would have to watch this family suffer another loss.

She picked up the letter and examined it again. Armed with the contents of such a note, she'd usually interview the parents of the missing girl as a first step, but she'd promised Josh she would wait.

She hated waiting and she was too keyed up to sleep. What had possessed her to agree to his request? She didn't have to wonder. She knew why. Like many of the parents who received these notes, Elise had been paralyzed by guilt—the guilt of confronting the woman whose husband she was responsible for taking away. Plus, it was difficult to argue with a man who was practically holding you up. And the blue of his eyes hadn't helped, either.

She rubbed a spot on her temple where a drum line seemed to be playing. Why was she letting this man affect her so? It had to be the concussion impacting her judgment. That mixed with the crazy traumatic shock of discovering she was investigating the disappearance of the daughter of the man who'd saved her life.

But she couldn't allow guilt to rule over her life. She had an investigation to perform and her first step was the first step. There was no way around it, and she didn't need Josh Adams to oversee her interview with Candace's mother. In fact, it was better that he wasn't there.

She made her way outside to her SUV and climbed in.

No one told Elise Richardson how to conduct her investigation...not even Josh Adams.

She punched the home address from Candace's file into her GPS and started the car.

Minutes later, despite several moments of light-headedness when she'd nearly driven off the road,

Elise arrived at the home of Patti and Candace Adams. She parked her car at the curb and stared at the single-story house. The blue shuttered windows and flower-lined sidewalk broke her heart into a million pieces. Was this the same house where Max had lived? Or had this home been purchased after his death? Which-ever, his widow had raised their daughter alone in this house, and that was Elise's fault.

She had to face this if she hoped to get anywhere on this case. Her personal life and professional life were at a crossroads, intersecting at the worst pos-sible point. She couldn't rule out Candace as a victim of the human trafficking ring without gathering the details she needed, and gathering those details meant interviewing the victim's mother.

She jammed the SUV into Park and got out, facing the house. She smoothed her jacket and braced her-self for the meeting, pushing past a rush of dizziness along with the knot in her stomach. She could do this. She had to do this.

Patti Adams—a petite woman with short dark hair and brown eyes made red from crying—answered the door, and Elise introduced herself.

"Josh told me the FBI was in town," Patti said. "Please come inside."

Elise stepped into the small but open living area. A decorated Christmas tree stood in the corner, and on the mantel sat a photograph of Max holding a baby that had to be Candace. He was notably absent from more recent photographs and no one had to tell Elise why.

"Thank you for coming," Patti stated, inviting Elise to sit. "I thought everyone had given up on looking for Candace."

There were a thousand questions that ran through her mind. She wanted to thank this woman for the sacrifice her husband—her family—had made for her all those years ago. But she could see the lack of recognition on her face. Josh had told her the FBI was in town, but he hadn't told her yet who the FBI agent was.

She couldn't be sure if she was relieved or disappointed.

She pulled out her notebook and turned her attention to the matter at hand. "When was the last time you saw her?"

"The day she vanished. We'd stayed up the night before decorating the Christmas tree. We got into an argument and the next morning she said she was going to walk to school instead of riding with me. I know she made it to school, but she never came home." Patti took a deep breath, choking back sobs. "I can't believe the last words I may have spoken to my daughter were angry words." Tears pooled in her eyes. "Excuse me." Patti jumped up and disappeared down the hallway.

Elise glanced at the photos layered around the house. The frames missing a father screamed at her to look at them, to see what her actions had caused, a family missing their husband, father and brother.

She glanced up at the photo on the mantel then stood to get a closer look. The only picture she had of Max was a cutout from the newspaper account of the story. In her mind, his face was grainy and unclear, but this photograph, taken with his daughter on her fifth birthday, was clear, like the one at the police station. She could see the bright blue of his eyes, the dark color of his hair. The glint of happiness in his face. He'd had no idea his life would change so dramatically only a few months later.

"That's my late husband." Patti spoke from behind her. "Candace's father. He died not long after that photograph was taken." She picked up the picture and ran her finger over the lines of his face.

"His eyes remind me of Josh's."

"They're a family trait. Candace has them, too. Bright blue." She handed Elise a photograph of Candace, an awkward-looking redhead with braces and those same blue eyes her uncle and father possessed.

"How did he die?" That question slipped out, but she didn't take it back, knowing it would help her to examine what she saw in Patty's face when she answered.

"He died a hero." Patti replaced the photograph. "He was taking night classes. He wanted to finish his degree because he said it would help him provide for his family. The police said he saw a girl being abducted and stepped in to help her. The attacker shot him."

Elise shuddered against the roar of emotions Patti's story brought up. She shook it off. She needed to get away from all these memories and focus on the missing girl. "What did you and your daughter fight about?"

"You have to understand my husband died many years ago. It never crossed my mind that I might ever want that again with someone else."

Elise breathed in. "You fell in love."

"No, nothing like that…at least, not yet. I mean, we're not in love. I don't think we are." She shook her head to clear it. "It's much too early for that, but I had met someone. Candace was not happy with the idea of me dating again. After all, it's been she and I for as long as she can remember. This was all just so unexpected. I mean, I've known him forever. I can't even explain when something changed between us, but it's exciting. For the first time in a long time, I found myself smiling and wearing mascara again."

Elise was grateful to hear Patti was once again finding love. She was also more than a little relieved. If Patti was moving on, it helped Elise's case when Patti learned the truth about her.

She found herself wishing she could talk to Candace about the situation. Her own parents had divorced when Elise was a child and she'd struggled with some of the same emotions, watching her father remarry. It had often been a tumultuous situation, but as an adult, Elise understood the need for Patti to crave adult companionship and romance.

Didn't she crave the same thing?

She pushed that thought away. She'd dated on and off, but no relationship had ever seemed interesting enough to make those cravings take center stage. Her work had always occupied her mind, and most men were turned off by the content of what she saw on a daily basis. Still, she noticed Patti blush and smile as she talked about this new relationship, and her heart waned a bit. Maybe she did crave that kind of relationship…someday.

Her eyes caught on a photograph of Josh smiling at her from the mantel. She remembered the broad shoulders that merged into muscular arms and strong hands. He'd been a steadying presence for her, one that she'd desperately needed and was thankful to have had. And those eyes that could captivate any woman.

A chill rushed through her and she pushed away the thought of those eyes locked on her and the intensity of his gaze.

Yes, she understood Patti's smile.

She forced her focus back to the matter at hand. "May I see Candace's room?"

Patti led her down the hall. "I picked up the room before I realized Candace was missing, but I placed the clothes I washed on the bed."

Nothing seemed out of place. It looked like a normal fifteen-year-old's bedroom with posters hung on the wall and books lining the shelves.

"Did she own a backpack?"

"Yes, she had it with her that morning. It's pink and gray. I haven't seen it since. Daniel believes she took it with her."

"What about her schoolbooks? Were they all accounted for?"

"I'm not sure. She usually had algebra and biology homework. I know she brought those books home most days, but I don't know if she had them that day."

Elise searched through Candace's desk drawers but found nothing unusual. "Are any of her clothes missing?"

"Only what she was wearing that morning—her faded jeans, a purple hoodie with the school's name and her Skechers."

"The police report indicated one of Candace's friends told her she was running away from home."

Patti shook her head. "What teenager doesn't threaten to run away every now and again? I know she didn't mean it."

"Was she having any problems you knew about at school or at home?"

"We were definitely at odds lately, but I thought it was just normal teenage stuff. It certainly wasn't anything big enough for her to leave home. Besides, if she was having a real problem, she would have talked to Josh about it."

"Josh? Not you?"

"No, Josh was her confidant. Since he got out of the army and returned home, he's been like a father to Candace."

"How long has he been back?"

"Nearly a year. He returned to Westhaven to help me with Candace."

"Not many men would make that kind of sacrifice, especially for a child that isn't theirs."

"That's Josh. Family means the world to that man."

She could imagine that in him. She'd already seen his passion for finding his niece. It was a nice trait for a man to possess. But if Josh had left the army to help her care for her daughter, how close were they?

She pushed that train of thought away. What did that really matter to the investigation?

She made a note to question Josh more about his military involvements. He'd been vague in the car yesterday, but if she was going to investigate all possibilities, that included his time in the military. Could someone be using his niece to get back at him? Or to blackmail Josh? It was a lead she had to at least rule out.

"Josh said you're the principal at the high school Candace attended?"

"That's right. I've worked there since before Candace was even born, but I was promoted to principal three years ago."

"Do you have any enemies that might want to harm you or use Candace to harm you?"

"Me? No! I live a quiet life, Agent Richardson."

"Any particular students or parents who have given you any undue trouble lately?"

"We always have our issues but none I can think of."

"What about your staff and faculty? Is there anyone who jumps out that has been outspoken or threatening toward you or your daughter recently?"

"No. Nothing." Her eyes widened with surprise and fear. "Do you think this happened because of me? Is someone targeting me?"

"I simply have to ask. Josh mentioned a particular biology teacher?"

Patti nodded. "Peter Larkin. Josh feels he's inappropriate with the girls."

"You don't?"

"I haven't witnessed anything out of the ordinary and we've had no complaints about him. For some reason, Josh has fixated on him."

Was there a personal history between Josh and this Larkin? She would have to investigate that further. Perhaps his accusations were a way of getting back at an old adversary.

She hesitated before jotting down a note to ask Josh about that. He didn't strike her as someone so vindictive, but then again, she had to remind herself that she didn't really know him. Just because he'd risked his life yesterday to rescue her didn't mean he didn't have skeletons in his closet.

"Are there any friends or relatives where Candace might have gone?"

"Josh is the only family we have, and Candace didn't have a lot of friends. She was very shy."

"What about boyfriends?"

"She didn't have a boyfriend. As I said, she was awkward. I think it was difficult for her to make friends with her mother as the principal. Josh got her a cell phone for her birthday and Daniel… Chief Mills… checked her calls, but there weren't any numbers we didn't recognize and it's probably off because they can't track it. He said they also checked her computer and didn't find any suspicious emails. That's odd, isn't it? If she ran away from home, wouldn't we find something indicating where she went, a browser search or something revealing an area she was heading?"

Patti Adams had done her homework. It seemed as if she'd checked all avenues available to her.

They both turned at the sound of a car outside. "That will be Josh now. He thinks he has to check up on me."

Elise closed her notebook. Josh would not be pleased to find her here, but she reminded herself she wasn't in town to please Josh Adams.

Josh bit back anger as he pulled up to Patti's and noticed Elise's SUV parked by the curb. What was she doing driving, and more important, why had she gone behind his back and met with Patti? Why hadn't she waited as he'd asked? The truth was foul on his tongue. She was FBI. They did what they wanted, no matter who it hurt.

He couldn't believe he'd actually started to trust her.

He found them in Candace's room. Elise was digging through Candace's dresser.

"Josh, I wasn't expecting you," Patti said as he entered the room.

"I imagine you weren't," he said, his eyes shooting darts Elise's way. He'd actually begun to trust her. So much for that.

Elise stood. "I think I have all the information I need. Thank you, Mrs. Adams, for answering my questions and letting me look around."

Patti grabbed her hand. "Please call me Patti. And thank you, Agent Richardson. Thank you for not giving up on my little girl."

Elise visibly stiffened as Patti hugged her tightly. "I'll do my best to find her," she responded before hurrying out.

Josh turned to Patti. "I'll be right back. I want to talk to Agent Richardson." He followed Elise out the door and down the driveway. "What did you think you were doing?"

She turned to face him, her hazel eyes daring him to question her again. "I was doing my job...interviewing the girl's mother."

"Stop calling her 'the girl.' Her name is Candace." He raked his hand over his hair. He hadn't wanted this. He'd wanted to give Patti a heads-up before Elise swooped in upon her. "What did you say to her?"

"Only what was pertinent to the case."

"You gave me your assurances that you would wait."

"I know. I'm sorry. I shouldn't have agreed to that. Time is too valuable to waste on our personal concerns."

"What if she had suspected who you were?"

"But she didn't." She folded her arms. "For what it means, Josh, I am sorry about your brother. He was a real hero."

"Yes, he was. And now his daughter is missing. This family cannot lose another member, Elise. You find her. You owe it to us to find her."

Josh stormed back toward the house, his anger still burning that Elise would go behind his back that way. What if Patti suspected who Elise really was? He had no idea how she would react.

He turned back to remind her not to let on to Patti who she was when he spotted a car slowing down as it approached the house. As if it were happening in slow motion, Josh saw the window lower and the barrel of a gun pushed through. A moment later the explosion of gunfire filled the air.

Chapter Three

Elise felt Josh's weight as he grabbed her arms, threw her to the ground and leaped on top of her, shielding her with his body. The air around them lit with rapid gunfire, screams and the roar of a car engine taking off. Amid all that, Elise heard the rapid beat of Josh's heart, felt the warmth of his breath on her neck and inhaled the musky scent of his cologne. So why, in the middle of a firefight, was it the feel of his chin stubble against her skin that caused the hairs on her neck to stand on end?

As quickly as those sounds filled the air, they ended until only screams coming from inside the house were audible.

Josh leaped to his feet and rushed back inside. Elise followed him to find a terrified Patti crouched beneath the kitchen table, her eyes wide with fear.

Her hands shook as she clasped them together, trying to stop the overwhelming sobs that racked her body. Josh reached for her and she allowed him to pull her into his comforting embrace. Elise couldn't help but notice how the woman calmed. Josh and Patti seemed to have a very close relationship. Elise remembered what Patti had said about finding love again with someone she'd known for a long time. Could she have been talking about Josh? It made sense. He'd left the army to help her raise her daughter and she'd had nothing but good things to say about him.

Elise should be happy for them, but instead a twinge of jealousy swept through her as she remembered the way her hair had stood on end or the feel of his touch. What would it feel like to have those strong arms wrapped around her for more than lifesaving benefits?

She shook away those thoughts. Josh and Patti deserved to find happiness with one another…especially after she'd cost each of them a vital part of their lives and left a hole where Max should have been.

She turned her attention back to the practical matters at hand. "Did either of you get a look at the shooter? The make of the car? Anything?"

Patti shook her head. "I didn't see anything. I was hiding."

Josh squeezed her hand. "You did the right thing." He looked at Elise. "I think it was the same car that tried to run you down, but I can't be certain. I only got a glance."

"I was thinking the same thing. Regardless, this was no random drive-by shooting. They were targeting us, and I believe it may have something to do with Candace's disappearance. Someone is trying to stop us from investigating. I think it's safe to say we're dealing with more than a runaway situation."

You owe it to us to find her.
Elise couldn't get Josh's words out of her head as

the police arrived and started surveying the scene. He was right. She owed this family much for her part in Max's death. Finding Candace was the least she could do. She only hoped she could uncover what had happened to this girl.

Statistics were not on her side. If Candace had been abducted by the ring she was tracking, then it was likely she had already been moved out of town, out of the vicinity, probably even out of the state. But the trafficking ring wasn't necessarily what had caused Candace to vanish. There were all kinds of dangers for a young girl to fall into. Josh suspected this teacher, Peter Larkin, and Elise could hardly wait to question him about the girl's disappearance. Of course, if Candace had indeed been abducted by someone she knew, her chances of survival decreased. Elise hadn't wanted to tell Josh that, but statistically speaking, Candace's chances for survival were not good.

The best option for Candace was that she had run away from home, but this family seemed so certain that wasn't the case. However, Chief Mills seemed convinced that was what had happened. In fact, the missing persons file he'd opened on Candace focused very little on other, more sinister avenues of investigation. She caught the chief's gaze and saw accusation in his face. This incident would only add to his suspicion that she'd brought this trouble to town with her.

She pulled out her phone and dialed Lin's number. She needed someone to give her theory some credence and trusted Lin's discernment.

"It's not enough," he told her. "There's nothing conclusive that this shooting had any connection to the missing girl. It's just as likely to do with the uncle as it is with her."

"But it's the same car that tried to run me over, Lin."

"And who pulled you out of danger? Think about it, Elise. He was there. They could have been targeting him then and you got in the way." Lin chuckled. "You do have a way of tripping over danger."

Elise hadn't considered that aspect. Josh had stated he was on his way to find her when the car approached her. Was it possible they were targeting him? It seemed a logical angle to follow.

"But why trash my hotel room and steal my files?"

"They didn't know why you were in town. For all they knew, you could have been investigating whatever he's involved in. It makes more sense than a human trafficking ring you can't prove exists is trying to shut you up or scare you off."

Elise suddenly felt defensive. "Just because I can't prove it yet doesn't mean it doesn't exist."

She heard Lin pecking at the keys of his computer. "Let me do a background on the uncle—"

"His name is Josh Adams."

"Right. Perhaps Uncle Josh has more going on than we know…" She heard him typing again. "Like a Special Forces background."

She was stunned by that piece of news. "Josh was Special Forces?"

"Yes. The Army Rangers."

Elise glanced across the yard at Josh, who was giving his statement to one of the officers on the scene.

The Rangers were often called into perilous situations. He could have been part of a dangerous mission or had a high-level clearance. He might have made enemies during his time in the service, enemies that wouldn't hesitate to use his family against him.

Perhaps Lin was right when he said the man in the car had been after Josh. He'd been nearby when the car tried to run her down and with her here at Patti's house when the same car fired at them. He'd tracked Elise down before anyone else even knew she was in town. He'd been the one to press for the investigation into Candace's disappearance. He, more than anyone, was adamant that something had happened to his niece. Did he know more than he was letting on? Was he hiding something, something about his time in the military that he couldn't share?

She gritted her teeth. He'd been vague in the car when she'd asked about his time in the military. And she'd let it pass.

Stupid, stupid, stupid.

She flushed with embarrassment, realizing she'd allowed a flash of attraction to someone she hardly knew to cloud her judgment. What would Lin think of her if he knew? She would be a laughingstock at the Bureau.

"Thanks for your help, Lin."

"Be careful," he said before hanging up.

Elise slipped her phone into her pocket. At some point, she and Josh were going to have to have a further conversation about his military past.

Josh had been in plenty of firefights in his time with the Rangers, but none that elicited the kind of fear he felt tonight. This wasn't right. This was a drive-by shooting in his own hometown, at his sister-in-law's house, involving civilians, people he cared about.

The police surveyed the scene, gathered evidence

and took their statements about what had happened, but Josh knew they wouldn't be much help. He hadn't got a good look at the car or the inhabitants, and none of Patti's neighbors reported seeing anything out of the ordinary before the shooting. Josh watched the forensics team pull bullets from the house, the Jeep and Elise's SUV. Surprisingly, both vehicles still ran, although Daniel was less than thrilled about the damage to his Jeep. Fortunately for Josh, he was more concerned about Patti's safety. He insisted she not stay at the house alone, and Patti agreed to go stay temporarily with a friend.

When they were gone, Josh inspected the damage and knew they'd been fortunate no one had been hit. Bullet holes lined one side of the house and had busted out the front windows. Those would need to be boarded up before he could leave.

Elise approached him as he was searching through the shed for wood and nails to secure the house.

"I'm heading back to the hotel," she told him.

He was glad for once that she had her own vehicle because he wasn't sure he wanted to be alone with her in such close quarters.

"Don't worry," she told him. "We'll find out who did this."

She reached out to him, but her hand on his arm wasn't enough to reassure him.

He bit back his anger aimed at her. Why had she gone to Patti's alone? Had she brought danger to his sister-in-law's house? And what if he hadn't been there when the gunfire began? Would she have been killed? Would Patti?

She must have sensed his resistance because she

didn't leave immediately. Instead, she turned to him and said uncertainly, "I want to go to the school tomorrow and interview Larkin."

As much as he wanted to be there for that, he wasn't sure he could continue on with Elise if he couldn't trust her. But he couldn't give up on finding Candace either and he still needed the FBI resources to do that, especially now that the stakes had been upped by tonight's shooting.

He needed to remain close to her. Plain and simple. "You shouldn't be driving. You still have a concussion. Give me a few minutes to board up these windows. Then I'll drive you back to the hotel."

"I have my SUV. Plus, I still wanted to stop to get a new computer."

"Then I'll follow behind to make sure you get there safely."

He secured the windows then made sure Elise made it safely to the hotel after a stop at the office-supply store before heading back to his apartment. Tossing his jacket onto a chair, he fell onto his couch. He rubbed his hands over his face, frustration washing over him. He'd been on rough missions before, assignments where the waiting for intel was frustrating and painstakingly difficult, but he'd always been assured that his part of the mission would eventually occur. Now, in this situation, he was on the sidelines. He should be out combing the area for Candace, but without search parameters, he would be hunting futilely. He was as much in the dark about her whereabouts as anyone else and he hated it.

He picked up his phone and dialed the number of his buddy and fellow former army ranger. After the fatal final mission that had decimated their ranger squadron, Colton had lost his faith and fallen hard into drinking and gambling until Josh and the remaining members of their squad joined in an intervention that sent Colton into therapy. He recovered both his faith and his sobriety, but not before he'd lost his ranger status and ultimately left the army. Unlike Josh and others who'd taken jobs in the security industry, Colton had retired to a cattle ranch in Georgia.

"Josh-u-a!" Colton exclaimed when he answered. He had a habit of stretching out Josh's name into three syllables. Josh grinned at the familiar expression of greeting. When Josh explained the situation involving his missing niece, his brother and even the arrival of the unexpected FBI agent, Colton was quick to offer his assistance. "Do I need to come help with the search?"

"Right now, we don't even know where we're searching," Josh told him, not at all surprised by the offer. His brothers-in-arms remained a close-knit group even though they'd gone their separate ways.

"We've all been in situations where we've had to work with officials from the various three-letter agencies that we weren't thrilled with, but we make it work because we have to. Stick with the FBI agent. Don't let her make a move without you. And remember, Josh, to let God's word light your way. We know better than most that when you're moving in the dark, you take it step by step."

Josh twirled the key he wore on a chain around his neck as a reminder of his ranger days and the command his squad leader always imparted to them from

Psalm 119—*God's light is a lamp unto your feet. He will guide our paths always.*

He'd repeated that verse whenever things on the mission got patchy, when they couldn't see the wisdom of their actions, reminding his men that God could see all things no matter how dark the night or how hopeless the situation seemed. God's guidance was the lamp that lit their paths, one step of faith at a time.

His squad leader had also recited those words to them only hours before the ambush that claimed six members of their squad including him. If God had truly seen that coming, Josh wondered again why He hadn't stopped it. A single interpreter that had double-crossed them had changed everything. For that matter, why hadn't God stopped whatever had happened to Candace or acted to prevent Max's death?

"What I wouldn't give for a pair of God-centered NVGs," Josh commented, referring to the night-vision goggles the squad used to see in the dark.

"We have to trust those above us."

That was the rub and Colton knew it as well as Josh did. They'd trusted those above them…and they'd been left abandoned in the fire.

"Even when we can't see the big picture," Colton finished. "Besides, we have a Commander in Chief that will never leave us and never forsake us."

Josh nodded, understanding Colton was referring to Jesus as Commander in Chief. Josh wished he had a quarter of Colton's renewed faith.

"I'm six hours away, but I'm on the road the moment you give the word."

Josh thanked him then hung up, as always feeling better after speaking with Colton. It was a nice reminder that he wasn't alone, despite how isolated he felt in this life he'd chosen.

When he'd first returned to Westhaven, he'd expected to step right back into his old life, but he was no longer the kid who'd cruised the streets after sunset. He no longer cared about football, a staple of small-town life while he was growing up. And despite stepping back into civilian life, he didn't feel as if he fit. He was still the square peg being shoved into the round notch. He hadn't yet been able to recapture the feeling of belonging that he'd had in his youth…or with his ranger team. He was acting a part, the part of a man he thought he should be instead of the man he really was. That man he kept hidden deep, deep inside. No one here would understand that man, the soldier who'd made the choices he'd made or known the consequences he'd faced. No one in Westhaven understood that the danger and risk were not to be feared but just another issue to confront…no one with the possible exception of Elise.

Was it possible she was a kindred spirit even if she was a three-lettered agent? Being FBI, she would understand the order, the risk and the chain of command. She would know the structures of missions and about risking her life for a greater purpose. He stared past his ribbons and his medal of honor to the photograph of him and Max as teens. Even if she'd never lost a brother, she might understand losing a brother-in-arms.

He sighed wearily and rubbed his eyes. Was he actually thinking Elise Richardson might understand him? The woman who'd taken his brother from him? Could he ever find it in his heart to forgive her for her role in Max's death? Why couldn't he get past this bitterness that had taken root inside of him? She wasn't really responsible. He knew that. Max had died doing what Max had always done—helping others.

He propped his elbows on his knees and leaned into his hands. He was tired of the bitter taste of unforgiveness in his mouth. He was tired of pretending to be someone he wasn't. He was ready to find the joy and comfort of life he knew he should have. "God, release me," he prayed. "Your word is a lamp unto my feet, and I will follow Your lead."

Even if that first step meant trusting Elise Richardson.

Elise was setting up her new computer equipment when someone knocked on the hotel door. She opened it to find Bobby Danbar.

"A delivery came for you, Agent," he said, holding out a FedEx envelope.

Her flash drive.

Thank you, Lin.

She took the envelope and set it on the table. She hadn't yet confronted Mr. Danbar on spilling the beans about her being in town. Now seemed to be as good a time as any. "Come in, please."

"Is there something else I can do for you, Agent?" he asked, stepping into the room and surveying, perhaps looking for something that needed repair.

She pasted on her best interrogation look and faced him. "As a matter of fact, there is, Mr. Danbar. I've heard rumors around town that you were bragging that the FBI had checked into your hotel."

His eyes grew wide at her accusation and he had the good sense to look ashamed. "I may have let that slip while I was out drinking with some friends. I apologize, Agent Richardson."

"Make certain nothing else slips out while you're out drinking, Mr. Danbar."

"Yes, ma'am." He hurried out the door and closed it behind him.

Elise opened the envelope, confirming it contained her flash drive. She spent the next few hours reloading her computer and printing out photographs on her new mobile printer. She taped up several of girls who she was convinced had been abducted as part of this human trafficking ring. She added the photo Patti had given her of Candace. Finding these girls was the key to finding Candace or vice versa. There was an evil presence simmering beneath these cases, one she had yet been unable to uncover. These girls needed her to stop this.

She closed her eyes, the memory of that fateful night ten years earlier still so vivid in her mind. She'd been minding her own business when the stranger tried to abduct her. She could still feel the weight of the man's hand as he grabbed her, still hear her own screams for help ringing in her ears, still feel the hardness of the gun against her skin. The sheer terror and panic that had grabbed hold of her had never completely dissipated. Had it not been for the intervention of Max Adams, Elise was certain she wouldn't have made it out of that situation alive.

She sat on the bed and stared at each of the girls' photos she'd taped to the wall. Each one of them knew that feeling, that same feeling she'd experienced, and much worse.

She couldn't…she wouldn't…give up on finding them.

* * *

Josh spent the morning going over security specs for a client trip to Baghdad. Like so many of his ranger buddies had done, he'd gone into the security business. It was what he knew. He knew how to spot evil and protect from it.

Yet he hadn't been able to protect Candace...or his squad.

That cold reality pressed into him, causing him to question his competence and go over the specs one more time to make certain he'd accounted for all contingencies.

He didn't like the thought of leaving the country with Candace still missing and he'd briefly thought of handing off the assignment to someone else. The trip was still a month away, but he might still if she hadn't been found by the time he had to leave. But it seemed now that the FBI was in town investigating perhaps things would move more quickly.

He shuddered, thinking on all the evil things that could have happened to Candace. Whether she'd run away from home or not, evil knew no boundaries. He quickly pushed those thoughts from his mind. He would drive himself nuts pondering all the things that could have happened to her. Instead, he had to forge ahead, reminding himself that she was out there and he could find her...even if he hadn't so far.

He should be grateful that the FBI was in town looking for Candace. It was more than anyone else had done, but he couldn't get past the fact that it was Elise Richardson. Was this some cosmic joke that God was playing on his family? But he'd decided to trust Elise and he meant to do it.

When he arrived to pick her up, Elise seemed steadier on her feet and didn't require his assistance to walk to the car. He was glad for the distance. Things between them had got too cloudy, and being so near to her had only blurred the lines. He had to keep reminding himself who she was—the woman who'd caused his brother's death—because he was surprised by the intensity of his attraction to her. She was someone he could see himself falling for in another time and place, but despite her involvement in his brother's death, she was a woman who put her life on the line every day and he wasn't going to set himself up to lose someone else he cared for.

She popped a couple of Tylenol as he drove to the high school and parked. He hadn't seen her take anything stronger, although he knew she had to be feeling that concussion. She was devoted to staying alert so she could find Candace.

Patti was waiting for them with a copy of Candace's class schedule and the combination to her locker. "I looked through it when Candace first went missing, but I didn't remove anything."

Elise thanked her then followed him to Candace's locker. He had it opened in moments. On first glance, he saw normal locker stuff—schoolbooks, notebooks and a sweater hanging on a hook.

Elise took the schedule Patti had given her and compared the books in the locker to her class schedule.

"What are you looking for?" Josh asked her.

"Both her biology and algebra textbooks are missing."

"Is that important?"

"A girl who is going to run away takes the schoolbooks out of her backpack before she leaves. I don't see these books in here and I didn't see them in her bedroom, either."

He hadn't even thought about that. If she'd run away, she wouldn't have taken her books with her.

The bell rang and kids began to pour into the hallway from the various classrooms. Josh scanned their faces, looking for one in particular. Brooke Martin. Elise had said she wanted to speak to the girl. "There she is." He pushed through the crowd of kids. "Brooke!"

The petite blonde stopped and turned worried brown eyes on him. "Mr. Adams. What are you doing here?"

"This is Elise Richardson. She's with the FBI and is here looking into Candace's disappearance."

The girl's eyes widened and she frowned. "Why? Candace ran away."

Elise stepped up beside him. "I'd like to talk with you about the last time you saw her and also about the note you gave the police."

Brooke frowned and became jittery. "I have to get to my next class."

"This is important," Josh said.

"And it won't take long," Elise assured her.

Still, Brooke hesitated. "I should phone my father first. He wouldn't like me talking to you without him." She pulled her cell phone from her bag and began dialing.

Josh didn't like the way she was acting. This was Candace's best friend. Why wouldn't she be happy to help in any way she could? "Does she seem edgy to you?"

He could see Elise had her doubts but was reserving her opinion. "Being questioned by the FBI can make anyone nervous. She may be worried about getting Candace in trouble."

Brooke turned back to them. "My dad doesn't want me talking to you. He said I've already told the police everything I know. You can get my statement from them."

"Can I speak to him? Is he still on the phone?"

"No. He said I should go on to my next class."

She turned to leave but Josh reached for her arm. "Brooke, please reconsider. Think about how your family would feel if you were missing. Candace's mother is worried about her and so am I. We just want to bring her home."

"She's not in any trouble, Brooke," Elise said, playing up that angle. "Neither are you if you're covering for her."

"I'm not covering for her." She fidgeted with her books nervously.

Elise didn't seem to notice. Her tone softened and she inched toward Brooke as if they were old friends just catching up. "Did she tell you where she would go if she ran away? Was she heading anywhere specific?"

"She always wanted to go to Florida."

Josh shook his head, knowing that wasn't true. Candace had never expressed an interest in going to Florida. If anything, she was always fond of the mountains.

"Brooke, have you spoken to Candace since she disappeared? Has she tried to contact you?"

"No."

More lies. Josh was certain of it. He knew the way she fidgeted and twirled her hair were telltale signs that she was thinking about her answers. Surely, Elise noticed, too?

Elise handed Brooke one of her business cards. "I'd like you to call me if you remember anything that might be helpful."

Brooke nodded, and although it looked as if she wanted to bolt away, she hesitated long enough to ask one more question of Elise. "Are you going to find Candace?"

"If I find something to indicate that she didn't leave of her own free will, I will use every resource the FBI has to bring her home." Everything from her stance to her expression showed her resolve, her determination to find out what had happened to Candace, and Josh felt heat rise on his neck. How could he have doubted her? It sometimes seemed she was the only one on his side…on Candace's side.

Brooke hurried to her next class, her expression at Elise's response one of concern and anxiety instead of appreciation.

Elise turned to him. "She knows more than she's letting on."

Josh bit back a retort. He wanted to push Brooke, to demand she reveal what she knew, but he, like Elise, knew that would only shut her down. Elise had already shown restraint and compassion in dealing with Brooke. But Brooke was supposed to be Candace's best friend. Why wouldn't she want to do anything and everything to bring her home safely?

A sick feeling raced through his gut. There were only two reasons he could think of for Brooke to remain quiet—either she was afraid of something or she already knew Candace was not coming home safely.

He raked a hand over his face and blew out a breath. "Should we try to talk to her again?"

She nodded. "Maybe she'll respond better in a more private environment. I'll ask Patti if she has a study hall. Away from the crowd of kids, she might open up more."

Josh scanned the hall again, spotting Larkin standing outside his classroom. His gaze landed and lingered too long on one female student passing by. Josh felt sick watching this man.

He'd been all over the world and seen evil, and Peter Larkin was the worst kind—the kind that preyed on innocence. He bit back anger, and his muscles tensed. If this man had done something to harm Candace…

Elise followed his gaze. "That's Larkin?"

He clenched his fists as he nodded. Watching this man made him physically ill. Every girl in this school was at risk with this man around. Why wouldn't anyone believe him?

But Elise would believe. He knew she'd seen what he had. She'd seen Larkin's true self.

She placed a reassuring hand on his arm. "If he did something to Candace, I will find out."

He believed her. One thing he'd come to learn about Elise was that she was determined. He liked that. She now knew the kind of man Peter Larkin was, and she wouldn't give up on making sure he didn't harm anyone else.

Larkin kept glancing their way as kids herded into classrooms and the bell rang, but when the hall was clear, instead of going back into his classroom, he came toward them.

"Let's go." Josh cupped her arm and led her away.

Another confrontation with Larkin wouldn't do any good. Elise had seen the man for what he was and that was what mattered.

"Are you following me now?" He looked at Elise. "Does he have you believing his lies?" He kept up with them as Josh hurried down the hall with Elise in tow, but Larkin didn't give up. "I won't be harassed this way!"

Josh couldn't take his feigned innocence anymore. He stopped and faced him. "I know you did something to Candace. If I find out you hurt her—"

Larkin got in his face. "How dare you accuse me!"

"That's enough, both of you," Elise said, stepping in between them.

Larkin pushed her, shoving her back against a row of lockers. Josh heard the slam of her body against the metal and the groan of pain it elicited.

This man had taken his niece, had harmed his family and now had shoved Elise. He reacted instinctively, grabbing Larkin by the shirt and ramming him against the same row of lockers. He pressed his arm into Larkin's neck, essentially pinning him there.

This man would not harm one more person he cared about.

Chapter Four

"Stop it! Both of you stop it!" Patti pushed through the crowd of kids that had formed and pulled Josh's arm away. "What is wrong with you two? Josh, let him go."

His adrenaline level began to fall and the look of disappointment on both Elise's and Patti's faces was evident. He released his hold and turned to Elise. "Are you okay?"

"I'm fine," she said, climbing to her feet.

Patti turned to address the crowd of students. "The excitement is over. Everyone return to your classes."

As the crowd dispersed, Larkin rubbed his neck where Josh had shoved his arm against him. "I should press charges."

"You're not going to do that," Elise told him. "You just assaulted a federal agent." She flashed her FBI credentials.

"That was an accident and you know it was."

"I'm conducting an investigation into Candace Adams's disappearance, Mr. Larkin, which means I'm asking questions of all of Candace's teachers."

"My answer is the same today as it was when the

police questioned me. I don't know anything about Candace's disappearance."

"Then you won't mind answering my questions."

"Fine," Larkin stated, "but right now I have a class to teach."

"I can wait."

"I have fifth period free."

"I'll see you then."

Josh watched him return to his classroom and shut the door behind him.

He glanced around at the empty hallways. The disapproving look on Patti's face spoke to him. "How am I supposed to keep the kids from fighting when my own brother-in-law and one of my teachers are brawling in the hallway?"

"I'm sorry that happened, Patti." He turned to Elise. "Are you sure you're okay? It sounded like he pushed you hard against that locker." He cupped her face, noticing the way her green eyes flickered. She trembled beneath his hand.

"I'm fine."

He doubted that was true. She'd taken blow after blow, all for the sake of him and his family, yet she kept going. He was torn between his desire to let her loose to do her job and her obvious need for rest. "Don't worry. I'll make sure he doesn't lay a hand on you during the interview."

Elise looked at him with apologetic eyes. "I don't think you should be there when I interview Larkin."

"I want to be there."

"There is clearly intense animosity between the two of you. Your presence will only shut him down."

"You don't really think he's going to admit to hurting Candace, do you?"

"It isn't what he says. It's what he doesn't say. I'm going to hang around the school and try to speak with Candace's teachers and other students. Why don't you come back and pick me up later?"

She was dismissing him? That wasn't going to happen. "I'm not leaving. Someone has tried to kill you twice. I won't leave you here unprotected."

"Nothing is going to happen to me at the school surrounded by all these people. I'll be fine."

Patti spoke up. "Agent Richardson is right. Your being here, your accusations against Mr. Larkin, won't help. They will only make the situation more volatile."

"All I've done is try to help find Candace."

"I know you have, and I appreciate it, but Josh, she's the FBI. She's trained for this. Please. I know you want to do everything you can do to help Candace. Right now, what you can do is leave and let Agent Richardson do her job."

Her rebuke stung him.

But Elise's face softened and so did her tone. "Josh, give me a chance to handle this my way. This is what I do. Let me do it."

He rubbed his face. He hated being left out and he didn't like Elise confronting Larkin on her own, but he had to admit she was right. Larkin was not going to open up with him around, especially not after what had just happened between them.

He reluctantly nodded his agreement.

"I'll have the AV room cleared for you," Patti told Elise. "You can conduct your interviews in there."

"That'll be fine." She turned to Josh and gave him a

reassuring smile. "Don't worry. If Larkin is involved, I'll find out."

He walked outside to the Jeep and got in, slamming the door hard. His mind was already mentally ticking off equipment he had in his footlocker at home that might be helpful. His fingers turned the key on his neck, ready to pull it off and use it. He was certain he had listening equipment in there that could give him access to Elise's interview with Larkin. But what good would that do? She'd been right when she'd stated it wasn't what he said that would give him away.

He leaned against the steering wheel, realizing that she was also right about his being there causing Larkin to shut down. He'd already confronted the man on three separate occasions, and it had accomplished nothing. He wasn't used to this process. It wasn't what he'd been trained for. He was trained for taking action, and not knowing what was the right action to take was the most frustrating part of this entire situation.

He longed to act, but his actions had no purpose. He needed Elise and her three-letter agency connections to point him in the right direction.

Elise spent the rest of the afternoon trying to form a profile of Candace Adams. What she found from speaking to Candace's teachers was a shy girl who was an above-average student. However, recently her grades had begun to suffer.

Elise strolled the halls of the high school, noticing the stringed lights and Christmas decorations that had been hung. It saddened her to think of all the girls that would not be home for Christmas this year, including

Candace. How would her family survive a Christmas without her?

She'd seen the frustration on Josh's face, but she couldn't give in. If Larkin knew something about Candace, he would clam up the moment Josh turned those accusing eyes on him. Josh was a man of action, but right now what they needed was patience and a sharp investigative eye.

She hoped she was up to the task.

When Larkin entered the AV room, Elise didn't speak immediately except to suggest he sit down. She spent the next few moments perusing the file in front of her, allowing silence to fill the room and the tension to build. It was a common ploy meant to make people uncomfortable and on edge.

And it worked. Larkin squirmed under her apparent lack of questioning. He jiggled his knee up and down and his fingers drummed against the table. Once or twice, he rubbed his balding head anxiously. Finally, he sighed loudly, and when Elise still didn't react, he gruffly demanded her attention.

"Do you have questions for me, Agent?"

She glanced up at him then back to her file without a word.

"I don't know why you've brought me in here. I barely knew that girl."

"She's one of your students."

"She's in one class along with thirty other kids. She didn't stand out."

Elise looked up from her files and fiddled with her pen. "Yet didn't you single her out to help tutor Ben Massey for extra assistance?" She'd discovered that bit of information while speaking with other students in Candace's class.

He fidgeted at that reminder and tried to cover his previous statement. "She had the highest grade average in the class. He needed the help. It doesn't mean I know what happened to her."

"I didn't ask if you knew what happened to her."

"Isn't that why you're here? Investigating her disappearance? The officers I've talked to said she ran away. Since when does the FBI investigate runaways?"

"My reason for being here is none of your concern, Mr. Larkin. Your only job is to answer any and all questions I choose to ask to the best of your knowledge."

He fidgeted again. "I still don't see the point. I barely knew that girl."

"What about Brooke Martin? How well do you know her?"

"I—I don't know. She's in one of my classes, too."

"The same class as Candace?"

"That's right."

"So I take it you don't get very invested with your students. Why did you become a teacher? Was it so you could have summers off?"

She knew her questions were abrupt and off-putting, but she wanted to see how Larkin responded to pressure. She already knew he was a lech…but was he a predator, as well?

"I enjoy teaching," he stated matter-of-factly. "I'm very invested in my students."

"Of course, you're right. That was my mistake. In fact, I've learned from several people that you often keep students after school for special attention. Many of the girls commented on it."

He glared at her. "As I've stated, I'm very invested in my students' progress. Some of them need extra help, which I am more than happy to offer."

"So you offer your personal assistance?"

"Of course."

"But not Ben Massey? You passed him off to Candace. Is it only the female students you personally give your after-school attention to?"

He squared up against her accusation. "I've done nothing wrong, Agent."

Elise studied him. "Not yet."

He sighed, a weary, frustrated sigh. "I thought you were here to ask me about Candace Adams. I have no idea what happened to her. I'm sure Principal Adams and her brother-in-law brought you here to pin something on me. As if with all the other girls in the school I would obsess over Candace. Do you know Josh has attacked me twice? I should be the one pressing charges against him. He's got a vendetta against me and I haven't done anything. You know you can't believe anything he says about me, right?"

Elise stood. "That's all the questions I have today, Mr. Larkin. I may contact you again if I need anything further."

He remained seated. "I still don't see why the FBI is investigating. The girl ran away. Everyone knows that."

Elise leaned over the table and locked eyes with him. "Let me make myself clear, Mr. Larkin. If I find anything linking you to this girl's disappearance, I will be all over you and every detail of your life. I will leave no stone unturned to make certain you pay for any harm you've done to this or any other girl."

She walked to the door and held it open. Larkin stormed out. She shuddered at the idea of being anywhere near the man. He was certainly sleazy and inappropriate, neither of which was against the law.

Now she only had to prove he was a predator, as well.

Elise finished her interviews then gathered up her notes, including the writing samples she'd requested and received from several of Candace's teachers. She hoped to compare the writing from the samples to the runaway note to confirm Candace had actually written the note herself.

She wasn't expecting to find differently. In fact, if the samples showed Candace had not written the notes, that would indicate to Elise that she was not a victim of the trafficking ring and her attention would turn more likely to another suspect, namely Peter Larkin. His interview had raised more suspicions. Josh had been right to suspect him of something…but was it the trafficking ring she'd been investigating, or was he simply a predator of his students? She would conduct a more thorough search of his background, including contacting past employers to see if he'd ever been accused previously of inappropriate behavior with his students.

Her phone beeped, indicating a message had been received. She assumed it would be Josh letting her know he'd arrived. Instead, she found a message from Lin containing an attachment. His message said, Uncovered information on Uncle Josh. Elise noticed the attachment was labeled *Army Ranger Incident Report*. She'd suspected there was something about his time in the military he'd been reluctant to expound on. Now it appeared her suspicions were on target. But could the incident referenced in this report contain the information that he'd been so determined not to share?

She opened the file. Words like *inaccurate intelligence*, *commander incompetence* and *multiple fatalitics* jumped out at her. Elise quickly closed the file and put away her phone. She felt as though reading it would violate some unspoken agreement she had with Josh.

Still, she had a duty to uncover any evidence that might have a connection to Candace's disappearance and she couldn't rule out Josh's time in the service... especially now that she knew about his Special Forces background and the incident report.

Still, she hesitated. It just felt wrong.

It would be better if he shared this information with her. But she owed a debt to Candace and Patti, too. Not only was she determined to uncover this ring, but from the moment she'd discovered Candace was Max Adams's daughter, Elise had vowed to find her. She owed a debt that couldn't be ignored, and she couldn't keep that promise without thoroughly investigating every angle of potential danger that might have impacted Candace. She would give Josh the opportunity to tell her the details of this report before she read it, but she would have to know the truth about it one way or another.

She headed toward the outside doors to wait for Josh.

The matter of Candace's missing backpack and schoolbooks still bothered her. If Larkin had abducted Candace, what had he done with those? And did he even possess the means to secure a girl against her will? She needed to find out more about his home environment, but if she shared her plans with Josh he would insist on tagging along. She would have to come up with an excuse so he wouldn't know what she was doing. It wouldn't work being stuck in a vehicle with him for hours, his blue eyes piercing into her in an enclosed space. Those eyes…she could lose herself in those eyes and in his fierce gaze. She couldn't help admiring his passion for finding his niece. Like her, he recognized evil when he saw it. She was sure that was from his time in the military.

But she couldn't bear spending so much time with the brother of the man she'd killed. She was getting too close to Josh. It was beginning to affect her judgment. Why was she relying on him so much? It did feel good to have someone believe in her again, to have someone on her side. She'd been working on her own for so long.

Her phone beeped again and this time it was Josh letting her know he'd arrived to pick her up.

"How did the interview go?" he asked when she answered.

"You mean did he confess to harming your niece?"

He grew impatient. "Elise, please don't keep me in the dark."

"Is it true you attacked him twice?"

"No! I've never laid a hand on the man except for today, and believe me, it has taken every ounce of strength and restraint I possess to keep from doing so."

"He said you did."

"Well, then, he's a liar in addition to a predator." She heard the bite in his voice and knew he was telling the truth.

"I believe you."

"About him being a predator?"

"About it taking all your strength and restraint to keep from attacking him. I only spent a short time with the man, but I could shower for a week and not wash away the ick. I can't believe he's still teaching."

"There haven't been any complaints about him except from me, and since I don't have a child in the school, the school board won't listen to me. Without a complaint from a parent, they won't do anything. Besides, Patti says she's never seen anything inappropriate. I was beginning to think I was the only one who saw it." He hesitated. "In fact, I was beginning to wonder if I was just imagining something wrong so I would have someone to target my frustration at."

She understood that comment. It was easier to be angry when there was a visible target. It was much harder when justice seemed so far-reaching and unattainable. Hadn't she discovered that with this ring? She had no suspect to target, no visible trail, only an instinct and a gut feeling that she was close to uncovering an evil that had been lurking beneath the surface for too long.

"What's our next step?" Josh queried.

Our next step.

She smiled, liking the idea that she was no longer working alone. Someone believed in her and what she was doing. She had to admit it felt good to have Josh on her side. She changed her mind about excluding him and was about to share her thoughts on how they could uncover more information when someone grabbed her from behind. Elise tried to scream, but her assailant pressed his hand over her mouth, preventing it. Her cell phone slipped from her hand, hitting the floor with a thud, and she heard Josh's voice calling frantically to her through the phone.

"Elise? Elise, are you there? What's happening?"

Her assailant stuffed a rag into her mouth then threw a bag over her face and everything went dark. He pushed her to the floor. She reached for her gun, but he knocked it from her hand. She struggled to overpower him, but his weight on her arms and legs was powerful as he tied her hands behind her back.

Her assailant dragged her down the hallway and out the door. She felt concrete stinging into her back. She heard the sound of voices of kids in the distance. She was in the parking lot. If he managed to get her into an automobile and out of the parking lot and away from the school, she was in real trouble.

Her only hope now was that Josh would reach her before that happened.

Josh leaped from the Jeep, the phone still to his ear. He couldn't hear a struggle anymore. The last thing he'd heard sounded like doors closing. He scanned the parking lot and spotted a figure moving in the afternoon sun with what looked like a person slung over his shoulder. He was headed toward the woods.

Elise!

He ran toward them, leaping from behind the assailant and kicking his legs out from under him, catching Elise when he dropped her. The man hit the ground then scrambled to his feet and took off running. Josh carefully set Elise on the ground, grabbed the bag from her head and pulled the rag from her mouth.

"Are you hurt?" He used his knife to cut the restraints around her hands.

She shook her head. "I'm fine. Go!"

He took off running after the assailant, chasing him into the woods. Josh still hadn't got a view of the man's face, but he committed what he could to memory—tall and thin, almost lanky in build, approximately six foot three, long dark hair, narrow shoulders and a tattoo on his left upper arm. The man leaped onto a hill and Josh followed suit, running full out, something he hadn't done in quite a while. There was a time when he could run at his max speed even in the high elevations of the Afghan mountains, but he'd been a year out of training and had a knee injured by shrapnel in the attack on his squad. He would never be able to chase this man down.

He changed tactics, stopping and reaching for his knife again. He threw it, his aim true and straight. The knife dug into the lower back of the assailant, causing him to hit the ground. He quickly scrambled to his feet again and came up cursing.

He pulled the knife from his back and turned on Josh with it.

Josh caught up with the man, getting a good look at his face. This was a hand-to-hand encounter now and this guy had no idea who he was messing with.

Josh landed a couple of shots, kicking the knife from the man's hands, then knocked him down, too, before a shot rang out, zinging past him. Josh fell, taking cover as his eyes scanned the tree line for the source of gunfire.

The skinny guy got up, wiped off his pants and grinned as if knowing that shot was meant for his protection. Obviously he was right because no other shots rang out as he took off running again.

Josh started up once more only to be met with another gunshot. This one hit a tree nearby. He took a chance and jumped behind a tree as shots rang out again. He used the trees for cover as he made his way up the hill. Movement and shouting caught his attention. He rushed up the hill noting two men, one holding a rifle, jumping into a gray car and speeding away.

This hadn't been a single-assailant assault. These men had come prepared to take Elise hostage and do no-telling-what to her.

He headed back down the embankment and rushed through the woods to where he'd left her, stopping only to pick up his knife.

Elise had moved to lean against a car. He noticed blood on the ground around her. The restraint he'd cut from her earlier was a common zip-tie restraint often used by police and military. They were quick, simple to use and effective to keep a person immobilized.

A chill ran through him at the thought of what could have happened to her. "Are you okay?"

He looked her over and didn't see any real injuries except the scrapes on her arms. His mind flooded with images of what could have happened to her. What if he hadn't been here yet? What if he'd been just a few minutes later?

But who were those men? And why were they after Elise?

And did it have anything to do with Candace's disappearance?

Josh whipped his arm around her back and helped her to her feet, but pain ripped through her thigh as she placed pressure on her right leg.

He stiffened at her cry of pain. "Am I hurting you?"

She motioned toward the back of her leg where the metal shard had cut her. Her pant leg was wet with blood. Her assailant had probably reopened that wound when he'd dragged her across the concrete. She braced herself for the pain. "I'll be fine." She took another step, but even with his strong arms surrounding her, the pain was unbearable.

Finally, he moved his hands beneath her knees and swept her up into his arms. "It'll be easier if I carry you."

She felt ridiculous being toted but was amazed by the strength of this man. He carried her with seemingly little effort. She felt the muscles in his arms and back tense and placed her arm around his neck as he carried her, noting the span of his shoulders. This was a man, a powerful, strong, muscular man, and she soaked in the feeling of being nestled safely by his embrace.

He carried her into the school and placed her on the couch in the front office, making certain her leg was raised on the arm, then fetched her a cup of cool water that helped soothe her raw and ragged throat. She hadn't been able to scream because of the gag, but her throat was still sore from trying.

She leaned back onto the couch and relaxed. Her mind insisted on recounting the incident, analyzing the players and trying to comprehend how it fit into Candace's disappearance, but her body complained, demanding a moment of peace and restoration. She closed her eyes and tried to concentrate on her breathing. She heard Josh speaking—she assumed on the phone because she didn't hear another voice—to Chief Mills. Soon, the police would arrive and she would have to recount the incident again and again.

However, as she replayed the incident in her head, the only image she could call to mind was of Josh and the expression on his face as he pulled off the hood. The painful look in his blue eyes had stunned her—worry and anger clouding his face before he took off after the assailant, his long, muscular legs quickly closing the distance between her and the woods.

Her phone rang, jolting Elise awake. She hadn't meant to doze off, but the startling ring brought her back up. She jumped around, searching for her phone.

"I have it," Josh stated. "I retrieved it while you were sleeping." He glanced at the screen. "It's the hospital."

Elise nodded. "That's Nurse Stringer calling to check on me. Every three hours like clockwork."

Josh smiled then answered the phone. "Carolyn, how's it going? This is Josh Adams." He paused for her to speak.

Elise interrupted. "Tell her I'm fine. No headache, no dizziness, no blurry vision."

He relayed her message then hung up. "Did I just lie to Carolyn Stringer?"

"I'm fine, Josh."

They heard someone approaching, and Elise tensed and raised herself up on the sofa. She relaxed again when she saw Chief Mills enter.

Josh relayed what had happened from his perspective, and then the chief turned to her.

Elise struggled to remember the moments before her assailant had come up behind her. Had she heard anything out of the ordinary? Had there been any unusual sounds or scents? She couldn't think of anything that would help.

Josh was more helpful, having gone face-to-face

with the assailant, and he'd even obtained a sample of his blood with his knife. "I didn't recognize him. He was young, probably only in his early twenties, and he had a tattoo on his arm."

Chief Mills snorted then scrolled through his phone until he reached a photo. He showed it to Josh.

"That's him," Josh confirmed. "Who is he?"

"Taylor Johnson."

Elise recognized the name. "His fingerprint was identified in my hotel room. It seems Taylor may be the key to solving Candace's disappearance."

Chief Mills wasn't convinced. "We don't know he had anything to do with Candace's disappearance. All we know is he is targeting you for some reason. This could still have only to do with you. So I have to ask you again, Agent Richardson—is it possible this is related to another case?"

"No." She was less convinced this was the result of someone following her to town now. "This is a local boy. You said you know him from previous run-ins. We have to find him now. I, for one, am ready to get to the bottom of this."

Patti rushed into the office and regarded Elise on the sofa with her leg up and the presence of both Josh and Daniel. "What's happened?"

Josh answered her. "Someone tried to kidnap Elise."

"What? Where?"

"They attacked me as I was leaving."

Her eyes widened. "You were attacked inside the school?"

"If Josh hadn't been there…" She glanced his way, hoping a look could convey the gratitude she felt toward him. He'd saved her life. Again.

"Who did this?" Patti demanded. "Does this have something to do with Candace?"

"I saw one of the guys, but he wasn't alone. He took a shot at me while the other guy fled."

Patti sat down, visibly upset. "I can't believe this happened on school property. Who would do this?"

Josh glanced at Elise and she knew they were thinking the same thing. "Where's Larkin?"

Patti raised her head. "We had a staff meeting after school ended, but he was so agitated after your interview that he said he had to go home."

Josh turned to Elise. "He could have been the one shooting at me."

"Now wait a minute," Chief Mills stated. "Let's not jump to conclusions. All we know for now is that Taylor Johnson is involved. Once we find him, we'll discover who else is involved."

Patti got up and moved to the couch, noticing Elise's leg. "Do you need to go to the hospital?"

Despite the pain, Elise wasn't keen on spending another evening in the ER. "It's fine. I just need to stay off it for a while."

"Why don't you stay at my house for the night," Patti suggested. "We'll take good care of you, won't we, Josh?"

She glanced in Josh's direction and saw him nod.

It was a nice offer and Elise knew it came from the heart, but she didn't think she had the strength to spend an entire evening with this family she had caused so much heartache. "Thank you, but I'll go back to the hotel."

"Do you think it's a good idea for you to be alone?" Josh asked. "They might come back."

Elise pulled herself up. "This time, I'll be prepared."

"I'll have increased patrols around the hotel," Chief Mills stated. "Plus, we already have the BOLO out for Taylor Johnson. I'll let you know if we get any hits."

"I'll drive you to the hotel," Josh told her.

He hugged Patti a moment longer than Elise thought was necessary, causing her to wonder again just how close they were. But what did it matter to her? They deserved to be happy, didn't they? And their being together made sense. Hadn't Patti told her that Josh had become like a father to Candace? Still, a pang of jealousy pulsed through her.

"I'll come by later and check on you," he promised Patti.

Patti pulled her keys from her pocket and pressed them into his hand. "Take my minivan." She looked at Elise. "It will be easier for you to get in and out of than the Jeep with that leg."

Josh helped Elise to her feet, placing her arms around his neck, and she leaned on him for support as she limped out to the parking lot. She couldn't help remembering the feel of his arms on her as he'd carried her to the office, and now, his muscles hard and strong as they bore her weight. She had come to depend so much on him in such a short time.

He helped her into the van and she buckled herself in as Josh crawled into the driver's side, pushing the seat back to fit his long legs. "Ready?"

Elise put her hand out as he reached for the ignition, now certain she wanted him involved in what she was about to do. "There's someplace else I want you to take me." It was time to let him in on her true plans for the evening. "I want to stake out Peter Larkin's house."

Chapter Five

It was odd to see Josh behind the wheel of Patti's minivan, clearly a family vehicle. He looked surprisingly comfortable managing it, and Elise giggled at the way it seemed to fit him.

"What's so funny?" he asked.

"Nothing." She felt heat rise in her face as she imagined Josh with a load full of kids in tow. It was a nice image and surprisingly one that appealed to her.

She sipped her coffee that was now cold and tried to focus on the matter at hand—watching Larkin.

His house lights were on and they could see him inside through the front window sitting in his recliner watching television. Nothing out of the ordinary. But she knew from experience that things weren't always what they seemed.

Elise leaned over, examining the one-story home. Like most of his neighbors, Larkin had strung Christmas lights on the house and set out lawn ornaments, but it was the layout of the house that captured Elise's attention. There wasn't much room for someone to keep a young girl against her will without alerting the neighborhood.

"He has a garage," Josh noted.

"Could there be a basement?"

Josh shook his head. "Mississippi soil moves too much. Most places around here don't have basements."

"It's possible he has a storage area or other place where he could keep his victims."

"What about a hunting camp?" Josh asked. "The woods around here are covered with them."

"Do you even know if Larkin hunts?"

Josh's eyes grew fierce as he stared at the house. "He's a hunter. Maybe he doesn't hunt wildlife, but I can recognize a hunter."

"Your instincts are no more admissible than mine. And they won't get us a warrant to search his home, either." She had to find some way to gather more information about Larkin.

After a while of uncomfortable silence between them, Elise glanced at Josh. She needed to clear the air about what had happened with Max.

"I really like Patti," she said instead. "She seems like a strong woman."

"Yes, she is. She's had to be."

"Josh, about your brother—"

"Don't, Elise."

"I need to say this. I am so sorry for what happened. I am so sorry that he died protecting me."

He gripped the steering wheel until his knuckles turned white. Then he turned to look at her. She braced, expecting a tirade, but then he took a deep breath and let it out, and all anxiety seemed to fade from his body.

"I've spent a long time trying to blame you, but Max died doing what Max did—helping people. He saw someone in trouble and he stepped in." He sighed. "But how can I be mad at my own brother? The truth is he didn't do anything I wouldn't have done."

"Only he had a wife and child at home."

"That's true. He wasn't thinking about them. Do you have a family, Elise?"

She shook her head. She'd been on her own most of her adult life and she didn't consider her father's new family hers. "Only a great-aunt who sends me fruit-cake at Christmas."

"Have you ever thought about starting a family?"

She was floored at the question. "I—I don't know. I haven't given it much thought. I've been so focused on my career."

"How could you even think about having a family knowing you would be placing them in danger because of your job?"

She saw where he was headed with this conversation. "Most of the agents I know have families, Josh. Celibacy is not a requirement for working for the FBI."

"But is it smart? How can you justify bringing that danger home to your family every night?"

"The world is full of danger. You could be killed driving to the store for a milk run."

"Or intervening when you see someone in danger."

So they were back to Max.

"He wasn't on duty," Josh said, "but he was always a cop. That didn't end when he went off duty."

"I suppose we have to rely on our training to protect the people we care about."

"What about God? Do you believe in God, Elise?"

She was taken aback by his question. It seemed so out of the blue. She struggled with how to answer. God hadn't been much of a consideration for her in a long time.

"I've always quoted to Candace Psalm 119 about the word of God being a lamp onto my feet. I told her it meant that God should decide our steps. Even when we can't see several feet ahead, we have to trust that He is leading our path and that His ways are good. I confess, I'm having trouble believing that now."

She shook her head. "I've seen too much to believe in a loving God. How can a loving God allow the atrocities of this world without extracting vengeance? Where's the justice for Max or for Candace or the other victims of human trafficking? Where's the justice for the millions of women kidnapped into sex trafficking every year and forced to spend their lives in bondage?"

"Vengeance is Mine, says the Lord."

"No, Josh, vengeance is mine. I will hunt down each and every predator I can and I will make them pay for their crimes. God doesn't have anything to do with it."

"I think He does. He's got you, Elise."

She was uncomfortable with his assertion. God hadn't recruited her to the FBI. Lin Wildwood had. Max's murder had sent her into law enforcement, and the FBI seemed a natural extension of her desire to help those in trouble. God had nothing to do with it.

Either the night air or the turn of their conversation sent chills through Elise. She reached to adjust the heater at the same time Josh did. Their fingers touched and he smiled and squeezed her hand, causing her heart to jump at the amused glint in his eyes.

She was way more interested in this guy than she

needed to be. After all, he was settling down, ready to start a family, probably with Patti and Candace. Besides, he certainly could never have feelings for her, not after her involvement in his brother's death. Still, she took pains to keep her distance from him. She didn't need the involvement or the reminder of how his blue eyes made her knees go weak.

Josh Adams was off-limits.

The stakeout was a bust. Larkin had done nothing but watch TV for several hours then turn in for the night. He didn't act like a man with something to hide, and Elise was beginning to question his involvement in Candace's disappearance. She unlocked the door to her hotel room and they went inside.

Josh glanced at the photographs of missing girls she'd taped up and rubbed his face. "I need some fresh air," he stated before opening the door and stepping out again.

Elise understood. She saw the frustration gnawing at him at the lack of progression at finding Candace. Perhaps a break was just what they both needed.

She followed him outside and sat beside him on the stairs.

He fingered the slender chain with a key around his neck and his voice was grim when he spoke. "It's hard when I see evil winning. It's hard to hang on to my faith at times like these."

Elise motioned to the key. "Is it symbolic or does it open something?"

"A little of both. It's a reminder to me of who I am, but also to keep my eyes on God instead of on the road ahead of me. God guides us one step at a time, but if we aim our eyes to the road, all we see is darkness. If we turn our eyes to the Lord and step out in faith..." He shook his head. "It seemed so much easier when I was walking into darkness and had no choice but to trust God to guide me. Here, I see the road. I see each step I take. It's so easy to take my journey into my own hands."

Elise glanced at him. "How do you do it, Josh? How do you have such faith? That's something I gave up on a long time ago."

"I confess I've had my doubts from time to time. My last mission with the Rangers, we lost six men—six good men with families and futures. I couldn't even wrap my brain around why they believed they could have it all—a wife, a family—and not put them in danger. I lost my ability to make decisions in the field. I was surrounded by men who had families back home, and every decision I made, every call, put them at risk. So I left. I came back home to take care of Max's family as I should have done from the beginning. But here is not that much different. There's still danger lurking everywhere I look, evil hidden behind every corner." He raked a hand over his face and sighed then twirled the key around his neck. "Sometimes it gets to be more than I can handle. That's when I cling to this, this symbol of faith I learned in the army. Some days, it's the only way I can force myself to go on."

"I'm sorry about your friends that died."

"My brothers-in-arms chose that life. Their wives knew the danger, but I don't understand how they lived with it. I saw the notes and letters they got from their families, from home, and I'm jealous because I don't have that, but at the same time, I know I could never place a family of my own in that kind of risk."

"That's why you never got married?"

He nodded. "I had the job. It was my life for a long, long time. I even pushed Patti and Candace out to a point. I couldn't care too much for them without opening them up to risk. Now I see they were at risk all the time anyway."

She hated to broach the subject, but this was as good a time as any, and Josh seemed receptive to talking about it. Plus, the case against Larkin seemed cold. They needed a new direction. "Was there anything about that last mission, or any of your missions, that might have followed you home?"

He turned his gaze on her. "You think this has something to do with me?"

"Your job as a ranger placed you in compromising parts of the world doing classified missions and even now you still travel to dangerous parts of the world and interact with risky people. And it's your niece that's mysteriously disappeared, and you're convinced beyond all doubt that she didn't run away from home even though everyone else is convinced she did. Plus, you've been around during every single attack. I'd be negligent if I didn't at least investigate the possibility."

Josh glared at her eye-for-eye for several seconds then turned away.

"I can't stand to lose one more person, Elise. Now you're telling me that my very presence in my niece's life could have put her in danger? I can't handle that."

"Then let me rule it out."

He glared at her again. "What does your gut tell you? Did Larkin kidnap Candace or not?"

Honestly, her gut was telling her this all had nothing to do with Josh's army career or an inappropriate teacher at school. Her gut still screamed this was about a human trafficking ring, but the evidence seemed to be pointing her in other directions. She'd vowed after Allie Peterson to always trust her gut, but she had to concede the truth. "My gut is not evidence."

"You're not answering my question. Do you believe Larkin kidnapped my niece?"

He wasn't going to give up until he got an answer, only he wasn't going to like the one she had. "I don't think he had anything to do with Candace's disappearance."

He sighed wearily, her words sinking in. He rubbed his face again then nodded toward her. "I'll answer whatever questions you want to ask me about my time with the Rangers."

She was right and he knew it. She needed to explore all avenues, she needed to be able to discount all possibilities, and although he knew this had nothing to do with him, he also knew his perspective wasn't the best judge right now. Hadn't Colton advised him to let Elise do her job?

A rip of shame rushed through him. What if Candace had been abducted because of him? What if this did have something to do with his time as a ranger? What if it was tied to that final, devastating mission? Was it possible one of the terror cells he'd been flown into was targeting him? The idea brought a shudder of possibility to him. They were never truly out of danger. No one was ever truly out of danger.

And he thought of his friends, his brothers, he'd

lost. Was it possible one of their family members blamed him and was retaliating?

The more he thought about the possibilities, the more he knew he had to allow Elise to investigate them.

She cautiously placed her hand on his arm. "Whatever you tell me, Josh, stays between us unless I discover it has something to do with Candace's disappearance."

He glanced over at the children's playground. Even now he couldn't turn off the switch in his mind that kept him from imagining the obstacle courses with their hills and ropes and hurdles. The calluses on his hands were healing without the constant weight lifting or pistol shooting. His body may be losing its purpose, but his mind and soul would always be a ranger.

"I was part of a Special Forces team. Our last assignment as a team was to track down members of a terror cell believed to be hiding in the Afghan mountains. These were high-profile targets and my team was up for the task. We went in with a CIA liaison, three interpreters and a band of tribal warriors."

"What happened?"

"We were betrayed by one of the interpreters, who was actually an enemy spy who'd infiltrated our ranks. His reports led our squad into a trap. Six of our members were killed. We walked right into an ambush while the interpreter escaped into the mountains and I'm sure was proclaimed a hero by his countrymen."

Elise took down some notes in her phone. "I'm going to find out if we have any intelligence on this spy or this terror cell to make certain they aren't targeting US servicemen." Elise touched his arm in a comforting manner. "I have to investigate this possibility, but let me do some background work before we assume the worst."

"I should call my ranger brothers to make sure they haven't had anything unusual happen."

"That's a good idea. I'll send this information to my partner so he can get started on this angle." She stopped then reached for his hand and squeezed it reassuringly. "I'm sure this has nothing to do with Candace. We will find her, Josh."

He watched her hurry away to start digging into his life. He closed his eyes and tried to breathe.

He couldn't be responsible for losing another person he cared about.

When he walked back into the room, Elise was on her hands and knees pulling back a piece of carpet beneath which she'd apparently hidden some files. She pulled out a folder.

Josh knelt down and touched the carpet. "You tore up the carpet. Bobby isn't going to be happy."

"Bobby doesn't have to know. You can't even tell it's been pulled up, especially when the chair is placed over it." She pulled the armchair back to the spot to prove her point. "Safe and sound. You and I are the only ones who know it's there. Besides, now if someone tries to break in and steal my files, they won't get them."

She handed him the manila envelope she'd removed from her hiding spot. He turned it over and saw the words *Army Ranger Incident Report*. He knew what was inside. The incident report on his last mission. "You read it?"

"My partner at the FBI emailed it to me. I printed it

out, but I didn't read it. It doesn't make sense from an investigative standpoint not to read it," she said, "but it felt wrong, like a betrayal."

It meant a lot to him that she hadn't read it, and he was glad he'd told her. He reached for her hand then pulled her into a hug. It felt good, it felt right, to have someone on his side. Plus, it confirmed what she'd already said. If she'd really believed Candace's disappearance had anything to do with his time with the Rangers, he knew she would have read the report regardless.

Matt Ross was only one of two members of his ranger squad who was still in the service. Josh phoned his cell, prepared to leave a message in case Matt was on assignment. He was surprised when his friend answered the phone.

"What's up, Josh?"

Josh explained the situation with Candace and asked if he'd run across any trouble. He'd already spoken with four of his former teammates, and none of them had reported having any trouble that could be linked back to their final mission.

Matt was no exception. "Nothing out of the ordinary. How are you holding up?"

"I feel better knowing this isn't about me, but it's frustrating being unable to find her."

"How's the knee, Josh?"

He reached out and rubbed his knee. The cold air and his recent sprint with Taylor Johnson had about pushed it to its limit, but he was thankful that was the only injury he'd sustained in the attack. "Still there."

"We'll be recruiting for new rangers in a few

months. We could use instructors to train them. I've left you a spot open if you want it."

Matt had been after him to return to the army and to the Rangers. He'd been the one who'd tried to talk Josh out of leaving in the first place. "No, thanks, Matt. I don't think I'm up for it."

"It's still a few months away," Matt insisted. "Maybe you'll change your mind."

Josh thought about the offer after they'd hung up. It would be a good job for him with his bum knee, but he still couldn't see himself going back to that life. He couldn't see the point of training others to make the ultimate sacrifice, not when he no longer believed in it himself, and especially not now when he could finally see a future with a family as a real possibility in his life. He wouldn't—he couldn't—risk that.

Josh stopped by Patti's house and was surprised to see the Jeep parked in the garage. He'd left it with Patti to drive when he'd taken her van, but she was supposed to be staying with her friend. He went inside, finding her there hand-washing dishes that he knew couldn't be dirty.

"This is my home," she told him when he questioned what she was doing. "I want to be here in case Candace comes home."

He understood that sentiment, but he didn't like her staying by herself after what had happened.

He watched her scrub a plate so hard he was certain she was scrubbing off the pattern. But he understood. She was doing whatever it took to occupy her mind, to keep her from focusing solely on her missing daughter. He admired her tenacity and her determination to keep it together despite the passing hours without information about Candace.

He reached for a towel. The least he could do was help her, especially if it turned out he was responsible for Candace's disappearance. Patti handed him a wet plate and he dried it off. It felt nice to be here in the warmth of family…even if their family was incomplete.

"Any news from Agent Richardson?"

He shook his head, hating to disappoint her with his negative response.

But Patti was stronger than he gave her credit for. She simply turned back to her dishes. How had she survived all these years without Max? Raising a daughter as a single parent after all she'd been through? Seeing her reminded him of those six other wives struggling to raise a family after the deaths of his brothers had left them widowed.

He remembered what one of the wives had told him the day of her husband's funeral about how the ancient Egyptians, when the pharaoh died, would bury his wife alive with him. She'd told him how cruel that used to sound to her, but now, as she watched her husband laid to rest, all she longed to do was jump in and die with him.

He glanced at Patti. Had she ever felt that, longing to die along with Max? He'd never had the courage to ask her. And would he ever find that kind of love?

"I like her," Patti stated, handing him another dish.

"Who?"

"Agent Richardson. She seems nice."

He nodded. She did seem nice.

"Don't you think she's cute? I love the way her nose crinkles when she smiles."

He grinned, having noticed that himself. "She is determined."

"Spunky. I would describe her as spunky. I'm glad she's on our side." She gave him a long look then smiled, an amused glint in her eye. "You like her."

Although it was more a statement than a question, Josh wasn't sure how to respond. He couldn't deny his attraction to Elise, but too many obstacles stood between them. "Nothing can happen with me and Elise."

"Why not?"

He kept silent about her involvement in Max's death and focused instead on the other obstacle between them. "I want a wife I can be assured is coming home to her family at night."

"She puts her life on the line to help people…like you used to and like Max did."

"And Max didn't come home, did he?"

He tossed down the towel and raked a hand across his face. He hadn't meant that to sound so brutally honest, but it was the truth. He leaned against the counter and tried to contain the emotion that threatened to bubble up.

"Max didn't die because of his job. He died because of who he was. Do you think he wouldn't have stepped between an innocent girl and an armed gunman even if he were an accountant? If he hadn't, he wouldn't have been the man I fell in love with."

He looked at her, wondering what she would think if she knew that innocent girl she'd just mentioned was Elise. How would she react to that revelation, and would it change her opinion of Elise?

It was time to find out.

"She's not who you think she is."

"Who? Elise? What do you mean? Is she being deceitful?"

"No, nothing like that." He chose his words carefully, believing he'd already said the wrong thing. This was a tactful situation and he had to handle it carefully. "She knew Max. They had a history."

Patti looked at him, her expression one of sudden apprehension. "Define *history*."

"Elise was the girl Max died saving."

He couldn't read the expression on her face as she digested that information. She crossed the kitchen away from him and folded her arms. "And why did you two feel you had to keep this information from me?"

"I wasn't trying to keep it from you. I just didn't know how to tell you."

She grabbed the keys from the counter and walked out, getting into her van and starting the engine. She was gone before he could stop her. But he was pretty sure he knew where she was headed—to confront Elise.

What had he been thinking telling her that? He reached for his phone and quickly dialed Elise's number to give her a heads-up.

The knock on her hotel door was no surprise after Josh's call. Elise braced herself and opened it to find a red-eyed Patti standing on the breezeway.

Patti stared at her for several moments before crossing the threshold and throwing her arms around Elise, hugging her tightly.

Elise was dumbfounded. She'd expected anger,

tears and angry accusations. She hadn't expected bear-hugging.

Finally, Patti broke the embrace and took her hands. "I honestly had no idea what I would say to you after Josh told me about your history with my husband."

Elise rushed to defend herself. "Patti, I am so sorry about Max. If I could go back—"

"Hush," Patti insisted. "We can't change the past and I know you never intended any harm to come to Max. This world is full of evil, and our family knows firsthand. Max was always one to stand up for others, and even though I miss him terribly, I'm proud to know he died defending what he believed in."

Elise wiped away the tears streaming down her face. "Then…then you're not angry at me?"

"Angry at you? Elise, I'm thankful. If Max hadn't intervened all those years ago, you wouldn't be here today to search for our daughter. I'm so thankful that the Lord has us all in His hands and His plans. I just don't know why Josh felt he had to keep this from me. It gives me hope. It gives me wonderful hope that my daughter will be returned to me safely."

Elise grimaced at being considered a part of God's plan. She was there for a reason, and it had nothing to do with God's will. But she wasn't going to argue with Patti over her faith. The lady needed something to grant her hope.

Elise squeezed her hand and made her a promise. "I will do everything in my power to bring Candace home."

Chapter Six

Josh received a call from Daniel the next afternoon letting him know the preliminary lab report from the blood collected from Josh's knife was in. He swung by and picked up Elise then headed to the police station.

Elise looked over the results and compared them to the local file the police had on Taylor Johnson. "The preliminary reports show the same blood type. That along with the identification Josh gave us is enough to issue a warrant."

Daniel leaned back in his chair. "Unfortunately, we still haven't been able to locate Johnson. And according to his landlady, he hasn't been at his apartment in days. We're unlikely to find anything by searching there."

Despite that news, Elise was determined. "He's the key. I know it. We've got to find him. Have you checked for credit-card usage?"

"He doesn't have a credit card and there's been no usage on his bank account. There's also been no activity on his cell phone and his car hasn't been located."

"What about family members?" Josh asked. "Have they had any contact with him?"

"If they have, they're not telling my officers."

"Extend the range searching for his car. We should include all areas between here and New Orleans. And I have a way of determining where Taylor's loyalties lie. I want to pull Peter Larkin's phone records."

Josh was intrigued. "What are you looking for?"

"If Taylor was basically a henchman working for whoever would hire him, I want to see if there is any indication that he's had contact with Peter Larkin."

Daniel shook his head, unconvinced. "If Larkin was involved in Candace's disappearance, why would he hire anyone, much less Taylor, to do work for him? Someone who would turn on him in the blink of an eye?"

"Is it possible they're working together? There was another person shooting at me," Josh stated. "He covered Taylor's getaway."

"We can do a test to see if Larkin has fired a gun recently," Elise said.

Daniel shook his head. "Not unless he agrees to it. We don't have enough evidence to compel him."

Elise grinned and headed for the door. "Then I'll ask nicely."

Josh followed after her. He knew her well enough by now to know that this was not going to go well.

Peter Larkin was in the teachers' lounge when Josh and Elise arrived at the school to question him. He glared at them as they entered. "Agent Richardson, Josh, what do you want now?"

Elise stepped forward. "Perhaps you heard about

what happened here at the school yesterday afternoon?"

"No, what happened?"

"Someone tried to abduct Agent Richardson," Josh stated.

Elise stared at him then punctuated one word. "Tried."

"I chased the guy through the woods."

Larkin shook his head. "And you think it was me?"

"No, I saw the guy. It was a man named Taylor Johnson."

"Then go arrest him."

"We will when we can find him."

Larkin got irritated. "Why are you here?"

"Taylor had an accomplice. He took a couple of shots at me."

"Too bad he missed."

Elise got right to the point. "We'd like to run a test to prove that you haven't shot a gun recently."

Larkin shook his head. "No."

"I'm sure you'd like to prove that you were not involved in the attempted abduction of an FBI agent, Mr. Larkin. This test could point the spotlight away from you."

He picked up his coffee mug and refilled it before heading for the door. "I said no. Now, if you'll excuse me, I have a class to teach."

"I can get a warrant and compel you to take this test," Elise warned.

He stopped at the doorway. "Then come back when you have the warrant." He walked out.

Josh moved toward her. "What do you think?"

"I think we still need to find Taylor."

* * *

Josh was trying to catch up on his work later that afternoon when his cell phone rang.

He recognized Daniel's number. "Hey, what's up?"

"I need you to come to the school," Daniel stated. "It's Patti."

Those words got his attention. Josh closed his computer and pushed it away, reaching for his keys. "What happened?"

"She attacked Larkin."

Josh phoned Elise as he was jumping into the Jeep and she agreed to meet him at the school. He kicked himself. He should have known better than to leave Patti alone.

He rushed into the office and found Patti sitting on the sofa, her head resting on the back of the couch and a wet cloth over her forehead. She looked drained and defeated. Beside her, the school nurse was taking her blood pressure. Daniel stood a few inches away, taking down notes.

Josh sat on the other side of Patti and took her hand. "What happened?"

She removed the cloth and stared at him, her eyes full of regret. "I'm sorry, Josh," she stated. "I just kept thinking this man knows something about my daughter. I only wanted to get him to tell me where she is." She placed her hands over her face and sobbed.

Josh pulled her toward him and wrapped his arms around her, doing his best to comfort her. He glanced up and saw the sympathy of the school nurse and Daniel. And he spotted Elise standing in the doorway, her face drawn in a frown. He knew seeing Patti so distraught was upsetting to her as well, and he appreciated how she'd already come to care for his family. At the same time, he also noticed the determined lines of her face and worried when she turned and marched out of the office.

"I'll be right back," he told Patti, getting up to follow Elise out. He found her headed down the hall and knew she was heading toward Larkin's classroom. He rushed to catch up with her. "Where are you going, Elise?"

"Where do you think?"

He grabbed her arm, spinning her to face him. "Confronting him won't do any good. Aren't you the one who told me that?"

She folded her arms, stubbornly sticking to her decision. "I don't care. I'm tired of the bad guys always winning. I can't take it anymore. He won't get away with this, Josh."

He pulled her into his arms and held her, her shoulders shaking as she fought back sobs.

The door to the faculty lounge opened and Larkin stepped out, his face scratched and his eye blackened. Patti had done a job on him and Josh couldn't help but be proud. At the same time, he felt Elise stiffen as she spotted him.

Larkin glared at them both. "I didn't have anything to do with your niece's disappearance," he insisted, "and I'm tired of being accused. Keep your sister-in-law away from me," he stated. "And you can let her know I will be filing a complaint not only with the police but also with the school board. She won't be principal for much longer."

It was already dark when Elise stopped by Patti's house, anxious to see how she was doing after the incident at school. The other houses on her street were lit up with Christmas lights, but Patti's lights hung limply from the house, unlit. Elise approached the house and raised her hand to knock on the door then stopped, spotting Patti and Josh through the recently replaced front window. Josh had his arms around her and had pulled her into a hug. The intimacy they seemed to share struck at her, reminding Elise of the mystery man Patti said she'd spoken to Candace about the morning of her disappearance. Hadn't she said she'd known him for years?

Josh.

Shaken by the display and even more by the upsetting flow of jealousy pulsing through her, Elise backed away from the door. She couldn't go in there now, not after seeing them that way, not after the intensity of jealousy that plagued her.

What was the matter with her? What difference did it make if Josh hugged his sister-in-law? There was nothing between her and Josh. There couldn't be, not knowing her hand in Max's death. She should be happy for them, finding one another after all these years. And once Candace was home, they would be one big happy family…just as they should have been before Max's death.

She shuddered, realizing that if Max hadn't died, he would be with Patti, and Josh would be free to love her. Ironically, her role in Max's death had not only ruined one family, but had also ruined any future she might have had with Josh. She supposed she deserved it. This was just another consequence of that night all those years earlier.

She jumped, startled by the crunch of leaves behind

her. She reached for her gun and stepped off the porch. A dark figure moved away from the house and Elise quickly moved toward it, her gun ready and drawn, her senses on high alert.

"FBI. Freeze!" she called out, but the person took off.

The light from the porch brightened up the night, causing her eyes to lose focus on the figure of a man running. Elise took off after him as Josh and Patti stepped out onto the porch.

Josh fell into step beside her. "What is it?"

"Someone was there." She moved toward the neighbor's house and hugged the brick outer wall as Josh joined her. Together, they moved to the side of the house, in perfect sync. Elise raised her weapon, ready to use if necessary.

A lone figure turned the corner then stopped when he saw the gun aimed at his head.

"What's going on?" he demanded.

Josh pushed Elise's gun down. "It's only Patti's neighbor Mr. Franklin." He turned to the startled man to explain. "We heard an intruder."

"There's no one here but me."

"You didn't see a dark figure moving around?" Elise demanded.

"I didn't see anything except a gun pointed at my head."

Despite Josh's reassurance, Elise was hesitant to put her gun away. She'd seen someone lurking around. She was sure of it.

"It's okay, Elise. Mr. Franklin has been Patti's neighbor for ten years." He apologized again then headed back to Patti's. Elise followed him, scanning the area. "What did you see?"

"Just someone lurking around the house. I didn't see who it was."

He glanced at his sister-in-law standing on the porch looking anxious. "I'll stay here tonight just in case."

Elise stiffened at the reference. She hadn't meant to hand him such a suggestion. Was this genuine concern for his sister-in-law, or was he jumping at the chance to spend more time with her? She tried to push off her frustration as she followed him back to the house.

Patti rushed off the porch and greeted her. "Elise, I'm so thankful you were here."

She didn't want this woman's gratitude. In fact, she didn't want anything from this woman, yet she couldn't rationalize her feelings. She liked Patti, but because of her closeness to Josh, she didn't want to like Patti.

It was all so confusing.

"I think I should spend the night," Josh suggested.

"Oh, really?" Patti seemed hesitant at the choice.

"On the couch, of course," Josh told her. When she still seemed hesitant, he questioned her. "What's the problem, Patti? I've stayed over before."

"I know. It's just that was when Candace was here. It doesn't seem right for us to spend the night in the house alone together. Maybe Elise would stay instead."

Elise nearly choked at her words.

"I'll be perfectly safe with Elise in the house with me."

Elise quickly scanned her brain for reasons why that would not work, but the look of concern on Josh's face and his pleading gaze changed her mind.

"I would feel better knowing she wasn't alone."

She felt like pounding her feet and throwing her arms and whining that she didn't want to stay in the same house as Josh's girlfriend, but she also knew how childish that sounded. It sounded silly even in her head. She couldn't blame Patti for falling for this handsome former ranger. She only wished she didn't have to be around to see it.

Elise bolted awake from her position on the couch. She reached for her weapon and jumped up at the sound of someone in the kitchen. She was surprised to find Patti preparing a glass of warm milk.

She felt foolish jumping to such conclusions. This entire case had her on edge, but she couldn't be so trigger-happy. She had to somehow find her bearings.

Patti offered some milk to Elise. "I couldn't sleep. I haven't had a full night's sleep since Candace vanished."

Elise joined her at the table. For the first time, she noticed the strain on Patti's face, the deep lines punctuated by sadness and grief. She was used to seeing this woman so strong, so solid even in the face of her daughter's abduction. Tears slipped down Patti's cheeks as she looked at Elise and gave an apologetic smile. "I just want her to come home. Do you believe she ran away?"

Elise struggled with what to say. Running away meant her daughter had chosen to leave on her own. It was essentially a rejection of her mothering. But not running away implied something bad, possibly fatal, had happened to Candace. Elise understood the concern.

"No," she stated honestly. "I don't believe Candace ran away."

She nodded. "No, neither do I. I know my little girl, Elise. She can be a hothead, just like her father was, like Josh is at times, but she cools off quickly. She wouldn't have stayed away like this. Something has happened to her and it terrifies me to think about all the awful things it could be."

Elise put her arms around Patti and hugged her tightly. "I will find her."

She pushed Patti to return to bed and try to get some sleep, but Elise knew sleep would likely not come. She doubted she would return to sleep, either. Her head was killing her and Nurse Stringer would be burning up her phone in another few minutes anyway.

She searched the cabinet for painkillers then poured herself a glass of water and swallowed two Tylenol, knowing it wouldn't make the pain go away, but hoping to dull it somewhat.

She heard a light tapping and saw Josh through the window standing at the back door. She unlocked it and let him inside.

"What are you doing here?"

"I saw the light on."

"From where?"

"I was in the Jeep parked across the street."

How had she not realized he was out there? That said more about her concussion than about his ranger training.

"I couldn't leave not knowing you were safe."

She wanted to find comfort in his words. *Not knowing you were safe*. He'd obviously meant that in a plural form of you, as in her and Patti, and meant, Elise was certain, *without knowing Patti was safe*. Her mind told her that was ridiculous. They were in the Deep South. If he'd really meant to imply them both, he would have said "y'all," but she argued with herself that his military training and traveling all over the world had trained the y'all right out of him.

"I'm sure you're worried about Patti."

He snaked his hand gently up her arm. "I'm worried about both of you, Elise."

She stiffened. "I can take care of myself." Her insinuation might have had more meaning if he hadn't saved her life more than once in less than a week. His hand remained on her arm, growing more and more heavy with every moment he failed to move it. She glanced down at his hand and then up at him, his blue eyes as intense on her as his hand was on her arm.

He moved his hand up her arm and touched her face. Oh, how she could lose herself in this man, in his strength, in his power and his gentleness. How could he be such extremes and how could she find them so appealing?

She knew he was about to kiss her, so she pulled away from him. "What about Patti?"

"What about her?"

"Are you sure you should be here with me in her kitchen? You two seemed pretty cozy earlier when I came by."

Recognition dawned in his eyes and he grinned, an amused twinkle in his eyes. "There's nothing between me and Patti except friendship."

"It looked like there was more."

"She's my sister-in-law, my brother's widow, the

mother of my niece. But it's nothing romantic. There never could be."

"Why is that?"

He smiled and gently brushed her lips with his finger. "Because you, Elise Richardson, have captured my heart."

He leaned in and kissed her and she melted against him, her heart soaring. She was right. She could lose herself in this man completely and not have a care in the world.

The buzzing of her phone interrupted them. Josh laughed at Nurse Stringer's timing. "I'll be outside if you need me," he told her before disappearing through the door.

Her phone buzzed again, but Elise took a moment to recapture her breath before answering it.

The next morning, Elise set her laptop up at the kitchen table. How odd it was for her to be inside Max's home and to feel as if she belonged there. She should have felt like an interloper, but she didn't. This felt like home and it had more to do with Josh than anything. She could see herself stepping easily into this life, into this family and into his life, but she had to keep reminding herself that what she imagined was just that…an imagination. Although he couldn't deny an attraction to her, Josh would never be able to get past her involvement in Max's death to let himself fall for her. And even if he could, there was still the matter of her job with the FBI. He might have left a dangerous life behind, but she hadn't. Would he ever be comfortable knowing she placed herself in danger every day on the job?

Her phone dinged and she picked it up, expecting it to be Lin calling to talk about one of the reports or Josh, who'd gone home to clean up, checking in. She smiled at that option, welcoming the soft sound of his baritone voice despite her doubts just moments ago.

She saw it was a text message from an unknown number.

This is Taylor Johnson. I want to make a deal. Meet me at Shadow Lake by the old fishing bridge.

Elise's heart jumped. Taylor wanted to talk? Did he know something about Candace's disappearance? Would he implicate Larkin?

Logic told her she should phone Chief Mills or the police at least, but she didn't want to scare this boy off. He'd contacted her instead of the police. Elise thought about phoning Josh but didn't want to waste the time for him to get there. She needed to go now before Taylor changed his mind. Josh would be angry, but she couldn't think about that. If Taylor Johnson was ready to give up Larkin, she couldn't waste any time.

She scribbled out a note for Patti, who was sleeping, then hopped into her SUV. She wasn't familiar with the area, so she entered the location into her GPS and followed it toward Shadow Lake. When she spotted Chief Mills's familiar Jeep, she pulled up next to it and parked.

"What are you doing here?" she demanded as she got out and faced Josh.

"I received a text from Taylor Johnson saying he wanted to tell me who had Candace."

She glared up at him. "And you weren't going to tell me? You just came on your own?"

"What are you doing here?"

"I received a similar message. So where is he?"

"I haven't seen him."

"Maybe he changed his mind before I could get here."

Josh shook his head. "I don't like this."

Movement from the brush caught their attention. Elise turned and saw a lanky man walk from the woods. He held something white and raised his hands high in the air.

"You came," he said. "Good."

Josh and Elise headed toward him.

"You said you know who has my niece," Josh said.

He held out a piece of paper. "I'm supposed to give this to you."

Elise took the envelope from him and ripped it open. She pulled out a typewritten note.

"'I can get to anyone anywhere.'" She glanced up at Taylor. "What is this supposed to mean?"

"I was just told to give you that. I'm the messenger."

"Where is my niece?" Josh demanded again.

"I don't know. I just do what I'm told."

He started to turn and head back into the woods.

Elise pulled her gun and aimed it at him. "You didn't think you were really going to walk away, did you?"

He turned to her and grinned, still certain in his getaway. "I'm not alone, Agent Richardson."

A shot rang out, slicing between Elise and Josh and slamming into her windshield. She ducked as Taylor laughed.

"I told you I'm not alone."

Shots rang out again, this time hitting Taylor multiple times. Elise crouched by her car while Taylor was racked with bullets. Josh grabbed her and crouched beside her, his eyes scanning the woods for the gunman as best he could without raising his head. After a moment, the gunfire stopped. Taylor lay motionless on the ground.

Josh leaned against the truck then pulled out his phone. "I'll call Daniel."

Elise stared at the paper in her hands. Taylor had been more than the messenger. He'd been the message, too.

Elise eyed the body on the ground, shot three times in the back.

She glanced up at Chief Mills. "Whoever made that shot was no novice. Does anyone know if Larkin has any background with guns?"

"None that we're aware of."

Nothing pointed completely at one person. She still had no solid proof that got them any closer to Candace, Larkin or the trafficking ring. She was no closer to unraveling this mystery than she was when she'd first come to town.

She noticed Josh draw near the perimeter. He stared out into the night.

Elise walked up to him, sensing that something was bothering him.

He turned toward her. "Someone took Candace, and if Taylor was involved and they killed him, they could have already killed Candace."

She wanted to tell him differently, but she couldn't.

The chances of finding his niece alive diminished daily. Ironically, being abducted by the trafficking ring seemed to be her best chance of still being alive, yet gave them the worst chance for locating her.

"We'll find her," Elise assured him, more intent than ever to do just that. She touched his arm for comfort. He turned and put his arms around her, drawing her into an embrace.

She'd started this journey determined to make up to Max. Now she wanted to do this for Josh…regardless of whether or not they could ever have a future together.

Elise parked in front of her hotel room. Although she'd spent the past two nights at Patti's, she didn't yet feel comfortable enough to let her hotel room go. It mixed too much of her professional and personal lives.

She thought of Josh and the kiss they'd exchanged and realized that line was already tangled.

Elise went inside, locked her hotel room door and pulled up a piece of the carpet where she'd hidden her most recent notes. She read through them again. Somewhere in these interviews had to be a clue she was overlooking, some link that answered the question as to what had happened to Candace. Candace's case shared so many of the same elements as her other missing girls. Her eyes kept focusing on Brooke Martin. She suspected Candace's best friend knew more than she was letting on. If only Elise could speak to her again, this time in depth, perhaps she could uncover information that might lead to Candace's whereabouts.

Her phone rang and Elise answered it without checking the caller ID.

"Agent Richardson? It's Brooke Martin." Elise perked up. She'd just been hoping for another chance to speak with Brooke and now the girl had presented herself. Did she have something else to offer? Elise wondered if her father was aware she was calling.

"Yes, hello, Brooke. What can I do for you?"

"I—I need to talk to you. It's important. There's something I didn't tell you. It's about Candace…and Mr. Larkin."

Elise sat up. Was this the break she'd been searching for?

"What about Candace and Mr. Larkin?"

"I lied when I said he and Candace didn't spend much time together. In fact, she stayed after school the day she vanished because he wanted to talk to her." Elise heard the choke in her voice. "I think he did something to Candace."

"Do you have a reason to suspect he would hurt her?"

"Yes." She choked again before dropping a bombshell. "Because he's been hurting me, too."

Excitement revved through Elise, the same excitement she felt whenever a lead opened up to break a case. This girl could be the answer to finding Candace.

"I'd like to talk with you some more, Brooke. Where are you now?"

"I just left the school. I don't want to go back that way."

"Tell me where you are and I'll pick you up."

"I'm walking down Lake Road toward downtown."

The road from the school heading into town. She

could be there in less than ten minutes. "I'm on my way."

She hung up with Brooke and grabbed her purse, hurrying down the steps as fast as possible. She hopped into her SUV. As she drove, she dialed Josh.

"Brooke Martin just confessed that Larkin assaulted her. She says he was hurting Candace, as well. I'm on my way to pick her up now."

"Where is she?"

"She just left the school on foot." A call beeped in. Elise glanced at the screen. "It's Brooke." She switched lines. "Brooke? I'm on my way."

"He's following me, Agent Richardson! He's in his car. He's chasing me!" Terror ripped through the girl's voice.

Elise's excitement turned to fear for the girl. "Who is following you, Brooke?"

"Mr. Larkin. He stopped me on the road and tried to make me get into his car. I got scared and ran into the woods. He's following me."

"Hold on, Brooke. I'm nearly there." Elise gunned the accelerator, thankful the road was clear. "Stay on the line with me, Brooke."

"He's here," she whispered. "He— *No!*"

Her scream reverberated through the phone. Elise heard the sound of the cell phone hitting the ground and Brooke's screams of terror. "Leave me alone! Let me go! Help, Agent Richardson! Help me!" Then the cries ended and Elise heard nothing.

Dread rushed through her. This couldn't be happening. She had to get there faster.

She zoomed past the school, passing Josh and the Jeep coming from the opposite direction. She slammed on the brakes, screeching to a stop in the middle of the road. She jumped out as Josh did the same. She hadn't passed the girl.

"Did you see her?" Elise asked, her heart pounding with worry and fear.

"No, I didn't see anyone."

There was no way Larkin or Brooke had got past them both. She scanned the area. Brooke said she'd run into the woods. Elise called her name but received no response. Nothing seemed to move in the woods along the road.

Josh rushed up the shoulder of the road, searching and calling her name. Elise took the other side. The girl had to be somewhere out here…unless Larkin had found her. And based on what Elise had heard, she feared he had.

She spotted something on the grass a few feet from the road. She slid down the embankment and rushed to it. She grabbed it, recognizing it as Brooke's purse.

Josh followed her. "Did you find something?"

She showed him the purse and saw the same look of horror in his face that she felt in her soul. This couldn't be happening again. Not again. She'd lost another girl.

"He took her," Elise told him. "Larkin just abducted Brooke Martin."

Chapter Seven

Nervous excitement lit through Elise as she waited for the confrontation about to take place across the street. She watched a group of local police officers all dressed in their SWAT gear move into position to storm Peter Larkin's home. Beside her, Chief Mills supervised the operation while Josh paced anxiously behind her. She knew he longed to be the one bursting into that house ready to strike.

She shared his desire. Had it not been for her injured leg, she might have insisted on being part of the team. Instead, she satisfied herself with coming in afterward. She was allowing Chief Mills to lead this operation. All she'd asked was that she could be a part of it. He'd reluctantly agreed, and she knew it was only because he was hoping to avoid a full-scale FBI presence in town. She didn't bother telling him that wouldn't happen.

"His car is parked in the driveway. He's in there," one of the officers voiced into the mic. That surprised Elise. Why would he be at home? He had to have known Brooke had alerted her. She'd been screaming into the phone for Elise to help.

Elise pushed away that terrible, helpless memory. She hadn't been able to prevent Brooke's abduction, but she would find her and have her home for Christmas and bring her assailant to justice.

Another officer peeked inside and relayed what he saw. "I have visual. He's inside. He's asleep in the recliner. No one else appears to be in the room."

Again Elise was struck with the oddity of Larkin's behavior. How could he be kicking back in his recliner after just abducting a girl not more than an hour ago? Josh moved to stand beside her, his arms stiffly folded across his chest. Anxiety poured off him and Elise longed to place her arms around him and try to reassure him, but she was too conscious of the presence of Chief Mills. Such an intimate gesture would surely be noticed and might affect how others saw her as a professional.

The lead officer gave the signal, and Elise heard the sound of the door being kicked open then the officers spilling into the house.

"What's going on?" Larkin demanded. "What are you doing?"

Chief Mills waited until he got the word that the house was clear before he allowed them to cross the street.

The head SWAT officer approached them. "The rest of the house is empty. No sign of the girl."

Larkin, who was already in cuffs and being walked to a police cruiser, glared at her and Josh. "You're making a mistake," he insisted. "I haven't done anything."

That lit the fire under Elise, who moved toward him. "You were following her. I was on the phone with her. She told me it was you. I heard her screaming for help."

"No, no. I haven't done anything. I wouldn't hurt Candace."

"This isn't just about Candace anymore. You abducted Brooke Martin. Now tell me where she is."

Larkin looked her square in the eye and seemed surprised by her accusation. "I haven't seen Brooke since third-period biology."

She motioned for the officers to lead him away. She had to be missing something. There had to be some evidence in this house to lead them to where he was keeping Brooke and possibly Candace.

"What now?" Josh asked her.

"Now we dig into his background. He must have a shed or a storage unit somewhere where he's keeping these girls."

She noticed a downcast expression on Josh's face and knew he was thinking about Candace. She touched his arm reassuringly, no longer caring about anyone's opinion but his. "We will find them," she told him. "We will find them and bring them both home."

Elise drummed her fingers against the table as Josh paced the police station. She should be happy that Larkin had finally been arrested and sat in a jail cell, but she couldn't get past the details of the night. Larkin had kidnapped Brooke Martin in broad daylight, stashed her and then gone back to his home and stretched out in his recliner to watch the night's programs? It didn't make sense. Who behaved that way?

And why would he abduct another girl when he already had the FBI snooping around?

Chief Mills appeared from an interrogation room. He looked tired and frustrated.

Josh met him. "Well?"

"He won't give up anything. Keeps insisting he went straight home after school ended."

Elise expected nothing less. "And we haven't uncovered any rentals or storage units where he might have hidden Brooke."

"It has to be close," Josh added. "Or else he wouldn't have been able to get back to the house so quickly."

A commotion in the front of the station caught their attention. Josh and Elise followed Chief Mills to the source—Rick Martin, Brooke's father, demanding answers about his daughter's disappearance.

"I want to see him," Martin insisted. "I want to see the man that took Brooke."

"That's not a good idea," Chief Mills said. "We're still questioning him."

"I can get him to talk," Martin stated. "He will tell me what he's done to my little girl."

Elise had seen grieving fathers before, but it never got easier to witness the pain in their expressions or the angry helplessness they felt. She stepped forward. "Mr. Martin, we are doing everything in our power to find Brooke."

He turned his angry eyes toward her. "You should have protected her," he said. "You're the FBI. It's your job to protect her, but you failed." He spit the last words out at Elise and they hit their mark, digging into her heart.

Yes, she'd failed. She'd failed to protect Brooke.

She'd failed to find Candace. She'd failed to uncover the human trafficking ring. Her entire FBI career was one big failure.

She tried not to let him see how his words affected her, pasting on a calm expression. "We're going to do our best to find your daughter, Mr. Martin. Now, if you'll excuse me, I'm going in to question Mr. Larkin."

She took the file from Chief Mills and headed away quickly, before any of them could see the tears that threatened her composure. She closed the door that led to the interrogation rooms and leaned against it, pushing back the wave of emotion that threatened to explode inside of her.

She didn't need Rick Martin to remind her of her failures. She had a sea of regrets and unsolved cases to do that for her. The list of girls that she hadn't been able to find lined her wall and her memory. She even had an official reprimand from her FBI supervisor and an order to stop using FBI resources to chase after a trafficking ring that, in his mind, didn't exist.

The door pushed open and Elise quickly wiped away tears that had spilled out.

Josh's arms surrounded her. "He shouldn't have said that. This is not your fault."

"He's not wrong. I should have done more to protect Brooke."

"Don't lay this all on yourself, Elise. I've been telling Daniel for weeks that Larkin was a predator. No one listened…no one except you. You saw him for what he is. That's more than anyone else has done."

She stared at the teacher through the two-way glass as he sat hunched at the interview table. He looked defeated and weak, certainly not like a predator. But she rationalized he preyed on young girls. He was only weak when he was challenged by adults who could fight back.

She opened the interview room door and stepped inside. Larkin looked oddly hopeful when he saw her. "Agent Richardson, I did not do this." His eyes pleaded with her for understanding. "I would never lay a hand on either of those girls. You're making a mistake."

She hardened her expression as she sat down across from him. "I was on the phone with Brooke when you grabbed her."

"I didn't," he insisted. "It wasn't me."

"Are you claiming Brooke was lying?"

"All I know is I didn't take her." He slammed his hands against the table. "You have to believe me!"

Elise tried to remain calm against his outburst.

"Tell me where you put her. Make this easier on yourself. If she's found safely, it will look better for you. Let these families have their daughters back before Christmas."

"I can't tell you where she is because I didn't take her."

They continued the back and forth until a man in a suit entered. "Don't say anything else," he told Larkin. "I'm Mr. Larkin's attorney."

Chief Mills followed him inside and addressed Elise. "We have to let him go."

She jumped to her feet. "What? Why?"

The attorney spoke. "All the police have is your word that Brooke named Larkin in her abduction. She was not found at his residence and you have no proof that he had anything to do with her abduction." He motioned toward Larkin. "Let's go."

Larkin stared from his lawyer to Elise and then to Josh, who stood in the doorway. "Of course. You're trying to set me up. Josh has been convinced since day one that I had a hand in his niece's disappearance and now he's convinced you, too." Chief Mills unlocked the restraints and Larkin motioned to his lawyer. "Let's get out of here."

Elise watched him walk out, a smirk crossing his face as he stopped at Josh in the hallway.

"Nice try," he told Josh, "but this won't stop me from filing charges against your sister-in-law."

Elise touched Josh's arm, a new determined fire igniting inside of her. Larkin would not get away with this. She would make certain he was brought to justice.

"This isn't over," she assured Josh. "This is far from over."

After another sleepless night, Elise spent her morning studying the photos of missing girls on her wall. She'd moved back into her hotel room after Brooke's abduction in order to give all her attention to the case. All her patterns, all her suspicions about Candace appeared to match those of these girls, but she couldn't deny the facts—Brooke had mentioned Larkin by name and his involvement in Brooke's abduction offered more substance to his involvement in Candace's disappearance.

Had she imagined the connection? Had she looked for patterns where none had existed? Were her supervisors right? Was she chasing after something that didn't exist?

A knock on her door caught her attention. She glanced at her watch. Seven a.m. was far too early for visitors. She was a morning person, but no one else in town knew that about her. She glanced through the peephole and spotted a tall, lanky man with sandy-brown hair. Her heart leaped.

Lin!

She threw open the door and he smiled at her in his nonchalant manner.

"What are you doing in Westhaven?" she asked.

"I was worried about you. I thought I would drive down here and see what kind of mess you were getting yourself into." He slipped out of his coat and examined her wall of photographs.

"Does Micah know you're here?" Their supervisor was convinced Elise was chasing after ghosts, and she knew he would never allow Lin to come.

He folded his arms, his stance strong and solid. "It's none of Micah's business what I do during my Christmas vacation."

"You took vacation days? You shouldn't have done that." But it meant the world to her that he had. Now, if she only had something to prove her point about the ring—but she didn't.

The moment Brooke had screamed Larkin's name, Elise had known this case was unlikely to link to the trafficking ring she'd been investigating. She had gathered information about his past employers and would look into any links between Larkin and the other missing girls, but it seemed unlikely he had anything to do with the missing girls in other towns. She'd simply uncovered a predator who liked young girls.

"We've had a break in Candace's case," she said, pulling off the photograph of Candace. "Another girl has gone missing, abducted in broad daylight while

I was on the phone with her. She claimed her biology teacher was hurting her and had hurt Candace, as well. So it looks like I won't find that connection I was searching for in Westhaven."

"What about the abducted girls?"

"Brooke's been missing for twenty-six hours now. So far, we haven't found anything to lead us to discover where she's being kept. Candace vanished nearly three weeks ago."

"So I'm confused, Elise. You said yourself this case has nothing to do with the trafficking ring and it clearly falls outside the scope of the FBI, yet you're still involved. Am I missing something?"

"You're right. It's not an FBI case, but I'm not acting in an official FBI capacity anyway."

"Yet you're still here?"

"I made a promise to find this girl, Lin. I owe it to these people to do whatever I can."

"Is this about the uncle?"

She felt her face redden, embarrassed that Lin would make such a suggestion and even more that it might be true. She owed a debt to this family, but she also knew she couldn't, wouldn't, leave Josh until she'd fulfilled her vow. "I told you. I owe this family."

"Why? Who are they?"

"It's personal."

"So it is about Uncle Josh."

"No. It's about so much more."

It was time Lin knew the truth about what had driven her into an FBI career. She poured out the story to him about Max, about Candace and Patti, and even about Josh.

"So you can see why I owe these people, Lin. I can't leave until I find her."

He sighed and picked up her notepad from the bed. "These are Larkin's past employers?"

"Yes. He worked at three other schools before coming here. I was about to contact them to discover if there were any similar accusations during his time at those schools."

He picked up his phone and his jacket. "I'll help you with the research, but can we at least go somewhere with decent coffee while we work?"

Elise grabbed her jacket, thankful for Lin's understanding and support.

Around noon, Elise knocked on Josh's apartment door, and after a moment, it opened and Josh stuck his head out. "Elise, hi." He rubbed his eyes and raked a hand through his mussed hair. It was obvious she'd woken him.

"I tried to call but you didn't answer. I hope it's all right that I just came over."

"Absolutely." He pushed open the door and motioned her inside. Dressed in only his jeans and a T-shirt, he padded across the floor barefoot as he headed to a small kitchenette. "Would you like coffee?"

"No, thanks."

He nodded but poured himself a cup. "I staked out Larkin's house last night, hoping to keep an eye on him or maybe get a clue as to where he's keeping Brooke or Candace, but he never returned home. He's gone."

She held out a file to him. "I looked into Larkin's employment history. It seems he was asked to resign from three separate schools for what they deemed inappropriate behavior with students. And if he agreed to leave quietly then they wouldn't notate the reasons in his file. Thankfully, we were able to speak with someone who knew the details before they closed for the Christmas break."

He skimmed through the file. "No one ever pressed charges?"

"No. The schools probably wanted to handle the problem internally. And because they did, it didn't show up on his references when he was hired here."

He closed the file, anger clouding his face. "And because these places didn't want to rock the boat, they released this monster to prey on my niece."

"The thing is, Josh, there's been no history of kidnapping or violence toward these girls. It doesn't make sense that he would change his pattern of behavior so drastically."

"Maybe he just never got caught before."

"I'll see if I can find any girls that went missing in the areas during the times he was teaching at each school." She pulled out her phone to call Lin, thankful again for his help. He was putting himself on the line for her using FBI resources when he was supposed to be on vacation, but she knew he would do it.

"I'll go get dressed," Josh said, disappearing down the hall.

She gave Lin the search parameters and he promised to let her know if he found anything.

As she hung up the phone, Elise noticed the small Christmas tree in the corner and the gifts beneath it. She spotted one with Candace's name on it and her heart broke. She noticed the display over the mantel. Josh's citations and medals as an army ranger were numerous and positioned beside a photograph of him and his brother. Family was important to this man, and Elise liked that. She also noticed a group photograph she assumed to be his ranger squad. She ran her fingers over the photograph, shuddering in the knowledge that most of these men didn't make it home to their own families.

"It's all about the blood," Josh said, startling her from the doorway. He'd thrown a button-up shirt on and slipped into his boots.

She replaced the photograph. "I'm sorry. I wasn't prying."

"Blood. It's what ties a family together." He motioned toward the picture. "We fought together, ate together, bled together. Do you have a partner, Elise? Someone in the FBI that always has your back?"

"Yes. His name is Lincoln Wildwood." Lin was the only person she'd trusted solely...until now.

"Imagine if you had fourteen of him. That's what it's like being a ranger."

"Do you keep up with them?"

"Absolutely." He fingered the key at his neck. "Those of us that survived the attack, most, like me, have taken civilian jobs or just retired altogether, but they still have my back and I have theirs whenever, wherever. With one call, I could have five fully decked-out former rangers combing every inch of this area."

She could imagine such a sight. But it made her wonder. "Why haven't you?"

The smile faded from his face. He sat down and glanced up at her. "We have no idea where to start searching. Besides, what if you're right, Elise? What if this is about me? About my time in the army or even my security work? I've already put Candace in danger. I couldn't ask my brothers to take on that risk, as well."

"So that idea wasn't quite as preposterous as you wanted me to think, was it?"

"Of course it wasn't. I knew it was always a possibility. I think that's why I've felt so paralyzed lately. My stomach has been knotted for weeks worrying about what calamity I might have brought down on my family. I don't understand how people live like this, constantly worried that every move they make could mean placing the people they love in danger."

"I suppose when you have a dangerous career, you're always aware that something bad could happen."

He looked at her, studying her for several long moments. "What would you be willing to sacrifice, Elise?"

"To stop innocent children from being sold into prostitution? I would sacrifice everything, even my life, in order to protect one child."

He rubbed his face and stood, his back to her. "You would sacrifice all that to help people who would just as soon spit at you as thank you?" The bitterness in his tone dinged her heart, and she knew he was referring to his time in Afghanistan. He was hurting so badly at the loss of his friends, his brothers. "It doesn't make sense to me anymore."

She placed her hands on his back, hugging him from behind. "Sacrifice never does make much sense."

"And what if you had a husband at home and a child? Would you expect them to sacrifice you, as well?"

"This is more than just a job to me. I don't do it only to earn a paycheck. I do it because I have to, because I feel it's my calling in life. There are young girls suffering and it's my job to find them, to help them. I hope that my family, if I ever have one, would understand that. I hope they would know that my sacrifice made a difference in someone's life."

He seemed to ponder that thought. Then he shook his head. "I used to believe that. I used to think the same way, but I don't anymore. I went to six funerals in as many days. I watched wives and children cry for husbands and fathers, and I watched most of my squadron lose lives and careers."

He stepped away from her, away from her embrace. His wide shoulders carried a heavy burden, and Elise knew they couldn't hold one more.

"It's not that I don't want you because I do. You're beautiful and smart and so kind. And you have this amazing zeal and passion for your work. The truth is all I want every waking moment of the day is to be in your presence, to soak in your perfume and to wait anxiously for you to smile and brighten my entire day."

Elise's heart soared at his words even as the painful reality of where he was leading sank in.

"But I can't. I can't lose another person I love. I can't let myself go there."

She understood. He wouldn't ask her to choose, but that was in essence her choice. Better to pull away now before things got too entangled, before their hearts got too involved.

"I understand." She grabbed her file folder and rushed out of his apartment before the depth of his eyes caused her to question the path she was on.

* * *

Josh ignored the shrill ring of his phone. He wasn't in the mood to speak to anyone. A few hours of peace was all he desired to process what had just happened between him and Elise. Was he making a mistake letting her go? His head swam with confusion. He could so easily see this woman stepping into his life and becoming important to him.

He rubbed his eyes, admitting the truth. She was already important to him.

He shouldn't have allowed that to happen, but it had sneaked up on him so subtly that he hadn't even noticed.

But he'd been honest with her about his feelings. He could get past her connection to Max, but he simply couldn't deal with her dangerous lifestyle. He'd had his share of putting his own life and others' at risk. He couldn't continue to live that way, and he couldn't live with the ever-present fear that one day she might not return to him.

His heart simply couldn't take that kind of heartbreak again.

But why did denying his heart hurt so much, too?

His phone rang again and this time he picked it up. He didn't recognize the number, but he'd got into the habit of answering it regardless. What if it was Candace calling him for help and he didn't answer because he didn't recognize the number she was calling from? Selfishly, he realized he'd spent the afternoon out of contact. What if she'd needed him then?

He answered the phone, holding out that one bit of hope that he would hear her voice on the other end of the line.

"I—I was going to leave a message," an unfamiliar male voice stated. "I wasn't expecting you to answer."

"Who is this?" Josh demanded.

"No one. I mean, I don't want to get involved in this, but I thought you should know Peter Larkin has a storage shed outside of town in the woods surrounding Shadow Lake. It's on the north side near a cluster of fallen trees." He rattled off coordinates to the shed.

"Who is this?" Josh demanded again, his heart beginning to beat faster with excitement.

"I—I told you. I don't want to get involved. I just thought you should know."

Josh heard a click and knew the man had hung up.

Excitement lit through him. This could be the break they'd been searching for. He hadn't recognized the caller or the number, but it didn't matter. If it led to finding Candace and Brooke, the tipster could remain anonymous for all he cared.

Elise spent the afternoon at the café with Lin, pretending everything was fine as they pored over statements, background checks and property holdings on Peter Larkin, although she doubted he really believed it. He knew her so well after all the years they'd been partners.

It was late when she finally excused herself and retired to her hotel room.

She was surprised to realize how emotional Josh's words had made her. She hadn't meant to fall for the handsome soldier, but somehow she had anyway. That only served to prove to her how entangled her personal and professional lives had got. It was a good thing Lin had arrived with fresh eyes to go over her work. She needed to distance herself emotionally.

Her phone rang and she reached for it, noticing Josh's number on her caller ID. Her heart leaped. Had he changed his mind? Had he decided losing her now was greater than losing her later? Her heart raced as she hit the answer button.

"Josh, hi." She tried to keep her voice steady and calm instead of shaking in anticipation as it was.

"I have news," he told her. His words were quick and excited. "I got a call, an anonymous tip. Larkin has a shed in the woods. That has to be where he's keeping the girls."

Elise perked up. "Who told you this?"

"I don't know. He said he didn't want to get involved, but he thought we should know. I called Daniel. We're going to drive out there and check it out."

"I'm on my way," Elise said, hopping to her feet, excitement bubbling through her. This could be the break in the case they'd been hoping for. But she couldn't help but wonder who'd called in the anonymous tip.

She texted Lin and met him downstairs. Together they hopped into her SUV and drove to the police station. Josh and Daniel were waiting outside, a map spread across the hood of his cruiser.

Josh looked up as they arrived. Surprise lined his face when he spotted Lin.

"Josh, Chief Mills, this is my partner, Agent Lin Wildwood. He arrived in town this morning to help."

Lin offered his hand and Chief Mills took it. "Looks like you might have arrived just in the nick of time."

Lin nodded and offered Josh his hand. "Glad I didn't miss the excitement."

Josh shook his hand then pointed them toward the map. "We've identified where the shed should be located based on the coordinates our anonymous tipster gave us. Daniel called the county clerk's office and the paperwork was recently submitted showing a dwelling there under Larkin's name." Josh folded up the map. "I'll lead the way in the Jeep. Daniel, you follow." He turned his gaze her way. "Elise, you want to ride up front with me?"

She hesitated. At this point, she would rather face an armed gunman than the blue of Josh's eyes, especially after the way they'd left things. She had to keep her distance if there was to be no future for them.

"I'll ride with you," Lin stated, giving her an out.

She nodded and silently thanked him. "I'll ride with Chief Mills." She slid into the passenger's side of the police cruiser and buckled in.

Josh and Lin headed for his truck and got inside. Chief Mills stepped into the driver's side of the police cruiser and started it up, following behind the Jeep as they headed out of town.

As Josh turned off the highway and onto rougher road, Elise held on tight.

The chief seemed to be in a talking mood. "I've known Josh for a long time. He's a good man but he's been through a lot recently. But I know him pretty well, Agent Richardson, and I can tell he's falling for you."

She shook her head. "No, he's not. Not anymore."

Ahead of them, Josh pulled up to a clearing containing a shed. He stopped his truck and jumped out. Elise, Lin and Chief Mills got out, too. A padlock was on the door, so Chief Mills went to the trunk of his cruiser and produced a pair of lock cutters. He handed them to Josh.

"We'll cover you," Mills said.

Elise pulled her weapon and trained it on the doors as the others did, mentally preparing herself for what lay inside. Was Larkin hiding out? It seemed unlikely since the lock was on the outside of the door. But what would they find inside?

Josh glanced back at them before pressing down on the pliers and cutting the lock. In one swift motion, he pulled it off and pushed open the door.

Elise swept the dark interior with her flashlight. She saw an old mattress on the floor and a stack of blankets. The smell was foul and the temperature cold. If someone was being kept in here they would be at the mercy of the outside temperature. December weather in Mississippi wasn't as cold as in other parts of the country, but thirty-to-forty-degree temperatures at night would still be cold for someone locked inside here.

"Agent Richardson?" The voice that called to her was small and still.

Elise swept her light toward it and caught sight of a small frame huddled against the wall, her blond hair straggly and her clothes torn.

Brooke!

They'd found her.

Chapter Eight

Elise examined the shed further while Josh stayed with Brooke. In the distance, sirens loomed, closing in on their location, answering Chief Mills's call. Elise spotted blood on the concrete and a mattress in the corner. This place was used to terrorize a young girl. Her blood boiled. Larkin would not get away with this.

"The ambulance just pulled up," Josh said from the doorway.

Hopefully the forensics team would be able to find fingerprints, blood samples and other specimens to use against Larkin. Elise watched as two paramedics hovered over Brooke, taking her vitals. She was now their greatest evidence against Larkin. A victim who'd survived to identify her predator.

Elise swept her flashlight over the inside of the shed again and spotted something in the corner. She moved toward it. She picked it up, recognizing it as the backpack Brooke had carried the day she'd tried to interview her. But the light shone on another object. Elise bent down and picked it up. Another backpack, this one gray and pink…like Candace's. Elise unzipped it and found it loaded with a biology book and an algebra book. Her heart thudded against her chest. She didn't call Josh over, not yet, not until she knew for certain to whom this backpack belonged. She pulled out a notebook and opened it, finding pages with Candace's name scrawled on them.

She stared out of the shed at Josh sitting by Brooke's side, her protector. This news would devastate him, but perhaps it would also bring him and Patti a sense of closure.

As she walked toward him, Josh spotted the backpack in her hand. All the painful emotions he'd tried hard to contain forced their way into his expression. "Where did you find that?"

Brooke looked up at her, sadness lining her young face. "That's Candace's backpack."

Elise nodded then knelt beside the girl. "I found it in the shed. Was Candace in there with you? Did you see her?"

Brooke shook her head. "He said he killed her. He told me he killed her and he would kill me, too, if I didn't do what he said."

Elise saw a tear escape Josh's eye. He swiped at it as he raked his hand over his face and turned away.

She wanted to rush to him, wrap her arms around him and offer him comfort, but she didn't. Instead, she focused on the cuts and bruises and the cigarette burns on Brooke's arms. She'd been tortured and beaten and possibly more.

"He can't hurt you anymore, Brooke. You're safe now. Can you tell me who did this to you?"

She needed her to say his name. She needed her to

identify him without confusion. Brooke was now their greatest piece of evidence against Larkin.

The girl fingered a lock of hair then looked at Elise, her chin quivering with fear. "It was Mr. Larkin. He grabbed me while I was walking to meet you. He locked me in the shed. He did terrible things to me." She broke into sobs and Elise immediately reached to hug the girl.

"You're safe now. No one is going to hurt you again." The paramedics motioned that they were ready to transport Brooke to the hospital. She was in for more poking and prodding and examination there, all in an effort to gather as much evidence as possible against Larkin. "These paramedics are going to take you to the hospital. They'll take good care of you and I'll meet you there."

She grabbed for Elise's jacket. "Can't you come with me?"

Elise longed to get over to Josh, to offer him comfort and sympathy. She knew he was hurting, having got evidence that Candace was not coming home. She wanted to be there for him…but as she looked into the trusting eyes of Brooke and realized the girl was bonding with her, she knew she had to accompany her to the hospital. Brooke needed to be questioned about her ordeal, and Elise needed to be the one to do it.

"I'm scared, Agent Richardson," Brooke whispered. "Please don't leave me."

Elise squeezed her hand reassuringly. "I'm not going anywhere." She would do whatever it took to put Larkin away for what he'd done.

"Brooke!"

Elise looked up at the call as did Brooke. Her father was rushing toward them. However, instead of being relieved to see him, Brooke tensed and inched closer to Elise.

"Brooke, are you all right?" Rick Martin reached his daughter and swept her into a hug.

"I'm fine," she told him

"Who did this, Brooke? Who hurt you?"

She glanced at Elise then back to her father. "It was Mr. Larkin from school."

Rick Martin turned a hard stare on Elise. "The man you let go? Surely now you have enough evidence to lock up that maniac."

Elise nodded. "Chief Mills has a team headed to his house right now. If he's there, they'll take him into custody."

He took Brooke by the shoulder. "Let's go home."

"Wait, Mr. Martin." Elise rushed after them. "Brooke needs to be evaluated by a physician. There are tests they need to perform on her."

"My daughter has been through enough already. I'm not putting her through a bunch of unnecessary medical procedures."

"The more evidence we collect against Larkin, the longer they'll be able to keep him locked up. Don't you want to know if Brooke was assaulted—" she glanced at Brooke "—sexually?"

"My daughter's statement that he abducted her will be enough to put him away."

"Mr. Martin, please be reasonable."

He stopped and turned to Elise. "I've made my decision, Agent Richardson. I need to get her home and get her cleaned up. She needs a chance to have a normal life. Can't you understand that? This ordeal is over. It's your job to catch the bad guys, so go do your job."

He walked to his car and opened the door for Brooke. The girl glanced her way before getting into the car, and Elise thought she saw a look of fear on her face.

She pulled out her phone and called Lin, who'd gone with Chief Mills to Larkin's house. Today had been a victory in that they'd found Brooke, but how could they celebrate when Larkin was not yet in custody?

"Please tell me you have good news," she said when he answered.

Lin sighed wearily. "I'm afraid not."

"You didn't get Larkin?"

"No, we got him all right. Elise, Larkin is dead."

When Elise arrived at Larkin's house, a crowd had already gathered on the street. Josh and Elise got out and moved through the crowds, beneath the police tape toward the garage where Lin and Chief Mills were waiting for them.

"What happened?" she asked the chief, who pointed inside the garage. Elise spotted Larkin's car parked there, with a figure slumped over the steering wheel. Exhaust fumes still filled the garage, and Elise had to cover her mouth and nose to keep from inhaling the toxic stench.

She examined the body, disappointed by this event. She'd hoped to have Larkin taken alive. Now would they ever know what had happened to Candace? Would her whereabouts be forever hidden because of Peter Larkin's cowardice?

She tried not to move the body, to preserve the integrity of the crime scene, but she checked for marks along his wrists and ankles or anything to indicate he was bound and then placed into the car. She saw none. It appeared this was just what it seemed—an accused man taking the easy way out.

Elise followed the chief into the yard, taking a deep breath to dispel the gagging harmful gas from her lungs and nostrils.

"Looks like suicide by asphyxiation," Lin stated. "He was in the car with the engine running and the garage door closed. The car was still running when we arrived."

"How long had he been in there?"

"Don't know yet, but there was still a quarter of a tank of gas left according to the gauge. Who knows if it was full or not."

"I didn't see any marks indicating he was bound."

"Any chance he was already dead when he was placed in the car?" Chief Mills asked.

She knew he asked the question purely for the purpose of covering all the bases. He wanted this to be just what it looked like and, for once, she was able to accommodate him. "He has bruises around his eyes indicating carbon monoxide poisoning. I imagine that will be his cause of death. And I saw no indication he was bound, but an autopsy may find differently."

She heard the crowd murmuring around the house. Peter Larkin had committed suicide—nearly as good as a confession, as far as the townspeople were concerned.

And to Chief Mills, too. "He knew he wasn't getting out of these charges."

He was satisfied. Larkin had kidnapped Brooke,

and the backpack they'd found suggested he'd kidnapped and killed Candace as well, then taken the easy way out when his crimes were discovered.

It all made sense.

It was simple and logical. Chief Mills seemed satisfied. Lin seemed satisfied.

Why, then, did it seem to Elise that this loose end had been hand tied just for their satisfaction?

Josh parked his truck in Patti's driveway and cut the engine, but he made no move to get out. "How can I go in there and tell her Candace is dead? I don't know how to do that."

Elise covered his hand with hers. "You don't have to do it alone."

His shoulders shook as he fought to control the emotions she knew were flowing through him. It wasn't fair for this family, for Josh, to have to go through this again. They'd already lost Max. Why did they have to lose Candace, too?

She was angry. Angry at God for allowing this. Angry at Larkin and those like him who used people for their own corrupt needs and then discarded them. These were the kinds of people she'd devoted her life to fighting against. These were the people who needed justice, and she vowed she would get vengeance for them.

She leaned over and hugged Josh, and he took her into his arms, his grasp strong and pressing as his ragged breath. She held him. It was all she could do for him now.

He broke their hold when the porch light came on and the front door opened. Patti stood at the door. Obviously recognizing the car, she headed toward them, but stopped as if realizing something was wrong when they didn't get out right away. Josh wiped his face, opened the door and stepped out. Patti must have seen the truth written on his face because her eyes widened and a retching sob shook her entire body so violently that Elise worried she might hit the pavement. But Josh rushed to her and held her as she cried.

Elise's anger continued to burn against Larkin and against God as she watched. What kind of God allowed such evil to win? Both Josh and Patti believed God guided their lives, but what kind of plan could God have that involved the murder of this child and the further devastation of this family?

Elise holed up inside a spare office at the police station and scanned through the evidence against Larkin again—Brooke's statement, the processing of the shed, Taylor Johnson's death. Something was wrong and she couldn't shake the overwhelming feeling that this entire situation was too well wrapped up. There were always questions remaining after an investigation ended. The motives, the undiscovered evidence. Where were they? The only piece of evidence unaccounted for was Candace's body. After the Allie Peterson case, she'd promised herself she would follow her gut, and now her gut was shouting volumes.

Lin knocked on the door and she waved him inside. He'd been there with her tying up the case. "I'm sorry it didn't turn out better."

The building was quickly filling up with volunteers ready to help comb the woods for Candace. But they were looking for only a body now. No one expected to find her alive. "Chief Mills is calling in search dogs to scour the area around where they found Brooke."

He gave her a sideways glance. "Elise, we can't save everyone."

"I know that, but lately it seems I can't save anyone, Lin."

"You saved Brooke. Your gut told you she was in trouble and you were right."

"But I interviewed Larkin. Why didn't I see what he was capable of?"

"He fooled you. That's all."

"He didn't strike me as all that smart."

"Perhaps that's part of his persona. He may actually have been smarter than he looked. That's how he's scraped by all these years. Either way, I'd say this case no longer fits the criteria for your human smuggling ring."

"No, it doesn't."

"What are you going to do now?"

She understood his question. What were her plans now that this case had exploded in her face? She hadn't uncovered any evidence of a trafficking ring. She hadn't been able to save Candace. She hadn't even been able to protect Brooke from Larkin. She'd failed on all accounts. Was it time to return to the FBI? To what extent? She was a failure. What would the FBI want with her now?

"Elise, it's time to come home. Your theory hasn't panned out. It's time to come back to the Bureau and do some real good."

She saw his insistence. He still believed in her, wanted her back. Still, she hesitated. "I may take another couple of weeks." This case had left a stench around her and she needed to distance herself from it. She'd got too close to this case, to this family, to Josh, and it hadn't been good for anyone.

She noticed Josh enter the police station. Lin followed her gaze.

"Excuse me," Lin said. "I need to speak with Chief Mills before I leave." He nodded to Josh as he left the office and Josh entered.

She stood to greet him, resisting the urge to reach out to him, to give the comfort they'd shared. The emotional turmoil this family had been through wouldn't end with Larkin's death. In fact, without a body to bury, their grief might be lasting. "How's Patti?"

"She'll be better when she can bury her daughter."

He didn't have to say the words for her to know that he would be better then, too. Despite his time as a ranger, witnessing multiple deaths, the deaths of those closest to him, including Candace's, was devastating.

"I have something I need to confess to you, Josh. I feel like I misled you when we first met. I didn't come here as part of an FBI investigation in human trafficking. I came here alone, having taken a leave of absence from the FBI three months ago. There was never an official FBI investigation into Candace's disappearance. Perhaps if I had told you the truth earlier, you could have done something else besides pin all your hopes on me to find her."

"I'm glad you told me, but I don't think it would have made a difference. It only reinforces what I knew all along. You were the only one who did anything to find Candace. For that, I'm grateful."

"I wish I could have done more."

"You did all you could. I don't think there's anything more you could have done, Elise. I suspect Candace was dead long before you came to town." He moved away from her. "What will you do now? Go back to the FBI?"

"I'm not sure. I really don't know what good I could do there."

"Then stay here with me."

"What?"

"I can't bear to lose anyone else I care about, Elise. Maybe…maybe there is a chance for us."

If you don't return to the FBI.

He didn't say those words, but she heard them regardless. He'd already shared his fears about her job being dangerous. It wouldn't be fair to him to continue on with a dangerous job. But if she'd already decided she wasn't going to return to the FBI… She sucked in a breath. How could she weigh the benefits of an FBI career against her love for Josh Adams? But how could she go back to that life where every decision she made seemed to be the wrong one?

He looked at her, his eyes pressing into hers as he moved closer to her. Suddenly, his arms were around her, pulling her against him, and he was claiming her lips. All thoughts of the pain of this case subsided and she lost herself in his embrace. He was her rock, her solid stone that would keep her anchored and safe.

Her mind spun with this new revelation. She could have a future with Josh. It wasn't too late. This new wrinkle should have made her decision easier… Then why didn't it?

He pulled away from her but locked his fingers with

hers. "I told Daniel I would come by the search area. I think he wants me there as the face of the family."

She nodded, knowing it was necessary for him to go, and also she knew he wouldn't give up until he found Candace's body. She silently prayed they would find her. She prayed they would finally find the closure this family so badly needed.

"I should go by and see Patti."

"She's at the school." He must have seen Elise's surprised expression. "She said she couldn't stand being at the house alone. She needed to occupy her mind. It's the last day of classes before Christmas break."

She nodded. "I'll go by the school."

He kissed her again then was gone, leaving her to make her decision.

She drove to the school and was heading inside when she spotted Brooke leaning against the school building on the sidewalk.

Elise approached her, surprised to see the girl at school. "What are you doing here?"

She appeared nervous as she spoke to Elise. "I had exams. I didn't want to miss them."

"I'm sure you could have gotten an extension for the tests."

"I—I wanted to get them over with. My dad said we might not come back after the break. We might be moving again."

Elise was saddened to hear that. Brooke needed help getting over what Larkin had put her through. She needed counseling and a support structure she doubted the girl would receive from her father.

But there was no need for Brooke and her family

to stay. She wouldn't have to testify now that Larkin had committed suicide. There were no legal reasons for her to stay. And the memories would haunt her for the rest of her life.

Elise could still see the fear that gripped her eyes, pain that would not go away for a very long time. She reached out for Brooke and the girl flinched. "He can't hurt you anymore, Brooke. You're safe now."

"I know that," she said, but the confidence in those words didn't reach her eyes. "That man can't hurt me again."

But she was still hurting. That man, that experience, would continue to hurt her daily.

"You still have my number, Brooke. If you need anything, even just to talk, call me."

The girl glanced around nervously then took a step closer to Elise as if she had a secret she was hesitant to share. She opened her mouth to speak but was cut off by the sound of a horn blaring.

Elise saw a beat-up Chevy causing the noise and a young man only a few years older than Brooke behind the wheel pressing hard on the horn to get their attention. Brooke moved away from her and Elise saw her shut down. Whatever had been on her mind, whatever she had been about to share with Elise, was gone.

"I have to go," she said instead, rushing toward the waiting car.

The boy got out and met her. "What did she want?"

"Nothing," Brooke told him then waited as he opened the door for her. Once she was in the seat, he slammed the door and turned back to Elise, glaring. He was a young man, not much older than Brooke, but the scowl on his face and the missing teeth as he sneered at her indicated past drug use. This wasn't the kind of boy Brooke needed to be associating with.

Elise moved toward the car. "Who is this?" she asked Brooke through the open window.

"My cousin Roy."

Roy flashed a smug grin then walked back around to the driver's side and got in. He roared away a moment later before Elise could ask any further questions.

Something about this situation felt wrong. What had Brooke been about to say before Roy's arrival, and why had his presence shut her down? Was the girl hiding something about Larkin? Elise realized suddenly what bothered her about the case against Larkin—it all hung on Brooke's assertion that Peter Larkin was the man who attacked her and killed Candace. Did the girl know more about the situation than she was letting on? Had her father convinced her to remain quiet about what she knew?

Elise had nothing but her gut to go on, but her gut was telling her loud and clear that Brooke Martin might still be in trouble.

What are you doing, Josh?

He closed the door to his truck but didn't turn the key. Instead, he leaned against the steering wheel and tried to pull his thoughts back to a rational, coherent process instead of the jumble Elise Richardson made him.

He'd nearly lost her, and the fear that notion sent flooding through him was almost more than he'd been able to bear. But it had simultaneously given him the desire to hold her tightly to make certain nothing happened to separate them and driven him to flee from her and the feelings she evoked in him.

The thought that he could lose her—the thought that he could lose anyone else—was more than he could stand.

He drove home, the pulling in his heart still present as he imagined himself walking through his empty apartment. What would it be like to have someone to come home to? A female presence to add life to his shell of an existence?

He could see Elise stepping easily into that role. Slowly, he felt the life returning to him the more he was with her, the longer her influence, her beauty, was around. Her passion and determination were infectious and he'd been stung.

But what would he do if he lost her? If something happened to her?

Or worse, if she left on her own?

He didn't know which was worse. He only knew that thinking about her leaving town stabbed him harder and sharper than his knife in its sheath.

He pulled up at his apartment and found a group of trucks parked in the lot and a bunch of familiar faces gathered together.

He knew them in a moment. Matt, Colton, Levi, Garrett, Blake—his ranger brothers, always there for him when he needed them.

"What are you all doing here?" he asked as they gathered around him.

Colton spoke up. "We're here to help with the search." He squeezed Josh's shoulder. "We'll find her and bring her home."

And even though he knew they were looking for only a body now, it meant the world to know his brothers had his back.

Elise knocked on Patti's office door.

Her face was drawn as she stared up at Elise with reddened eyes and a slight I-will-be-fine-eventually smile on her face. "I couldn't stay at that house alone," she said, pulling together a stack of papers to file. "It was too quiet. Besides, this is exam week and I'm down a teacher. So if Josh sent you here to take me home, I'm not going. Not yet."

"Josh didn't send me. I wanted to check on you and he said you were here. How are you holding up?"

She stopped then lowered herself into a chair, the stack of papers still in her arms. "I don't know. I suppose I knew this was coming. She'd been gone too long, but I still held out hope. Now that's gone, too."

"Patti, I'm so sorry."

She stared up at Elise and frowned. "I thought God sent you here to bring my baby home. I thought you were part of His plan."

"I wish I were," Elise said, and she meant it. She wished there was a greater hand at work to bring Candace home. "I saw Brooke as I was walking in."

"Oh, yes, Brooke." A flash of grief passed through her eyes and Elise was sorry she'd mentioned the name. Brooke had come home to her family, while Candace had not. "I didn't get a chance to check on her myself. I'm a little surprised she was back to school already. How was she?"

Elise hesitated, not wanting to burden Patti any further, but she needed to know more about Brooke if she was to put to rest the unease growing inside of her. "A boy just a few years older than Brooke picked her up. She said he was her cousin, but he seemed overly protective for a cousin, almost as if I was snooping around his property. Can you tell me about her family life?"

"Not much. Truthfully, Brooke spent a lot of time at our house with Candace. I often thought she didn't want to go home, but I chalked it up to them being friends and not wanting to be apart. You know how teenage girls can be."

"Have you ever met her parents?"

"Only her father. Brooke's mother left them years ago."

"What do you think of Rick Martin?"

Patti sat down in her chair. "Let me put it this way. I think Candace wanted to set us up so she and Brooke could be sisters. I politely but firmly informed her that wouldn't happen, but I was always pleased to allow Brooke to stay over whenever she liked."

"Do you suspect he's abusive?"

"No, just very involved in her life, but also very emotionally distant. Brooke had to call him whenever she arrived and when she left, and he would text her a lot while she was at the house. He was always checking in with her. It didn't seem to me to be out of concern. It seemed overly protective. In fact, it was downright controlling."

"Patti, did the police look at Brooke's father or her cousin as suspects when Candace disappeared?"

"I don't know for sure. I know they spoke to him. But there was no reason to believe they had anything to do with Candace's disappearance, especially after Brooke's statement that she ran away."

"If Brooke knew her family had a hand in harming Candace, she may have reason to cover it up by telling that runaway story."

"You suspect she's covering for them?"

"Or she's too frightened to tell the truth. I want to speak with her more in depth."

"You know her father wouldn't let you speak to her before. What makes you think this time will be different?"

"Because this time I'm going to their house, and I'm not leaving until I'm convinced Brooke is safe."

Patti picked up the phone. "I'm calling Josh."

Elise stopped her. "Don't call him just yet."

"Elise, you should wait and let Josh go with you."

"I'm only going to talk. I'll be fine."

Elise walked out. This situation with Brooke bothered her. She was certain Brooke had wanted to tell her something, something secretive, something her family wouldn't want her to expose. Was there more to the story with Larkin? Or was someone else hurting this girl, someone else she hadn't yet revealed?

One way or another, she would find out. She wouldn't let another girl slip through her fingers the way Allie Peterson had and the way Candace had.

Elise got into her car and started the engine. Only then did she realize the confusion and disorientation of the day had finally subsided. She knew who she was. She might not always be FBI, but she would always fight to protect girls in danger no matter what the cost to her.

Her heart tore at the realization.

There could never be a future between her and Josh.

* * *

It was dark when Elise found the house. She pulled into the long driveway. The house sat back on a lot and the closest houses were a good trek away. With no street lamps this far out, Elise relied on her headlights. She parked, noticing no outside lights on the house. She left her headlights burning but also grabbed her flashlight from the glove compartment before getting out and heading toward the house.

She knocked and heard movement from inside, but no one answered.

She knocked again. "Brooke? It's Agent Richardson. I'd like to speak to you again if you don't mind."

She heard movement again then a pounding, causing her head to jerk up and her heart to race. Elise pulled her gun. That sounded like someone hitting the floor. Something was going on inside and it didn't sound good.

She reached for the door handle and it turned. She pushed open the door, cautiously glancing around.

"Agent Richardson with the FBI," she announced. "I'm coming inside."

The room was nearly cleared out with only two chairs and a card table and boxes stacked against the wall, but the room stank of cigarette smoke and the haze of it met her as she pushed open the door, evidence that someone had been here very recently. She hadn't imagined hearing someone inside. One chair was back-side on the floor, obviously knocked over in the rush to get out when Elise knocked.

"Hello," Elise called to whomever was there. "I was just dropping by to check on Brooke. I don't want any trouble."

No response, but she sensed someone was inside.

She checked the bedrooms and found mostly boxes. It looked as if the Martins were preparing to leave town. Was it because of what had happened to Brooke? Or was it because the family had something darker to hide, like her suspicion that someone was still hurting the girl?

She pushed open a bedroom door and found what had probably been Brooke's bedroom. The walls were pink and the curtain frilly. She checked the closet and found girls' clothes. On the dresser was what looked to be the purse she'd seen Brooke carrying earlier that afternoon. So they had come back to this house. But now where were they? And why could she not push away that nagging suspicion that something in this household wasn't right?

She checked the other two bedrooms and found no one. She moved toward the kitchen. The cabinets were cleared out and even the refrigerator was empty. Wherever this family was, wherever they were going, she needed to find them in order to make certain Brooke was safe. Even if her suspicion that someone was still hurting Brooke was wrong, the girl needed counseling to deal with what she'd been through. Not only had she been abducted and abused by someone she'd trusted, she'd also lost her best friend and dealt with the knowledge that she could have been killed, as well.

Elise turned to leave, but tripped over a rug on the floor and fell. The rug slid, revealing a cellar door with a locked padlock.

A secret door!

She saw a set of keys hanging on the wall and grabbed them. They fit into the lock. She pulled off the padlock and opened the door to reveal a set of stairs leading underground to a basement-like area. But why keep it padlocked?

Elise pulled out her flashlight, drew her gun and headed down the steps. She scanned the area with her light but saw only a bloodstained mattress thrown into the corner and a makeshift toilet.

Movement from the opposite corner startled her and she turned her light and weapon that way.

A figure shielded her eyes against the light. "Agent Richardson? Is that you?" The voice sounded so young, so innocent.

Brooke.

Elise moved toward her, her gun held high and her suspicions on full alert. "Are you hurt? Who did this to you, Brooke? Who locked you down here?"

The girl's eyes pooled with tears. "Agent Richardson, I'm sorry."

"There's nothing for you to be sorry about, Brooke. You didn't do anything wrong."

"I did really want to talk to you," she said, tears streaming down her face. "I wanted to tell you the truth, but they wouldn't let me."

"Who wouldn't let you, Brooke?" Elise's mind raced with information. What truth was Brooke trying to share with her? And who was the "they" who wouldn't let her? Larkin? Her family? Or someone else entirely?

"I wanted to warn you, but they said you were getting too close. They said you were going to ruin everything. They had to make you look at someone else."

Larkin. It had all been a ruse to turn Elise's attention toward Larkin and away from the real culprits. Brooke had not been abducted that day. Someone had planned her abduction…and called in the anonymous tip that led them to find her. Had they also killed Larkin to cement his guilt, or had he taken that measure on his own after realizing that he was being so efficiently framed for something he hadn't done?

She stared around the dirty, damp basement room. Brooke's family had been keeping her locked up. They'd done this to her…assuming they were actually her family.

Brooke had said it. Elise had been getting too close. She'd been too close to uncovering the trafficking ring. Brooke was just a pawn, another victim of the trafficking ring. She was certain that was what was behind this. She was being kept prisoner, released only to do what she was told—to lure girls into captivity.

"I'm going to get you out of here," Elise assured her, lowering her weapon.

Brooke's eyes grew wide with fear. "I don't think so. Neither one of us is going anywhere."

"What do you mean?"

Movement on the steps grabbed Elise's attention. She swung around, raising her gun, only to have it knocked out of her hand. Her flashlight went flying, too, casting the cellar into darkness. As Brooke screamed, someone grabbed Elise. She was overcome by the smell of cigarettes and beer. Pain ripped through the back of her head. Then the darkness changed and the fight left her body as the last remnant of light faded and complete darkness enveloped her.

Chapter Nine

Josh spent the evening reminiscing with his buddies about old times, then the morning coordinating a search area through the woods surrounding the shed where Brooke had been found. It felt good to have his team with him, and after trading stories all night, he was confident they would uncover something that would lead them to find Candace's body.

He and Matt were just returning from an uneventful search when Josh's phone rang.

"This is Carolyn Stringer over at the Medical Center," a lady said when he'd answered. "As you know, I've been calling Agent Richardson every day since she left the hospital."

He was only too aware.

"Well, today is the last day we had scheduled to phone her, but she doesn't seem to be answering our call. We've tried multiple times."

"I haven't spoken to her since yesterday."

"I've called the paramedics, but I thought you might know something. Please let us know if you hear anything."

"I will." He hung up and dialed Daniel's cell phone.

"I take it you've heard?"

"The hospital called me. How long has she been out of contact?"

"They spoke with her last yesterday afternoon but haven't been able to reach her since. I had an officer meet the paramedics at the hotel, and she's not there, but neither is her car. It's possible she just finally decided to ignore Nurse Stringer's call."

"No, she wouldn't do that." Josh knew she found those calls annoying, but she hadn't ignored them. In fact, she'd gone out of her way to make certain the nurses knew she was fine.

"You said her car was gone? Maybe her phone died and she hasn't been able to get in touch. I'll check Patti's and the school."

He hung up and turned to Matt. "Elise is missing."

"You go," Matt said. "We'll stay here and keep searching."

He ran to the Jeep, dialing her cell phone number as he hopped inside. As Daniel had stated, the call went straight to voice mail. "Elise, call me when you get this," he said after the beep.

He drove by the hotel. Her SUV was gone, but that didn't stop him from pounding on her hotel door without response. He went to the office, intent on getting Bobby to open her room so he could make sure she was okay, but the office was locked up tight.

He jumped back into his truck and dialed again, this time calling his sister-in-law's number. Patti answered after two rings. "Patti, have you seen Elise? I've tried calling her cell phone and she's not answering."

"I haven't seen her since yesterday afternoon."

"Did she say anything to you about where she was headed when she left?"

"Um…no, nothing." Patti's voice held a note of nervousness. His sister-in-law had never been good at hiding things. She hadn't had the practice he had. He could almost see her fidgeting as she spoke and nervously pushing a strand of hair behind her ear.

"I'm on my way over." He clipped off the call and threw the Jeep into gear. Patti's nervousness mixed with Elise's failure to answer her phone and Daniel's concern was enough to prick his senses. Something wasn't right with this situation. He needed to find out the truth from Patti, and he was best at doing that face-to-face.

He roared into the driveway and jumped out. Patti was waiting for him, her hand in the air as if trying to bat off his questions.

"I wanted to call you, Josh, but she insisted I not. She wanted to go alone."

His heart kicked up a notch, sensing a not-so-good response. "Where did she go, Patti?"

"She was worried about Brooke Martin. She said she was going to her house to check on her."

"When?"

"It was after school let out yesterday."

His gut twisted.

Something was wrong.

No one had seen or heard from her in over eighteen hours. That was too long for her to be out of touch.

He turned and walked back to his truck, Patti following behind him.

"Where are you going?" she asked.

He didn't care that their future together was unresolved. He wasn't going to lose someone else he cared for.

"I'm going to the last place I know she went—to see Brooke Martin."

As consciousness slipped back into her, Elise was aware only that she was lying on something cold and wet. She moved her arms and lifted herself. Her head felt as if it was going to burst with pain. Her world spun and her hand flailed for some stability.

"Are you okay?" a voice asked, full of concern.

She jumped, scrambling to a sitting position and reaching for her gun only to discover it was gone. "Who's there?" she demanded. Through blurry eyes, she saw the outline of someone sitting a few inches away.

"You've been unconscious since they lowered you down."

Elise used her hands to steady herself as the world spun and nausea rolled through her. What had happened? How had she got here? Memories flooded her. She'd been searching Brooke's home and found the cellar. Then…blackness. Someone had hit her from behind. That explained the weight of pain across the back of her head.

She struggled to focus against the nagging darkness to get a better look at her companion. "Who are you?"

The girl leaned forward into a stream of light and Elise noticed red hair, braces and a purple hoodie.

Candace?

Could it really be her? Was she alive?

If Brooke's abduction truly was staged, then so probably was Candace's death.

"Roy brought you in last night. I thought you were dead at first. Then I wondered if you would ever wake up."

Elise used the wall as support as she crawled to her feet. They were on a dirt floor and the walls surrounding them were damp and cold. Elise stared up at the only light that shone. It came from a circular area several feet up and opened up to blue sky. Elise quickly realized they were underground, probably in an old, abandoned well…a perfect spot to hide abducted girls for the trafficking market where no one would ever look and no one would hear them if they called for help.

"Roy?"

"Roy Martin. Brooke's cousin."

Elise looked at the girl. It was indeed Candace. The girl's red hair was streaked with blood and dirt, but other than being dirty and bruised, she didn't seem to have sustained serious injury.

"Where are we? Still at the Martins' house?"

"No. Somewhere else. I'm not sure where. There's a cabin, but otherwise the area is surrounded by woods."

"How long have you been down here?"

"I don't know. A while."

"Where's Brooke? Is she here?"

"No."

"I found her locked up at her house."

"I know. She's the one who recruited me."

"What do you mean recruited you?"

"It's her job. They let her go to school so she can find girls like me who would be good candidates."

"They? Brooke's family did this? Her father, her cousin? They're the kidnappers, not Larkin?"

"It's mostly Brooke's dad, Roy and another man. I heard Roy call him Jay. There used to be another guy named Taylor, but I haven't seen him in a while."

Elise nodded. She knew why. Taylor Johnson had been used to make a point.

"But there's someone else," Candace told her. "There's someone else in charge. An older man. I don't know who he is, but he made me write a letter to my mom. He made me tell her I was mad at her and I wasn't coming home." Tears slid down Candace's face. "She must think I hate her."

"No, she doesn't. She didn't believe the letter, Candace. She knew something had happened to you. She knew you wouldn't just leave and not come back. She and Josh, they never gave up hoping they would find you."

But Elise's suspicions about the notes were right. Someone—whoever was in charge—had forced Candace, and probably the other girls, to write those letters.

She'd been right about the trafficking ring, too, but it was little consolation when she was trapped underground by the same ring no one else believed existed.

"They were going to move me, but Brooke overheard them say it was too dangerous right now. Are you the FBI lady she told me about?"

"Brooke talked to you about me?"

"Yes. She said you were here to find me. They don't lock her up here because she can't get away. Sometimes she comes and talks to me."

"Have you seen Brooke since I arrived?"

Candace shook her head. That wasn't a good sign. Wherever Brooke was, she was in danger. But before

Elise could worry about her, she had to find a means of escape for them.

Climbing up the walls would be impossible, and even if she placed Candace on her shoulders, the opening was still too high for the girl to reach.

They were trapped.

"Don't worry. An FBI agent can't just go missing. They'll be out looking for us. Help will be here soon."

Candace seemed comforted by her words, but Elise knew they were empty assurances. She'd told Lin she was taking a few weeks to reevaluate her direction, which meant it would be weeks before he realized Elise was missing. And after the way she'd left things with Josh, he would probably believe she'd made her decision and gone back to the FBI. He would take her disappearance as a rejection of him. No one would be looking for her.

They were on their own.

Except maybe…for God.

Was it possible she was still a part of the plan Patti had mentioned? He had guided her to find Candace and to find her alive. Was that merely a cruel final joke in His cosmic plan? Or was God really with them? Was it possible He cared more than Elise had thought? Did He have a plan for getting them out of this situation?

She wasn't yet ready to pin all her hopes on divine intervention, but she wasn't above accepting God's help in escaping if He offered it.

Josh gripped the steering wheel as he drove the winding country roads that led out of town, following the GPS directions from the address Daniel had given him for the Martins. They lived in a rural area south of town and Josh spotted deer several times in the woods along the road. He briefly wished he had his rifle with him to take out a few. It was easy hunting this time of year.

He found the house and pulled into the driveway. He got out and knocked on the door. Rick Martin answered the door barefoot and without a shirt, but sporting a beer in one hand and a cigarette in the other.

Josh got straight to the point. "I'm looking for Agent Elise Richardson. I was told she came by here last night."

"Nope," Martin said. "Nobody's been here."

"She was coming to talk to Brooke."

"She's not here and she hasn't been here."

Josh bit his tongue, his instinct itching to grab something and beat the information out of this man. He calmed his thoughts. This wasn't a terrorist or even a suspect in anything. He couldn't allow his emotions to guide his actions. He had to remain calm, despite this man's lack of forthcomingness.

"Were you home last night? Maybe someone else saw her?"

He turned to two young men sitting at a card table inside. "Either of you see that lady FBI agent come by here yesterday?"

One of the boys shook his head. "Haven't seen anyone around here."

Josh noticed the other hesitated, stopping the game for a moment before resuming and agreeing with the other boy. "Haven't seen nobody around here," he echoed.

"What about Brooke? May I speak with her?"

"She's not home," the boy answered. "She spent the night with a friend."

"What friend?" Josh asked. "What's her name?"

He glanced Josh's way. "Didn't ask and she didn't offer." He dropped the game controller and stood, coming to the door. "Besides, that lady wouldn't have talked to Brooke because her dad wouldn't have let her."

Josh didn't like the way this boy cocked up as if he was all important and in charge. "That was when she was a witness to my niece's abduction. My understanding is that Agent Richardson was worried someone might still be hurting Brooke."

The boy gave him a sadistic grin. "My cousin don't concern you."

"She does if someone is hurting her."

Rick Martin stepped in. "That's enough, Roy." He addressed Josh with his final comments. "Agent Richardson is not here and she hasn't been here," he said before slamming the door in Josh's face.

Josh turned and walked slowly down the unsteady porch. The steps wobbled beneath his feet. He scanned the yard, noticing the junk cars and car parts scattered across the lawn and the wooded areas surrounding the tract of land.

This place was out in the middle of nowhere. No street lamps and no neighbors to witness anyone's comings and goings.

He had no reason not to believe the Martins when they claimed not to have seen her. But this was the last place he knew Elise had come.

A shadow crossed over the opening of the well. Elise scrambled to where Candace was sleeping and nudged her awake. They both looked up to see Roy Martin peering over the edge.

"Hello there, ladies." He tossed down a rope ladder and pointed at Candace. "Climb up."

She looked to Elise, fear pooling her blue eyes.

Elise hated to be split up, but she knew they had no choice. Besides, if there were any chance for escape, it would be up there and not down here. "If you have the opportunity to run, take it," Elise whispered to her.

Candace nodded her understanding then took hold of the rope ladder. Elise stood holding the bottom so it wouldn't slip beneath her and cause her to fall. Once Candace was safely to the top, Roy grabbed her arm, causing Candace to cry out in pain.

He glanced back down the well at Elise. "Now you, too. Climb."

She chewed her lip and bit back the fear that crawled up her. This couldn't be good. They'd held Candace here for weeks and now suddenly they were calling them both out? Still, she grabbed the rope and started to climb. At least they would both be out of the well. Escape was probably their only chance, and they wouldn't be able to escape while they were stuck at the bottom of an abandoned well.

She reached the edge and crawled into the intense brightness of the afternoon sun. Roy grabbed her arm and pulled her to her feet. Elise noticed Candace being held at gunpoint by another man about Roy's age, obviously the guy named Jay Candace had mentioned. She didn't recognize him, but she memorized every inch of his face in case she got out of this situation and needed to identify their abductors.

Roy pressed the cold metal of his gun into Elise's

side. "There's someone who wants to meet you, Agent."

He motioned for Elise to move and led her toward a cabin while Jay pulled Candace along behind them. While they walked, Elise scoped out the area. Candace had been right. They were no longer at the Martins' house. They were in an open area surrounded by woods. Two pickup trucks and a high-priced sedan sat in front of a cabin. If they could get loose and run into those woods, they might be able to hide long enough to stay safe or run across a hunter who could help them.

But as Elise's feet hit the cabin steps, their chances for escape dwindled.

Roy pushed her up the steps and into the cabin, through the door and into a large, well-decorated room. He pulled out a chair at the dining table and ordered her to sit. In front of her on the table was a pad of notebook paper and a pen.

The letters. They were going to make her write a letter.

Roy walked over to a closed door and knocked softly. "We're ready," he called to whomever was inside.

Elise held her breath. She was going to see him… the man behind all of this…the man she'd been chasing after for months…the man responsible for all the missing girls on her wall.

The door opened and a man exited. Elise couldn't see his face as he stopped to speak with Roy. She strained her neck to see him…to see his face.

She didn't have to wait long.

Roy stepped out of the way and Elise got a good

look at the man who was heading up this trafficking ring.

He smiled at her, a smile so familiar that it was sickening to remember. A smile that she now knew hid only lies and betrayal.

Bobby Danbar.

"I'm sorry it had to come to this, Agent Richardson," he said as he approached the table. "I had hoped you would take what we gave you and be satisfied and leave town."

She glared at him. "What you gave me?"

"Mr. Larkin. We practically spoon-fed him to you. You had everything you needed to close down your investigation, but still you kept pushing and probing. You've made quite a bit of trouble for us, Agent Richardson."

Had he been behind it all? Had he staged the break-in at his own hotel? "Glad to help."

"It's time for you to disappear."

He pushed the pen and paper toward her.

She knew where he was headed. The same way he'd forced the girls to write runaway letters, he wanted her to write a letter stating she was leaving, so no one would suspect she'd been abducted.

But she was not a child to be terrorized. She was a trained federal agent, and she wasn't writing anything for this man.

She stared at him, determined not to relent. "I won't do it."

"I thought you would say as much. That's why she's here, too."

He nodded at Roy, who grabbed Candace and raised the gun to her head. Candace cried out in fear.

Elise understood the threat. Write the letter or he would kill Candace. But being sold into prostitution might be a fate worse than death. Still, this wasn't the time to make such decisions. She had to keep them both alive long enough for someone to find them.

Reluctantly, she pulled the paper toward her and picked up the pen.

He smiled. "That's much better, Agent Richardson." He sat on the table overseeing her. "Now, you'll write only what I tell you to write. Any tricks and the girl will die. Understood?"

Elise nodded and began to write as this man dictated her goodbye letter to Josh. When she was done, he produced a typewritten letter stating her intention to resign from the FBI and instructed her to sign it. Elise did as he asked, knowing Candace's life depended on her being compliant.

When she was done, he picked up the letters and placed them into an envelope. "I'll be sure and mail these for you," he said smugly.

"What's going to happen to the girls?" she asked him. She had no reason to believe that she would make it out of this alive, so she hoped he might feel at ease to speak freely.

"You should know, Agent. You've been on our trail for a while now. Brooke and Candace will be moved to another location once we're convinced the authorities are off our trail. You've made quite a mess for us." He motioned toward Candace, who was still at the mercy of the man with the gun to her head. "I only hope the police are satisfied with the evidence we planted indicating she was dead. I'd hate to have to provide them a body to find. It would cost us a good deal and I don't like to waste merchandise."

"She's not merchandise. She's an innocent young girl."

He snorted. "Not for long." He walked over to Candace and touched her hair, twirling it around his finger. "A pretty young thing like this can bring us big money on the market."

He was talking about trafficking Candace. She'd been right all along about the human trafficking ring, though it didn't make her happy to know that. But at least Candace was alive…for now.

"And what about me? What will you do with me?"

He sneered at her. "For all the trouble you've caused me, I'd like nothing more than to put a bullet in your head. But I have my orders, too. The boss wants to see you. He wants to take care of you himself."

So he wasn't the man in charge. "Who is your boss? Who do you work for?"

"I'm only a supplier. I don't get the names of the big guys. Only now, I have to move my operation because of you. If word gets out, no one will do business with me. That's why I have no choice but to clean up the mess you've made."

"You had Taylor Johnson break into my hotel room and steal my files."

"Of course. I had to know if you were onto us, if that was why you'd come to town. Unfortunately once I knew you were here to investigate my operation, I was forced to put Roy Martin on the job."

"Trying to run me down?" She flashed Roy a smug smile. "He failed."

"Yes, he did. Because of that Josh Adams. He's always sticking his nose into everyone else's business."

"I thought he was your friend."

"No, those Adams boys were never concerned with me. They had everything. They had the family, the popularity, the good looks. But neither one of them ever knew how to keep their noses out of other people's business."

She was stunned by this revelation. Had Max been onto Bobby's operation? "Max was investigating you?"

"I was just beginning to branch out then. My cousin had turned me on to a drug ring operating in the area. Max got a little too curious, so we had no choice but to take him out."

Elise's mind was reeling. Bobby Danbar had hired someone to kill Max. Had she simply been in the wrong place at the wrong time? Or had they counted on Max's police instincts to lure him into the dangerous situation?

Lin was right. She did have a way of tripping over danger.

Candace cried out. "You killed my father?" Tears streamed down her face, and she was sobbing so badly that her body shook. It was a shock for anyone. All she'd ever known was that her father died a hero. Now to learn that he'd been coldly murdered was heart-breaking.

Bobby stood and addressed Roy and Jay. "Take them back to the well."

Roy grabbed Elise's arms and pulled her to her feet, pushing her out the door and back down the steps. Elise could hear Candace crying behind them. When they reached the well, Roy pulled his gun and pointed it at Elise. "Go." She grabbed the ladder and climbed down, her gaze striking Candace and the gun at her head. They knew she wouldn't try to escape with Candace's life at stake. Candace followed down after her, and Roy hauled the ladder back up when Candace reached the bottom.

Elise reached for her as the girl slid to the floor, her hair hanging in shambles around her face. Elise sat beside her, wrapping her arms around the girl's shoulders.

"He killed my dad," Candace said. "I've always blamed my dad. I've spent so many years being mad because he left us. Now I realize he never stood a chance. He was never coming home." She turned those bright blue eyes on Elise. "And now neither are we."

Josh headed back through town toward the police station. He'd swung by the homes of several of Candace's teachers he knew Elise had interviewed, hoping at least one of them had spoken to her. He hated bothering them the first day of their Christmas break, especially when all their answers had been the same—no one had seen her—but he was desperate for information on her whereabouts.

He passed the hotel and still didn't see her SUV, but he did see Bobby's sedan pulling into the parking lot. He turned sharply, hoping his friend had some information about her.

"I've been trying to phone you, but you didn't answer."

Bobby pulled out his phone and examined it. "Sorry. I put it on silent earlier. I've been doing some Christmas shopping this morning for the family and didn't want them to find out. What was so important?"

"I'm looking for Elise. I've knocked on her door several times, but she hasn't answered and no one has seen her for a while."

"I'm not surprised. Agent Richardson checked out yesterday."

His words were like a punch in Josh's stomach. "She checked out?"

"Yes. She packed her stuff into her SUV yesterday evening and left." He reached into his jacket pocket and pulled out an envelope. "She asked me to give this to you."

He tore open the envelope and pulled out a hand-written letter letting him know she was leaving town now that the investigation was over.

So while everyone in town was searching for her, she'd packed up and left with only a letter as explanation? "She left this? You saw her?"

"Yes, she handed it to me when she checked out. I promised to give it to you if you came by."

Josh stormed back to the Jeep, anger biting at him. How could she leave without a word to anyone? And why leave so abruptly? He'd poured out his heart to her, promising a future together if she stayed.

He opened the letter and read it again, his mind turning over and over at the words.

It was true. Elise had left town.

She'd made her choice and was gone.

He'd lost her.

"So you're the one who broke it off?" Colton asked as he knelt down to examine the ground for evidence of fresh tracks.

"I guess I did," Josh said. He hadn't come right out

and given her an ultimatum—the FBI or him—but he might as well have.

Finding nothing, Colton stood and moved on through the woods. "Yet you're upset that she left town without telling you?"

His mocking tone didn't escape Josh's notice. "I know it doesn't make sense, but I didn't think she'd leave. She didn't even say goodbye to Patti."

"She left you a note."

The note. Elise's letter mocked him. He'd reread it once or twice, noticing the fine lines of her handwriting, searching for something, some clue or reason as to why she'd left so suddenly without a word, without even giving him an opportunity to apologize.

"But Patti said Elise believed someone was still hurting Brooke Martin. She said she was heading to the Martins' house. The woman I know wouldn't just leave without knowing Brooke was safe. But the Martins insist she was never there."

"If you keep focusing on it, it'll drive you crazy," Colton warned him. "Maybe Patti misunderstood, or maybe the Martins lied. Either track her down and make sure everything is fine or else forget about it." He checked the time on his watch. "Let's head back to base camp and see if any of the other teams have found anything."

They trekked back to where a makeshift base camp in the search for Candace's body had been established. There was no good news from the other teams, but some volunteers were still out searching.

Josh decided to take a break and drive over to Patti's. Maybe Elise had said something more that she'd forgotten or maybe Colton was right about her misunderstanding. All he knew for certain was that his mind just wasn't going to rest until he put these pieces together.

He parked at the curb, recognizing Daniel's squad car in the driveway. His heart jumped. Was there news? Had they found Candace? He'd just left the search area. Why hadn't they called him?

Patti opened the door for him. Her face was drawn and tight from crying. Her days of being strong were over. Her hope had ended the day they'd found Candace's backpack in Larkin's shed.

Daniel stood by the fireplace, almost in front of the photo of Max and Candace. His face was drawn, as well.

"What's going on?" Josh asked. "Do you have news?"

He dug his hands into his pockets. "It's not what you think, Josh. We haven't had any headway in our search for Candace."

"Then what is it?"

He glanced at Patti then back at Josh. "There is something I need to tell you. Patti and I talked, and we both agree we want to be the ones to tell you before you hear it from someone else."

Josh glanced at Patti, who moved to stand beside Daniel. "We weren't trying to keep it a secret," she said. "We just hadn't had the opportunity to tell anyone."

He noticed the way Daniel reached out for Patti's hand and held it firmly as he talked. "You're a couple?"

Daniel nodded and looked at Patti. "We didn't mean for it to happen, but it did. We haven't told anyone… except Candace."

"Candace knew?"

Patti's chin quivered. "I told her the night before she disappeared. She was so angry at me."

Daniel rubbed his face. "I suppose that's why I was so convinced she ran away. She was so angry. And then when we received that letter . . . I've already expressed my regret to Patti, but I'm sorry, Josh. You tried to convince me and I didn't hear you."

He shook Daniel's hand and let the man know there were no hard feelings. He hugged Patti and wished them both well. He wanted nothing but the best for Patti, and he knew Max would be pleased that she was finding love again.

He walked out to the Jeep and got inside but didn't start the engine right away. The letter—Candace's runaway letter. He'd forgotten about that. Had Larkin forced her to write it? And how had Brooke got ahold of it to turn over to the police?

But if Candace had written a letter, had Larkin forced her to do so before he killed her? He tried Elise's number again. He needed to speak with her. Was it possible Larkin was the suspect she'd been tracking all along? Why wouldn't she have told him about the connections with the letters?

He remembered the file she'd kept on her leads. After her hotel room had been broken into, she'd hidden the file. Had she taken it in her haste to leave?

He pulled out the letter from his pocket and stared at it, suddenly realizing the letters were the key. If someone had forced Candace to write a runaway letter, could they have also forced Elise to write one? He pulled it out and reread it, this time looking for details instead of feeling the emotions of the words.

Was this letter evidence that she'd been abducted, too? That suspicion was growing inside of him. He felt the urge to rush back inside and spill out his suspicions to Patti and Daniel, but they would probably just think him crazy and brokenhearted. He needed proof that she hadn't left on her own...and he knew just where to find it.

Bobby shook his head. "I don't know why we're doing this," he said as he slid the key into the lock and the door opened. "I told you she left. I saw her drive away with my own two eyes."

Josh pushed past him into the hotel room. All her belongings were indeed gone. Her photos had been removed from the wall and her bags were missing.

"I told you," Bobby said. "She packed everything and left."

Josh gazed at the corner. Elise had hidden her files under the carpet. If they were still there, he would know she hadn't left on her own. She would never have left them, and if someone else had packed up her room, they wouldn't have known to look for them there.

He pulled out his knife.

Bobby jumped, startled. "What are you doing with that?"

Josh knelt by the corner and used the sharp end to pull back the carpet. He spotted the brown color of the folder she'd used. He reached for it, pulling out the file.

She hadn't left on her own and now he had his proof.

"What is that?" Bobby asked him.

"Evidence Elise hid. She wouldn't have left town without these files."

That meant someone else had packed up her hotel

room. Had they also forced her to write that letter? But who had access to the hotel room? And how had Bobby watched her drive away with his own two eyes?

Suspicion dawned as he realized there was no way Bobby could have seen her, yet he'd been the one to give Josh the letter and he'd had access to her hotel room to clean it out.

He turned to look at his friend and found the man standing over him, a gun now in his hand. "You just can't leave well enough alone, can you?" he said as he slammed the butt of the gun into Josh's head and knocked him to the floor.

He thought of Elise as darkness cloaked over him, smothering every thought he had.

Chapter Ten

Blood trickled down Josh's face as the light of consciousness seeped through. He opened his eyes, his head pounding at such a simple idea as moving. He ignored the pain, pushing himself up to a sitting position. He was still in the hotel room, but Bobby was gone.

He pulled himself to his feet and struggled to regain his balance.

Bobby had sucker punched him. Bobby, whom he had considered a friend, had betrayed him. Had he hurt Elise? Had he hurt Candace? Josh bit back anger as he carefully took the steps to the ground floor. He rushed to the office only to find it locked up. He stumbled back to the Jeep instead.

Bobby Danbar was his key to finding Elise.

Bitter anger rushed through him at the realization that he'd been betrayed again by someone he'd considered a friend.

He dialed Daniel's number and spilled out what had happened when he answered.

"He didn't kill you," Daniel stated, "which means he'll have to leave town quickly."

"He's already got an hour's head start," Josh said, estimating how long he'd been out cold.

"I'll send a patrol out to his house."

But Josh doubted he would be there. "He has to have a place where he's hiding these girls. I think he used to have a hunting cabin near the river."

"That's on the opposite side of town from where we found Brooke and where we've been searching for Candace."

Josh knew that was by design. Bobby had planned all of this down to the last detail. He must have framed Larkin for Brooke's abduction and planted the girl in a shed on the other side of town, keeping search crews far away from where he was really keeping his victims. But that didn't explain why Brooke had identified Larkin as her attacker. Had the two men been working together? Did this have something to do with the human trafficking ring Elise had been investigating? And had she finally stumbled across it?

"Where are you now?" Daniel asked.

"On my way to my apartment." He needed to make the stop to grab his gun and his gear.

"Meet me at the station," Daniel stated. "We'll get a team together and go find that cabin."

"No," Josh said. "This isn't a time for patience. It's a time for action. Bobby knows I'm after him now. He'll be looking to get out of town quickly and that might mean tying up loose ends before he does." And Elise was likely that loose end. "He already has an hour's head start. I can't wait anymore."

He hung up as he roared into the parking lot of his apartment. He rushed up the stairs and to his bedroom, pulling open his closet and reaching into the back of it. He pulled his army chest out then ripped the key from his neck. He'd locked up this part of his life for a reason, but he'd clung to the key, unable to give it all up completely. Now he knew why. This trunk and its contents were a part of him. Giving it up completely was impossible, like losing an arm or a leg. He'd been walking around with a part of himself missing. And he'd wanted Elise to do the same. He'd asked her to give up the part of her that made her unique, the very part that caused him to fall in love with her. Of course she'd gone to see Brooke. She'd stuck her neck out again for a girl in trouble. It was who she was, and he knew she would never stop taking those risks as long as it meant protecting those in trouble.

He turned the key and the padlock clicked open.

God, I need Your help.

He pulled off the padlock and slowly, cautiously opened the hood of the trunk. He ran a hand over the folded clothes and properly stowed equipment. He touched the cold metal of his gun, then picked it up. It felt like an extension of his hand, an extension that had been missing for too long.

He set it on the bed and reached for his tactical gear, his NVGs and boots. He'd trained for this mission. He'd tracked down terrorists hiding in the mountains of Afghanistan. He could certainly track down domestic terrorists hiding in his own backyard, woods he knew like his own hand, land he'd spent his childhood growing up, playing on.

He gathered up his gear and set out.

He would track down these menaces who had invaded his hometown and taken those he loved. He would find them and make them pay.

He had a new mission now, and no one would prevent him from completing it.

He heard a knock on his front door. He opened it and saw Daniel and Patti waiting for him. Behind them, in the parking lot, were Matt, Colton, Levi, Blake and Garrett.

"I called them the moment I hung up with you," Daniel said. "They dropped everything and met me here. I made a few calls. Bobby has a hunting cabin on the north side of town." He spread out a map across the hood of the Jeep and pointed to a particular area. "It's an ideal place to keep someone hidden…if she's still alive."

"She's alive." He refused to accept the alternative. "And I'm going to find her and bring her home."

Evil would not prevail this time.

"Well, you aren't doing it alone," Levi stated, and the others nodded. "We're coming with you."

Daniel picked up one of the guns from Josh's bag. "I'm coming, too." He planted a kiss on Patti's lips then walked to the Jeep, getting into the passenger's seat.

Josh wasn't going to argue with his brothers or with Daniel. The truth was he could use all the help he could get to find Elise.

A shadow crossed over the opening. Candace scooted closer to her and gripped her arm. "Someone's coming."

Elise hugged the girl as they both stared at the opening. But instead of Roy Martin or Jay or Bobby, they spied a wisp of blond hair above them. Brooke! She held a bottled water and some crackers, which she tossed down to them.

Elise was relieved to know the girl was safe…at least for the moment.

Candace scrambled to her feet, ignoring the water and crackers. "Brooke, help us, please."

"I'm sorry," the girl cried. "I tried. I tried to help." She glanced at Elise. "I really did want to talk to you that day. I wanted out."

"Please, Brooke. Please help us."

Elise understood Brooke was frightened and trapped, but she'd already broken rules. She'd stolen water for them and tried to speak with Elise. It was possible she was capable of more than she thought she was. And it looked as if she might be their only hope for escape. "You can still get out," Elise told her. "I can help you."

Her chin quivered as she shook her head. "No, it's too late. He'll never let me go."

"I can get us out of this, Brooke. I can get us all out of this. But first, you have to help us. Do you see the ladder? Is it close by?"

She glanced around, scanning the area, then shook her head violently. "I can't. They'll catch me. They're all inside packing up. They're getting ready to leave town."

Which meant time was running out for them. "I can help you get out of this, Brooke, but I need you to trust me. We need that ladder."

Brooke still hesitated, peering around nervously. Whatever her relationship to these men—Elise doubted she was actually Rick Martin's daughter; she was more likely an innocent child who'd been abducted and forced to do his bidding—she was so ingrained in this life to be afraid of these men that she was taking a risk even speaking with them. But without her help, Elise didn't know if they would escape this prison.

Candace stepped forward. "She can help us, Brooke. You said yourself that she could help. We don't have to be alone anymore."

Brooke rubbed her hair, obviously torn by fear and the desire to help. She glanced around, her eyes darting anxiously.

Elise felt Candace's sob when the girl vanished from view. She placed her arm around Candace's shoulders and tried not to despair herself. She had to remain calm for Candace's sake if they hoped to get out of this alive.

And she did have hope.

As crazy as it seemed to her, she'd finally found hope that they weren't actually alone in this. The hours in darkness with nothing but her thoughts and a shivering teen by her side had given her time to ponder her predicament. Was it possible that God had had her back all along and she simply didn't realize it? She was where she needed to be, wasn't she? With Candace. She'd found the girl alive and that had to count for something. Surely God wouldn't bring her this far only to allow Candace to die now. No, whether Elise lived or died, shared a future with Josh or not, she had one purpose and one purpose only—to return Candace home to her family.

Brooke appeared again, this time heaving the heavy ladder over the edge. It bounced several times as it hit the wall before the end finally reached the ground.

"Hurry," Brooke hissed from above, "before they come."

The rope ladder was like a beacon of hope. They

had a chance. Elise pulled it toward Candace and the girl started climbing, a new, hopeful, quick step to her ascent now. Elise was only inches behind her. She spotted Brooke reaching out her hands and grabbing Candace's, pulling her up and over the well's edge before they both looked back down at Elise climbing up.

"Hurry," Candace said, motioning excitedly with her hand.

Elise climbed up the ladder as quickly as she could.

Suddenly both girls jerked their glances away, terror fixed on their faces. "Someone's coming," Brooke announced.

They'd run out of time.

"Go," Elise commanded them. "Run. Get away. Both of you."

"We can't leave you," Candace insisted.

"Yes, you can. Run and get help. I'll be right behind you."

They took off running. Elise reached the edge of the well just in time to spot them heading for the woods, Roy Martin hot on their heels.

"Get back here!" Roy shouted, stopping to raise and point his rifle at the fleeing girls.

"Hey!" Elise shouted, grabbing his attention momentarily as she climbed out of the well. He glanced her way then quickly turned back and took a shot. Candace flinched but kept running, disappearing into the woods. But Brooke screamed and hit the ground. Elise could hear her pleas for help as Roy rushed over to her, yanking her to her feet before backhanding her.

"Leave her alone!" Elise shouted, running toward them.

Someone grabbed her from behind, knocking her

down. Elise hit the ground then swung over kicking, but Jay grabbed hold of her arms and pinned her easily.

Roy dragged Brooke over to them then tossed her to the ground, still crying in fear. He motioned to Jay. "Go find the other one," he ordered and the young man grabbed a rifle from the back of the truck and rushed into the woods.

Roy dug his fingers into Elise's arm. "You thought you could get away from us? You're never getting out of here." He yanked Elise to her feet then pushed her forward until her legs hit the cold concrete of the well. He shoved her over the edge.

Brooke screamed. Elise reached for something to stop her fall, but only the smooth walls met her hands. She hit the bottom with a thud and a sharp loss of breath. She gasped, trying to recapture it even as pain ripped through every inch of her body. Finally, her breath caught and she glanced up at Roy and Brooke watching her, he with a look of satisfaction on his face, she with a look of terror. Elise hated to think what punishment she would receive for helping them.

Roy kicked the ladder from the top, and Elise watched it fall as if it were in slow motion. Each inch seemed to seal her fate. It landed with multiple thuds at her feet.

"Try getting out now," he told her. Then he turned his attention to Brooke, slapping her so hard and so loudly that Elise felt it. "I'll teach you to defy me." He hit her again.

Elise clawed at the dirt walls, but the loose earth gave way beneath her feet, causing her to fall back into the hole. She was helpless to intervene.

She heard the sounds of flesh on flesh and knew

Brooke was getting a beating. Finally, the noise stopped…and so did Brooke's sobs of pain.

Elise heard Roy's voice overhead but she couldn't see him. "Did you find the girl?"

"I couldn't find her," Jay stated. "But we'll keep searching. We'll find her."

At least Candace had got away. If she could find help…

Elise stared up at the blue sky overhead and wondered if what Josh had said about God guiding their steps was right. Did He have a plan for them? Was He with Candace right now in the woods? For Candace and Brooke's sake, she hoped He was. She lifted a prayer toward the sky just in case.

"Please let her find help."

Josh concentrated on the road ahead, clutching the steering wheel with a grip that turned his knuckles white. How could he have been so stupid believing that letter? What if he hadn't put it together? What if he was too late?

He parked the Jeep a quarter mile from the cabin and hopped out. Three trucks pulled in behind his vehicle and his crew spilled out, quickly gathering up their gear. "We walk from here. We'll go in on foot and scout the area."

As much as he wanted to barge up there and take back what Bobby had taken from him, he knew it wasn't smart. He had no idea where Elise was being kept and no idea about the layout of the cabin or the surrounding area. If he hoped to bring Elise home safely, he would have to be smart.

Daniel and Matt pulled out the map of the area

and studied it before deciding the guys would break up into two-man teams and spread out to set up a perimeter while Daniel stayed by the trucks to establish a base point.

Levi patted Josh's arm reassuringly. "Don't worry. He won't get through us."

Josh nodded his thanks, but he knew first they had to establish that Bobby…and Elise…were still at the cabin and hadn't got away before they'd arrived.

Colton followed Josh as he pushed through brush. They were only a few hundred feet into the woods when movement grabbed their attention. Josh raised his weapon and saw Colton do the same. His heart raced at the thought that they'd already been discovered. Had Bobby established his own perimeters complete with guards? Did he have that many people working for him? How had such a large organization operated right under their noses?

He noticed fresh footprints on the ground. The tracks looked small, too small to be a man's prints, but he estimated they'd been made less than a half hour ago. He followed the trail to a pile of rocks a few feet away where the footprints disappeared. He scanned the ground for more tracks, but they were gone as if whoever had been there had suddenly vanished.

A scream erupted behind him and he turned in time to see someone jump from behind a tree and attack Colton, swinging a big stick at him. Colton quickly grabbed the small figure and held her as she twisted and turned, trying to escape his grasp, her red hair swinging back and forth as she jerked and struggled to slip free.

Josh's heart skipped a beat as he recognized the

purple sweatshirt, jeans and Skechers sneakers belonging to his niece.

"Candace?" he said, incredulous. Could it really be her? Alive?

The girl's head jerked at her name and she stared at him, past red, stringy hair with intense blue eyes that matched his own. Yet she stared at him as if she, too, couldn't believe what she was seeing.

Colton loosened his hold on her as Josh slipped his weapon over his shoulder and approached her. "Candace?" He reached out and stroked her hair. "It's me, Candace. It's Uncle Josh."

Recognition seemed to dawn in her eyes. "Uncle Josh?" The fight gushed from her and she fell into his arms, clinging to him and sobbing.

His heart swelled as he held her, speaking soothingly. "You're safe now," he promised, a wave of overwhelming gratitude rushing through him. "No one will hurt you again, Candace. I promise. You're safe."

He silently praised God for His mercy and grace in sparing Candace. He'd brought the girl through, leading her to safety when they'd all given up on her being found alive. Josh knew as she did that she could have come upon anyone in these woods. Plenty of people were looking for her, but they weren't all good. If she'd escaped, her captors were likely in the woods, too, searching for her.

"Let's get her back to the base camp," Colton suggested.

Josh agreed. He had to get her to safety. He picked her up and carried her through the woods, back toward their base point.

He stumbled into the clearing and rushed to the

Jeep, settling Candace into the back. Colton called to Daniel to grab a bottle of water, and he handed it to Josh. He opened it and gave it to Candace, who drank in the cool water.

"I don't believe it," Daniel said when he saw her. "I don't believe it."

"We found her wandering in the woods," Colton told him. "She slipped her captors."

Daniel knelt beside her. "How did you do it?" he asked her. "How did you escape, Candace?"

She drank down the water but stopped and looked at them all. "I had help. Some lady from the FBI saved me."

Josh's gut tightened. "Elise? You saw Agent Richardson?"

She nodded. "She saved me. She told me to run and I did. I ran so hard. They came after me, but I hid and they didn't find me."

Excitement bubbled through Josh. Elise was alive and he'd been right. She was right here in Westhaven. They hadn't taken her away yet. "Where is she now, Candace? Where is Agent Richardson?"

The girl's eyes darkened and her face drew up.

"I'm sorry, Uncle Josh, but I think they killed her."

Her words nearly knocked him to his feet. Josh fought to catch his breath as Candace's words reverberated through him. It couldn't be true. It couldn't be. Elise could not be dead.

Colton took over where Josh's voice failed. "What do you mean by you think they killed her?"

"Roy saw us trying to escape. He shot at us. Brooke and Agent Richardson, they were right behind me, but didn't make it. Neither of them made it out."

"What else, Candace? What else can you tell us?"

"I don't know. I ran away like she told me to do. I heard gunshots. When I stopped to look back, I saw Brooke on the ground, and I didn't see Agent Richardson."

Colton reached into a pocket and pulled out a pencil and a small notebook. "Can you draw me a map of the cabin and where you were being held?"

"I don't know. Maybe."

He scribbled out a makeshift drawing of the cabin and the surrounding area and showed it to Candace. "Can you tell me where they kept you? Where they kept Agent Richardson?"

Her hands shook as she took the notebook, but she studied it then pointed to an area south of the back of the cabin. "There's an abandoned well behind the cabin. That's where they held us."

Colton smiled at her. "Good girl. Now, can you tell me how many men there are?"

"I only saw four men—Roy, Jay, Brooke's father and the main guy in the cabin. He mostly stayed inside and let Roy and Jay do the work."

Candace answered their questions like a trouper, providing valuable information they would need to mount a rescue. When he'd finished asking her questions, Colton relayed several key details to the other members of the team over his radio headset.

He pulled out the map Candace had helped him construct. "Josh, we'll cover you while you go to the well and retrieve Elise. Once she's safe, we'll draw in on the cabin and its occupants."

"You're leaving me?" Candace asked, aiming her

question at Josh. She fell into his arms again. "Please don't leave me, Uncle Josh."

His heart broke at the thought of leaving her, but one of the women he loved was safe. It was time to retrieve the other one. "Daniel is going to be right here with you. You won't be alone. And Colton and I will be back soon."

She clung to Josh and he hated to release her. "Please don't leave me."

"I have to go find Elise before it's too late. She might be scared or injured or worse. I have to find her, Candace."

"I'm scared, Uncle Josh." She seemed to choke over her next words. "He said he killed my dad."

That revelation threatened to knock him to the ground. Did she mean Bobby? Had he killed Max? Could it be true? But why would he tell a frightened little girl such a thing unless it was? The bitter taste of betrayal hit him again, but he glanced up and saw Colton's expression that clearly communicated he didn't have time right now for grief and anger. He had to keep his head about him if he wanted to get Elise back alive.

He leaned down and faced Candace, trying to turn his tone to one of comfort. "I know you're frightened, but remember what the Bible says… Let God guide your path."

"Let God guide your path." She spoke the words at the same time he did then smiled, a reminder of how many times she'd heard that verse quoted to her.

"The Bible says God's word is a lamp onto my feet. That means we often can't see where we're headed, but God knows. He knows each step we take before we take them. He led you to me, and now Daniel will keep you safe."

She reluctantly pulled away from him. "I'll be praying that you find her."

Josh watched her as he and Colton headed out.

He thought about her last words. She would be praying he found Elise. He prayed that, too, but he added one condition.

He prayed he would find her alive.

"Agent Richardson."

She glanced up at Bobby Danbar staring down at her. Roy was at his side.

"You've caused us all sorts of problems. Because of you, we're shutting down operations here sooner than we'd planned. And the first rule of shutting down operations is to tie up loose ends."

He motioned toward Roy, who placed something large over the opening.

"What are you doing?" Elise cried, scratching at the walls as the object filled more and more of the open space, then buried Elise into darkness.

He was closing up the well and leaving her to die.

"No!" Elise clawed at the dirt walls, trying to climb up. All she managed to do was loosen the dirt around her. And what would she do if she made it to the top anyway? The opening was blocked.

"Somebody help me!" she screamed over and over again until her throat was raw and sore.

This was it. This was where she was going to die. Her only hope was that Candace would get away and bring back help. But would the girl even remember how to get back to her? And would help arrive in time?

Why had she even been brought here? Why had God even allowed her to connect with Josh? To find a chance at love only to have it ripped away?

Why had God allowed this to happen to her? She pondered that thought. All the terrible things God had allowed in her life had led her to this. She should be angry at God, but she couldn't be. She'd found the trafficking ring. She'd helped Candace escape. And no matter if she died or not, she'd shut down this ring in this area. Girls here were safe. Even if her death was the cost.

She was willing to pay it.

But what if God had intervened? If He hadn't allowed the mugging or Max's death? She might never have become an FBI agent. She wouldn't have been here to help Candace and she would never have met Josh.

Yes, she was thankful for her suffering, thankful for the guiding hand of the Lord. Josh was right. *We might not see all the steps ahead, but we have to follow Him one step at a time and allow His goodness to light our path, even when we can't see it ourselves.* She had been a part of God's plan all along.

She crouched down and covered her face with her hands. She was on her own. Even if Candace managed to get away, even if she found help, the air in this well would certainly run out before anyone could arrive.

This was it. This was where she was going to die.

She wiped away tears that rolled down her cheeks and thought of the future she would miss. The next kiss with Josh, planning a future, perhaps kids and a home of her own. She saw her future slipping away, her dreams, her desires.

What would happen to her now? She vaguely remembered something she'd heard repeated at funerals about closing your eyes in this world and waking up in Heaven. Would it be that simple?

Not for her. Not for someone like her. After all she'd done wrong, after the way she'd lived her life, why would God want her?

There is no condemnation in Christ Jesus.

That verse from Romans pulsed through her mind. She'd heard her mother recite it again and again when Elise was a child. But could she believe it? Was it possible God really wanted her even after all the bad choices she'd made and all the consequences that resulted? Could God forgive her? Redeem her?

She lifted her head toward Heaven and cried out.

God, do You want me? God, can You love me?

A peace fell over her. God's everlasting patience was there waiting for her to want it. She imagined His hand reaching for hers. All she had to do was grab for it, accept his offer of everlasting life and grace.

"I accept," she whispered and felt her life opening to the grace He'd sustained her with.

It no longer mattered what lay ahead of her if she made it out of this well. If Josh chose never to forgive her, she would survive. If her career was over, she could still have a future.

But none of that mattered now because she was in this hole, this grave that would be the end of her.

She closed her eyes as the weight upon her chest grew heavier and heavier with each breath. She'd told Josh she would sacrifice her life to protect innocent girls, and now it looked as if that would be the cost of saving Candace. If it was, so be it.

Some sacrifices were worth making.

* * *

Josh moved through the woods in the direction Candace had instructed. He stopped when he came to a clearing ahead of him and crouched at the perimeter. He peered around and noticed a car he recognized as Bobby's black sedan and a truck he remembered seeing at the Martin home parked in front of a cabin.

Lord, help me find her.

Candace had said Elise was being kept inside an abandoned well. He pulled out his binoculars and scanned the area, finding it on the back side of the property toward the tree line, right where Candace had indicated.

His brothers' voices echoed in his ear as they each reported back over the radio. The perimeter was secure. No one was getting in or out while his team was there.

Colton appeared quietly beside him. "That must be the well your niece mentioned," he said, motioning to the same area Josh had scoped out. "There's no easy access to it. You'll be a sitting duck out there if anyone in the cabin walks out."

He agreed with Colton's assessment. There was no cover around the well. It was away from the tree line in an open area. Still, he had no choice but to take the chance.

"I'm going," he stated.

Colton nodded then spoke into his mic, alerting the team that the plan was about to go into action.

"I have a clear view into the cabin," he heard Matt say. "I have visual on four souls. Looks like they're clearing up evidence."

"Four people. That confirms what Candace told us," Colton said to Josh. "Let's hope they don't wander outside." He raised his weapon and trained it on the cabin. "Go."

Josh took off for the well, moving as cautiously and quickly as he could. He was an open target and he knew it, but he also knew his team had his back. They would see someone coming before he would.

As he approached the well, he saw it had a cover over the top of it. They'd closed it up. Panic struck him. Had they done that with Elise inside? Or had they moved her after Candace escaped?

He dropped his gun and leaned down, pushing the heavy iron cover until it gave way and moved. He pushed it off and it hit the ground with a thud. He shone his light into the well. He saw her half sitting, half lying against the side.

"Elise!"

She didn't move when he called her name. He had to get down to her, but he didn't see any way back up. A rope ladder lay at the bottom near Elise's foot.

He pulled out his grappling harness and attached it to an iron pipe, probably where they'd secured the ladder when they needed it. Then he rappelled down the well. She still didn't move as he reached the bottom.

He bent down and touched her cheek, his heart ready to burst through his chest with worry and relief. Her face was warm and he could see her shallowly breathing in and out. He wasn't too late.

He spoke her name again. "Elise. Can you hear me?"

Her eyelids fluttered then opened and she gazed up at him from weary eyes. "Josh? Is that you?"

"It's me. I'm here."

"Candace?"

"She's safe. She's with Daniel."

"What about Brooke? Where's Brooke?"

He hadn't seen Brooke, but he didn't want to worry her. "We'll find her. We'll find her together."

But first they had to get out of this well.

"You came for me," she whispered.

"Of course I did. I'm not letting you go that easily, Elise. I love you."

She smiled. "And I love you."

"That is all so sweet." Colton's voice sounded in his ear. "But perhaps we could get on with the rescue. What's your status?"

Josh grinned, remembering his mic was on. "On our way up." He helped Elise to her feet. "I need you to climb, baby. Can you do that?"

She grabbed the rope but looked so weak he wondered if she would be able to pull herself up.

"You can do this," he assured her. "I'll be right behind you."

She pressed her foot against the wall and started to climb but made it only a few steps before she slid back down. "I don't think I can."

Josh pressed against her back. He wasn't going to let her give up. "You have to do this. You have to escape. Think about Brooke. We have to get out of this well so we can find Brooke."

His words seemed to give her renewed energy. She pressed her lips firmly and grabbed the rope with renewed strength and began to climb, slowly but surely making it to the top. He climbed up behind her, quickly scaling the wall to the top.

"What's our status?" Josh asked into his mic.

He heard the word *clear* from each of his team

members. All they had to do now was to get safely into the woods and then they could move in on Bobby and the others. He took hold of Elise's arm. "Let's go," he said, leading her toward the woods away from the cabin.

But she stopped and turned back toward the cabin. "Brooke. We have to go get her."

"First we have to get you to safety. Then we'll go in after Brooke."

She shook her head firmly, her face set. "I'm not leaving without her."

Josh crouched, pulling Elise down with him. They were sitting targets out in the open, but he recognized the determination on her face. "Does anyone have visual on the girl?" he asked into his mic.

"Negative. No visual on the girl," Matt said. He had the best view into the front room of the cabin, but that didn't mean Brooke wasn't tied up somewhere out of visual range. The rest of the team echoed Matt's status.

Josh scrubbed his hand over his face. He wanted nothing more than to get Elise out of danger, away from this cabin and Bobby's reach.

Elise looked him square in the eye as if sensing his desire to toss her over his shoulder and haul her out of danger's way. A fire lit in the brown of her eyes. "I won't leave without Brooke."

She reached for the gun at his side then stood and rushed in the direction of the cabin.

"You're made!" Matt's call rang in his ears. "They spotted movement in the window. They're armed and heading out the back door. Get down now!"

Elise was too far away to hear the warning, and

calling out to her would only attract further attention their way.

Josh did the only thing he could do as the back door of the cabin opened and the barrel of a gun poked out.

He tackled her as gunfire sprayed.

Elise hit the ground and rolled as the bullets from the shooter's gun sprayed over them. Josh jerked then fell to the ground, his gun flying out of his hand. Anger and adrenaline rushed through Elise as she saw Josh lay unmoving on the ground, blood pooling around his shoulder just above his bulletproof vest. He'd come to rescue her only to get shot.

She rushed to him and rolled him over. He was unconscious and unresponsive and blood was flowing onto the ground around him, but she couldn't tell where it was coming from.

She glanced back at the cabin and saw Jay and Rick dead on the ground outside the cabin door while Roy was crouched down still shooting. A moment later, the crack of gunfire took him out, too.

"Help me! Please help me!"

Elise heard the cry over the sound of rapid gunfire. *Brooke!* The girl was inside the cabin. Elise crawled forward until she could see into the cabin. She spotted Bobby on the floor, crouched beneath a table, his arm wrapped tightly around Brooke and a gun to her head.

"Tell them to stop firing," he called to Elise. "Tell them to stop or I'll kill her right now."

Elise scrambled back to pull Josh's earpiece and mic free so she could use them. She had to stop Josh's team from firing on the cabin. Not only because of Bobby, but because Brooke could be injured by their gunfire.

"Stop firing," she called into the mic. "He has a hostage inside the cabin. Please stop firing. You could hit her."

"Hold your fire!" She heard the call over the radio. "Stand by. Elise, it's Colton. What do you see?"

"He has a hostage inside. It's Brooke. He has a gun to her head."

"How is Josh? From here, it looks like he's not moving."

She glanced down at him. No, he hadn't moved since the moment he'd gone down. "He's unresponsive and he's losing blood."

"We're on our way toward you," Colton told her. "Stay where you are."

Once the gunfire stopped, Bobby poked his head out, the gun still pressed into Brooke's head. "That's better," he shouted, obviously feeling more in control now with his hostage's life to bargain with. He pointed the gun at Elise. "Now you come in here with me, Agent Richardson."

"Stay where you're at, Elise," Colton shouted in her ear, obviously having heard Bobby's demand over the mic. "Do not—I repeat, do not—go into that cabin."

Bobby glared at her, then pressed the gun harder against Brooke's head, causing the girl to sob even more. Her chin quivered and tears flowed down her face.

"Please help me," she begged. "Please help me."

"Do not do it, Elise," Colton's voice commanded her. "We're nearly to you."

She kept her eyes on Bobby and Brooke as she slowly stood, not wanting to give him any reason to doubt her intentions. She was going to do what he said. She wouldn't do anything to risk Brooke's life. Perhaps she could convince him to let Brooke go and use her as a hostage instead.

Colton kept hollering in her ear, and it didn't take long before she heard his voice behind her instead of only through the mic. She also heard the sounds of footsteps heading toward them. She peeled her gaze away from Bobby long enough to see five men dressed in full gear, rifles trained at them, heading her way.

Bobby saw them, too, and dug the gun into Brooke's head. "Stay back," he shouted at them. "Stay back or I'll kill her." He glared at Elise. "Get inside or I do it right now."

There was no way she was going to let him hurt another girl.

She dropped the gun and radio and slowly stood, her hands raised to show him she was unarmed.

Colton was only feet away from her. "Elise, do not do this."

She glanced back at Josh still unmoving on the ground. She was nearly certain he was dead, and without him she had only one thing left to live for—protecting this girl from a madman.

Bobby grinned as Elise closed the cabin door on his order, effectively shutting out the team surrounding the cabin.

"Good. Now sit in the chair," he said, motioning to a straight-backed chair. She did as he commanded and sat down.

"How could you do this, Bobby? How could you betray your friends this way?"

"I have my own family to look out for. I provide for them any way I can."

"Even by kidnapping and murder?"

"When you have a family, perhaps you'll understand the lengths you'll go to in order to get them what they need."

"You can let Brooke go now. You have me. What's a better hostage than a federal agent?"

He glanced out the window at the activity of the team then swore. "They've got the place surrounded. But they won't fire, not while I've got you both inside. They won't take the chance on hurting one of you. I don't care what kind of sharpshooters they think they are."

He closed the curtain then paced the floor in the kitchen, dragging Brooke along beside him.

Elise noticed her face was pale and red from crying but she appeared to be uninjured. That was good. They might need to run to escape. It was good to know Brooke was capable of running.

"It's going to be okay," Elise told the girl, trying to keep her calm. "We're going to get out of here."

Brooke sniffled back a tear but nodded her understanding. "Did—did Candace get away?" she asked.

Elise smiled and nodded. "She's safe."

"Bobby! Bobby, it's Chief Mills." His voice reverberated through the empty cabin as he stood outside surrounded, Elise was certain, by the Rangers. "We need to talk this out, Bobby. The cabin is surrounded. There's no way out."

Elise saw him tighten his grip on the gun at Brooke's head. "Stay back," he hollered out to Chief Mills. "I'll kill them. I swear I will."

"Tell me what you want, Bobby. How can we end this without more bloodshed? These boys out here, they're just itching to take you out. You just killed one of their own. It's all I can do to keep them from barreling into that cabin guns blazing."

Killed one of their own?

Elise's blood went cold. She knew he was talking about Josh. Bobby had killed Josh. She couldn't hold back the sob that broke through her. Josh had died trying to rescue her.

"You tell them to stay back," Bobby hollered to Chief Mills. "I have hostages!"

"There's no way out now except by negotiating through me. You know me, Bobby. You know I won't let anything happen to you if you cooperate by releasing the hostages and coming out peacefully."

She looked at Bobby, who was studying the scene outside. This man had betrayed his friends. He'd hidden like a snake in plain sight. He'd plotted and schemed to hide his criminal endeavors and then exploit young girls for money. And now he'd murdered Josh.

She wouldn't let him get away with it.

She leaped from her chair, rushing him and knocking him to the ground before he realized what was happening. The gun fell from his hand as he hit the floor, but not before he fired off a round. Brooke screamed but broke free and ran out of sight.

She vaguely heard a commotion outside and knew the gunshot had grabbed their attention, but Elise was more focused on scrambling to reach the gun that had slid across the wood floor before Bobby could reach it and use it on her.

She kicked him and lunged for the gun, coming up several feet short when he gripped her leg and jerked her back toward him. He grabbed a handful of hair and dragged her back to him before pinning her to the ground. He smacked her hard across the face. Pain ripped through her and the floor seemed to move with the impact of his hand. She groaned and tried to focus on Brooke moving quickly out the back door of the cabin with the aid of an infiltrating figure decked out in ranger gear. The image blurred and she wasn't even sure of what she'd seen as she forced her eyes to try to focus. Had it been an illusion? She hoped not. She hoped Brooke was safely out the door.

Bobby grabbed Elise by the chin and forced her to look at him. "You've been nothing but trouble to me since you came to town." He pressed the gun into her head. "Any last words?"

Everything around her blurred except the gun's barrel. She tried to push it away without success. "Don't kill him." She addressed her words to Josh, who stood behind Bobby, his rifle trained directly on the man's head.

"What the—?" Bobby glanced behind him and Josh slammed the butt end of his rifle into Bobby's face, sending him sprawling across the floor.

Josh picked up the gun Bobby had dropped. "Why can't I kill him?"

"Because I need to question him," Elise said, trying to sit up. The floor spun again and she felt herself falling. Before she could, Josh was beside her, cradling her in his arms.

"Take it easy. You're safe now."

She tried to focus on his face, on those blue eyes,

but nothing made sense to her. She'd seen him on the ground, unmoving. She'd suspected he was dead, and Chief Mills had confirmed it. How could he be here now? Was she hallucinating? She reached up to touch his cheek, to feel flesh and confirm what she was seeing. He covered her hand with his and kissed her palm.

"You're safe now," he whispered. "Everyone is safe."

She leaned into his arms, no longer caring if her eyes were lying to her. Whatever the truth was, she was in Josh's arms, hearing his voice whisper sweet words to her. There was no place else she'd rather be.

She slipped blissfully into unconsciousness.

"The ambulance is on its way," Colton told Josh as he sat holding Elise in his arms. "It'll be here within minutes."

He'd wanted nothing more than to kill Bobby when he'd seen him with a gun to Elise's head. Instead, Bobby was outside, being cuffed and read his rights by Daniel. He would stand trial for his crimes. He would pay for his betrayal.

Josh heard the wail of the ambulance sirens and carried Elise outside, stretching her across a gurney as the EMTs took over her care. He'd seen the blow Bobby had given her and was surprised she'd remained conscious as long as she had. She'd fought for Brooke, and he'd expected nothing less from her.

He checked on Brooke, who was sitting on the edge of the other ambulance, an EMT treating her wounds.

"How is Agent Richardson?" she asked, her voice young and innocent and frightened.

"She's going to be fine," he assured her.

"She saved us all," Brooke said. "She saved us all."

The EMT from Elise's ambulance stepped over to him. "She's awake, and she's asking for you."

He headed to her side, and when he saw her awake and recognition in her eyes, he leaned over and kissed her long and hard, rejoicing when she matched the intensity of his kiss. He broke from her and gazed at her, his hand stroking her hair and face.

"I thought I'd lost you there for a minute," he said.

She gazed up at him, her hazel eyes filling with tears. "I thought I'd lost you, too. I thought you were dead."

He saw the pain in her eyes and wished she hadn't had to go through that, but knew the ploy of having Daniel announce he was dead had thrown Bobby off, giving her an opportunity to get Brooke away from him.

Then her face set obstinately. "Remind me to read Chief Mills the riot act when I see him."

Josh didn't envy his friend when Elise got through with him. He'd seen how tough she could be when crossed. He glanced back and saw Bobby being led away by two city officers. Anger bit at him again at the betrayal they'd all endured because he hadn't seen Bobby for what he was in time.

"Tell me again why I couldn't kill him," Josh said, motioning to Bobby.

"He kidnaps young girls and sells them to a buyer. I need to know who that buyer is. My human trafficking case just got a huge break."

"And if he refuses to give up his dealers?"

She smiled at him sarcastically and patted his arm. "Then you can kill him."

He shook his head at her wit. "You FBI types are always making promises you can't keep."

She touched his face, turning it toward her as she stroked his stubbled chin. "I promise you this and I intend to keep it. I love you and I will never leave you again."

Josh reached for her and wrapped his arms around her, kissing her like a man who'd been denied water and finally found a spring.

Epilogue

"Are you on your way?" Josh asked over the cell phone mounted to her dashboard.

Elise smiled and assured him she was nearly to Westhaven. She'd had to return to FBI headquarters to explain about the trafficking ring she'd uncovered. Because of Bobby's cooperation, they now had several good leads to follow and evidence of a human trafficking ring that spanned multiple states.

She had news about Brooke, as well. She'd been identified as a child abducted seven years ago from a small town in West Virginia. Elise couldn't imagine all the girl had been through, but she would soon be reunited with her real family in time for Christmas.

When she arrived at Patti's house, she noticed several other cars parked out front. The Christmas lights had been rehung and in the darkness hid most of the damage to the house. Elise knew this house, like this family, would be repaired and continue on. They were strong and they would endure.

Elise caught a glimpse through the window of the family decorating the Christmas tree. Candace looked happy, smiling and horsing around with Josh while Daniel and Patti held hands as they watched.

Josh spotted her through the window and stepped outside, pulling on his coat. "Hey, you made it." He pulled her to him and kissed her deeply. "What are you waiting for? Why don't you come inside?"

She'd had a lot of time to think on her drive over and one question continued to bother her. She couldn't spend any more time with this family until she knew the answer to it.

"I've been reinstated with the FBI and they've picked me to head up a task force on this trafficking ring."

"That's great news, Elise. Congratulations." He bent to kiss her again, but she pushed him away. "What's wrong?"

"You said you couldn't be with someone who would purposely put themselves in danger. My job, heading up this task force, could be dangerous."

She knew this wasn't the best time to bring this up, but she just couldn't—she wouldn't—walk into that house and pretend everything was wonderful if she knew after Christmas would bring her heartbreak.

"When I look at Candace, I know that you risked your life for her. Max risked his life for you. My ranger brothers and I risked our lives every day, but it was for a reason. I've always known that, but I suppose I lost the realization that there are things worth risking your life for. You do that every time you go after someone like Bobby. You brought home my niece. You restored this family, Elise. How can I fault you for putting yourself at risk when you saved someone I care about?"

"But that won't always be the case, Josh. Most of the time, these cases don't end well."

"It doesn't matter. If there's a chance you can help someone else the way you helped Candace, you have to do it."

"But can you love someone who continually places herself in danger?"

He smiled. "I can, and I do. I love you, Elise, risks and all." He leaned in and kissed her then smiled. "Now will you please come inside? It's cold out here all alone and this family isn't complete without you."

She snuggled against him and followed him inside, comfortable in the realization that she would never have to be alone again.

God had guided her home.

* * * * *